A year to remember!

It's been twenty-eight years since they were last together—and now one man will reunite them.

Gabriella, Beth and Georgiana have no idea that they have sisters they've never met— and a biological father who's still alive. Then Dylan Garrett from Finders Keepers Detective Agency gives each one the news. The revelations come just as each sister finds herself exploring a budding romance that might actually be headed somewhere. What a time for the perfect guy to show up!

This Christmas, three women reclaim their pasts in a bid to enhance their futures. And in the process, each stands to gain two sisters, a father and a lover!

Jasmine Cresswell is the multitalented author of more than forty novels. Her efforts have gained her numerous awards, including the RWA's Golden Rose Award and the Colorado Author's League award for best original paperback novel. Born in Wales and educated in England, Jasmine met her husband while working at the British Embassy in Rio de Janeiro. She has lived in Australia, Canada and six cities in the United States. The parents of four grown children, she and her husband now make their home in Sarasota, Florida.

Tara Taylor Quinn's love affair with Harlequin Books began when she was fourteen years old and picked up a free promotional copy of a Harlequin romance in her hometown grocery store. The relationship was solidified in 1993 when she sold her first book to Harlequin Superromance. Ms. Quinn has had thirty-two sales in less than nine years, and her books are sold worldwide, with many foreign translations. Her seven-book SHELTER VALLEY series has received several nominations for national awards— the most recent addition, *The Sheriff of Shelter Valley*, was released in October 2002. Tara's first romantic suspense novel for MIRA, *My Son's Keeper*, will be in stores July 2003.

Kate Hoffmann began reading romances in 1979 when she picked up a copy of Kathleen Woodiwiss's *Ashes in the Wind*. It inspired her to try her hand at her own historical romance. But when she gave that up to write a short, humorous contemporary novel, she found her métier. She finished the manuscript in four months, placed first in the 1993 national Harlequin Temptation contest and quickly found a happy home with the line. This talented award winner has gone on to write more than twenty additional novels. A former teacher, Kate has also worked in retailing and advertising. She now devotes herself to writing full-time and resides in Wisconsin.

JASMINE CRESSWELL

TARA TAYLOR QUINN

KATE HOFFMANN

TRUEBLOOD
Christmas

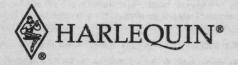

HARLEQUIN®

TORONTO • NEW YORK • LONDON
AMSTERDAM • PARIS • SYDNEY • HAMBURG
STOCKHOLM • ATHENS • TOKYO • MILAN • MADRID
PRAGUE • WARSAW • BUDAPEST • AUCKLAND

Special thanks and acknowledgment are given to Jasmine Cresswell, Tara Taylor Quinn and Kate Hoffmann for their contribution to *Trueblood Christmas*.

ISBN 0-373-83533-7

TRUEBLOOD CHRISTMAS

Copyright © 2002 by Harlequin Books S.A.

The publisher acknowledges the copyright holders of the individual titles as follows:

GABRIELLA
Copyright © 2002 by Harlequin Books S.A.

BETH
Copyright © 2002 by Harlequin Books S.A.

GEORGIANA
Copyright © 2002 by Harlequin Books S.A.

Visit us at www.eHarlequin.com

Printed in U.S.A.

CONTENTS

Dear Reader,

I was born in England, so I grew up with holiday traditions that are a little different from the ones that are familiar here in the States. Especially the food! In the nineteenth century, people in England used to eat roast goose for Christmas dinner. That passed out of fashion in the 1920s in favor of newfangled turkey, although a few families still cling to the old-fashioned favorite.

Even though most English people eat turkey on Christmas Day, their traditional holiday dinners aren't much like the one Ella has just finished serving in the opening Thanksgiving scene of her story. English people usually stuff the turkey with a puree of chestnuts, and a bread mixture that contains a great deal of sage. Instead of mashed potatoes, English families roast potatoes around the meat. And instead of green bean casseroles, brussels sprouts are probably the most popular vegetable. Sweet potatoes are almost never sold in England, except as an exotic import from the Caribbean, so there are no bourbon-glazed sweet potato pies, garnished with pecans and marshmallows. A sad loss, in my opinion!

As for dessert, English families still eat the traditional plum pudding, which doesn't contain any plums, and is rather like a boiled fruitcake, served warm. My children quickly decided that they much preferred being American when it came to dessert, and nowadays our family enjoys pumpkin or pecan pie, followed by lots and lots of Christmas cookies! Whatever your family's traditions, I hope this Christmas will be joyful for you, and that Ella's story will add an hour or two of reading pleasure to your holiday celebrations.

Sincerely,

Jasmine Cresswell

GABRIELLA

Jasmine Cresswell

For Vanessa and Skip,
who gave hope and love to a baby in need.

CHAPTER ONE

GABRIELLA PETRI ENJOYED feasting on turkey and all the trimmings as much as anyone, but having spent the past twelve hours supervising the preparation of 758 traditional Thanksgiving dinners, in three separate sittings, starting at noon and ending at seven, she was ready to throw up if she smelled any more gravy, or so much as glimpsed another platter of candied sweet potatoes decorated with pecans and marshmallows.

Trying to decide whether her feet ached more than her shoulders, or vice versa, she let herself into her town house in the Brackenridge Park district of San Antonio, sighing with relief as she was greeted by space, serene ivory walls and silence. Averting her gaze from the cartons of books still stacked against the far wall of her living room even though it had been six weeks since her move from Chicago, she hung up her jacket and made her way to the sofa, where the latest issue of *People* magazine beckoned enticingly.

Kicking off her shoes, she sank onto the sofa, hanging her feet over the armrest and wriggling her toes. After a few blissful moments of staring at the ceiling and thinking about absolutely nothing, she summoned the energy to sit up straight enough to check her answering machine for messages.

There were no calls. Which, given the pathetic state of her social life these days, was hardly surprising. Still, she would have expected her parents to call, even though she'd warned them twice that she would be working all day. Ella's mouth quirked into a wry smile. It seemed her mom and dad had actually paid attention for once, which had to be a first. Normally, they called on any and every holiday, from Christmas to Ground Hog Day, despite her warnings.

Truth be told, she was always glad that they did. As an only child, not adopted until she was four, she had long ago realized that keeping in close contact with her parents was more important to her than it was to many of her friends. In an odd way, she liked being scolded for not flying home, even if her parents ought to realize by now that in the hotel industry, Thanksgiving was one of the busiest periods of the year and the least likely time for her to take off on a vacation.

Ever since she could remember, Ella had wanted to travel, and she'd chosen to work in the hotel industry in part because she knew that she would be required to move often if she wanted rapid promotions. But itchy feet didn't mean that she liked to be out of touch with her family. Maybe the fact of being adopted made her especially grateful to Frank and Mary Petri, who had been willing to take her into their home and love her through thick and thin, despite the fact that Ella didn't conform very well to the type of daughter they'd always dreamed of raising.

Her mom—childless until she was forty—made no secret of the fact that she had longed for a daughter who would play with Barbie dolls, wear pink ruffled dresses, marry young, and produce a cluster of grand-babies for Mary to love. Sadly, Ella never came close to matching her mom's wishful blueprint. Frilly dresses made her itch, and she had preferred hanging upside down on the monkey bars to playing with dolls. Presented with Bridal Barbie on her ninth birthday, Ella had dutifully displayed the doll on the top of her chest of drawers and instantly escaped to play baseball with the Taylor brothers next door.

Her mother had sighed and lamented, but the following Christmas Ella received a catcher's mitt stamped with the Yankees' logo. Even as a child, Ella had realized what a generous gift that mitt was on her mother's part, and what a triumph of love over pre-conceived expectations.

You had to give it to her mom, Ella reflected. Mary Petri was an optimist to her core. She had never given up hope that one day her tomboy daughter would see the light and miraculously transform herself into Holly Homemaker. After years of delicate hints, Mary had recently abandoned any attempt at subtlety and now came right out every time they met or spoke on the phone, informing Ella that it was past time for her to get married and start a family. Other women juggled careers and marriage, Mary pointed out. Why couldn't Ella?

Ella had become very good at changing the subject.

Her dad, in his own quiet way, must have been equally disappointed with the daughter the adoption agency found for him. Under the pressure of paying the mortgage and putting food on the table, Frank had years ago set aside his dreams of becoming a professional tenor and resigned himself to earning his living as an electrician. But Ella knew how much he loved music, and guessed how he must have yearned for a child who shared his talent for singing and his passion for Italian opera. Unfortunately, what her dad had been blessed with was a daughter with a tin ear for music and a singing voice reminiscent of a bullfrog with laryngitis.

Still, for all their mismatched personalities, Ella had never doubted that her parents loved her, even when she was at the high point of her bratty teenager period. And it had been some high point, Ella reflected. There had been the spiked orange hair phase, the gold ring in her belly button phase, and the memorable weekend when she'd locked the door to her bedroom and painted the walls and ceiling in unrelieved black. Frank and Mary had weathered the dramas with remarkable aplomb, all things considered. They'd even bought her a package of glow-in-the-dark stars to stick on her black ceiling.

Ella glanced at her watch. Nine-thirty. That meant it would be eleven-thirty in Long Island, and much too late to call home. Her parents had always been early to bed and early to rise and now that they were both in their seventies, they got up with the dawn and were often in bed by nine. She would have to remember to call them tomorrow, before she left for work. Thank heaven, for once she didn't have to be at her desk until ten-thirty.

Picking up *People* magazine, Ella wriggled into a more comfortable position against the sofa cushions, but for some reason not even the article on Brad Pitt, her favorite fantasy hero, could hold her attention. She felt restless, she acknowledged. On the night of Thanksgiving shouldn't she be doing something more exciting, or at least more heartwarming, than vegging out and reading a magazine? She'd always been dedicated to her job, probably in reaction to her mother's firmly held opinion that all the evils of modern civilization could be laid at the door of women who put careers ahead of their families. But, despite her ambition, she'd never expected to find herself at thirty-two years of age, alone in a strange city, devoid of anything that bore even a passing resemblance to a personal life.

She was the youngest woman in the history of the Sedgwick Hotel chain ever to hold the position of deputy general manager and she earned an impressive salary. In her twenties, that sort of professional success would have been more than enough to keep her happy. But since her trip home to Long Island last Christmas, she'd found herself wondering just how much she'd sacrificed in pursuit of rapid career advancement.

Hot branding irons and truth serum wouldn't get her to admit as much to her mother, but Ella had actually reached the point in her life where she wished she could find a decent man to marry. She wasn't looking for the impossible. She didn't expect Prince Charming, or a head-over-heels, lasts-forever kind of love. She was just hoping to find a decent guy who would be a pleasant roommate. Someone who would be a friendly face across the dinner table, an intelligent companion for the occasional night out, and a good father to a couple of kids. That wasn't too much to ask for, was it?

Apparently it was. So far, she hadn't come close to meeting anyone she could imagine living with for the rest of her life. Except Josh Taylor, of course, and she'd trained herself never to think about him. Only a masochist would waste fifteen years of her life pining for a man who found her invisible, and Ella had no sympathy for masochists.

Bruce, the last guy she'd dated, had dumped her after he challenged her to a three-mile cross-country race and Ella had won. Since Bruce was handsome, aggressively hetero, and had a good job, her girlfriends all insisted she should have let him win the stupid race. Ella wasn't convinced. If she could only keep Bruce happy by pretending to be a slower runner than she really was, it didn't seem to augur well for the future honesty of their relationship. Besides, even though she wasn't holding out for blow-your-socks-off passion— unlike her mother, she was a realist—still, she couldn't help hoping that somewhere in the world there was a man who would generate at least a mild case of mutual sexual fever. And Bruce sure hadn't been that guy. Bruce was enthusiastic about sex, Ella had decided, chiefly because he so much enjoyed complimenting himself on what a great performer he was.

Now that she'd put down *People* magazine, the boxes of books loomed in her peripheral vision, demanding to know why she still hadn't unpacked them even though she'd transferred from Chicago six weeks ago, and had been moved into this town house for more than a month.

Ella glared at the boxes. "I've been busy, okay? I've worked five 60-hour weeks back-to-back, and I don't have the energy to go out shopping for bookshelves by the time I finally get through with work."

The boxes didn't reply, which had to be a good thing. Bad enough that she talked to packing crates; she'd really be in trouble if they ever started talking back. Ella got up from the sofa, finally acknowledging that she felt much too restless for celebrity gossip, however juicy. She realized that, despite having been surrounded all day by food, she'd eaten nothing, and she was hungry. Maybe that was what was making her so antsy.

She walked into the kitchen on a grazing expedition, but the fruit, cottage cheese and yogurt arrayed in the fridge didn't inspire her. Rummaging in the pantry, she took out the peanut butter, gleeful when she found a jar of gourmet strawberry preserves that one of the sous-chefs at the hotel had asked her to taste test. Hell, it was Thanksgiving, the national celebration of unhealthy eating. It was about time she joined in the fun.

Unfortunately, she only had nutritious multigrain bread in the house. Something white and gooey would have made a more satisfying sandwich. But even on healthy bread, the peanut butter tasted pretty darn good, especially washed down with ice cold milk. The perfect Thanksgiving dinner, she thought, leaning back in the kitchen chair and sucking jam from her fingers. There was nothing like a generous hit of fat and sugar to improve a person's mood.

She was licking peanut butter from a spoon and wondering if she could find the energy to take a bath—

something decadent, with scented bubbles—when the doorbell rang. Ella's heart skipped a beat. It was past ten o'clock, and she didn't know anyone in San Antonio well enough for them to come calling uninvited at this hour. She put down the spoon, throat constricting when she saw that she'd been careless enough to leave the chain off the door. She must have been even more exhausted than she'd realized, and the consequences could be horrible.

The doorbell rang again and a muffled voice spoke through the panels. "Ella, it's Josh Taylor. Are you there? I need to talk to you."

CHAPTER TWO

JOSH TAYLOR? Here? Ella's heart skipped another beat. If she had to choose between facing a mad rapist and Josh Taylor, she guessed she'd pick Josh, but it was a close call. She swallowed hard, resisting the urge to run and find a comb and some lipstick. Josh probably wouldn't notice if she came to the door looking like Morticia on a bad hair day, but it seemed typical of their wretched relationship that he would arrive when she was exhausted, sticky fingered, and smelling faintly of roast turkey. She debated taking the cowardly way out and pretending she wasn't home. Then, annoyed with herself for being such a fool, she reluctantly opened the door.

Josh, looking like a *GQ* advertisement for how the man-about-town dresses when paying impromptu house calls, stood on her tiny front porch, jacket hooked over his shoulder, his hand propped against the door jamb. The pose was elegant enough for a photo shoot, and the wind rumpling his thick, dark hair provided the perfect finishing touch.

Any other man she'd ever met would have looked ridiculous, self-conscious and affected. But she knew Josh had zero vanity about his appearance, and that the pose was completely unstudied. So he simply looked...*stunning* was the word that came to mind.

He was tall, with interesting gray eyes, and his lean build was muscular in all the right places, but he'd never been classically handsome. He still wasn't. Josh Taylor was, in Ella's considered opinion, something much worse: a living and breathing, walking and talking sex symbol. Which wouldn't necessarily have been a bad thing, of course, except that he'd made it plain on numerous occasions that he had no interest in her, sexual or otherwise.

He smiled at her, a thousand watts of undiluted charisma directed straight at her gut. "Hi, Ella. How are you? I'm sorry to arrive at this hour without calling first, but your phone number's unlisted." His voice washed over her, a husky baritone that never failed to produce an idiotic tingling in the pit of her stomach.

She ignored the tingling and returned his smile with an impassive nod. Josh had been driving her hormones crazy ever since she hit puberty, which meant that by now she had a lot of practice ignoring the various undesirable effects he produced on her nervous system. Last Christmas had nearly defeated even her iron self-discipline, but if she could survive that—and she had—she could survive anything.

"That's all right. Come in. What's up?" She spoke without warmth. She'd learned that when in Josh's company she had only two choices if she wanted to keep her feelings for him under wraps. She could either sound cold, or she could sound stupid. Cold seemed the better of two lousy choices.

He walked into the living room and she caught the

faintest hint of his cologne, something very expensive and subtly reminiscent of forests and freshwater springs. She scuttled sideways so that he wouldn't be rewarded with a whiff of stale parfum de giblets.

He headed for the sofa, but didn't sit down. She had the oddest impression that he was ill at ease, which was a state of mind she'd never previously associated with Josh, who had made it through high school anointed as the King of Cool. As far as she could tell from her distant observation point, he had effortlessly maintained the title ever since. The founder and CEO of a company that manufactured packaging materials for products ranging from medical equipment through computer components to Christmas decorations, he'd avoided the dot com crash and remained a millionaire. Soon after Ella arrived in San Antonio, he'd been voted number two on the list of Most Eligible Bachelors in Texas.

"Is something wrong?" she repeated, unable to think of any other reason he would come to call. He'd paid his dutiful, welcome-to-San-Antonio visit the first week she arrived in town. Josh had always been big on getting unpleasant chores over with as quickly as possible. Almost visibly gritting his teeth, he'd offered to show her the sights, since she was new in town and he'd been living in San Antonio for almost ten years now and knew some interesting, off-the-beaten-track places to visit. She'd thanked him politely, and told him she'd be in touch when her work schedule eased up a little. They'd both known she wouldn't be in touch, and that was the last time they'd spoken to each other.

Josh hesitated. "Actually, I'm afraid there is something wrong." He drew in a visible breath. "I've been rehearsing how to say this all the way over here, and I can't find any way to make the news sound better, so here goes. Your mother's in the hospital. She had a heart attack earlier today. I'm so sorry, Ella."

For a moment her mind went blank. She should have known something was terribly wrong, she thought when her brain started functioning again. Only a disaster would have kept her parents from calling on Thanksgiving.

Her mom was in the hospital. The peanut butter and strawberry jam churned ominously in her stomach, threatening to come back up, and she turned abruptly, hurrying into the kitchen for a glass of water.

Josh followed her, his gaze both sympathetic and unexpectedly gentle. "Here, sit down, for a moment, Ella. Take a couple of deep breaths."

He pulled out a chair for her and she sank onto it, oblivious to her surroundings. "A heart attack you said?"

"Yes—"

"Are they going to operate? Or did she have surgery already? How is she doing?"

"She's had surgery already and she's…holding her own."

Ella looked up quickly. "What does that mean? For goodness' sake, Josh, don't be cryptic."

"You're right, you need to know the truth. She had a triple bypass, but she came through okay, all things considered. Fortunately, Dr. Bitterman happened to be in the hospital when your mom arrived in the ER, and he's one of the best cardiovascular surgeons around. But I'm giving it to you straight, Ella. The heart attack was pretty massive.''

She swallowed, trying to find her voice. "How did it happen? When, exactly?''

"This afternoon. Apparently Frank came in from the garden and found her collapsed in front of the TV. That was about two-thirty, just as my parents were getting ready to join your parents for Thanksgiving dinner.''

Ella stared at him, her forehead wrinkling. The news that her mother had suffered a massive heart attack was too shocking to be absorbed, but she could grasp the fact that hours had passed and nobody had phoned to let her know. "Mom had the heart attack at two-thirty? My God, that's hours and hours ago, even with the time difference! Why didn't anyone call me, for goodness' sake?''

He didn't answer at once. Josh wasn't guarding his feelings tonight the way he usually did and, even though she was so worried, Ella could see that he was choosing his words carefully. And that wasn't a good sign, she reflected grimly.

"From what my father told me, it was an emergency situation,'' Josh said. "He and my mother arrived at your parents' house just as your dad was calling 911. Since the hospital's only ten minutes away, they decided it would be better to drive your mom straight to the emergency room in their car. There was no time for phone calls, even to you.''

Ella gulped. "Does that mean Mom was so bad they were afraid to wait for the paramedics to arrive?''

"Your mom was unconscious after she had her attack, and she quit breathing a couple of times," Josh admitted.

Ella's hand crept to her throat. "Oh, my God. Poor Dad. He must have been beside himself."

"Yeah, I'm sure he was. Frank is such a quiet, soft-spoken man that it's easy to forget how deeply his feelings run, but my mother did mention that he was almost catatonic with shock. When they got to the hospital and your mom was taken into emergency surgery, Frank wanted to call you right away, but with all the stress of the situation, he couldn't remember your new phone number. He tried calling Directory Assistance, but they insisted they couldn't reveal your number even in an emergency. That just made him even more stressed, of course, so my parents told him they'd take care of locating you. Knowing I live in the same town, they called my house and left a message on the answering machine asking me to phone them urgently as soon as I got home. I didn't get back until an hour ago, and I came over the minute I'd finished speaking to them."

"Thank you for that, Josh. I appreciate you bringing the news in person."

"You're very welcome, except that I wish it hadn't been such bad news."

Oddly, Ella was glad that she'd heard it from him. Maybe this was one of those rare situations where the fact that they'd known each other since she was in kindergarten outweighed the fact that she'd made a total idiot of herself over him all through high school, and had been trying to freeze a multitude of embarrassing memories into nonexistence ever since. When you'd been suffering from unrequited love since you were fifteen, there were a lot of embarrassing memories.

"I'm very grateful you came over here so quickly, Josh, but your parents shouldn't have bothered you. They could have found a number for the hotel where I work and reached me that way."

He smiled, but without a trace of his usual mockery. "Yes, of course they could, but I'm glad they didn't. If either of my parents was in the hospital, you'd want to know, wouldn't you?"

"Of course—"

"Then you must realize I would want to know that Mary has had a heart attack. Your parents and mine have been next-door neighbors for thirty years. Mary's a lot closer to me than half of my real family."

The numbness was fading just a little bit. "The fact that your parents were right there probably kept Dad from falling completely apart," Ella said. "If this had to happen, I'm so glad they were on hand."

"Yes, although they're almost as worried and non-functional as your dad. You can imagine what it was like for all of them. One minute the most important thing on their minds was whether they should play bridge or watch the football game once they'd finished Thanksgiving dinner. Moments later, they're wondering if your mom is going to survive long enough to make it to the hospital. It's not surprising that nobody was behaving too rationally—"

A terrifying thought struck Ella, and she reached out to clutch Josh's arm, something she would never have done in normal circumstances. "But Mom did survive, didn't she? Josh, tell me the truth. Don't try to be kind and hold back. My mom didn't…die…did she?"

He put his hand over hers, and she glanced down, startled. Normally, she would have jerked away from the contact. Tonight his touch felt warm and reassuring, and she left her hand tucked beneath his.

"Mary most certainly didn't die," Josh said. "In fact, the news is a little better now than it was earlier. I called my parents on my cell phone thirty seconds before I rang your doorbell, and Mary's condition had just been upgraded from critical to serious. It's the first step, Ella. She's a fighter. She'll pull through."

Ella lifted her gaze from their interlinked hands and stared blankly at the note on the fridge door reminding her to pick up her dry cleaning tomorrow morning on the way to work. She could no longer visualize a world in which such trivial tasks as picking up dry cleaning seemed important enough to merit a reminder note. She tried to think what she ought to do next, but her mind was jammed with terrifying images of her mother, frail and unconscious in a hospital bed. Mary wasn't tall, and her build was slight, but she'd always struck Ella as wiry, strong, and indomitable. How could her mother possibly be fighting for her life in the ICU? The whole idea was ridiculous.

"I'm guessing you'll want to leave for Long Island as soon as you can get a plane," Josh said, interrupting the depressing mental movie of her mom, suffering.

Of course! She needed to get home just as fast as she could. Why hadn't she thought of that for herself? Ella stood up and reached into the cupboard where she kept her phone directory. "Do you think I have any hope of getting a plane reservation at this hour? Thanksgiving's the busiest travel period of the year. Do planes even fly directly east out of the airport this late at night?"

"No, you'd have to go via Dallas, or possibly Chicago, and you probably wouldn't get an onward connection until morning. But I have a suggestion." Josh came and stood next to her, this time maintaining the eighteen inches of space that seemed to be their unspoken, but mutually agreed, barrier. How strange that both of them should be so uncomfortable at the prospect of accidentally touching each other, Ella thought. She'd never really noticed before that Josh avoided physical contact every bit as much as she did.

Then Josh spoke, and the thought skittered away, breaking under the weight of concern for her mother. "By a really fortunate coincidence, a friend of mine is flying his own plane back to New York City tonight. He's already had a flight plan approved to land at La Guardia Airport. That's not more than a thirty minute cab ride from the hospital if traffic's reasonable. I explained your situation to him, and he's more than happy to help out. He says the whole back of the plane is empty. It's a small jet, configured to take eight passengers. We could be at your mom's bedside in just a few hours."

Ella didn't stop to analyze Josh's offer, or to wonder at the amazing convenience that a friend of his just happened to be flying his own plane back to the New York area at the very moment she needed to get to Long Island. She turned to him, her gratitude so overwhelming that she forgot to insert the usual filter between her feelings and her voice.

"Thank you," she said huskily. "I'd love to take your friend up on his offer. I'm so glad you're here, Josh."

CHAPTER THREE

JOSH LET OUT A SMALL SIGH of relief when he saw the Learjet waiting on the runway as promised, wing lights glowing and engines revving. Now, if the pilot had just been given the crucial message that he was supposed to be one of Josh's best buddies, they should brush through the next stage of the journey without disaster. In a perverse sort of way, it was fortunate that Ella had been so devastated by the news about her mother. Her perceptions, normally razor sharp, were blunted by stress. With luck, she might not pick up on the fact that Josh hadn't told her the literal truth about why he just happened to have a plane ready and waiting to fly her to Long Island.

It was, of course, completely insane that Josh didn't dare to risk telling her the simple truth. Namely that he'd hired a private jet because he knew it was the best, fastest and most comfortable way to get to her mother's bedside, and he could afford the expense, so why the hell not. If she knew the truth, Ella would accept the ride because she was desperate to get home, but she would feel burdened by what she would consider his excessive generosity, and their already bleak relationship would take another step backward down the icy road of mutual misunderstanding.

Josh had decided some time ago that God must be female, otherwise Her life lessons couldn't possibly be so damn difficult to understand. Take his totally screwed-up relationship with Ella, for example. The brutal truth was that he was hopelessly in love with a woman who, on the rare occasions they met, afforded him about as much attention as she did the sports pages in last week's newspaper. She didn't even pay him the compliment of actively disliking him; she was merely indifferent to his existence.

In his saner moments, Josh realized his situation was far from unique. He accepted that men often had the misfortune to fall in love with women who didn't return the favor, and vice versa. He understood that half the world's art, music, and literature wouldn't exist if men and women managed to find the perfect mate the moment they started looking.

That didn't make it one damn bit easier to cope with his feelings. The irony of the situation was that he'd lived next door to Ella since she was four years old. He'd spent the next twenty-seven years ignoring her, before being smitten with something that had felt pretty damn close to a lightning bolt from the sky. If God wasn't having a private joke at Josh's expense, how else to explain that it had taken him a quarter of a century to realize that his soul mate lived next door? Okay, so he might be a bit of a slow learner where relationships were concerned, but twenty-seven years to notice that he'd fallen in love was flat-out ridiculous.

The lightning bolt of revelation had struck last Christmas when Josh had gone home for the holidays.

It had been his first trip home in three years and he'd almost canceled it. There was a mini crisis brewing at the factory and the demands of his work as CEO of his own company happened to be especially intense. Besides, much as he loved his family, he found all of them gathered in one place way too much of a good thing. That was why he usually preferred to treat his parents to winter vacations in the Bahamas, or the Caribbean, where he could catch up on family togetherness without the added pressure of staying in his parents' house. Last Christmas, though, his parents insisted that they didn't want a fancy vacation. They just wanted him to come home for the holidays.

Then, right at the last minute, Josh's longtime girlfriend developed the flu and didn't feel well enough to travel. So in addition to losing time he couldn't afford at work, and being polite when his parents invited every neighbor within a ten-mile radius to meet their millionaire son, he was also deprived of the buffer that would have been provided by Jenny's presence. Josh volunteered to stay in San Antonio with her, but she urged him not to disappoint his parents, especially since she felt rotten enough that all she wanted to do was to lie in bed and be left alone.

It was typical of Jenny's generosity that she wouldn't allow her own illness to interfere with Josh's holiday plans. He and Jenny had been dating on and off for over a year. They'd reached the point in their lives where the singles scene no longer held much appeal and they'd talked sporadically about their mutual desire to settle down. They'd never discussed specific marriage plans, but Josh was pretty sure Jenny would say yes if…when…he proposed. They both wanted children, they enjoyed the same books and movies and Jenny had no career ambitions. She would be more than happy to quit her job and stay at home, helping with the heavy social demands that came with him being the boss of his own company. In fact, Jenny was so pliant and easy to get along with that Josh would have been hard put to name a single issue on which she felt strongly enough to disagree with him.

It seemed a starting place to build a future, if not exactly the passionate relationship he'd once dreamed of finding. After hesitating for a couple of months, Josh had bought an engagement ring that he'd planned to give Jenny on Christmas Day, a traditional solitaire diamond since she was a traditional type of woman.

Then she got sick. Since Josh knew she would hate to receive a proposal of marriage when she could barely lift her head from the pillow without groaning, he decided to wait until the holiday was over before popping the question.

So he'd said goodbye to his probable wife-to-be and, thoroughly grouchy, had flown thousands of miles across country to spend Christmas with his parents in Long Island. On his first night home, in a feeble attempt to demonstrate some holiday spirit, he'd given in to his brother's teasing and kissed Ella under the fake mistletoe his mother had hung from the rec room ceiling.

The joke had definitely been on him. Within seconds of taking Ella into his arms, his sensible plans for a sensible marriage had exploded into chaos. The kiss was supposed to be casual. What else, for heaven's sake, when his kissing partner was Ella, the girl next door? What else, with a dozen of their assorted relatives laughing and cheering him on?

Instead, he touched his mouth to Ella's soft lips—and his world shifted on its axis. The kiss changed from casual to consuming in approximately one second. And then went on. And on. God knew how long he would have continued the kiss, or how passionately intimate it would have become, if Ella hadn't broken away and left him standing alone under the mistletoe, his knees shaking and his world shattered.

After their kiss, on the rare occasions over the next couple of days that Ella turned her incredible green eyes in his direction, Josh had barely been able to prevent himself from grabbing her and sprinting for the nearest horizontal surface in a room with a lock and key. In fact, a horizontal surface wouldn't have been necessary. Any room with a lock and key would have seemed like paradise, given the white-hot state of his lust.

Since he was, unfortunately, a civilized man, staying in his parents' home, he'd refrained from ripping Ella's clothes off—just barely—and had spent the rest of his stay sneaking awestruck glances at her, like a high school kid in the throes of his very first teenage infatuation.

It was as if he'd never seen her before. Which, to all intents and purposes, he never had. In Josh's mind, Ella had always been the scabby-kneed kid next door, four years younger than him on the calendar, a generation younger in his mind. To him, she was simply the girl his baby brother, Eric, had dated during the final year of high school, and the girl his parents loved like a daughter.

So it had been with gut-wrenching astonishment that Josh registered the incredible fact that all-elbows-and-knees Gabriella Petri had morphed into the most beautiful woman he'd ever set eyes on. Her body was still slender, but it now curved—fabulously—in all the right places. Her long dirty-blond braids had been converted to lush, chin-length waves, gleaming with golden highlights. And then, of course, there were those stunning green eyes that could reduce him to rubble with a single glance. What foxhole had he been living in while this miracle transformation was happening, Josh wondered. How in hell had he remained so blind for so long?

It wasn't just that Ella was beautiful, he discovered, or even that she was also whipcord smart. He'd always known that she was bright, and he'd grown accustomed over the years to hearing snippets of information from his parents about her latest academic or professional success. She didn't talk too much about her job when he was around, but what little she said showed how hard she worked and how ambitious she was. Unlike Jenny, her job was a lot more to her than a way to earn a living while waiting to get married.

Her opinion of social and political issues fascinated him. Even when he disagreed with her views, which was at least half the time, he found her take on the issues stimulating. Jenny's willingness to agree with him on every possible subject bored him, he realized belatedly. Harmony was all very well, but after a while it was like eating oatmeal without sugar, or even salt.

Ella not only had opinions she was willing to express, she was fun to be around. Josh noticed how kind she was to his parents, and how loving toward her own. She was a people person—not surprising, given that she'd chosen a job in the hospitality industry—and she even managed to be polite to Brittany, his incredibly annoying sister-in-law. Eric and Brittany had a three-month-old baby daughter, and Ella seemed genuinely entranced by the baby, although Josh wasn't quite sure what it actually did except eat, sleep and cry. The latter, it seemed, with far greater frequency than either of the former.

But Jenny was a kind person, too, and she also loved animals and babies, and yet Josh's heart didn't feel as if it would burst when he looked at her. Whereas just being in the same room as Ella made him ache all over. He wondered what the precise source of Ella's magical power over him might be.

He had found that question difficult to answer. In one way, he felt connected to her as he had never felt connected to any other person. In another way, she was utterly mysterious to him. What were her dreams? Did she want to marry and have children? Or was she dedicated to becoming the youngest president in the history of the Sedgwick Hotel chain? That was the trouble with knowing someone forever, Josh reflected. You forgot to check in and find out what had changed about them since you last slugged baseballs to each other twenty-something years ago.

The Taylors and the Petris more or less lived in each other's homes over the holidays, so he had plenty of opportunity to spend time with Ella and ponder why he was falling in love. He studied her intently, hungry for clues as to why he'd been attacked by this unbearable yearning. Ella was a lot more outgoing than he was, he concluded. She found it easier to relax in a noisy group, and she seemed to be much more tolerant of people's foibles than he was. But their fundamental personalities meshed. When he smiled at an incident nobody else seemed to find funny, he could almost guarantee that Ella would be smiling, too. More important, and despite her willingness to be sociable, he sensed a vulnerability deep inside her, a core of isolation that called out to his own barely acknowledged loneliness.

Neither his parents, nor his brother, nor the Petris ever gave any indication of needing to be alone, but Ella seemed to seek solitude at precisely the same times he did. When he felt the need to decompress from too much family togetherness, he would walk out onto the porch to gulp in some frosty winter air, and nine times out of ten, Ella would already be there.

But that, unfortunately, seemed to be the point where their miraculous harmony ended. She would be out on the porch, staring at the pine tree his parents had planted twenty-three years ago and which now spread massive branches across an entire corner of the yard. Leaning against one of the porch posts, with her arms folded across her chest, and her hands tucked under her sweater for warmth, she would look in perfect sync with his mood, the personification of the woman he wanted to spend the rest of his life with.

Except that as soon as she heard his footsteps, she would give him one of her quick smiles that didn't quite reach her incredible eyes and make some remark about feeling cold. Then she'd retreat inside the house again, leaving him in solitary splendor on the porch.

Which was exactly what he would have wanted any other year. In the period of his blindness, as he thought of it now.

They parted at the end of the holiday having barely exchanged a private word, Ella flying to Chicago in time to work the Sedgwick Hotel's hectic New Year's Eve schedule, and Josh to San Antonio where the shortage of raw material at the factory had turned into a full-blown crisis.

As their time together came to an end, he wondered how in the world Ella could look at him and not see that he was desperate for some sign from her—anything, however small—that would indicate that she'd felt at least a minor jolt from the lightning bolt that had burned him to the core.

The sign never came. In fact, the opposite happened. Ella carefully avoided giving him her standard kiss on the cheek when they said goodbye, as if she were afraid he might misinterpret the gesture and repeat his under-the-mistletoe performance. She didn't even offer to shake hands. Instead, she just stood in the hallway of her parents' house and politely wished him a safe trip, her voice cool, her gaze remote as it followed him down the path to his waiting limo.

So much for overwhelming passion, sparked by a kiss.

There was only one minor silver lining to the entire miserable experience. Painful as it was to break up with a woman he genuinely liked, Josh knew he and

Jenny should both be grateful that she'd succumbed to the flu on Christmas Eve, and that he'd postponed his plans to propose. Wiser than he had been only a week earlier, he realized—almost too late—that he and Jenny would have made each other very unhappy. They were two people who shared some superficial interests but had nothing in common at the deepest level, where compatibility really grew and wove together the roots of a marriage. He supposed there were some marriages based on friendship that worked out okay, but it wasn't what he wanted, Josh realized. He wanted passion and fire to warm his home and his life.

He wanted Ella.

CHAPTER FOUR

A GUST OF COLD WIND, blown in from the snow-covered prairie, struck Josh's face as they passed through the steel mesh gate onto the tarmac, returning him abruptly to the reality of the present. A man in a flight suit, holding a clipboard, was walking from the plane to greet them. He gave a friendly wave as he approached. "Hi, Josh. I've just signed off on the fuel, so everything's ready to go. You've made good time."

Josh glanced at the silver name tag pinned to the man's flight suit. David Lurden. "Hi, Dave." Josh shook hands and gave the man a light punch on the arm, as if they'd known each other for years. Thank goodness the guy had been smart enough not to wear his company's dress uniform, donning a nondescript beige jumpsuit instead.

"Traffic's light on the roads, as you'd expect at this time of night," Josh said. "This is my friend, Gabriella Petri. We're both really grateful for your offer to take us to New York. We sure do appreciate it, Dave."

"My pleasure. Good to meet you, Ms....um... Petri." Dave was no actor, and he stumbled as he spoke, but Ella, as Josh had hoped, didn't seem to notice anything amiss, despite the jarring formality in Dave's attitude.

"Please call me Ella," she said, shaking Dave's hand. "I don't know how to thank you for being so generous. I would have had a dreadful time trying to book a seat on a commercial airline at Thanksgiving. I'm just so grateful to you."

"No problem. My pleasure to help out, in fact. The…um…seats in back would be going to waste if you weren't in them." If Dave thought they were both nuts, he managed to conceal his opinion pretty well. His voice boomed with nervous good cheer.

"Well, then. Let's get on board, stow your bags, sir—" He caught the warning glint in Josh's eyes and quickly corrected himself. "We'll stow your bags, Josh, and I'll introduce you to my copilot, Bob Rainey. I'm not allowed to fly this plane without somebody available to take over the controls in case I have a heart attack or something—"

"Yeah, that seems smart," Josh interjected.

Ella turned to him, managing a smile, although it wavered a bit. "It's okay, Josh. I'm not going to fall apart because Dave mentions the words heart attack. I'm not that fragile."

Where worries about her mother's health was concerned, he thought she might be more fragile than she knew. But nothing would be achieved by suggesting as much, so Josh concentrated instead on getting them both settled onboard as swiftly as possible. The plane's cabin was configured to be practical for business meetings, with two blocks of double seats upholstered in gray leather facing each other across a central table, seating eight in all. Not the ideal arrangement for a nighttime flight, but at least the seats were spacious, well padded, and had plenty of leg room.

Once they were airborne, he found pillows and a blanket and offered them to Ella.

"You can stretch out and try to get some sleep," he suggested, glancing at the wall monitor which displayed their flight details, superimposed over a map of the States. "It's going to take at least five hours to reach New York, so you might as well get some rest."

She took the pillows and blanket with a murmur of thanks, but after less than ten minutes, she sat up again, pushing the blanket aside. "Can't sleep?" Josh asked softly, putting down the trade journal he'd been skimming.

She shook her head. "Every time I close my eyes, I'm swamped with images of my mother on life support. It's more exhausting than staying awake."

"Would you like a magazine? I saw copies of *Time* and *Newsweek* on the shelf by the minibar."

"Do you think we could just talk?" Belatedly, she noticed the journal open on his lap. "Oh, but not if you're catching up on your business reading. I'm sorry if I interrupted—"

"I'd much prefer to talk to you." Which was certainly the truth, Josh reflected, tossing the magazine aside. "I was already feeling bored with my own company. Tell me about your new job. Are you enjoying living in San Antonio?"

"I think I'm going to love it. But so far, other than the route to and from the hotel, I haven't seen much more of the city than the River Walk and the Alamo memorial. I haven't even been to the zoo, although it's so close to where I live. At least I already know I love the climate. After three years in Chicago, it's great to see so much sun, especially at this time of year.''

"Yes, it must be a pleasant change. Although there's a lot more to San Antonio than sunshine and blue skies. Or even the River Walk and the Alamo. You'll have to let me show you some of my favorite places when we get back.''

He'd made that offer already, Josh reminded himself, and Ella was no more likely to take him up on it this time than she had been before. He was suddenly impatient with his lack of courage. He was about to spend five hours alone with the woman he loved almost to distraction. Surely to God he could think of something more interesting to discuss than sightseeing in San Antonio.

Josh leaned back against the opulently cushioned leather seat and tried to appear relaxed. He was a man who enjoyed challenges, he reminded himself. He could do this, possibly even without making a total horse's ass out of himself. True, last month he'd had a meeting with the vice president of the United States and had felt significantly less nervous than he did right now. On the other hand, the worst Ella could do was freeze him into silence. Since she'd done that a few hundred times before, it wouldn't be a new or shocking experience.

He cleared his throat. "About six months ago my parents told me you'd met a great guy and were thinking of getting married,'' he said, taking the plunge and hoping his voice wouldn't squeak. "Bruce, I believe his name was. Is marriage to Bruce still a possibility even though you've moved away from Chicago?"

Ella looked startled by the abrupt change from social chitchat to a probing personal question, but at least she didn't give him one of her patented icy stares. In fact, she looked almost amused. "I should have realized Mom and Dad would report all the supposedly fascinating details about Bruce to your parents," she said ruefully.

He leaped onto her word choice. "Supposedly?"

She gave an embarrassed smile. "The truth is that my mother is so anxious for me to get married and start popping out babies that I get lectured every phone call on the need to find myself a nice man and settle down. In self-defense, I've taken to stretching the truth a tad where my boyfriends are concerned. If Mom thinks I'm making a serious effort to get myself married off, she eases up a bit on the nagging."

"That's a tactic I'll have to add to my repertoire," Josh murmured.

"You get nagged, too?"

"Nonstop. With many unfavorable comparisons to my brother Eric, and the fact that my sister-in-law is already expecting her second baby whereas I don't even have a steady girlfriend."

Ella gave a sympathetic sigh. "Then you'll understand why I pushed the truth about Bruce. He was an okay guy, I guess, and we dated for quite a few months, but we never came close to getting engaged. Then he dumped me about three months ago."

Dumped her? *Dumped Ella?* The man was clearly

insane. "You don't exactly sound devastated," Josh managed.

"Far from it." She grinned. "Actually, any woman who ends up married to Bruce will have to resign herself to living in a threesome—herself, Bruce, and his oversize ego. Speaking for myself, I'd prefer a marriage with just two people in it."

Josh returned her grin, perfectly willing to smile about Bruce now that he knew Ella wasn't in love with the guy. She'd also given him the perfect opening to ask another personal question, and he seized it. "But would you like to get married some day? If you could find the right man, that is?"

She hesitated for just a moment, as if not sure how much to confide in him. Then she nodded. "Yes, I love my job, and I enjoy the strokes—not to mention the paycheck—that come from having a successful career, but I'd like to be married one day, too."

"And have children?" Josh asked.

"Definitely. How about you?"

"I want to have kids," he said. "I'd like to have two, or even three. But it's nearly always the woman whose career gets put on hold when it comes to having babies, so I realize I may have to be satisfied with just one. If my wife is trying to juggle a demanding job along with being a mother, that's a lot of balls for her to keep in the air."

"You could help her out at home and ease the load a bit." There was a hint of challenge in Ella's voice.

"True," he said mildly. "And I could even afford to hire a cleaning service to take care of the house, but that sort of help only goes so far when you're getting up half a dozen times during the night to feed a newborn infant. It's tough to keep up in the workplace when you're barely functional from sleep deprivation.''

"You and your wife will be a lot luckier than most new parents, though. Because of your financial situation, your wife can afford to take time off from work without worrying about money to pay the bills.''

"You're right, that's a plus. And I'd definitely cut back on my work schedule. There doesn't seem to be much point in producing kids unless you plan to hang out with them while they're growing up.''

Ella looked at him, her expression revealing her surprise. Because he planned to spend time with his children, if he had any? Because he acknowledged that even in the twenty-first century, women still had a tougher time than men when it came to combining careers and children? Josh found it disconcerting to realize that Ella didn't know much more about his hopes and dreams than he did about hers.

"I imagine you want to continue working even if you do have children," Josh said. "My mother talks all the time about the success you've made of your career with Sedgwick Hotels.'' His mother talked so much about Ella for the simple reason that Josh had become incredibly skilled at steering the conversation in that direction.

She hesitated again. "Right now, I enjoy my job,'' she said finally. "But working in the hotel industry isn't what I want to do with the rest of my life.''

"With your managerial expertise, you'd be valuable

to almost any company. What sort of a change are you thinking of?''

''Nothing at all, unless I get married. Then, if we could afford to live on just my husband's salary— which is a big if, these days—I'd really like to change directions and stay home for a few years to become a foster parent. Maybe even go back to school so that I could get the qualifications to work with children who've been neglected or abused.''

''Does that mean you'd like to be a foster parent instead of having children of your own?''

Ella shook her head. ''No, I'm greedy. I want it all. I want to have the experience of pregnancy and giving birth, but I'd like to become a foster parent, too.''

Josh went to the minibar and selected a couple of sodas. Soda for him, diet soda for Ella. He might not know the secrets of her heart, but he had all the trivial stuff down pat. ''Wouldn't you find it hard to give the foster kids back to their birth families, maybe just when you'd started to love them?'' he asked.

''Yes, it would be dreadful. But in a way, that's the major problem facing the foster care system. The money foster parents receive barely covers expenses, and very few people are willing to tackle the job of raising kids on a temporary basis, precisely because it's so emotionally wrenching when the time to give them up rolls around. That means it's difficult to find decent foster homes for a lot of kids. Nowadays, any healthy newborn baby can find half a dozen couples who want to adopt it, but the picture's nowhere near as rosy if you're a kid in need of temporary care. While your mother's in jail, for example. Or if you're living with your grandmother, and she ends up in the hospital. And if you're unlucky enough to be orphaned or abandoned when you're a teenager—well, forget about finding a new family. You'd better resign yourself to living in some sort of institution or group home, because that's where you're likely to end up."

"You sound angry."

"I guess I am. Every child deserves to have at least one person in the world who really cares what happens to him, and that sure isn't happening right now. Kids in the child welfare system reach their eighteenth birthday, the government cuts off payments, and they're thrown out into the world to sink or swim on their own. No surprise, a lot of them sink." She shrugged, not quite managing to appear casual. "I guess some of my interest in the foster care system stems from the fact that I could have been one of the kids abandoned to the mercies of the child welfare bureaucracy if the Petris hadn't been willing to take me in."

It had never been any secret that Ella had been adopted by Frank and Mary when she was already four years old. Josh even had a vague memory of the day the Petris brought her home. He'd been eight at the time, and aggressively uninterested in boring things like girls. Then he discovered that Ella was better at catching baseballs than his brother Eric, also four, and he occasionally condescended to go out into the backyard and toss a few balls in her direction.

Beguiled by the unexpected memory, he felt his mouth curve into a smile. "You were a prickly little thing when Frank and Mary brought you home, but amazingly cute as I recall. Some other couple would have jumped at the chance to adopt you if they hadn't.''

''Maybe. At four, I was still easily adoptable. But a year later? Three years later? That might have been another story. Besides, what if I hadn't been cute? What if I'd been ugly from abuse and neglect? What if I'd been a real discipline problem? I'd still have been just as desperate for a home and people to love me.'' Ella lifted the top on her soda can and took a deep swallow. In part, Josh suspected, because it gave her something to do while she got her emotions under control.

She put down her soda before speaking again. ''I often wonder what sort of a family I come from. I wonder why they just…gave me away when my birth mother died. Were they all so desperately poor that they couldn't afford another mouth to feed? Or was my mother estranged from her family so that they weren't willing to have anything to do with me, just because I was her child?''

''Do you have any memories at all from the time before you were adopted?'' Josh asked.

''It's questionable how much a person can remember from that early an age. I don't have many memories, and what I do remember doesn't seem to tie in with the facts, so I've never paid much attention to the few snippets I can call up. For example, I have this vivid mental picture of a man walking through the front door and scooping me up into his arms, then swinging me around high above his head. Whenever that image flashes into my mind, I know the man is my father, and that I've been waiting eagerly for him to get home from work. Then there are these tiny wisps of memory I get of playing in the bathtub with another baby, younger than me. I can actually see us fighting for possession of a plastic boat, which was our favorite toy."

"What color is the boat?" Josh asked.

"Blue," she said instantly. She shrugged. "Okay, so the image is quite clear. Except neither of those memories makes any sense, because my biological father abandoned my mother before I was born and nobody's ever suggested that she had a second child by another man."

Which didn't necessarily prove much, Josh reflected, keeping his thought to himself. If Ella had a sibling who'd been adopted into another family, why would anyone at the agency mention it? "What did Frank and Mary tell you about your birth family?" he asked.

Ella's gaze softened at the mention of her adoptive parents. "Well, you know my dad. He's great at discussing music and sport. He's not so great at discussing personal stuff. As for Mary, she always claims that the adoption agency wasn't willing to provide any background information, except that my birth mother had tried her best to raise me, but she was poor, and then she got sick and died."

"It's a perfectly credible story," Josh said.

"Yes, I know, but somehow, I've never quite believed it. Mary isn't a good liar, and she squirms every time I ask a question about the circumstances surrounding my adoption."

"There could be a really simple explanation for that," Josh pointed out. "Perhaps Mary prefers not to be reminded that you were once part of another woman's family." Especially if Ella's birth mother had ended up in jail for some crime related to her extreme poverty, Josh reflected. Knowing Mary, he was sure she would do her utmost to shield her adopted daughter from information like that. Much better, from Mary's point of view, if Ella believed her birth mother was dead.

Ella nodded. "It could be that, I guess. But that brings me back to my original question. If my birth mother died so young, why didn't anybody in her family take me in? Didn't she have brothers or sisters? What about her parents? Were they both dead, too? If so, I must come from a rather short-lived gene pool."

"The story you've been told is the most likely one," Josh suggested. "If your mother's relatives were all too poor to take care of you, adoption would have been their best choice."

"Then why haven't those relatives kept in touch with me?" Ella unlocked her seat belt and got to her feet. She paced the small cabin, her head scraping the ceiling, making her look caged, as if her thoughts were chasing her. "If the only problem was that my birth mother and her family were poor, why haven't I been told their names? Why does everything about my past seem such a *secret?*"

Josh didn't let his sympathy show. Knowing that he felt sorry for her was the last thing Ella would want. "People weren't as open about adoptions in those days, you know that. Your birth family probably has no idea how to get in touch with you, even if they want to. I have a good friend in San Antonio, Emily Sutton. Well, Emily Chambers now, since she got married eighteen months ago. She's a really talented interior designer and we met five years ago when she redecorated my office. She's about your age, and she happens to be adopted, too. She recently found her birth mother and father after hiring a firm of investigators to do a professional search. When she was telling me the story of her search, she mentioned that it's only recently that adoption agencies have begun to encourage birth families and adoptive families to keep the lines of communication open. Before that everything was deliberately shrouded in secrecy. In fact, the details Emily's adoptive parents were given about her origins turn out to have been almost completely untrue. Mary and Frank may be in exactly the same situation."

Ella nodded. "I guess that sort of thing happened all the time up until a few years ago. And you're right. I shouldn't see mysteries where there's nothing but typical bureaucratic obscurity." She shrugged, halting her pacing at the entrance to the cockpit. "Anyway, this isn't the moment for me to start worrying about my birth mother. Mom would hate that, and she doesn't need anything else to worry her right now."

"Are you sure she doesn't want you to trace your birth family? You might be surprised by her reaction."

Ella shook her head. "No, I'm sure. About five years ago, I talked to Mom about getting in touch with the agency where I was adopted, but she was really unhappy with the suggestion. I was surprised at how passionate she was on the subject, actually. She pleaded with me to leave well enough alone and not to go poking into a past that was better left unexplored.''

''So you respected Mary's wishes and backed off?''

Ella pulled a face. ''You're giving me way too much credit, Josh. It wasn't so much about respecting my mom's wishes. To tell the truth, I got scared about what I might uncover. I began to wonder if my birth mother was a convicted ax murderer, or something equally awful. Mom was so adamant about not doing any research that it wasn't hard to figure out that she'd been told something pretty terrible about my background.''

For a second or two Ella looked so desolate that Josh forgot all about the No Touch Zone. He got up and crossed the narrow space separating them and put his arm around her shoulders, a gesture that was intended to convey nothing but comfort. He should have realized that feeling sympathy for her was no protection against the swarm of other emotions simmering just beneath the surface of his role as polite family friend. He felt a surge of electricity shoot up his arm at the contact, the jolt so powerful that it paralyzed his ability to move. Teeth clenched, he waited for Ella to back away as she always did whenever he came within touching distance.

But she didn't move. Instead, she turned slowly so that she was facing him, her back resting against the smooth wall of the plane, her breasts almost brushing his chest. He couldn't stand entirely upright in the small jet, so he was bent over her, increasing the intimacy of their position. Her green eyes were shadowed, but they met his gaze straight on and something stirred deep inside him. Josh held her gaze, his brain turning to mush. If he leaned forward even fractionally, they would be touching from shoulder to thigh. God, he wanted to kiss her! He sought to distract himself. What the hell had they been talking about? He was sure it had been something important.

A thought formed, fragile and insubstantial, but he fought to hold on to it, not letting it slip back into the pea soup that currently passed for his brain function. He pounded the thought into coherence: if he kissed Ella again, maybe this time there would be no magic and he would be released from her spell. Maybe he could finally rescue himself from his pathetic and painful state of unrequited lust...love...whatever the hell he wanted to call it.

His hand moved before he had time to censor the action, brushing against her cheek. She was pale with fatigue, but color rushed under her skin as he touched her. For once he didn't try to analyze the forty-five different explanations as to why she might be blushing. Without allowing any more time to second-guess himself, he bent his head and covered her mouth with his.

His heart moved into instant overdrive. He'd made a major mistake in kissing her, Josh realized. Far from breaking Ella's spell, the magic had returned, twice as powerful as before. When he kissed other women, he was able to control both his reaction and the intensity of the kiss. He could decide—with cool rationality—whether the kiss would be the prelude to a skillful seduction, or whether it would be just a kiss. He could decide if he would take total charge of the situation, or whether he would allow himself to drift in the pleasure of the moment, deliberately surrendering partial control. With Ella, the choice to surrender wasn't his. He felt helpless, and helplessness wasn't a sensation Josh was accustomed to experiencing in any arena of his life, especially in his emotions.

Her lips were even softer than he remembered, and they seemed to welcome him. Josh didn't tell himself to be gentle, or aggressive, or anything else. Such choices were beyond him. He kissed her hungrily, with aching demand, because that's what his body forced him to do. Her lips parted and he sank deeper and deeper into their kiss. Awareness of their surroundings faded. The taste and scent of her surrounded him until he was totally lost. Lost in the magic that was Ella.

He didn't realize that one of the pilots had come out of the cockpit into the cabin until the man had spoken twice. Ella tried to pull away, but Josh refused to let her go. Be damned if he was going to act as though they were teenagers caught making out behind the bushes in the school yard.

What the hell was the man's name? "Yes, Dave." Josh was amazed to hear that he sounded like a man in full possession of his faculties. "Did you want something?"

The pilot appeared unimpressed by what he'd seen. He'd probably witnessed many more startling activities in his private plane than a fully clothed man kissing a fully clothed woman. "We've had a report of some pretty bad air turbulence up ahead, sir—I mean,

Josh. We need you both to return to your seats and fasten your seat belts. We'll let you know when it's safe to move around again.''

"Thanks, Dave. We'll do that right away.''

For a man who'd lost his mind, Josh thought he sounded blessedly normal. Now if he could only remember how to walk without falling over his own feet, he'd be in great shape. If he didn't look at Ella for the rest of the journey, there was even a good chance that he'd have reclaimed minimal brain function by the time they landed at La Guardia. He could only hope.

CHAPTER FIVE

IT WAS RAINING when Ella and Josh landed at La Guardia airport, a penetrating drizzle that was almost more chilling than snow, but the temperature must have been a degree or two above freezing because there was no ice on the roads. A rental car was already waiting for them on the tarmac, its lights making a welcome glow against the leaden skies. In other circumstances, Ella would have found Josh's efficiency intimidating. As it was, all she felt was gratitude.

Despite the luxury of their flight, she was exhausted; more from stress than physical fatigue, she realized. By the time they left the airport it was the start of the early-morning rush hour, but they were driving against the main flow of traffic and they made good time for the fifteen-mile drive to Saint Luke's, near her parents' home in Port Washington. As the familiar scenery from her childhood sped by, Ella's nerves were stretched to breaking point. What if she arrived at the hospital and her mother was already dead? She could hardly bear the thought, and had no idea how she'd cope with the reality.

She had long since passed beyond the stage where she was capable of having even a semicoherent conversation, and she was relieved that Josh seemed to understand that the struggle to control her panic consumed all her mental resources. He made no attempt to talk to her, just quietly drove them to Saint Luke's. If Josh hadn't been there, Ella supposed she would somehow have pulled herself together enough to get from the airport to her mother's bedside, but she was sincerely thankful that she didn't have to put her survival skills to the test.

Having traveled so far, so fast, it was beyond frustrating to be met at the hospital by a blank wall of bureaucracy. They did manage to find out that her mother was alive, but according to the witch guarding the entrance to the intensive care unit, Ella wouldn't be allowed to see her until the early-morning routine was complete and the day shift of nurses had come on duty. Josh might not be admitted to Mary's room at all, since the doctor had specifically ordered a restriction on the number of visitors. As her punchline, the witch added a comment to the effect that visiting patients was a privilege, not a right, and Ella should come back in an hour, at which time visiting hours officially started.

While Ella was ranting and getting nowhere at the reception desk, Josh made a quiet detour and intercepted a nurse coming off duty. The nurse was much more sympathetic than the sour-faced gorgon in charge, and Josh extracted the information that Ella's mother had slept fairly well and that her father had spent the night in the visitors' lounge. About fifteen minutes ago, the nurse had heard Frank say he was going down to the cafeteria to get some breakfast, and they'd probably find him there.

Since they weren't permitted to visit her mother, Ella and Josh went down to the basement cafeteria in search of her father. The found him seated in a corner, rumpled and weary, his shoulders hunched and his expression miserable. He was drinking coffee and crumbling pieces of a Danish pastry across a paper plate, a newspaper lying unread at his side. Ella's stomach lurched when she saw how haggard her dad appeared beneath the stubble of gray beard, but he jumped up, beaming from ear to ear, when he noticed her walking toward him.

"Ellie, you've arrived!" He wrapped her into a bear hug, with a show of emotion that was quite unlike his usual taciturn self. "Well, you're a sight for sore eyes and that's a fact. I never expected to see you this early. I was afraid you wouldn't even be able to get a plane reservation, what with the Thanksgiving crush, and all."

Ella debated for a second or two about how to reply. During the final stage of the flight from San Antonio, cocooned in the darkness, with the memory of Josh's kiss burned into her, she'd had plenty of time to decide that her feelings toward Josh might be impossible to change, but she could surely find a better, more mature way to behave toward him. What she needed was a little less pride, and a lot less fear of making a fool of herself, combined with at least an occasional attempt at honest communication. And this seemed an excellent moment to start on the honest communication part.

"Josh hired a private plane for the two of us," she told her father, sending Josh a swift, sideways glance as she spoke. "As you can imagine, I'm really grateful to him. There's no way I'd have gotten here so fast if he hadn't been so generous."

Frank turned a bemused gaze toward Josh, who was making incoherent spluttering noises. "Hired a plane, eh? A whole plane, just for the two of you? That was good of you, Josh, a real fine thing to do. We're in your debt, that's for sure. Mary will be real appreciative when she hears."

Josh shuffled his feet and muttered something about no big deal, while Ella tried to absorb the astonishing fact that the King of Cool looked embarrassed and unsure of himself. If this was what a small dose of honesty produced, maybe she should try it more often.

Gathering her courage, she turned to look at him. "I know you didn't want me to realize how generous you were being, Josh, but the pilot was such a lousy actor, it didn't take long to work out what was going on." Amusement crept into her voice. "The second time he called you sir, then tripped over his tongue to correct himself, it was pretty easy to conclude that the guy didn't know you from Adam."

Josh gave her a wry smile. "Yeah, I was afraid you might notice that." He paused for a moment. "You aren't angry, then?"

"Angry?" It was bewildering to realize that Josh—sophisticated, always-has-his-act-together Josh—could be as clueless about her reactions as she was about his. "Why would I be angry because you've spent a fortune to help my family and then tried to make sure nobody would know what you'd done? Groveling with gratitude is more like it."

Josh made a dismissive gesture. "As long as you're okay with it, there's nothing more to be said. I'm glad I could help." He cut off any more thanks by pulling a chair across from another table and sitting down next to Frank. "So tell us about Mary."

"Yes, we want to hear all the details," Ella said, taking her father's hand, which was a better alternative than letting her fingers drum an anxious tattoo on the tabletop. Her father was already a nervous wreck, so he didn't need to see proof that she was pretty much in the same condition. "How's Mom doing this morning? Have you spoken to the doctors today? Have they said when we can expect to bring her home?"

Frank nodded. "I spoke to one of the residents and he mentioned five more days, provided everything goes okay, then at least six weeks at home to recuperate."

"Five days?" Ella gulped, not sure whether to be delighted or worried that her mother would be coming home so quickly after major heart surgery.

"You think it's too soon?" Frank's voice was sharp with anxiety.

"No," Ella said quickly. "I think it's fine. It must mean the doctors are pleased with Mom's progress."

Frank's face set into gloomy lines. "I'm not sure they are." It bothered Ella to see how far removed her dad was from his usual optimistic self. He gave a weary shrug. "You know what it's like nowadays. They want you out of the hospital as soon as you can walk to the bathroom and keep down solid food. No matter to them if you've got a two-foot-long surgical incision. They just give you pain pills and tell you to get on with it.''

"It'll be good to have Mom at home with us, though.'' Ella managed to sound upbeat, although she shared some of her father's anxiety. She hoped to goodness they'd be given a list of warning signs for any dangerous symptoms, not to mention guidelines for routine care. "She'll get better much quicker in her own home, in familiar surroundings.''

"I sure hope so.'' Frank shook his head. "If you'd seen her last night, Ellie, hooked up to so darn many machines and IVs, you'd have thought she'd be kept in here for a month or two at least.''

Ella asked many more questions about the surgery, trying to reassure herself that the procedure had gone well and that the prognosis was good. Finally Josh pointed out that fifty minutes had passed since the gorgon banished them, and that it was time to make their way back upstairs to the ICU.

"What was Mom doing when she had the attack?'' Ella asked her father as they waited for the elevator. "Was she lifting something heavy? She's always doing crazy stuff like that during the holidays. She climbs up into the attic and starts heaving all those old trunks around, looking for Christmas decorations—''

"No, she wasn't lifting anything,'' Frank said, holding the elevator door. "In fact she was resting. We'd finished cooking the turkey, and I'd lifted it out of the oven and set it on the counter to cool a little. Gerry and Barb—'' he nodded toward Josh as he mentioned the Taylors ''—your folks had just called to say they'd be over in fifteen minutes, bringing the sweet potatoes and the green bean casserole with them. Right after they called, Mary decided she wanted some more evergreens for the centerpiece on the table, so I went out into the backyard to cut her a couple of sprigs of pine. She'd been working nonstop all day, and I told her to sit down and put her feet up for a few minutes and take a peek at the newspaper, which she hadn't had time for, what with the cooking, and all."

They'd arrived on the ICU floor, but Frank was so caught up in his story that Josh and Ella had to take his arms and guide him out of the elevator. "When I brought the evergreens back into the house, I called out to Mary for her to come fix the centerpiece how she wanted it. I knew however I did it wouldn't be right." He gave a smile that quivered only slightly. "After forty-one years of marriage, I'm smart enough to realize there are some tasks no husband can ever complete to a wife's satisfaction, and arranging flowers is sure one of 'em."

"And that's when Mom had her heart attack?" Ella prompted.

Her dad shook his head. "The attack must have happened a couple of minutes earlier. She didn't answer when I called her name. I could hear CNN blaring on the TV—your mother's getting to be hard of hearing, you know, although she won't admit it—so I walked into the family room, and that's when I saw her."

Frank stumbled to a halt and it was a moment or two before he could go on. "Well, the long and the short of it is that your mother was on the floor and I could see we were in big trouble—"

Frank broke off, reaching into his pants pocket for one of the starched linen handkerchiefs Mary still washed and ironed for him every day. He wiped his glasses, then blew his nose, visibly pulling himself together. "Mary wasn't conscious when I found her," he said shortly. "Although it's all's well that ends well, I guess. Gerry and Barb arrived right at that moment. They got Mary into the car and we were at the Emergency Room in less than ten minutes. Thank God your mother was a nurse, Josh. She knew just what to do for Mary during the drive. I didn't even realize Mary was having a heart attack, but Barb recognized the symptoms right away."

The new shift had arrived on duty in the ICU and instead of a sour-faced witch at the reception center, there was a plump, pretty nurse who couldn't have been more friendly. She took all three of them to Mary's room, telling them to enjoy their visit, and delivering only one quick warning not to tire the patient.

After listening to her father, Ella thought she was prepared for whatever she would see, but she discovered right away that there was a shocking difference between watching a hospital drama on TV and taking part in the real-life version of open-heart surgery. Her mother, always tiny, appeared dwarfed by the medical equipment surrounding her. Tubes, lines, drips and monitor wires trailed from every part of her body, and although Mary was awake, and turned toward them as they came into the room, it was obviously an effort for her to speak. "Hello, Frank."

"Hello, Mary, love." Frank took Ella's hand and

drew her forward, directly into her mother's line of vision. "Look who's here to see you, Mary. It's Ellie. She just flew all the way here from San Antonio. Josh Taylor brought her."

CHAPTER SIX

"ELLIE." Her mom spoke in a raspy whisper, her vocal cords probably sore from the breathing tubes inserted down her throat, but her eyes lit up. "Oh, Ellie, sweetie, I'm so glad you're here."

Ella bent over and found a spot on her mother's cheek where there was room to kiss her. "And I'm glad to be here, too," she said, wondering how in the world this pale, fragile woman was going to be ready to come home in five days. She took her mother's hand and carried it to her cheek, trying to ignore the trail of IV lines and monitor wires. "How are you feeling, Mom? Did you manage to get some sleep last night?"

"Some, I guess. They gave me morphine."

"Well, at least that should have kept you happy!"

Mary frowned. "The drugs make it hard to keep your head straight, you know? I don't really remember what happened yesterday—"

"You scared us," Frank said with mock severity. "That's what happened. And please don't do it again, do you hear?"

Mary looked at her husband, still straining to remember the sequence of events. "It was Thanksgiving yesterday, wasn't it? Did Gerry and Barb come over?

I don't recall eating dinner...." Her voice faded to a painful silence.

Frank and Ella exchanged worried glances. "You didn't have Thanksgiving dinner, Mom. You were taken sick before you could eat."

"Oh, my!" Mary's thrifty soul was shocked. "Whatever happened to all the food?"

"Barb and Gerry cleaned up for us. It's all taken care of," Frank said. "The turkey's in the freezer. We'll eat it when you come home."

Ella dragged a chair across to the bed and leaned closer. Her mother wasn't wearing her glasses and she seemed to be having a hard time focusing. No wonder she sounded vague and out of it, Ella thought. On top of not being able to see clearly, she had a hearing problem, and she'd been pumped full of drugs that left her floating in la-la land.

Ella gently pushed a strand of hair away from Mary's eyes. No point in letting her mother fret about the gaps in her memory, she decided. Much better to keep her focused on the present, and the need to regain her strength. "Are they going to let you eat something today, Mom, or are they still feeding you nothing but clear liquids?"

"I'm not too hungry." Mary's gaze came to rest on her daughter's face and she finally gave a real smile. "So pretty," she murmured. "My little sunshine girl. You were always so pretty, right from when you were a tiny baby." As she spoke, her smile faded although her gaze remained fixed on her daughter.

"You didn't know me when I was a tiny baby, Mom. I was four when you and Dad adopted me."

Ella's attention was distracted and her response was automatic, or she might have been more tactful. She'd just noticed a huge bruise in the fold of her mother's arm where somebody had drawn blood, or tried to insert an emergency IV. The sight of the bruise made her feel slightly sick, especially when she contemplated the fact that this bruise was among the least of the hurts inflicted on her mother yesterday. She hated to think of how much pain her mother must have suffered.

Mary's head suddenly jerked against the pillow. "Mother of God, I remember what happened yesterday!" Her voice cracked. "My God, I saw your father...." She swallowed the wrong way and choked, her face contorting with pain.

In her entire life, Ella could never remember hearing her mother blaspheme, and the consternation in Mary's voice jolted her. "What are you talking about, Mom? What is it? Where did you see Dad?"

"It was on the TV news...." Mary clutched Ella's arm. "Got to tell you about the mistake...urgent...you have to know—" Mary's attempt to communicate ended in a strangled gasp and her eyes rolled back in her head.

Ella's gaze turned frantically from her mother to her father and back again. "Dad, what's she trying to tell us? What did you and Mom see on TV? Oh, my God, she's passed out. Is she having another heart attack?"

"Not again! Please, God, not again." His voice filled with despair, Frank clutched his wife's limp hand. "Get the doctors in here! *Now*. We need them now!"

Josh had already made his way to the head of the bed and pressed the red emergency button. "Stay with your mother," he said to Ella. "I'm going to the nurses' station to make sure they realize that we didn't push the button by accident." He ran out of the room.

Her mom was still breathing, Ella consoled herself. Then, even as she watched, cursing the fact that she had no idea what to do to help, a machine started to buzz, and then another, indicating that her mother's systems were performing erratically enough to set off warning bells.

Where the hell was the emergency medical team? Her father was talking insistently to his wife, telling her to hang on, that the doctors would be there in a minute, that she'd be feeling better again soon. Since Ella had no idea about the precise purpose of any of the machines, she realized she couldn't do anything more useful than follow her father's example. Leaning down, she put her arms around her mom as best she was able, taking care not to put any pressure on her incision. Then she mentally willed her to fight for her life, throwing in a few pleas to God for good measure.

The emergency medical team arrived with the crash cart and ordered them out of the room as they began to work on Mary. Realizing she was in the way, Ella reluctantly followed Josh and her father out of the room. A doctor came down the corridor at a run, pulling on latex gloves as he passed them. He rushed into Mary's room, kicking the door shut behind him. Ella found herself staring at the closed door in grim, anxious silence.

The weight of her fear was becoming oppressive

when Josh put an arm around her and her father. "Come on, we're not doing anything useful here. Let's go and sit in the visitors' lounge. Mary's in good hands. We should leave the medical people to work their miracles."

Frank shook his head. "You and Ella can go, but I need to stay here, close to Mary." He leaned against the wall, his gaze fixed hypnotically on the blank facade of the door to his wife's room. "They might need me. Mary might need me."

"You're right about that," Josh said. "But Mary needs you to be strong, not exhausted. The visitors' lounge is only six doors down, and they have comfortable chairs there."

Frank shook his head. "The doctors wouldn't be able to find us if there was an emergency."

He meant if her mother was dying, Ella thought, her stomach twisting into a giant knot. Her gaze flicked instinctively toward Josh and he gave her hand a comforting squeeze.

"Why don't you go and sit in the lounge with Ella," he said to Frank. "But I'll wait right here where the doctors can find me in a hurry. You and Ella really need to get some rest."

It took some skillful persuading, but eventually Frank agreed to accompany Ella to the lounge. He gave one last look at the door of his wife's room, shaking his head as he started to walk away. "Promise me you'll come get us as soon as that door's opened," he said.

"I promise." Josh laid his hand briefly on Frank's

arm. "I'll let you and Ella know the second there's any news."

It was a very long hour before Josh came to find them in the visitors' lounge. "Good news," he said, a smile lighting up his face. "Mary's doing fine. The doctors say she's stabilized and out of danger again."

"Thank God." Frank's whole body relaxed as he let out a sigh of relief.

"Dr. Bitterman arrived a while ago, and he wants to talk to you."

Frank's body jerked to renewed attention. "They need to do more surgery?"

Josh shook his head. "Not as far as I know. I think Bitterman just wants to reassure you that everything's okay. He's waiting for you and Ella outside Mary's room."

Dr. Bitterman looked more like a hobbit than a famous heart surgeon. He was about five foot seven, with bright-red hair and a face wrinkled into the puzzled expression of a shar-pei dog. He was also more talkative and friendly than Ella would have expected for a renowned surgeon. The good news, he told them, was that Mary hadn't suffered another heart attack. The bad news was that he believed she'd suffered a stroke.

"Fortunately, it was a very mild stroke," he said. "And she received treatment right away so, with luck, she's not going to experience any long-term consequences. We've already confirmed that there doesn't seem to be any paralysis."

"What about her mental faculties?"

The doctor gave Frank a reassuring pat on the

shoulder, although Ella noticed he didn't exactly answer the question. "If you're going to have a stroke, always plan to do it in the hospital, because we have lots of treatment options available for stroke victims nowadays, but they have to be administered quickly. Your wife was in just the right place at the right time."

Frank wasn't capable of responding to the doctor's attempt to cheer them up. "Can we see my wife now?" he asked.

"Yes, but just for a couple of minutes. She's sleeping, and I'd prefer that you don't wake her. This is going to be a tough few days, but she'll come through in the end. Your wife's a fighter, Mr. Petri, I already saw that yesterday. Cheer up. I'm optimistic that the eventual outcome is going to be positive."

CHAPTER SEVEN

ELLA HAD JUST FINISHED tying the laces on her sneakers when she heard a light knock on the back door. She opened it to find Josh standing on the doorstep, his breath misting in the cold morning air. He was wearing state-of-the-art running shoes, hand-stitched leather gloves, baggy gray sweats and a ratty hooded sweatshirt, stamped with the faded logo of a trucking company. He managed to make it look as if thrift store sweats were the only possible outfit to team with hundred-dollar designer gloves and two-hundred dollar sneakers.

He smiled at her, the usual ten thousand watts of sexual charisma. For some reason, instead of freezing as she usually did, today she just smiled back. "Hi, Josh."

"I thought you'd be getting ready to go for a run," he said. "Want to go with me? I was thinking of taking the loop around the park and coming back past the library."

That would be exactly four miles, less than her usual five-mile stint. On the other hand, she'd heard that Josh ran six and a half minute miles, which was a stretch for her, so maybe she should be grateful that he'd chosen the more scenic, but shorter, of the routes favored by local runners.

Oddly happy at the prospect of running with him, she grabbed a knitted cap from the hook by the door and pulled it over her ears. "You've got a deal. Let's go. I want to be back in time to cook breakfast for Dad."

"How long does that leave us?"

"As long as you need," she said blandly. "I don't want to push you."

He raised an eyebrow. "Is that a challenge, Ella?"

"Of course not," she lied, closing the kitchen door and dropping the key into her pouch. "I hear you routinely run three miles in less than twenty minutes."

"And I hear that you routinely win all the 10K races you enter."

She grinned. "That's because I'm smart enough never to enter one of the races where the real runners are competing."

He laughed, holding the gate open for her. "Ready?" he asked as they reached the sidewalk.

She nodded, hiding a smile when she noticed that they both set the timers on their watches as soon as they started to run. They jogged in silence through the streets leading to the park, building rapidly into a steady rhythm, their feet slapping in harmony against the damp pavement. Ella felt the wind whip against her cheeks, blowing away the headache she'd been fighting ever since she learned about her mother's heart attack. She'd been running competitively since she was fifteen, and found it the best stress reliever ever invented.

They reached the park and circled the pond where a small flock of Canada geese had decided to spend the winter, living on handouts from local residents. A boy walking his dog was heading toward them and by unspoken agreement they split up, letting him pass between the two of them. Josh was setting a grueling pace, but Ella had no intention of asking him to slow down. The geese would have to start laying golden eggs before she would inform Josh that she couldn't keep up.

At the three-mile mark, as they left the park, Ella could feel sweat pooling at the base of her spine, and her breath was beginning to come in short, hard pants.

"You okay?" Josh asked.

"Fine." They'd scrape her dead body off the pavement before she admitted that he was pushing her close to her limit.

They passed the library. Half a mile to go. The dead-body-scraped-from-the-pavement scenario was beginning to seem a more likely possibility with every passing yard. Ella tucked in her elbows, thought about the air flowing into her lungs, and concentrated on not breaking her stride.

They reached the end of their parents' street. Ella gave a mental crow of relief. She was going to make it! She ran the last two hundred yards in a final burst of speed and just had the presence of mind to click the timer on her watch before she collapsed against the fence, doubling over as she fought to suck breath into her laboring lungs.

When she could breathe again, she glanced at the timer on her watch. Twenty-five minutes and forty seconds elapsed time. My God, she'd run 6.25-minute miles, her best time over four miles since she left college! Elated, laughing with the sheer pleasure of success, she flung her arms around Josh and hugged him. "Hey, we did that in less than twenty-six minutes!"

"I know." He grinned down at her. "Damn near killed me, too."

"It did? You looked as if you could have gone another ten miles at the same pace, no problem."

"If that's how it looked, trust me, appearances are deceptive. I ran the last half mile on sheer willpower. Or maybe on the refusal to let you beat me." He brushed his thumbs across her cheeks, and for a moment she was sure he was going to kiss her. Then his expression smoothed into blankness and he dropped his hands to his sides, stepping a little away from her before speaking.

"I have to go back to San Antonio today," he said.

Ella felt a sharp stab of disappointment, although she knew it was unreasonable to wish that Josh would stay. He had already gone above and beyond the call of duty, and she should be grateful for that, not wish for the impossible. It was crazy of her to keep nurturing the hope that one day—some day—he would notice her as a woman, not just as the daughter of neighbors he'd known for thirty years. In fact, all things considered, maybe it was better that he was leaving. These past thirty-six hours had been a welcome break from the usual strain of their relationship, but his departure would prevent her building fantasies based on kindness and a couple of kisses that probably meant nothing to him.

"I'll be sorry to see you go." She thought—hoped—she managed to inject the right note of polite regret into her voice. "But, of course, I understand how busy you are, Josh. You know how much I appreciate everything you've done." Fortunately, since they'd just been running, she didn't have to worry about the catch in her voice. Josh would chalk it up to exertion.

"I have a couple of projects at work I really need to take care of, but I wouldn't leave until Monday if it was just to play catch-up at the office." Josh unlatched the gate, walking with her to the back door. "But I have to be in San Antonio tomorrow morning because of a promise I made to a friend. I mentioned her to you before, Emily Chambers."

Ella fished the key out of her pocket and unlocked the door. "I remember. You mentioned her on the plane. You said she was adopted, didn't you?"

"Yes. She and Jordan—her husband—had a baby daughter a couple of months ago, and I agreed to be the godfather. The christening is this Sunday, and I promised faithfully to be there."

"Of course you must go." Ella was pleased she could say that with genuine conviction. She walked into the kitchen, gesturing to invite Josh inside. "What's your goddaughter's name?"

"Sarah Marie."

"Sarah Marie Chambers?" Ella considered the names while she hung her jacket and hat on the peg next to the door. "That's pretty."

"Mmm, I thought so, too."

Ella opened the fridge and pulled out eggs and milk. "I'm going to whip up some scrambled eggs for Dad. Would you like to join us for breakfast?"

Josh shook his head. "Wish I could, but I need to get home. My mother's making pancakes, and as soon as breakfast is done, I'm leaving for the airport. With all the extra security, it can take a couple of hours to check in for a regular commercial flight these days, and my flight's scheduled for eleven-thirty.''

"What, no private jet this time?" Ella gave him an extra bright smile, so that he wouldn't see how very badly she wished he didn't have to go. Much better that he left before this dangerous blurring of the lines between friendship and sexual attraction progressed too far.

She opened the cupboard next to the stove in search of a pan for the eggs. "Have a safe trip home, Josh, and thank you again for all that you did for us."

He hesitated for a moment. "If you'd like me to fly back here next weekend, I could do it.''

"Oh, no, I couldn't ask you to do that. I know how busy you are—"

Josh took the pan out of her hand and set it on the stove. "Jesus, Ella, what is it with us? Why are we always so damned polite to each other?"

"Would it be better if we were rude?"

"Maybe. At least it would be honest." Josh gave a frustrated sigh. "For once, do you think we could have a conversation where we both say what we're really thinking?"

Ella's pulse, which had just slowed to normal, sped up again. "We could try."

"Okay. I'll start. About next weekend. If you would like the company, I can clear my schedule and fly back here on Friday night. Would you like me to do that?"

She drew in a deep breath. "Yes."

"Good. That's settled, then. Expect me some time next Saturday. Do you want me to let your boss know that it's going to be ten days or so before you're back at work?"

"Thanks, but I'm planning to call right after breakfast."

"Okay. See you on Saturday." He swung around, heading toward the kitchen door, and she reached out, stopping him.

"I know you don't want to be thanked, but I am grateful, Josh. The last thirty-six hours would have been unbearable without you."

He turned his head and his gaze locked with hers. "You're welcome."

Ella couldn't have said whether she moved toward Josh, or he moved toward her. Suddenly, they were in each other's arms, kissing with a passion and hunger that blotted out the world. His hands moved through her hair and over her face as the kiss deepened. The force of his demand pushed her against the counter, and the discomfort of the ledge cutting into the small of her back warred with the rush of almost feral desire that swept over her.

They broke apart, breathless, then came together again, but this time Josh dragged her against his body, so that all she could feel was the solid wall of his chest, the hard length of his thighs, and the magic of his mouth moving over hers. She sank into the kiss, drowning in feelings she had forbidden herself to acknowledge existed, much less to experience.

"Hello there." The sound of hands clapping jerked her back into the reality of her surroundings. She swung around, as embarrassed as if she'd been fifteen, and saw her father standing in the arched entrance to the kitchen. Josh moved away from her, muttering beneath his breath about never managing to kiss her without an audience.

Ella found her voice. "Er...hi, Dad. How are you this morning?"

"Not too bad, thanks, all things considered." Her father appeared amused. "I'd offer to go out and come in again, but I already tried that. Twice. You didn't seem to hear."

"I'm just leaving," Josh said, sounding nothing like his usual sophisticated self. "I'm...going back to San Antonio."

"I'm sure Ellie will miss you," Frank said. "I will, too."

"I'm coming back next weekend," Josh said.

Frank gave him a hearty clap on the back. "We'll both look forward to seeing you. Mary, too, I'm sure."

Josh left after a polite exchange of goodbyes. When they were alone, Frank directed a searching look toward his daughter. "Is there anything you'd like to tell me about you and Josh?"

"No, nothing. Absolutely nothing." Too late, Ella realized she sounded way too vehement. "We're just friends," she said. "You know, the kid next door, growing up together, all that stuff."

"Yes, I understand," Frank said. "I must say, that's exactly what the two of you looked like a few minutes ago. Just good friends."

CHAPTER EIGHT

MARY CAME HOME from the hospital on Friday, eight days after her surgery. She was tired and weak, and getting upstairs to the bedroom exhausted her, even with Frank and Ella both helping, but she was so glad to be home that once she was tucked into bed, her cheeks bloomed with a pink glow of happiness, and her mouth curved into the biggest smile she'd given all week.

Despite her mother's good cheer, Ella could see that the heart attack and stroke had taken a toll mentally, as well as physically. Mary's long-term memory had developed seemingly random gaps, and her short-term memory had been wiped clean. She had absolutely no recollection of the hours preceding her heart attack, which wouldn't have mattered much except that the gap seemed to worry her, and no amount of reassurance could convince her that she hadn't forgotten anything important.

The doctors had warned that mild depression and difficulty recalling the immediate past were often part of a convalescence after a major heart attack. Mary didn't appear to be suffering from any depression, unless her fixation on the trivial few hours missing from her memory banks was a form of depression. They had been trying to distract Mary without success for almost an hour when Frank made one final attempt to soothe her.

"Look, love, here's what happened, blow by blow. Nothing much but cooking, to tell the truth. First thing after we got up and had a cup of coffee, you made chestnut stuffing using your mother's recipe, then we put the turkey in the oven. After that we went over to the Taylors' for brunch. We came home around noon, and while you made your famous orange-cranberry relish, I set the table in the dining room with the good china. Then you settled down for five minutes with the newspaper. You were in the family room relaxing when you had your heart attack. There, that's about it."

"You weren't with me, though, when I had the attack."

"Well, I wasn't in the room, no. I'd just stepped outside into the backyard, that's all. We weren't apart more than ten minutes."

"It sounds like a regular Thanksgiving." Mary shook her head, as if she couldn't quite bring herself to accept that simple fact.

"It was a regular Thanksgiving, except for rushing you off to the hospital!" Frank smiled and patted her hand. "Quit with your worrying, love. As you can see, you haven't forgotten anything exciting."

Mary didn't respond to Frank's smile. Instead, her brow furrowed into a frown. "But there's something at the back of my mind. Something terrible that happened, only I can't recollect what it was." She looked ready to cry. "Darn it! Why can't I remember?"

"Because it's not important," Frank said.

"How do you know it's not important?" Mary demanded. "You have no idea what it is I've forgotten!"

"We can guess," Ella said, seeing how frustrated her father was getting. "Mom, your subconscious is probably trying to process the fact that you had a life-threatening experience. I'll bet that's why you have this feeling something terrible happened. It did. You had a heart attack."

Mary turned her gaze toward Ella. "You weren't here when I was taken sick, were you? You didn't come home for Thanksgiving this year?" Her mouth turned down at the corners. "Silly, isn't it? I can't even remember that."

"No, Mom, I wasn't here. I arrived later, after you were in the hospital."

"That's right, now I recollect. You came after the heart attack but before I had the stroke." Mary's hands plucked restlessly at a woolen thread in the afghan wrapped around her shoulders. "I know there's something important I needed to say to you, Ellie, but I can't remember what. It's bothering me. It's bothering me a lot."

Ella plumped the pillows behind her mother's head, a little alarmed at the way the conversation seemed to be moving in circles and going nowhere. Her mother had always been quick-witted, ready with a little joke, and this sort of helpless repetition was definitely not her usual style.

"I'm sure there's nothing important you need to tell me, Mom. We spoke just a couple of days before Thanksgiving. Give it a rest, and whatever's missing will probably come back to you.'' In an effort to coax another smile from her mother, Ella was desperate enough to introduce a topic she would normally have avoided. ''I expect you wanted to nag me about why I'm not married. You haven't lectured me about not giving you any grandbabies in at least a month.''

Instead of the chuckle Ella had hoped for, Mary's eyes filled with tears. ''I wish you would get married and have children, Ellie. Not for my sake, but for yours.''

''I plan to get married one day. Honest, Mom. I'm just waiting for the right man.''

Her mother's expression became pensive. ''I dreamed about the day you were born last night. Do you remember when Ellie was born, Frank? That was an anxious day, and no mistake. She gave us all a real scare, didn't she?''

Frank gulped, and Ella had the impression he was avoiding her gaze. She had no idea what Mary was talking about. How would her mother know anything about the day she'd been born? She and the Petris had met each other for the first time four years later. Hadn't they?

''Remember how the cord was wrapped around Ellie's neck?'' Mary said. ''The doctor was so afraid we were going to lose her. I'd been in labor so long, and then at the last minute, they finally told us there was this problem. We were so terrified.''

Frank cleared his throat. ''Yes, I remember.''

''I've forgotten the doctor's name.'' Mary's voice rose in panic. ''Do you remember what he was called, Frank? What was his name?''

Instead of looking utterly confused by her mother's questions, Ella saw that Frank was merely looking sad. "Dr. Giffens," he said. "That was his name."

"Dr. Giffens." Mary gave a sigh of relief. "David Giffens. You're right, that was it. Funny, I can see his face as plain as plain. It was just his name I couldn't recall. Well, all's well that ends well, I guess. Thank goodness Ellie arrived right as rain in the end."

Despite having totally misremembered the facts of Ella's birth, Mary finally seemed to relax, displaying no awareness of her confusion. She yawned, then closed her eyes. "Gee, I'm feeling real tired, Frank. I think I'll take a little nap now, if that's okay."

"It's fine for you to take a nap, love. Just what the doctor ordered."

Ella waited to be sure her mother was asleep, then followed her father downstairs to the kitchen, where he was puttering around making himself a cup of instant coffee. She knew he'd escaped the bedroom to avoid her questions, but this time she wasn't going to let her mother's statements slide by without comment, although her father was a man who found any form of confrontation acutely uncomfortable.

"What was that all about, Dad?" Ella asked. She realized her stomach was churning with nervous tension.

"Nothing important. Your mother's confused. You know that."

It had been an exhausting week, and Ella's store of empathy was wearing thin. "Dad, I hate it when you try to gloss over a situation and pretend there isn't a problem." She had to struggle not to raise her voice.

"Mom may be confused, but you aren't, and you were responding to her just now as if her questions made perfect sense."

Frank's gaze remained averted. "I didn't want to upset her. Her doctors said she needs to avoid stress."

"I understand that, but Mom isn't hearing this conversation. Why is she remembering giving birth to me when we all know that I was adopted when I was four years old? And who was Dr. Givens, for heaven's sake?"

"Dr. Giffens." Her father stirred milk into his coffee and took a scalding sip before answering. "We never told you before because this is a subject your mother doesn't like to bring up. Nor me, either, to tell the truth. In fact, I'm sure she'd never have breathed a word in normal circumstances." He fell silent.

"Breathed a word about what?" Ella prompted, striving for patience.

"The fact is, your mother got pregnant once, but the baby had the cord wrapped around her neck in the womb and we didn't find out until too late. Ultrasound wasn't routinely used in those days, you see. Anyway, our baby girl was born dead and your mother was never able to have any more children."

"Oh, no! I'm so sorry!"

Frank stared into his coffee. "What you heard her talking about upstairs...I think she was remembering the day she gave birth to our little girl, but she isn't strong enough to remember something sad right now, so her mind gave the story a happy ending. She grafted your adoption onto her memories of giving birth."

Ella felt tears prick at the corner of her eyes. "I'm

so sorry, Dad. Poor Mom. No wonder she prefers to forget what really happened.''

''Yes. It was a bad couple of years after the baby died,'' her father said, busying himself putting away the jar of instant coffee and returning the milk to the fridge. ''Losing a child is very hard, especially since we knew that she was healthy and perfect in every way, except for the problem with the cord. Anyway, we adopted you five years later when you were four, just like we always told you, and that healed a whole lot of pain.'' He gave a smile that wasn't quite steady. ''After all this time, Mary and I are so used to thinking of you as our daughter that I'm not surprised if she's gotten confused about who actually gave birth to you.''

Ella swallowed over the lump in her throat, emotions very close to the surface. ''You do know how much I love you both, don't you, Dad?''

''Yes, I do, and so does your mother. The feeling's mutual, you know.'' His smile grew stronger. ''Anyway, that's enough about the sadness of the past. Let's concentrate on the present and getting Mary well again. I know you'll have to go back to San Antonio in a few days, and I want to be sure I have the routine of caring for Mary down pat before you leave.''

The day passed with welcome placidity. Reading was still tiring for Mary, but after her nap she watched *Jeopardy* on TV, and the Taylors came to visit, the first in a stream of well-wishers. Having lived in the same neighborhood for thirty-five years, Frank and Mary were surrounded by old friends, and by the end of the day so many home-baked casseroles had

been delivered by anxious neighbors that Ella esti-
mated her father would be able to live for a month
without cooking.

Frank was watching the final round of a golf championship on TV when they heard noises from the bedroom overhead, where Mary was supposedly settled
down for the night. "Sounds as if Mom needs something and doesn't want to bother us," Ella said. "My
gosh, I can't believe she got out of bed by herself.
What is she thinking of?"

Frank started to get up, arthritis making him slow.
"I'll go—"

"No, you stay and enjoy your program." Since Ella
considered golf on TV pretty much the equivalent of
watching grass grow, she was glad of the excuse to
escape.

Heading swiftly for the master bedroom, she discovered that her mother was indeed out of bed and
rummaging through one of her dresser drawers.
"What is it, Mom? Do you need something? Let me
get it for you."

Mary turned to her, blind eyed, and Ella realized
her mother wasn't fully awake. "I have to find the
picture," she said, fumbling with the package she held
in her hands. "He'll need to see the picture."

Ella noticed that her mother was clutching a small
bundle of old photographs, wrapped in tissue paper
and tied with faded blue satin ribbon. She recognized
the collection, which she'd seen several times before.
It included pictures of Frank and Mary when they were
children, and sepia-toned portraits of their parents,
many of them taken in Sicily before the two sets of

grandparents emigrated to America some time during the 1920s.

Ella put her arm around her mother's waist. "Come back to bed," she said softly. "You didn't put on your slippers and you don't want to catch cold."

"I have to find the picture," her mother repeated, still sounding dazed and out of it. "Your father will need to see it."

"But there's no urgency, Mom. Dad can wait." Ella couldn't imagine why her mother was obsessing over old family photos unless her subconscious was sending out a message that this was a good way to cure some of the gaps in her memories. She guided her mother back toward the bed and reached out to take the bundle of pictures.

Mary snatched them away. "No, don't touch!"

"All right. I won't." Ella helped her mother into bed, and gently pulled up the covers, but her worry level ratcheted up a notch. The stroke really seemed to have inflicted some serious damage on her mom's mental abilities. It seemed to her that Mary's fixation on the past could only be damaging to her recovery, and she deliberately turned the conversation away from the collection of old photos. She talked about the neighbors who'd come to call, and mentioned the chicken pot pie she and Frank had eaten for dinner. The pie had been baked by Kitty Charzewski who was the neighborhood's best cook, and Ella jokingly warned that Mary would have to look to her laurels. She even brought up the fact that Josh Taylor was due to return to Long Island late tonight, and would be coming to visit the following. Anything to get her mother's mind running along a more productive track.

It was the mention of Josh Taylor that finally distracted her mother. "Now there's a fine young man, and such a success story," she murmured. "He's really achieved something with that company of his. Barb says he's thinking of taking it public when the economy gets back on its feet again. That'll make him a fortune, and the Taylors have shares in the company, so they'll be reaping a nice little nest egg. They helped Josh out when he got started and in exchange, he gave them ten percent of the company, you know."

"No, I didn't know. But I'm surprised you approve of him, Mom. You're always telling me that women should never trust a man who's too handsome."

"Josh Taylor isn't handsome," Mary said. "He's sexy."

"Is he?" Ella said airily. "I hadn't noticed."

"Then you must be blind or dead," her mother said with surprising tartness. "I gave you his address and phone number before you left Chicago. Have you been seeing anything of him now that you're in San Antonio?"

"No." Ella wished heartily that she had never mentioned Josh's name. She should have known it would trigger an inquisition. "My work schedule's so crazy and I'm sure Josh's is even worse—"

"So put some effort into adjusting your schedule, for heaven's sake. It's just as easy to fall in love with a rich man as it is to fall in love with a poor one, you know."

"Maybe," Ella snapped. "But you want me to

marry Josh, not just fall in love with him. And although it only takes one person to fall in love, marriage takes two.'' She stopped, appalled at what she'd tacitly admitted.

Fortunately for Ella, her mother wasn't alert enough to pick up on what had been revealed, and after a few more minutes pointing out Josh's many virtues as husband material, she dozed off.

Ella was finally able to remove the photos from her mother's grasp. She tried to find a place for them on the crowded nightstand, but between the glass of water, the lamp, the magazine and the tissues, there wasn't any space. Rather than putting them back in the drawer, she decided to take them downstairs with her. She always enjoyed looking through the pictures and, once the interminable golf program ended, she would ask her father if he could think of any reason why Mary might have been concerned enough to get out of bed in search of them.

When she got downstairs, Frank was snoring peacefully in front of the television. Ella knew he'd hardly slept for days, and she didn't have the heart to wake him. Pressing the Mute button on the remote, she sat down in the armchair, tucking her feet under her. Untying the satin ribbon and opening the tissue paper wrapping, she slowly leafed through the familiar photos, pausing to smile at her favorites: two-year-old Frank, hair slicked, looking miserable in a frilled white shirt, and Mary looking beautiful in her First Communion dress, an enormous satin ribbon tied in her dark curls.

At the bottom of the packet, Ella discovered something she hadn't seen before. Wedged between the covers of a stiffly posed wedding picture of Frank's parents was a photo that was new to her. Black-and-white like the others, it nevertheless appeared more recent. The photo showed a man in his thirties, wearing military uniform, standing behind and slightly to the left of a slender young woman, who was seated in a Queen Anne style chair, holding a baby on her lap. The baby was about nine months of age and had fluffy fair hair and wide round eyes. She was clutching a tiny teddy bear that the photographer had probably given her in an attempt to make her smile.

The woman's dress looked silky and expensive, and the man's uniform crisp and well tailored. Ella didn't know enough to identify which branch of the armed service he might be in, or what rank he might have attained. She wondered if this was a photo from the World War II era, although the clothes and hair didn't seem right for the 1940s. The woman had her hair styled into a puffy French twist, with dangling wisps at the front, a style that Ella remembered seeing in pictures dating from the late sixties or early seventies. The sort of hairstyle all the female aliens always had on the original *Star Trek* series, she thought with amusement.

Ella held the picture closer to the light, searching the features of both the man and the woman, trying to identify to which family they belonged. Were these people relatives of Franks', or of Mary's?

As she studied the man's face, she was swept by a sudden, intense feeling of familiarity. An image flashed across her mental screen, unexpectedly clear and vivid. The man in the picture was walking toward her, arms outstretched. As he came closer into view, she could see herself running toward him, feet flying. The man swung her up high over his head, twirling her around, both of them laughing out loud. She had no idea where they were, or who the man was, but she knew she was very happy and that she adored the man in uniform.

Suddenly feeling a little queasy, Ella put the picture down. Then, almost against her better judgment, she picked it up again, flipping it over to see if there was a studio name printed on the back or any indication of where the picture had been taken.

Gabriella, age nine months and two weeks, taken on our second wedding anniversary, April 12, 1972.

The inscription was written in a strong, masculine hand, using old-fashioned ink, and the individual letters had more character than she was accustomed to seeing in the Internet age of scrawled gel-pen messages. By the time she'd read the inscription for the second time, her hands were shaking so badly that she dropped the picture. Drawing a deep breath, Ella picked the picture up and very carefully slipped it back inside the cover of her grandparents' long-ago wedding photo. She wrapped the tissue paper around the collection, and was about to tie it up with the blue ribbon when she was seized by second thoughts.

Acting almost furtively—why she was anxious to avoid waking her father, for heaven's sake?—she quickly unwrapped the package and pulled out the inscribed photo, slipping it under her sweater. She retied the rest of the pictures into their package, feeling as guilty as if she'd stolen something.

Perhaps she had, Ella thought, torn between remorse and a hint of anger. Right at this moment, she had the uneasy suspicion that she'd just stolen back a piece of her own past.

CHAPTER NINE

JOSH ARRIVED at the Petri house the next morning while Ella was still in the shower. She came downstairs to find him sharing a cup of coffee over the kitchen table with her father. They were involved in a heated discussion about the outcome of the upcoming game between the Jets and the Broncos. She walked into the room just in time to see Josh slap down a five-dollar bill in support of his claim that the Broncos were going to win by seven points.

"Ha!" Frank exclaimed, pulling out his own five-dollar bill. "You're going to lose, you know. But I'm happy to take your money since you're determined to throw it away."

Josh grinned. "I'll remind you of that when the game's over and I've won." He looked up at Ella and his smile changed, taking on a subtle warmth that sent her heart into instant, pounding overdrive. "Hi, Ella," he said softly.

"Hi." She could feel her cheeks growing warm and she quickly turned away, trying to look casual as she walked over to the coffeepot and poured herself a mug of coffee. What was the matter with her? She'd been successfully pretending indifference to Josh Taylor for—oh, about fifteen years. Why had she suddenly lost a skill she'd been honing for half a lifetime?

By dint of keeping her back turned toward him, she managed to get out a question that sounded both casual and appropriate. "I hope the christening went off okay last weekend."

"Well, Sarah Marie screamed through most of it, so I can certify she has a healthy pair of lungs. And she didn't throw up on me, which Jordan says is a sign of almost unique good fortune on my part."

"Does she spit up a lot?"

"Yes, although apparently that's not a particular cause for alarm. I must say, I learned more about the causes and cures of projectile vomiting in infants last weekend than I ever wanted to know."

Ella laughed, her emotions finally under control enough that she dared to turn around and meet his eyes. "All in all, you sound as if you had a grand time."

Josh's gaze held hers. "Not really. I missed you."

So much for having her emotions under control. Ella felt her cheeks flame. She shot a horrified glance toward her father, who was eating Cheerios and doing a very bad job of pretending not to listen.

"It's…good to have you back," she stuttered. "Was your flight on time last night?"

"More or less." Josh had walked across the kitchen and was now standing right next to her. She wondered if he could hear her heart thumping.

"I came to invite you to have lunch with me," he said.

"Oh. Er…thank you. That would be nice." Ella

mentally gnashed her teeth. If Josh was attracted to dim-witted women who had trouble saying anything interesting, she should be doing a fine job of capturing his attention.

"Do you need a coat?" Josh pulled a set of car keys from his pocket.

"Well, yes—"

"Anything else you need to take care of before we leave?"

"You mean leave *now?* But it isn't even nine o'clock, and I have a bunch of stuff I need to do before I can—"

"I was planning to drive to Montauk," Josh said. "Even if we leave now, it'll be lunchtime when we arrive."

Montauk was on the easternmost tip of Long Island, a three-hour drive away. It was one of Ella's favorite places, even at this time of year, when the wind had a tendency to whip in from the Atlantic, and the sand dunes could look cold and bleak. It was also a time of year when there were fewer tourists, and—with only a little flexing of her imagination—she could take a wonderful mental journey back to the days when Montauk had been a remote Colonial fishing village.

Frank pushed his chair away from the table and carried his empty bowl over to the sink. "Go, Ellie. You need a break. Josh has just flown halfway across the country for the second time in a week, and you've been bearing the brunt of looking after your mother. You should both take a few hours to enjoy yourselves. Besides, it's time I took over here. You have to return to San Antonio on Monday, so this will be a practice run for me, to see how I cope when I'm on my own.''

Ella didn't need any more coaxing. She had begun to feel claustrophobic after nine days of high-pressure nursing duty. Running upstairs, she kissed her mother goodbye, grabbed her purse and her coat, and was back downstairs again in a couple of minutes.

For the first time since Ella had arrived in Long Island, the sun was shining steadily, albeit through wispy clouds, as Josh drove his parents' Subaru along the congested streets of Port Washington and onto the highway. Fortunately, the sun wasn't strong enough to entice drivers to make for the shore when there was Christmas shopping to be done, and the traffic heading toward the tip of the Island was minimal in comparison to the usual summer crush.

"Is there any special reason you decided to drive to Montauk today?" Ella asked.

Josh nodded. "Actually, there is. A friend—a business acquaintance of mine—has a cottage right on the oceanfront that he wants to sell. I'm considering buying it."

"As an investment? To rent out?"

"No, as a vacation place. I love San Antonio, but I miss the sea, and I've been thinking for a while that it would be good to have a place in this part of the country where I could chill out for a few days and see my parents all at the same time. I love them both dearly, but it's tough adjusting my lifestyle to their expectations, and although they don't say anything, I know they're hurt if I book into a hotel. When I heard about this cottage coming on the market ten days ago, it seemed as if it might be the perfect compromise. With e-mail and a fax machine to keep on top of any major crises at work, I'm hoping that I could make four or five trips out here each year.''

"It does seem like a great idea," Ella agreed. "What does *cottage* mean in this case, do you know? In Montauk, it could be anything from seventy-year-old kitchen fixtures and electrical wires dangling from the ceilings, all the way up to multimillion-dollar luxury retreats."

Josh grinned. ''Well, I'm looking for something in between. I've been told this place has three bedrooms, two and a half bathrooms, and was—quote—extensively renovated eighteen months ago. We're about to find out exactly what that means, I guess.''

"Even if the cottage turns out to be hideous, at least we get lunch and a trip to Montauk out of it. Did you have somewhere in mind for lunch?''

"Captain Teddy's has my vote.''

Ella smiled. "My favorite place. They make the world's best crab cakes, despite what those upstarts in Maryland try to claim.''

As the miles sped by, they spoke at length about her mother, about how her father was coping, and about the doctors' upbeat predictions for Mary's full recovery. Ella explained that her mother seemed to be doing a little better than the medical experts had expected in terms of regaining her physical strength, but that she seemed to be obsessively focused on the fact that she couldn't remember what had happened in the few hours preceding her heart attack.

"The doctors have told her this is normal for somebody who had a heart attack followed by a stroke, and so has Dad, but she doesn't seem able to let it go."

"I sympathize with your mom, though." Josh sped up to overtake a delivery truck. "It must be miserable to have gaps in your memories. Have you and your dad tried to fill in the gaps for Mary?"

Ella nodded. "We sure have. In fact, Dad has gone over and over the events of that morning with her, but she just doesn't seem satisfied. It's as if she thinks we're holding back something from her." She hesitated, on the brink of mentioning the odd little incident from the night before when she'd found Mary rummaging through her dresser drawers. The photograph of the young couple and their baby had haunted Ella to the extent that she'd slipped it into her purse. Having found this possible record of her past, she wasn't willing to surrender it.

In the end, though, she decided against saying anything, oddly reluctant to discuss the subject of her birth family with Josh. For some reason, it was an area that felt tender in relation to him, as if opening up that subject would expose vulnerabilities that she wasn't ready to confront, much less share with Josh. Which was definitely a strange feeling, given that Josh knew almost as much about her family background as she did.

Not in the mood to probe inconsistencies, Ella led the conversation onto a different track without much difficulty. Sexual attraction might leave her feeling permanently on edge when she was in Josh's company, but they'd known each other for so long that they had plenty of memories they could share and even laugh about, and she knew enough about the interests they had in common to have a wide range of subjects to choose from. Before long, she was so caught up in their conversation that she actually forgot to be tense. Because she'd spent so much time over the past few years suppressing her attraction for him, it was a pleasant surprise to rediscover the fact that she liked Josh almost as much as she lusted after his entirely gorgeous body.

The crab cakes at Captain Teddy's were as tasty as they both remembered, and the coffee had been immeasurably improved by the addition of an espresso machine and a waiter who knew how to use it.

Replete and very well content with the day thus far, they followed the directions to the cottage Josh had come to inspect. After getting lost twice, they found the house at the end of a quiet cul-de-sac that backed up to Long Island Sound. The tiny front yard had a scrimshaw path leading up to a wide front porch, decorated by an interesting piece of driftwood shaped vaguely like a porpoise. The timbers of the house were weathered, but there was fresh paint on all the trim and the wind-tossed shrubs looked neatly trimmed.

"It's pretty, at least on the outside," Ella said, looking around the yard, which was bare of color at this time of year, but appeared to have been planned with the withering salt air very much in mind. "How would you cope with the maintenance, though, if you're only here occasionally?"

"Apparently that's not a problem," Josh said, unlocking the front door. "There are plenty of reputable local companies who'll take care of the place for a reasonable charge. Right down to maid service and laundry, if that's what I want.''

The front door opened straight into the living area, which had no walls dividing the eating and sitting areas. Plank wooden boards must have been rescued from an older house and transported here, and instead of the fireplace being built into a side wall, it was built in the center of the room, dividing the living area from the kitchen. Sliding glass doors gave a view of the sand dunes, but although the sea was audible when Josh opened a window, it was invisible because of the height of the dunes. Still, with the afternoon sun shining through a skylight onto the oversize sofa and the sisal area rug, the overall impression was casually attractive.

''The kitchen is terrific,'' Ella said, pulling open a cupboard door and discovering a huge pantry. ''State-of-the-art appliances, plenty of storage, huge windows with another view of the dunes. It's great that you can see the fireplace from the kitchen, too.'' For a moment she pictured cooking a meal here and then curling up in front of the fire with Josh, and was swept by a feeling of wistfulness.

Josh lingered approvingly in front of a built-in wine cooler. ''The place certainly seems designed for easy living, and the decor is pleasant, but I wouldn't call it spectacular. Would you?''

''Not really, although it's better than acceptable. Way better. Were you looking for spectacular?''

He grinned. ''I haven't told you the asking price. Yeah, I guess I'm expecting spectacular. Let's take a look upstairs. According to my friend, the master bedroom is the real reason he bought this place.''

Upstairs they found a guest bedroom with attached bath, along with a room lined with bookshelves that was obviously designed for use as an office. They finally discovered the master bedroom tucked away at the back of the house. Josh pushed open the door and they drew in simultaneous gasps of sheer wonder. They were looking through a giant picture window that faced in the same direction as the backyard, but because the second story was nine feet above ground level, they now had a perfect view of Long Island Sound. The sea heaved and rippled, with the dunes providing foreground perspective and an ocean liner moving serenely in the far distance as the perfect finishing touch.

Ella was too awestruck to speak. She crossed the room, subliminally aware of the luxuriously thick carpeting at her feet, and the artful coloring of the walls, a shade of blanched yellow that mimicked the pale sands of Montauk's famous beaches. She stared out at the ocean, wondering how the current owner of the cottage could bear to part with a home that possessed such a perfect view, even if he did have to go to Singapore.

Josh came and stood behind her and she finally tore herself away from the hypnotic motion of the waves to turn and face him. ''It's beautiful,'' she said. ''Josh, I can't find the words to describe how perfect it is.''

''You think I should buy the cottage, then?''

''Absolutely. But be warned. Once it's yours, I'm

going to be angling for invitations to stay here on any and every occasion.''

"That would definitely be a bonus.'' He looked down at her, his gaze steady. "I wish we could spend more time together, Ella.''

She wondered what that meant, precisely. More time as in we're good friends who both like Captain Teddy's crab cakes? Or, more time as in I want you to share my bed? There was quite a lot of room for misunderstandings and mutual embarrassment in the spectrum between those two extremes.

Ella knew that she hadn't imagined Josh's lack of interest in her for most of her adult life. Until last Christmas, she was fairly sure that she could have lain naked in his bed and, if he'd come in and found her, he'd have handed her a robe and asked politely what she was doing there. Consequently, she'd learned to take steps to protect herself. It was no fun being tortured by his indifference. But last Christmas, she had began to wonder if perhaps something had—finally— changed in their relationship. When Josh kissed her under the mistletoe, she'd felt the flaring of a passion so intense and so immediate that she couldn't quite convince herself it was entirely one-sided. For a few mind-blowing seconds she'd allowed herself to hope that Josh might actually be experiencing the same sort of tempestuous yearning that she was feeling.

Then common sense had come to her rescue. Unwilling to be drawn any deeper into a pathetically one-sided love affair that was already damaging to her relationships with other men, she had ruthlessly suppressed the hope that Josh might finally have noticed that she was a woman, as opposed to the annoying kid next door.

So for eleven months, she'd avoided Josh with even greater determination than usual. Their Christmas kiss had cost her weeks of painstaking effort to recreate the illusion that she disliked him. When she was offered the promotion and transfer to San Antonio, she'd been determined to avoid laying herself open to any further damaging attacks of hope.

But now circumstance had thrown them together again, and even the most hardheaded examination of Josh's behavior over the past few days didn't support the view that he considered her nothing more than the kid next door. Josh had not only kissed her under the mistletoe. He'd kissed her on the plane, and he'd kissed her after they went running. When you got right down to it, every time he saw her recently, he seemed to kiss her. And she wasn't talking friendly, buss-on-the-cheek type of kisses. She was talking about curl-your-toes, curl-your-hair, curl-your-insides sorts of kisses. What's more, Josh had made several comments that indicated he was as frustrated by their dysfunctional relationship as she was. Including this latest remark that he wished they could spend more time together.

What did she have to lose by letting him know she cared? She was thirty-two years old, for God's sake. She had a successful career, a house that was hers and the mortgage company's, a new car that was hers and the bank's. Her life would go on if Josh rejected her. In fact, if he explicitly rejected her, spelled out the words, maybe she would even be able to move on and start a meaningful relationship with some other decent guy.

Ella gathered her courage in both hands. Instead of turning away, she met Josh's gaze. Instead of hiding her feelings, she laid them bare. For good measure, in case Josh turned out to be as bad at reading female emotions as every other man in the world, she reached up and clasped her hands behind his neck, pulling his mouth down toward hers.

"Kiss me, Josh," she said softly.

His lips met hers in the explosion of sensation that had by now become almost familiar. Not that familiarity lessened the impact of what happened. Ella's body shook, her stomach lurched, her heartbeat sped up, her skin turned hot and prickly. All the symptoms of a severe attack of flu, she thought wryly, before her thoughts spun off into a world where coherence was impossible, and all her senses narrowed down to the exquisite, supercharged agony of feeling Josh's mouth covering hers, and his body pressed hard against hers.

She didn't remember they were in a bedroom until her legs bumped up against something solid, and she realized Josh had been walking her backward to the bed. She fell back against the pillows, and Josh lay down beside her. He had been the object of her suppressed fantasies for so long, that she could hardly believe they'd reached this point so fast.

Then the craziness of that thought struck her, and she gave a little hiccup of laughter.

"What is it?" Josh asked.

"I was just thinking how quickly we went from being friends to being something else."

"Yeah, well, I'm known for moving fast." Josh's smile was tender. "Once I see the woman I want, I go after her, no holds barred."

"Twenty-eight years since we first met," Ella said, unbuttoning his shirt. "Yep, I can see you're a man who moves lightning fast."

He ran his hand suggestively down the length of her body. "Sometimes," he said huskily, "slow is better."

Ella had no idea if he proved his point. She had soon traveled so far beyond the point of rational thought that she could never quite recall how they went from teasing pleasure to passion so hot and fierce and primal that she heard herself moan, and then scream, and she didn't even care.

She had a suspicion that they might have reached their first climax in record-breaking time, because she did have a vague recollection of taking longer to reach orgasm the second time around. And the third time, she was actually able to enjoy a couple of leisurely erotic movements along the way.

Afterward, she lay against the pillows, exhausted and replete, not even attempting to analyze what had just happened between the two of them. The reality of making love to Josh was one of the few experiences in her life that far exceeded the fantasy.

So far, so great. The downside was that, after what had just happened between them, no amount of effort and no amount of self-hypnosis was ever again going to convince her that she wasn't in love with Josh Taylor.

CHAPTER TEN

EVER SINCE THEIR KISS under the mistletoe last Christmas, Josh had been fantasizing about the pleasures of having sex with Ella. Even so, it had never occurred to him that making love to her would be a transforming experience. Now, in the space of a couple of hours in bed, his world had changed. With the taste of her lingering in his mouth, and the feel of her body imprinted on his skin, he felt complete for the first time in his life. He finally understood the distinction between having sex and making love, and he was spellbound by the difference.

Turning onto his side, he propped himself on one arm so that he could feel the soft curves of Ella's body at the same time as he could see her face. At this time of year daylight faded fast and, as the pale winter sun sank beneath the horizon, the bedroom was filling with purple shadows that wrapped them in ever deeper layers of intimacy. Josh reached out, tucking a tangled strand of Ella's hair behind her ears, leaving his hand resting against her cheek.

"Marry me, Ella." The words slipped out, easy and natural. Unplanned, but exactly right.

Emotion flashed in her eyes, intense and brilliant. Josh thought he saw happiness and wonder before her magnificent green eyes darkened and she sat up, distancing herself from him in the king-size bed. Almost at once, she seemed to regret the distance. She stretched out her hand and laid it palm down against his chest, so that he could feel the beat of his heart throbbing against her fingertips. But he noticed that she didn't move back closer to him.

"I love you, Josh." Her voice was husky with the aftermath of powerful sex.

He put his hand over hers, smiling in relief. "That's really good news, because I love you, too. More than I ever thought I could love anyone."

She returned his smile with a nostalgic one of her own. "I think I've loved you since the summer after I turned fourteen, and you drove off to college, taking a piece of my heart with you."

He ought to have been happy to hear Ella had loved him for years. Instead, Josh had a terrible premonition that she was about to give him some cockamamie reason she wasn't going to marry him, even though she loved him. He soon realized that he was right to be worried. Wrapping herself in a sheet, Ella got out of bed and walked to the window, trailing yellow percale.

She spoke looking at the sea rather than at him. "We ought to call our parents to let them know we're going to be late home. You know how they'll worry. And we'll have to contact the maid service, too. The bed linen will need to be laundered."

"Screw the laundry." Josh followed her to the window, the air chill on his naked skin. "Could you please explain to me why in hell we're talking about maid service when I just asked you to marry me?"

"I guess...because I don't know how to answer you."

"Yes, Josh, I'd be thrilled to marry you. Let's set the date. There. Sounds like a great answer to me."

"It's what I want to say, but it isn't quite that easy."

"You love me. I love you. We're both single, and we have enough money to set up house. How difficult can it be to agree that we should be married?"

"Way more difficult than I ever dreamed. Marriage isn't just about being in love, Josh, at least not for me. It's about starting a new generation, joining our two families—"

"Agreed. But how does that pose any problems? Our parents, all four of them, will be over the moon when they find out we're getting married. I want kids. You do, too. We'll adopt if by some chance it turns out we can't have our own. What else is there to worry about?"

She avoided his eyes. "My biological roots. My genes."

Josh gave an incredulous laugh. "Honey, ask me how much I care about your biological roots!"

"Okay, I will. Think about it, Josh. Doesn't it bother you that we have no idea who gave birth to me? That I have no clue what my heritage is?"

"No, it doesn't bother me in the least. I could not possibly care less about something so irrelevant to our lives together."

"Are you sure it's irrelevant, Josh? I haven't any idea what sort of a genetic heritage I would pass on to our children, and I didn't fully understand how much that worries me until just a few moments ago, when you asked me to marry you.''

Josh put his hands on her shoulders, forcing her to turn around. ''You can't be serious, Ella! You're smart, kind and beautiful. You were the healthiest kid in the neighborhood, and if your biological grandmother died of breast cancer, or your great grandpa suffered from Alzheimer's, well gee whiz, I'm sorry, but that sure isn't a reason for you to refuse to marry me.''

Ella smiled, but her expression remained troubled. ''Okay, grandma and grandpa get a free pass. But the gene for Alzheimer's isn't the worst one I could pass on. What if my mother was a vicious murderer? What if my father was an alcoholic drifter, who stole to support his habit?''

''Leaving aside the fact that there's no scientific proof that there's any link between antisocial behavior and genes, why in the world would you make such melodramatic assumptions about your biological parents? Why not accept that they were poor and young but otherwise average folks, which is what you've always been told?''

Ella pushed impatiently at a strand of hair that had fallen over her forehead. ''I guess that's the heart of the problem. I've realized for the past couple of years that I don't believe the stories I've been told about my adoption. We discussed this a little on the plane coming out here, Josh, but I didn't tell you just how much all the inconsistencies about my adoption bother me. Frank and Mary Petri are good people, the salt of the earth, and they wouldn't tell lies unless they thought it was essential to hide the truth. There's some secret about my birth family, and I don't think it's pretty. In fact, I think it's downright ugly.''

"Okay, let's suppose you're right and there is an ugly secret in your parents' past. It's you I want to marry, Ella, not your ancestors. We're not medieval kings, trying to establish a dynasty. We're Americans, living in the twenty-first century. I don't give a damn who your birth parents were, so if you don't want to marry me, you'll have to come up with a better excuse than that. I don't care if your mom and dad had a fight one night and chopped each other up in little pieces. I don't care if your mother really didn't die as you've been told, but was sent to prison for stealing gold bars from Fort Knox—''

"What if she's incarcerated in a psychiatric hospital, frothing at the mouth and slashing at invisible goblins?''

"I—don't—care.'' He emphasized each word. "What I care about is having you as my wife. I want you to share my home and be the mother of my children. It's taken us about two decades longer than it should have to discover that we love each other. Now that we've found each other, for God's sake let's not walk away because you're worried about your genes. Let me count the ways that I don't care about your genes.''

Her eyes misted and she let out a long, slow breath. "You really mean that, don't you?''

"I really mean that.''

She straightened, as if a heavy weight had just been lifted from her shoulders. "Then maybe you could start your proposal over again," she said. "This time, I'll know how to answer."

He carried her hands to his mouth and pressed a kiss into each palm. "Will you marry me, Ella? Will you have my children and live with me so that we grow old together?"

She cradled his cheeks with her hands. "Yes, Josh, I'll marry you. More than anything else in the world, I want to spend the rest of my life with you."

Josh realized he was so happy and relieved that he needed to lower the emotional temperature. "Great." He kissed the end of her nose, deliberately casual. "Terrific. That's settled, then. When can we have the wedding ceremony? My calendar looks good for tomorrow."

Ella gazed up at him, torn between tears and laughter. "I think the state of New York requires a license. Ditto for the state of Texas. And our parents are going to want enough time to invite a gazillion guests, you know that."

Josh gave a resigned sigh. "You're right. Which makes me realize all over again how incredibly much I love you. I'm even willing to brave a family wedding that's been jointly organized by the Taylors and the Petris. Do you think we can set a guest limit of a hundred and expect any of our parents to listen?"

"Not a chance. A hundred barely covers the cousins and the neighbors." Her voice caught. "I do hope you won't regret this, Josh."

"Never." He kissed her lingeringly, then realized she was crying. Not the previous half laughter, half tears, but honest-to-goodness weeping. He stopped, appalled. "What's the matter, honey?"

"Nothing. I'm insanely happy, that's all."

He rolled his eyes. "Right. Of course. I should have known. It's only men who have this weird habit of laughing when they're happy and crying when they're sad."

Ella sniffed. "That's because men are astonishingly one-dimensional creatures when you get right down to it."

"Hah! Engaged less than two minutes, and you're already dissing me."

"I'm practicing for when we're married." She scrubbed away the last of her tears with the heel of her hand. "Seriously, there's something I want to show you, Josh. Let me find my purse. I left it on the kitchen counter, I think."

She hurried out of the room, the sheet still dragging behind her, and came back holding out a black-and-white photograph. "Just so that you'll know I'm not totally neurotic in suspecting I haven't been told the truth about my adoption. Take a look at this picture, Josh, then tell me if the stories I've heard about my birth mother seem credible. I'm almost a hundred percent sure the baby in the picture is me. But does the woman in this portrait look like a desperately poor single mom to you?"

Josh took the picture, which was of a young couple holding a cute dumpling of a baby with dimples and a mop of flyaway blond curls.

No, he thought. This didn't look anything like a portrait of an impoverished single mom. This looked like a prosperous middle-class couple, and the baby was wearing an embroidered dress that shrieked expensive, at least to Josh's untrained eye.

"What makes you think the baby in the picture is you?" he asked.

Ella made a quick twirling gesture with her hand. "Turn the photo over. There's an inscription on the reverse."

He flipped the picture and read the inscription. *Gabriella, age 9 months and 2 weeks, taken on our second wedding anniversary, April 12, 1972.*

Josh let out a long, slow breath. "Your birthday is June 30, isn't it? Same as my brother's."

She nodded. "In other words, nine months and two weeks before April 12. Just like it says on the back of the photo."

"The couple might not be the baby's parents," Josh suggested, without much conviction.

"Then who are they?"

"They could be godparents. Friends. Neighbors."

Ella shook her head. "Then the inscription wouldn't make sense, would it? The note deliberately relates to the baby's age to the couple's wedding anniversary, which surely suggest that the couple were her—my—parents?"

"Yes, I guess that would seem logical." Josh ran his finger over the child's face, seeking similarities to the four-year-old Ella he'd seen walking down the garden path to her new home, Frank holding one of her hands, Mary the other.

"Where did you get the photo? How long have you had it?"

"I just found it yesterday." Ella explained how she'd discovered Mary rooting around in her dresser drawers, and how she'd found the photo hidden inside the cover of a decades old wedding picture of Frank's parents.

"The man in the photo is wearing a military uniform," she said. "Do you think there's any chance we could trace him through his service records? I was hoping that an expert might be able to identify something about the unit or the regiment where he served just by the badges on the uniform. We could get the photo blown up to show more detail."

"It's an air force uniform," Josh said. "And see the two silver bars on his collar. I think that mean's he's a captain. I don't understand enough about the details of military insignia to be able to identify anything more. But I'll bet you're right. An expert in the field could tell us quite a lot about the guy's service record, just by looking at this photo."

Ella sat down on the edge of the bed. "I can't believe I just found out my biological father was an officer in the United States Air Force! Is that what we did, Josh?"

"I think so. Although we have to be careful we don't put two and two together and make five." Josh gave the warning without really believing it. He should have known that Ella was too smart and too levelheaded to get suspicious about her adoption unless she had cause.

Ella shivered, more from emotion, Josh suspected, than from cold. "The most logical conclusion to draw from this photo is that my mother wasn't poor, and she sure as heck wasn't single. In other words, some-body has been lying about why I was put up for adoption. I want to know why."

Josh sat beside her on the bed. "If you want to start an investigation to find out more about your biological parents, I'm with you a hundred percent of the way. I even know a great guy you can go and see in San Antonio who makes his living tracing missing people. His name is Dylan Garrett, he has a company called Finders Keepers and his track record in reuniting families is outstanding. He's the person who solved the case of Julie Cooper, the missing wife of Sebastian Cooper."

"I read about that when I first arrived in San Antonio and he seems to have done a brilliant job. Could we arrange to see him as soon as we get back to San Antonio?" Ella didn't try to disguise her eagerness. "It would be so great if he could discover the truth about my background before we're married."

Ella obviously felt an urgency to research her past that Josh didn't quite understand. Still, he realized it was easy for him to be bored by the subject of ancestral roots because he knew more than he wanted or needed to know about his own background. His father had made genealogical research one of his retirement hobbies, so Josh had not only heard ad nauseam about his parents and grandparents, he knew that one of his great-grandfathers had been a shoemaker and another had married a cousin of Lord Byron, along with a string of other facts that made not an atom of difference to his daily life.

Maybe helping Ella to find out something about her birth family could be his wedding gift to her, Josh thought. It seemed to be a gift she would appreciate a lot more than diamonds or pearls.

CHAPTER ELEVEN

JOSH AGREED they would tell their parents about their wedding plans as soon as they got home. Her mother was already settled into bed for the night when they finally got back to Port Washington, so Ella asked permission to bring the Taylors up to Mary's bedroom, then she and Josh broke the news of their plans to marry.

Both sets of parents were ecstatic. Both mothers cried. Josh exchanged an amused glance with Ella. "They're crying because they're so happy, right?"

"Right."

"Hey, I'm a fast learner."

Frank took the men downstairs, where they celebrated with a beer. Barb Taylor, Ella and her mother stayed upstairs and began a serious discussion about where the wedding reception should be held. "I think Josh wants the wedding ceremony to be quite soon," Ella said, as one local venue after another was discussed and dismissed. "So there's the question of availability as well as how much we like it."

"How soon is soon?" Barb demanded.

"Er...Christmas?" Ella murmured.

"Christmas!" Barb and Mary yelped simultaneously.

"Land sakes, Ellie, are you trying to give me a heart attack?" Mary said.

"Oh, my God, no—" Ella broke off, realizing her mother was teasing. "No," she continued more calmly, then laughed, because tonight it seemed very easy to laugh. "I guess Josh and I decided we've waited long enough, and it's time to get this wedding production on the road."

The Taylors didn't stay late, partly out of concern for Mary's health, but mostly because they were anxious to get home and start spreading the news. Mary was equally anxious to get on the phone, but once she'd called her sister in Larchmont and her brother in Saint Louis, she was persuaded to wait until morning to begin calling her long list of cousins.

When her mother was once again comfortably settled, Frank went down to the kitchen to make a nightcap of hot apple cider, and Ella followed.

"You couldn't have found a better tonic for your mother," her father said, putting a mug of cider in the microwave. "That's a good man you've chosen, Ellie."

"I'm very glad you and Mom approve."

He smiled. "Although something tells me you'd marry him anyway."

She returned his smile. "Yes, I would. I love him, Dad."

The microwave beeped and her father removed the mug of hot cider. "Do you want this? I can make another one for me."

"No, thanks. I'm fine."

"Well, I'll say good-night. Sleep well, Ellie." He

gave a rueful chuckle. "You'll need your rest. You know your mother is going to be firing off in ten different directions tomorrow."

"I figured as much." Ella hesitated for a moment, then decided there was never going to be a good time to broach the subject of the photograph, so she might as well do it now. She would feel deceitful if she hired Dylan Garrett to investigate without giving either of her parents the chance to comment. After all, as Josh had pointed out during the drive home, it was possible they'd somehow managed to misinterpret everything about the photo. She didn't quite see how, but it was possible, she supposed.

"Remember when we heard Mom moving around upstairs last night?" Ella opened her purse and took out the picture. "I think this is what she was searching for. Have you ever seen it before, Dad?"

Frank took the photo and stared at it in total silence for a full minute.

"Turn it over," Ella said, when the silence began to get to her. "There's an inscription on the back."

Frank turned it over and read the brief message. Then, still without speaking, he carefully wiped the table to make sure it was dry before setting the picture down. He pulled out a chair and sat down with a thump.

"What does it mean, Dad? The baby in the photo is me, isn't it?"

"She sure looks like you." There was a tremble in her father's voice and he suddenly sounded every one of his seventy-two years. "I've never seen this picture before. I don't understand what it means." He looked at her almost pleadingly. "Ellie, I swear I've never withheld information from you. This is the whole truth of what I know about your adoption. Your mother and I had been on the waiting list for almost two years, and I was thrilled when I came home from work the last Friday in July and Mary told me that the adoption agency had found a little girl for us, that you'd recently turned four, and that we were to go to a lawyer's office in Sands Point to collect you the following Monday."

"And that's where you picked me up. At the lawyers office." Ella had heard the story many times before, and everything Frank said was familiar to her.

"Yes. Mary and I were in the parking lot outside the lawyer's office at eight o'clock. The appointment was for nine, but we were so excited we'd been up since five in the morning, and we literally couldn't wait at home another minute. The lawyer called us in and we signed what seemed like a hundred pieces of paper. And then this woman walked through the door from an inner office, bringing you to meet us. She was holding your hand, but you were squirming, trying to get your hand away. That's when Mary got up from her chair and just kind of scooped you into her arms." Frank stopped and cleared his throat. "Then we brought you home with us, and you've been our daughter ever since."

"Did I cry, or ask for my mother?"

Frank shook his head. "You were a very quiet, sad little girl for two or three months, but you never spoke about your home life, and we for sure didn't probe. Then, gradually, you perked up. By the time we had our first Christmas together, you were a normal, noisy, happy four-year-old.''

''But did the adoption agency specifically tell you my birth mother was dead?'' Ellie asked. ''Did they tell you that she was poor, and that she didn't have any relatives who were able to take care of me?''

Frank nodded. ''Honey, that's exactly what they told us. What's more, I remember that among the papers the lawyer showed us was a release form from your mother's sister. She'd taken temporary custody of you when your birth mother died, and she was waiving all rights to have that custody made permanent.''

Ella frowned. ''Do you have a copy of that form? I've never seen it.''

''No.'' Frank shook his head. ''Remember they kept all the details secret in those days. I wasn't allowed to know the name of the family giving you up, and they weren't allowed to know the name of the family adopting you. That's just the way it was handled back then.''

He gave a despairing glance at the photo. ''I guess the lawyer and the adoption agency lied to us, that's all there is to it.''

Ella knew exactly why her father looked so distraught, and it wasn't because the agency or the lawyers had lied to him. It was because Mary must have lied to him, too, and he knew it.

She spoke quietly, although beneath the surface calm, her emotions roiled with gale force intensity. ''The agency can't have lied to my mother. Otherwise she wouldn't have this picture that she's kept hidden from both of us all these years. She must have known all along that my mother wasn't poor and single, but for some reason she kept the truth from you.''

"You're probably right.'' The concession was obviously painful. Frank swallowed, his Adam's apple bobbing. ''Why didn't she tell me? What is it they were all so anxious to keep secret from me? From you?''

"I don't know, but I have to find out.''

Her father sent her a pleading look. ''Don't ask your mother about it until she's better, Ellie. For one thing, she's still so confused that she probably couldn't give you any of the answers you're looking for—''

"Or maybe she could. I have the oddest feeling that it's something to do with my adoption that's worrying her so much.''

"Why would you think that? After all these years, why would she suddenly be worried? Even if it turns out your birth mother isn't dead, why would it matter? It isn't as if we're going to be fighting her for custody!''

Ella couldn't begin to think of an answer. ''Is there any chance that somebody phoned her while you were out in the backyard?'' she asked. ''Maybe somebody gave Mom a message from my birth family that shocked her so much it caused her heart attack.''

Frank shook his head. ''I don't believe there was a call. I was only outside a few minutes, and I was right up close to the house. My hearing's pretty good, always has been. I'd have heard the kitchen phone.''

He leaned across the table. ''Don't push this, Ellie. The doctors said Mary has to avoid stress until she's rebuilt her strength. Give her another month to get back on her feet and then show her the photo. It's been thirty years, honey. Waiting another few weeks isn't going to make much difference, is it?''

Almost anything she could say in reply would probably hurt her father's feelings, Ella reflected. If she told him that her decision to marry had left her feeling a hole where her roots were supposed to be, he would be devastated. If she admitted that she was angry with her mother for years of silence, he would be saddened to no real purpose. She ought to let him know that she was planning to take the photo to Dylan Garrett at Finders Keepers the second she could arrange an appointment, but she decided not to mention it.

Was this how Mary had rationalized keeping the photograph hidden? Ella wondered. Perhaps she'd made a spur-of-the-moment decision that it was in the best interests of her husband and new daughter not to reveal the truth. Then, as the years passed, revealing the truth had become more and more impossible.

Ella recognized that she was planning exactly the same sort of deception by omission, but she still chose not to mention Dylan Garrett's name to her father. And when they said good-night and went to their respective rooms, Ella made sure that she was the person who took possession of the all-important photograph. The bottom line was that she didn't want to be forced into a position where she would have to promise not to dig into the mystery of her past.

Because if she gave such a promise, she knew she would break it.

CHAPTER TWELVE

JOSH CALLED IN some favors and managed to set up an appointment with Dylan Garrett at Finders Keepers for seven-thirty on Thursday morning, only three days after Ella returned to San Antonio. Josh asked if she wanted him to accompany her to the meeting and, barely needing even a moment to reflect, Ella replied that she did. After years of coping perfectly well on her own, it was a little scary to realize how quickly she had come to feel that she wanted Josh at her side for any important event in her life.

Dylan Garrett's office, with its walls of natural stone and rough-hewn timber, made for pleasant surroundings in which to pour out the story of her adoption. Dylan struck Ella as an intelligent man, with a laid-back Texan friendliness that didn't quite disguise a hint of ruthlessness behind the easygoing facade.

All of them were pressed for time, so they didn't waste many minutes in social chitchat. After a brief exchange about the unusually cold weather and the offer of coffee or orange juice, Ella gave Dylan a concise account of everything she knew about her background. She had been awake since dawn rehearsing exactly what she wanted to say, and she thought she did a pretty good job of covering everything relevant without sounding obsessive about her fear that Mary Petri had spent the past three decades covering up some terrible secret.

Dylan listened without interruption, his attention sharply focused, jotting the occasional swift note onto the legal pad in front of him. When she'd finished, he gave her an encouraging smile. "In comparison to some adoptees, you have quite a lot of facts for me to work with. I'm optimistic I'll be able to come up with some solid information for you, Ella. The fact that you have a photograph of your parents is a big help. Do you have a copy of it with you?"

"Of course." Ella handed him a manila envelope. "I already went to the drugstore and made an enlargement on one of those instant photocopy machines. The original picture is in the envelope, too, so that you can check out the inscription."

Dylan drew out the two photos and put them side by side on the desk in front of him. He glanced briefly at the images, then flipped the original photo over and read the inscription. Suddenly frowning, he turned the picture back again and studied it intently. After less than a minute, his head jerked up and he stared at Ella and Josh as if they'd sprouted rabbit's ears in the middle of their foreheads.

"You said your adoptive mother had a heart attack over the Thanksgiving break. Did you mean actually on the holiday itself?" Dylan, who had been so attentive while Ella told her story, didn't wait for her to respond. Instead, he got up from his desk and started rummaging through a pile of magazines stacked on his credenza.

"Yes. Mary sat down to read the paper after spending the morning cooking, and she just collapsed, right there in the armchair."

"While she was reading the paper?"

"Well, yes. That's what we think happened, although nobody was in the room at the time and Mary doesn't remember."

"She must have seen the news about Henderson," Dylan muttered to himself. "Must have been a hell of a shock."

"What must have been a shock?" Ella asked.

Dylan pulled copies of *Time* and *Newsweek* out of the magazine pile and set them on his desk. "Haven't either of you watched any TV or read the newspapers since your mother had her heart attack?" he asked.

Ella blinked at the seeming irrelevance of the question. "I watched the final round of some golf championship with my Dad, and a couple of *Frasier* reruns with my mother. Other than that, I haven't even had time to catch the weather forecast. Between Mom's heart attack, catching up at work, and trying to stop our two sets of parents planning a wedding that would be excessive for the heirs to a medium-size kingdom, my days have been so crammed I can barely stay awake long enough to brush my teeth before I fall into bed at night." And the fact that once she was in bed, Josh was there with her, meant that sleep was reduced by another couple of hours while they made love. Not that she was complaining about that part of her schedule.

"How about you, Josh?" Dylan turned as he spoke.

"I'm guessing you haven't been paying much attention to the news over the past couple of weeks?"

"You're right," Josh said. "I'm usually a news junkie, but it's been one of those periods at work where we seem to be proving Murphy's law that whatever can go wrong will go wrong. Between scrambling to correct a hundred-thousand-dollar error in the order for one of our biggest clients, and two trips across the country in the space of a week, I think aliens would have had to land on the White House lawn before I'd have paid real attention."

Dylan suddenly laughed. "You know, I think you've both missed something that as far as Ella is concerned is almost as extraordinary as aliens landing on the White House lawn. You need to catch up on your current events reading." He pushed the magazines across his desk, *Time* toward Josh and *Newsweek* toward Ella. Then he tipped his chair back and rocked gently, looking very pleased with himself.

Dylan Garrett might come highly recommended, Ella thought, but she was beginning to find his behavior distinctly odd. Catch up on their current events reading? Was he nuts? Only politeness drove her to pick up the magazine and glance at the cover.

Her heart stopped beating for a moment, then raced forward in double time. The cover carried the picture of a man in late middle age, wearing military uniform. His hair was gray and close cropped, his eyes a piercing blue. He stood with a ramrod straight spine and stared directly—almost defiantly—into the camera. At his side an elderly man, with stooped shoulders and a shock of white hair, clutched a briefcase in one hand

and a fistful of documents in the other. The white-haired man seemed to be waving the papers in triumph. The background to the photograph appeared to be the steel bars of a high gate, very possibly a prison.

It wasn't hard to guess that one or both of the men had just been freed from captivity. Ella looked over at the magazine in front of Josh, and saw that his cover bore a similar picture.

Her hands were suddenly sweaty with tension, but she spoke coolly. Her reaction to stress always tended to be withdrawal into a state of unnatural calm. "Who is the man in the picture?" she asked Dylan.

"His name is Brad Henderson. He used to be a major in the US Air Force. Actually, about a week ago I believe his rank was reinstated. His story has been plastered over every media outlet in the country. It's hard to believe that you avoided seeing or hearing anything about it."

Josh frowned. "The name does have a familiar ring to it. I believe I caught the tail end of an interview on *Good Morning America*. He's just been released from prison, hasn't he? Something about being wrongly convicted years and years ago?"

"Right," Dylan said. "Major Henderson was arrested by the United States government in 1975 and charged with multiple counts of espionage, along with aiding and abetting the enemies of the United States, and assorted other crimes. He was convicted and served twenty-eight years of a lifetime sentence before his release early on the morning of Thanksgiving Day."

Josh frowned in thought. "In the TV piece I saw,

he was talking about how angry the public was at the time of his arrest, and how he was lucky to have avoided the death penalty. I got the impression he was one of those golden people who had the world at his feet until he blew it all, and then the public really turned on him.''

Dylan nodded. ''You've hit it. There's nothing like a hero gone bad to rile people up. Henderson was a combat pilot in Vietnam and he'd won medals for bravery. Then he was accused of selling the plans for a top secret fighter jet to the Soviet Union. It was rumored that he'd betrayed the names of several of our agents working undercover in Eastern Europe and that nineteen people had died because of his treachery. The country was still reeling from the mess in Vietnam, it was the height of the Cold War, and the public felt betrayed. They were baying for Henderson's blood. If he hadn't had a brilliant lawyer, he probably wouldn't be alive today to enjoy his vindication.''

Ella's mouth was so dry that her tongue felt as if it would stick to her teeth if she tried to speak. She was very glad for the mug of coffee she'd accepted earlier, and took several sips before she managed to unglue her vocal chords. ''Why was Major Henderson released from prison after all this time? If his appeals were unsuccessful in the past, why were they successful this time?''

''The government has finally admitted they made a terrible mistake. With the fall of the Soviet Union, and the opening of the KGB archives, new evidence became available two years ago which not only proves conclusively that Major Henderson wasn't guilty, but also names the real culprit who sold the plans for that fighter jet.''

"They've known for two whole years that he's innocent and they've only just released him?" Ella was incredulous.

Dylan gave a quick shrug. "You know what government and the courts are like. Never admit you're wrong until you absolutely have to. Which I guess is the way it should be, or the system would collapse. It's taken his lawyer two years of nonstop legal wrangling to get the miscarriage of justice acknowledged, and his client released. The icing on the cake is that the lawyer has managed to get back pay for twenty-eight years, plus interest, paid into Henderson's bank account. Not exactly recompense for all those lost years, but at least the poor guy is going to have enough money to enjoy his new freedom.''

"How did the real culprit get away with it for so long?" Ella asked, her stomach churning. "How could the prosecution and the jury all make such a terrible mistake?"

"Remember Henderson was tried by a military court, not a civilian one, so the rules of evidence weren't as favorable to him. The bottom line seems to be that the Soviet Union planted false information to incriminate Henderson and the Air Force investigators fell for it. The Soviet government was desperate to protect their asset, a man called Ronald Muir, who was one of Major Henderson's colleagues, and a true believer in the Communist cause. Muir was such a valuable source of information that the Kremlin didn't care who suffered in their efforts to protect him.''

"Is Ronald Muir in prison now?" Ella asked. "I sure as heck hope he is."

Dylan shook his head. "Before Muir can be tried, much less incarcerated, he has to be found. The government issued an arrest warrant over a year ago, long before they were willing to exonerate Henderson, but somebody must have tipped Muir off, because he fled the country about two hours ahead of the feds. And so far, he's managed to stay hidden."

Ella knew she would worry later about the missing Ronald Muir. For the moment, she could think of only one thing. "Do you think Brad Henderson is my father?" she asked Dylan. Her body felt stiff and awkward with shock, and the question sounded more aggressive than she intended.

"Yes, I do."

Ella picked up the magazine and examined the cover photo again. "I guess he does look like an older version of the man in my photo, and I know the dates fit with what we know. Still, it's a huge leap to conclude that Major Henderson is my father...."

Although it might explain why Mary had suffered a heart attack, Ella reflected. That must have been what Dylan was muttering about earlier. If Mary knew that Major Henderson was Ella's father, it would explain why she'd wanted to keep the past hidden. No child needed to know that her biological father had been a reviled traitor. But having kept the secret for so long, if Mary had picked up the newspaper on Thanksgiving Day and read that Henderson had been released from prison with a full government pardon, it could easily have been enough of a shock to send her into cardiac arrest.

"I'm almost certain Major Henderson is your father, Ella." Dylan spoke gently. "If you look at the articles in *Time* and *Newsweek,* you'll see they've reproduced some photographs of Major Henderson's family. When you see those pictures, Ella, you'll understand why I'm so sure we've found your father."

Josh, whose fingers weren't shaking like Ella's, found the photo spread in his magazine first. He handed it to Ella and she stared at the glossy pages with such intensity that they blurred beneath her eyes. Blinking, she refocused and the images swam into view.

The largest picture was in color, and showed Major Henderson and his wife sitting on a blanket under a giant maple tree. It was a sunny day, obviously warm, and they were wearing shorts. A wicker picnic hamper could be seen in the corner of the photo. A baby, perhaps a year old, was standing with one hand on her mother's shoulders, a dandelion in her other hand, tickling her mother's chin. A toddler, somewhere between two and three years old, was leaning back against Major Henderson's chest, her gurgles of laughter almost visible she was laughing so hard. Henderson had his arms tight around the little girl, and his chin nuzzled her fluffy curls.

That's me, Ella thought, staring with hypnotized fascination at the picture of the little girl in Henderson's arms. That's me with my mother and father and my sister.

Another wild thought buzzed into her head. Good

grief, she had a sister! Swallowing over the lump in her throat, she reached out toward Josh, glad when she felt his fingers wrap firmly around her hand. Right now, her whole world was tilting, and she needed anchoring.

A second snapshot showed the same family group at Christmastime, with the two little girls decked out in velvet dresses, and a pile of gift boxes at their feet. A third insert reproduced the very same portrait Ella had found in Mary's dresser drawer, while the final photo was of a young baby, with the squished, otherworldly look of a newborn. A notation beneath the picture indicated that this was the youngest of Major Henderson's three daughters, photographed in the hospital just after she was born.

Good grief, she had *two* sisters, Ella thought in disbelief. For an only child to become one of three sisters all in the space of a few minutes required quite a mental adjustment!

Henderson was already on trial by the time his third child was born, and he'd never been allowed to hold the baby, whom he'd seen only once, when he attended his wife's funeral, shackled hand and foot. He and his wife had wanted to call the baby Catherine, after her grandmother, but he had no idea if that was the name she had actually been given.

Her emotions might be racing full speed ahead, but her thought processes must have been crawling along at a snail's pace, Ella realized, because it was only when she saw the caption under the photo of her baby sister that she asked the obvious question.

"What happened to my mother? Why didn't she

take care of the three of us after my father was sent to prison? Why doesn't he know what his own child was named? Didn't my mother send him a letter, even if she couldn't bear to visit him?''

Dylan hesitated for a second or two, long enough for Ella to hazard a guess at what he was going to say. ''I'm so sorry, Ella, but your mother died.''

''How did she die?''

''According to the media reports, it was one of those fluke accidents of labor and delivery. The doctors knew your sister was in the wrong position for a normal delivery and so they scheduled a C-section. It should have been routine, but it wasn't. If I'm recalling the accounts correctly, your mother's uterus ruptured, they couldn't stop the bleeding, and she died in the delivery room.''

Mary had lost her baby, and she had lost her mother, Ella thought, as a wave of sadness washed over her. In the twentieth century, giving birth wasn't supposed to be that dangerous.

Dylan pushed back from his desk, tactful enough to realize that Ella needed some down time to assimilate everything she'd been told. ''I just heard the sounds of my assistant's arrival. I need to confer with her for a few minutes, if you'll excuse me. Why don't I leave you two to read the articles? You'll see that Major Henderson is desperate to be reunited with his three daughters. His lawyer has actually set up an 800 number for people to call if they have any information that would help him find his lost daughters.'' Dylan gave a chuckle. ''I think he's going to be real happy to take your call, don't you?''

CHAPTER THIRTEEN

By THE TIME Ella arrived at the hotel later that morning, there were three urgent phone messages from Mary, all asking her to call immediately. "Your mom called at eight, eight-fifteen and again at eight-forty," the front desk clerk said. "She says not to worry, there's no problem with her health, but she needs to speak with you ASAP. She said to tell you it was real important, Ella."

Although her mother and Barb Taylor were both obsessing about Ella's failure to treat the problem of finding a wedding dress with sufficient seriousness—not to mention ordering a cake and deciding on a color scheme—she knew that Mary would never intrude with personal calls into the workplace unless it was a genuine crisis.

There wasn't much doubt what her mother was calling about, Ella reflected wryly. She could only be grateful that the second time around Mary had apparently managed to hear or read about Brad Henderson's release from prison without almost literally dying from the shock.

She dialed her parents' number and the phone was snatched off the receiver almost before it had time to ring. "Mom? It's Ella."

"Ellie, thank God you've called. I've remembered what it was I'd forgotten! Oh dear, I don't know how to begin telling you this. It's about your birth family. The fact is, I knew a little bit more about them than I ever told you. Your father says you've seen the photograph I've kept hidden all these years, the one when you're a baby—"

Mary paused to draw breath and Ella broke in. "Mom, I think I know what you're going to say. I've read the articles in *Time* and *Newsweek* about Major Henderson's release and seen the pictures—"

"Then you must have guessed by now that he's your father."

"He's my biological father, Mom. Frank Petri is my father, and you're my mother."

Mary burst into tears. "But we should never have had the chance to raise you! Ellie, I feel so terrible now I know the poor man was innocent! All those years in prison, denied access to his beautiful girls, and he'd never committed the crime. If we'd only known the truth back then!" Mary was crying hard and Ella could hear her father making comforting noises in the background.

"Mom, you can't blame yourself for accepting what ninety-nine percent of the people in this country believed was true."

Mary was obviously having a tough time getting control over her runaway emotions. "When I adopted you, I thought it was for the best, I swear. Your mother's own sister told me that your father was so notorious, and so hated, that the best chance of happiness for all of you girls was to be adopted and brought up in families where you'd never know the truth about your parents."

"Mom, I understand that you did what you thought was right. Honest." During the drive into work from Dylan's office, Ella had wondered why she didn't feel more angry about the fact that Mary had obviously known at least some of the truth and had lied all these years to conceal it. Ella had eventually decided that in Mary's shoes, she'd probably have done the exact same thing. Given that Major Henderson had been accused of causing the deaths of nineteen brave people, she had to acknowledge that her childhood had been happier for her ignorance. As a teen, she would have had a miserable time coping with the knowledge that her father had betrayed his own country.

"What I don't understand is why the adoption agency told you the truth about my background but not Dad. He didn't know anything about Major Henderson, did he?"

"No, and Frank's very angry with me." Mary made a sound that was as close to a sob as a laugh. "Good thing I had a heart attack and he doesn't dare get on to me the way he'd like to."

"Why did you keep the truth from him?" Ella asked. Her parents always seemed to share every detail of their lives and it was hard to visualize her mother keeping such an important secret from her husband.

"Well, you'd have to go back in time to understand how angry people were with Major Henderson. And the truth is, your dad was as angry as everyone else. The Taylors were the same, and you know they're not folks to condemn without knowing all the facts. In fact, Frank was so angry with Henderson. I was afraid that if he knew the truth he wouldn't agree to the adoption. And Ellie, I wanted you so badly to be my own.''

''I'm surprised the adoption agency agreed to go along with the deception,'' Ella said.

''The truth is, you weren't adopted through an agency,'' Mary said. ''Although Frank never knew that. He was working long hours, trying to get his business established, and I took care of all the paperwork, so he never realized the lawyer's office where we picked you up had nothing to do with Catholic Charities. We'd filled out all the forms to go through the agency. We'd done the home inspection and been approved, but they didn't have any babies for us. They said we might have to wait another three or four years before our name came up, and there was a chance we might be considered too old. They liked the adoptive moms to be under forty, and I have to say, you can see why. That's why it seemed truly like a gift from God when Heather Cooper asked me if I'd be interested in adopting you.''

''Mom, back up! Who is Heather Cooper?''

''She's your aunt. Your birth mother's older sister. Mrs. Cooper was divorced, living in a house in Sands Point near your parents, and I worked as her housekeeper for about five months. I had no idea she was connected to the Hendersons and you can be sure she never told me. Then one day, I went to her house and found her arguing with Lorraine. Lorraine is your birth mother.''

''Yes, I know. Her name was in the magazine articles I read.''

"Well, Lorraine's picture had been splashed all over the TV and the newspapers back then, so I knew right away who Heather's visitor was. Imagine! I was in the same house with the notorious Lorraine Henderson. That's as much thought as I gave it right then, except to think that Lorraine was even prettier than her pictures. And pretty soon, I figured out Lorraine and Heather were sisters."

"You said they were arguing. What about, do you know?"

"I do know, because Heather was screaming she was so angry. There was no way to avoid hearing what she was saying. She told Lorraine she was a fool to believe in Brad's innocence, and they ought to move to Australia where they could start over without anyone knowing who they were. Lorraine said Heather was free to move any time she pleased, but Lorraine was staying right where she was because she and her children had nothing to be ashamed of. Except, maybe, the rotten way their government and the American people were treating Brad Henderson."

"And did Heather Cooper follow her own advice and move to Australia?"

"I wouldn't know." Mary sniffed disparagingly. "But I do know she moved from Sands Point as soon as you three babies were adopted. Which was as lickety-split quick as Heather could make it after her sister died."

"Do you know who adopted my two little sisters?"

"I wish I did, Ellie, but I don't have an idea who took them. I offered to adopt all three of you. Frank and I would have been thrilled, even if it would have busted our budget, but Heather said she was a trained psychologist, and she'd decided it would be best if you were split up and given new identities, even new names, so that you could start your lives fresh, not tainted by your father's crimes and your mother's death. I didn't agree about splitting you up, but your sisters were already gone, so there wasn't a darn thing I could do about it. I didn't change your name, though. I figured your mother had never done a thing wrong except marry a traitor, and if she wanted you called Gabriella, then that's what you were going to be called."

Tears sprang into Ella's eyes and she blinked them away. "I'm glad you kept my name, Mom."

Mary was silent for a long moment, and when she spoke again, her voice was heavy. "I wanted a child so badly that I ached, Ellie. You have to forgive me if I maybe didn't ask all the questions I should have. There was something about Heather Cooper that I didn't trust, and I never thought she had the best interests of you babies at heart. But I didn't care what private agenda Heather was following. I just wanted you."

"And you got me. Including all those wonderful teenage years when you had to put up with me finding myself. Remember when I painted my room black? Including the ceiling?"

Mary laughed, as Ella hoped she would and the conversation continued, with her mother sharing all the details of the adoption that she had for so long kept to herself. Finally, Mary asked the inevitable question.

"Are you going to make arrangements to see Major Henderson?" she asked.

"I already tried," Ella said, deciding there was nothing to be gained by prevaricating about how badly she wanted to make contact with the man who had seemed to love her so unreservedly when she was a baby.

Mary gulped. "D-did you speak to him already?"

"No. I expect you know that Henderson's lawyer set up an 800 number for people to get in touch with him. But when we tried to call, we discovered the number had been disconnected. Then Josh had the idea of calling directly to *Newsweek,* and an editorial assistant there told us the lawyer's office was flooded with so many calls from people claiming to be Henderson's daughters that the entire staff of the law office was doing nothing but answering the phones."

"So what are you going to do now?" Mary asked.

"Josh and I are working on it. We went to see a man called Dylan Garrett this morning. Dylan's an ex-cop, now a private investigator, and he just cracked one of the biggest kidnapping cases to hit Texas in recent years, so his name carries a lot of weight in law enforcement circles. He's promised to have us in touch with Major Henderson within the next twelve hours. I'll keep you posted, Mom. If Major Henderson contacts us, you and Dad will be the first to know."

CHAPTER FOURTEEN

MAJOR BRAD HENDERSON—it amused him that the air force had restored his rank—had once been a trusting soul, with a naive faith in the goodness of humanity. Wrongful conviction and twenty-eight years of incarceration had taken care of all the trust and most of the faith. The death of his wife and the loss of his children had taken away love and hope, leaving very little behind. Brad would be the first to admit that these days he was a pretty cynical guy. Unfortunately…fortunately…he wasn't sure which, the prospect of being reunited with his daughters had sparked a dangerous flicker of hope. A hope that needed to be contained, or it would burn away the protective layers of ice that had numbed his feelings for so many years. Brad had no interest in reacquiring the capacity to be vulnerable.

Allen Kemp, his lawyer, was screening the deluge of applicants with great care, and Brad's attitude as he interviewed prospective "daughters" was a mixture of distrust and caution, liberally laced with suspicion. So far, he had already undergone five meetings with young women who turned out not to be his children. Despite the lure of his money, three of the women had actually been genuine in their belief that he was their father. In one case, Brad had decided there was a possibility that the young woman might indeed be his youngest daughter, Catherine. DNA tests had proved conclusively that she wasn't. Brad hadn't allowed himself to feel disappointment because that would have acknowledged the existence of hope.

With every expectation that this meeting would be as abortive as the others, Brad strode through the San Antonio airport in search of a cab. His lawyer had arranged a meeting for him with a woman called Gabriella Petri, and it was scheduled for noon at the Hyatt Hotel located on the famous River Walk. The Petri woman apparently worked for the Sedgwick Hotel and had originally suggested meeting there, but Brad wanted a more neutral ground than her place of employment, and the Petri woman hadn't objected. His plane had been half an hour late landing in San Antonio, but he'd factored air traffic delays into his schedule, and he would get to the hotel on time. An officer and a gentleman never kept a lady waiting, he reflected ironically.

Allen had made sure Ms. Petri clearly understood Brad's rules for meeting with prospective "daughters." Any leaks to the media concerning the meeting and it was instantly canceled. The meeting was to take place in a hotel reasonably close to the airport, to make it quicker and easier for Brad to get out of town. He also stipulated nowadays that the meeting would take place in a public area to prevent any possible accusations of misconduct or inappropriate behavior. This latest rule had been formulated in response to claimant number two who, immediately after being rejected as a daughter, had filed a lawsuit accusing Brad of sexually assaulting her. If they couldn't get their hands on his two million dollars' worth of back pay one way, Brad mused, some of his ''daughters'' were obviously determined to get it another.

Brad got into the cab and gave his destination. "How long to get to the hotel?" he asked the cabbie.

"Half hour, mebbe. Depends on traffic."

Brad quelled a faint stir of anticipation. His lawyer had been optimistic that this Petri woman might be the real thing, but Brad had refused to get his hopes up. Much better to expect the worst and then you weren't knocked sideways when it happened. He was through with sunny optimism. He'd tried that experiment with Lorraine, and didn't intend to repeat it. After a childhood spent in foster homes, and a gut-wrenching tour of duty in Vietnam, it had taken him quite a while to believe that a woman as good and as beautiful as Lorraine Fletcher could possibly love him.

Once they were married, and his first daughter was born, healthy and perfect, Brad had made the terrible mistake of allowing himself to believe that Lorraine was right, and happiness was possible. He often wondered if any married couple had ever been more in love, more blissfully compatible, than the two of them. The four years between Gabriella's birth and his arrest shimmered in his memories like a jewel in a pool of mud. But, much as he yearned for those halcyon days, he wasn't going to let himself become an easy mark for crooks and con artists. Or even for needy young women trying to find their biological parents.

Allen pointed out that the Petri woman had been

adopted when she was four, and that the adoption had taken place in Sands Point, New York and that she'd sent him a copy of a photo she had in her possession that was identical to the one that had appeared in various magazines and newspapers. Her adoptive mother had worked as a housekeeper for Heather Cooper. There really did seem to be strong links. Plus she was apparently engaged to a man who was reputed to be a millionaire in his own right, so Brad had to conclude that she wasn't in this for the money. All in all, it did seem as if this woman might truly be the one. The first of his daughters to be reclaimed.

Brad fought grimly against the flicker of hope that was determined to burn, weakening him. Coincidence proved nothing. He was a living testament to that, or he wouldn't have spent the past twenty-eight years watching the seasons change from behind a barbed wire fence. No way he was going to acknowledge this woman as his daughter until they had a DNA test to prove his paternity. And then he might ask for a repeat test from another lab.

Better not to think about the details of this Petri woman's life and how neatly they fit with his eldest daughter's. Better to concentrate on the scenery. Tight-lipped, Brad stared out of the window at highways and strip shopping malls that still looked bizarrely unfamiliar to him. He'd been arrested when Barry Manilow was the country's most popular singer and *All in the Family* was the most popular show on TV. He'd come out of prison to a world where popular music seemed to consist of streams of foul language without the inconvenience of an attached melody, and the most popular shows on television were about undertakers, mobsters, or single women who spent their entire waking hours thinking about sex. Sometimes, Brad reflected ruefully, he felt every one of his sixty-five years. And he wasn't entirely sure that the time warp was all due to prison.

The cabbie drew to a halt under the hotel canopy. "This is it," he said. "The River Walk. Hyatt Hotel."

Brad paid the fare—he'd become fairly good at hiding his sticker shock at twenty-first century prices—and walked into the hotel lobby, keeping his dark glasses in place. These days, he could never be sure he wouldn't be recognized, and he was beginning to develop a reluctant sympathy for movie stars who suddenly snapped under the glare of constant intrusion and hit paparazzi over the head with their own cameras.

A two-story sculpture of fountains and waterfalls decorated the hotel lobby and tumbled attractively into the waters of the River Walk. Brad forced himself to slow down and admire the view for a moment. Most civilian decor beat the cinder blocks of the prison rec room, but this was especially attractive.

Allen had arranged that he would meet with Gabriella Petri in the restaurant on the main level, and he steeled himself to face disappointment as he walked across the atrium to the designated spot. He told himself that it didn't matter if the Petri woman turned out to be another fraud, or even just another well-intentioned adoptee mistakenly believing she'd found her father. He would keep searching and eventually he would find all three of his girls. That was his life's goal, however long it might take, and he was determined to achieve it.

The restaurant was open to the lobby, and he could see several people clustered around the pasta bar, all clearly intent on eating lunch rather than waiting to meet anyone. His gaze flicked to the side of the restaurant, where a man and a woman sat on opposite sides of a small table. They had tall mugs in front of them, but neither of them seemed to be drinking. Allen had told him the Petri woman would be bringing her fiancé to the meeting, so this was probably the couple he'd come to meet. Part of the reason Allen had insisted they needed to establish contact with the Petri woman right away was that her fiancé was a prominent figure in San Antonio, the CEO of his own company and a millionaire in his own right. Not the sort of person to have any interest in scamming Brad out of a few thousand bucks, or to waste time with a woman who had neurotic fantasies about being the daughter of a minor celebrity.

None of which meant that this woman actually was his daughter, Brad reminded himself, and he wasn't going to let down his guard for a second. He was hardened, prison tested and dedicated to conducting this search rationally.

The woman's back was turned toward Brad, but as he entered the actual restaurant area, the man at the table caught sight of him and murmured something to the woman. She immediately pushed back her chair and stood up, turning around so that she could see him.

Brad stopped breathing. Rationality took wing and flew somewhere far, far away. The woman in front of him was Lorraine returned to life. A couple of inches taller maybe, her hair a little darker, her eyes a fraction more brilliantly green, but from the tilt of her head to the half smile on her lips, it was his own Lorraine, just as she had lived in his memory for twenty-eight long, bitter years.

Brad's head started to swim and he clutched a nearby decorative railing, steadying himself. He had to remind himself to draw breath. Plastic surgery can make anyone look like anyone, he thought wildly. Think DNA testing. Think *proof,* you fool.

"M-Major Henderson?" The woman stepped toward him, her hands hanging uncertainly at her sides. "I'm Gabriella Petri."

God, she even had her mother's voice. Hope exploded inside him, blasting away the protective barriers he'd so carefully erected. "Gabbie?" Brad said hoarsely. "Oh, my God, Gabbie, is it really you?"

"I...I think maybe it is." Tears brimmed, then spilled out of her gorgeous green eyes and he reacted on one hundred percent emotional instinct, not an atom of reason or caution involved. He opened his arms and she moved into his embrace as easily and naturally as if they'd spent a lifetime exchanging hugs.

After a very long moment, she stepped back and he was able to look at her again. He touched her elegantly high cheekbones, marveling at how the baby dimples had transformed themselves into this vision of adult femininity. Her lashes were still just as long and thick, he noticed, her skin still as soft and smooth. "You have no idea how glad I am to have found you, Gabbie."

"Yes, I do. Because I feel the same way." She smiled as if she couldn't stop.

He wanted to say something wise. Something that would make up for the twenty-eight years he hadn't been there. But all he could think of was how much he loved her, and how incredibly much he'd missed her and her sisters all these years. "You're so grown-up, and beautiful!" he said. "Have you any idea how much you look like your mother?"

"Do I?" Her eyes lit up. "Josh mentioned that I looked like her, after he'd seen the pictures in the magazines—"

"Josh is your fiancé?"

"Oh, yes. We're getting married the day after Christmas. It will be so wonderful if you can come to the wedding. I can't believe that we found you in time!"

She turned, leaving her arm linked with his, and Brad felt his heart swell until he was sure it couldn't hold any more emotion without bursting out from his chest. "This is Josh Taylor," she said, gesturing toward the table. "My husband-to-be."

There was a world of pride in her voice as she said Josh's name, and a universe of love. She smiled as the man at the table stood up and held out his hand.

"It's an honor to meet you, sir. Ella has been counting down the minutes for this moment."

The guy was good-looking, with decent manners, and—if Brad could still judge such things—expensive clothes, even if they were casual. Josh picked up an envelope from the table and extended it toward Brad.

"We're confident that you're Ella's father, sir. But

I guess you'd like to have something more to go on than gut instinct. There's a letter in here from the Petris giving all the details of Ella's adoption, along with the photograph Mary Petri took from Heather Cooper's house at the time the adoption was being discussed. There's an inscription on the back of the photo, and you might recognize the handwriting. At least that way, you'll know the photo is genuine, not some copy we faked from a magazine. Plus the Petris have lots of snapshots they took of Ella when she was four and had just left your home. That should reassure you that she's the same child."

"And of course I'll take a DNA test if that's what you want. Mr. Kemp, your lawyer, said that you wanted hard evidence."

"That all seemed a lot more important before I met you," Brad said wryly.

"But since the DNA test is so simple to take, we might as well do it," Ella said.

"I guess." Brad took the package, more because his daughter seemed to expect it than for any other reason. From the moment he saw her, he'd felt an absolute conviction that this was his child, a conviction that had been entirely lacking with all of the other women he'd interviewed. He pulled out the familiar photo and turned it over, seeing his own handwriting on the picture that he and Lorraine had given to her sister. Back in the days when he'd been crazy enough to trust the scheming, conniving bitch.

"Were the Petris good parents to you?" he asked, dreading her answer. Heather, he was sure, had been capable of giving his babies away to the first person willing to accept them.

"They were wonderful. I couldn't possibly have asked for better people to adopt me."

"I'd likė to meet them. Tell them how much I appreciate all they've done."

"They're very much looking forward to meeting you. My mother—" She broke off, embarrassed.

"Honey, she *is* your mother." It hurt Brad to admit that Mrs. Petri was his daughter's mother, but he'd learned the hard way that glossing over the truth did nothing to change it.

"Well, I was going to say that my mother can't travel because she had a heart attack over Thanksgiving, but she's getting stronger every day, and she's hoping that when the wedding is over, you'll stay with her and my da—"

"With her and your father," Brad prompted, although it damn near killed him.

Ella nodded gratefully. "Yes." She smiled. "Although, be warned. They're hauling out the family picture albums and getting ready to tell you all the stories about how cute I was in fourth grade."

"There's nothing I'd like to hear more." This time, Brad was entirely sincere.

"But let's not do it here," Ella said. "Would you come home with me and Josh, so that we can spend some time together? If you could spend the night—if you're not too busy—we would love to have you."

If he wasn't too busy? Too busy to spend time with his eldest daughter, and the guy who looked as if he might be quite decent son-in-law material? Brad laughed. God, he thought, how long had it been since he laughed with so much genuine happiness?

"I think I can clear my schedule," he said, taking his daughter's arm and tucking it under his. "Let's go home, Gabriella. We have a lifetime of catching up to do, so let's get started."

Dear Reader,

I believe in the magic that Christmas weaves around the season. I also believe in Santa Claus because Santa Claus is a doer. He know about the magic of love; he sees a need and addresses it, and he enriches the life of someone else just because he knows he can. Santa Claus wants only to make his small portion of the world a better place, to make the few people with whom he comes in contact a little happier for his having been there. He's *anyone* who believes in the power of love.

I'm delighted you're visiting with us this Christmas season. I've spent a lot of time with the Trueblood folks this past year and was excited to have a chance to visit them again—even if only peripherally.

And in the meantime, I have someone else for you to meet, someone I hope you'll approach with an open mind and heart—my heroine, Beth. So many of us suffer from some kind of self-doubt or low self-esteem at some point in our lives, and many of us are lucky enough to recover from that. Some people don't recover, and they must learn to compensate in order to lead productive lives. These people contribute, they serve, they laugh and work and live, and we never know the effort it takes them to do simple things. Such is the case for Beth. She struggles daily with her issues, but she nonetheless manages to be productive and ambitious.

I know people like this. I imagine you do, too. Or perhaps you're one of them. If so, my heart is with you, as is my admiration. I wish for you, as I do for Beth, healing that makes the fight no longer necessary, or at least, less frequent and strenuous. My holiday message for you this year is one of hope.

Merry Christmas!

Tara Taylor Quinn

BETH

Tara Taylor Quinn

CHAPTER ONE

"BETH? I'm sorry to bother you, but I thought you might want to see this."

Twenty-eight-year-old Beth Chenoweth looked up at the smartly dressed middle aged woman standing in her office doorway. Her administrative assistant was holding a facsimile. Smiling at Nancy, she held out her hand. "What is it?"

It couldn't be good or Nancy wouldn't be bothering Beth. But dealing with problems came with the territory of being executive director for a multimillion dollar organization.

"That group of charter schools in Arizona has filed a suit against us, claiming restraint of trade."

"Get Kyle on the line, will you?" Beth asked even before she'd read the fax. If a suit was being threatened, she needed to speak with their lawyer.

Nancy moved farther into the spacious and elegantly furnished Victorian office, located only a minute's walk from downtown Victoria. Once at the desk, she dialed their lawyer's number, while Beth perused the fax. The state of Arizona had a large number of charter schools, due in part to the state's laws concerning them, and had been presenting a challenge to The Parents of Gifted Kids, and Beth in particular, for more than a year. They wanted to use the lobbying powers of PGK to fight for rights and further their cause in the state legislature.

Because PGK was a proven force in educational legislative battles, the Arizona faction wanted Beth to approve blanket memberships to the organization for any student and parents of students attending their schools. But they didn't meet the membership requirements because they weren't strictly dealing with gifted kids. PGK, now in it's fiftieth year, was an organization that served the needs of parents of gifted kids.

After a conversation with Kyle that netted her a letter to the Arizona schools in hopes of having the suit dropped, Beth decided not to walk the half block to the park for lunch, even though the fall day was perfect for such a stroll. Instead, she proofed her article for the seventy-five-page PGK membership journal that her staff produced in-house every month. The park had been inviting when she'd walked by it on her way to work that morning. But she had responsibilities to attend to and that took priority.

"How'd the interview with CNN go this morning?" Nancy was in the doorway, a folder in hand.

"Good," Beth hardly looked up from the article. She'd promised it to Bob Lane, her editorial director by two. It was almost that now. "The usual. Lots of questions about the external economic value regarding our influence over governmental lawmakers and educational governing boards around the world."

Nancy came in and took a seat in the high-backed floral print chair across from Beth's desk. "I've got your itinerary for the trip to San Francisco." She set the folder in front of Beth.

Beth had been trying to forget that she was leaving in the morning.

"You got Joe?"

"Yes, he's meeting you at the strip at nine." Nancy sat down. "I've been meaning to talk to you about that. Costs are rising so much, I'm just wondering if you wouldn't rather use someone closer to home. Seattle, maybe, or someone here in British Columbia?"

Beth shook her head.

"It can't be easy for you to pay a private pilot to come all the way from Oregon...."

With one glance, Beth quieted her assistant. "I live simply, and alone," she said, completely firm on this one. "I make a very generous salary and have a trust from my father, as well. I can afford Joe."

Smiling, Nancy said, "I know you said your friend from Seattle recommended him, but he must be some guy to keep you going back to him for, what, five years now? Ever since you got this job, at least."

"I trust him," was all she said. Nancy had no idea, and never would, that it was *that* trust alone that got Beth off the island. Her friend from Seattle had actually been her psychologist and had recommended Joe because she'd had another client who'd gone to him. And been pleased.

Not that Joe knew any of this.

It was only because of Joe that Beth had been able to take this job that she so loved. She'd been ecstatic when, upon graduation from the University of Victoria with her graduate degree in social work at the young age of twenty-three, she'd been approached by Parents of Gifted Kids. PGK was a highly respected organization that had helped her throughout her own school years. She'd been ecstatic because she could do work she loved and remain at home in Victoria, a place she couldn't leave.

And then she'd heard that the job entailed traveling to various conferences throughout the year. She'd been ready to turn it down, but then Dr. Lamont told her about Joe.

Traveling was hell. She only did it when she absolutely had to. And only for the job that gave her life significant meaning. The job she loved made the occasional trek into darkness necessary, and Joe made it possible.

"I think I'm going to fire Susan," Nancy said.

"Okay," Beth looked over from the article she'd been sightlessly gazing at. "Why?"

"She's been late three times this week and I just received another member complaint about rude treatment they'd received on the phone."

Frowning, Beth flicked her hair back over her shoulder. Susan, their receptionist, had been with them for a couple of years. "That makes four in the past six weeks. Seven in the past year." Her phone line was blinking. She probably had thirty messages waiting for her. "And she's had three warnings."

"I'll tell her tonight before she goes home."

"Give her two weeks' severance."

"With the documentation I've collected we don't have to do that."

"Do it anyway." Beth turned back to her computer.

"Yes, ma'am."

Nancy got up to leave. "Can I get you any lunch?"

"No. I had a granola bar." She looked over at Nancy again. "Any word on when the system will be up and running for online membership applications and dues?"

"They're saying by next Monday. The new Web site went up today. Take a look at it when you get a chance. Your idea of online member discussion boards was great. There are already more than one hundred hits."

Nodding, Beth made a mental note to do just that before she went home.

But first she had an article to finish, a state senator to call, and two superintendents of school waiting to hear from her. Not to mention the employee evaluations she had to present—and all those messages.

JOE HOLDEN confirmed that the gauges all read within range and leaned back in his seat, a hand on his jean-clad thigh, letting the automatic pilot do its thing. It left him time to concentrate on the woman in the co-pilot's seat of the private jet he flew for a living.

At least she looked more relaxed, than she had when they first took off.

Beth Chenoweth, the slim, elegantly controlled woman sitting beside him, was one of his longest standing clients. And the one who interested him the most.

She'd told him the last time he'd flown her—just six weeks before—that there was no significant other in her life.

He'd found that hard to believe. While he and Beth didn't speak of personal things, over the years he'd come to think of her as a trusted friend. Someone whose opinion he valued. Just like he valued her honesty, her work ethic, and her kindness.

"I remember the first time I picked you up," he said, speaking into the microphone just beneath his bottom lip. "You held your carry-on clutched up against you for the entire two-hour flight."

"How could you tell?" she asked. "I was sitting back there where I belonged." Her voice was loud and clear—and sexy in an innocent kind of way—over the headset.

"Back there" was the four large seats where his passengers usually sat. It was equipped with a television and mini-bar.

He indicated the mirror above them.

"You watched me?"

Hoping he wasn't making a mistake, showing too much of his hand, Joe nodded.

"The whole time?"

"Pretty much."

"Then I guess it's a miracle we got there safely since apparently neither of us was flying this thing," she muttered, but she wasn't frowning. In fact, with that slight little tilt of her lip, she looked like she might be fighting a grin.

Hot damn.

"So, you meeting someone for a hot date in San Francisco?" He was leaving her there on Thursday, and would pick her up for the return flight on Sunday.

She shook her head.

"Don't tell me it's *another* convention," he said softly, knowing that, despite the noise in the cockpit, his voice would travel just fine through the headset.

"Okay, I won't."

He studied her, the soft golden curls of her hair flowing from beneath the headset and over her shoulders, and waited until she glanced his way.

"It is, though, isn't it?"

"I'm the executive director of a multimillion dollar international organization, Joe. Parents of Gifted Kids is active in lobbying for educational rights in Canada, every state in the United States and around the world. The scope of our mission is tremendous and it's part of my job to see that the needs of our members are represented. Yes, it's another convention. I'm presenting a workshop to the California Educators Association."

The organization certainly treated her well, allowing her to charter a private jet every time she traveled for them.

"I didn't mean to make you defensive."

She looked out the side window. "I know," she said sighing. She paused. "I overreacted. I'm sorry," she added with the candid honesty that was only one of the many things that attracted him to her.

He wanted to ask what had made her overreact.

"So, do you fly commercial when you go on vacation?"

"No."

"You take the ferry off the island?"

"No."

She turned away from him again, her movements stiff.

"I've been flying you for almost five years," he said, not sure why now was the time he had chosen to push her. "But never for pleasure. Surely you've had a vacation."

"I vacation at home."

His skin tingled as her voice, coming so intimately in his ears, washed over him.

"You don't want to see the world?"

"I love all the world I see in Victoria."

Odd. Joe couldn't imagine a life without new vistas to explore.

The fuel gauge was showing a little lower than it should be. That was odd, too. Joe hadn't gassed up his own planes in years, but he always topped it off before he left, just to be sure. He'd have to get the gauge checked before he took off from San Francisco. Thank goodness he didn't have another flight booked until the following morning. There were days when he barely had time to let a passenger deplane before he was off on another trip. And if there was one thing Joe hated it was to be late.

"So how's Joshua?"

"Fine."

"Really?"

"No."

"Still having trouble in school?"

He took over from the autopilot. "And at home."

"Have you had him tested yet?"

"He doesn't need any testing. The boy is just re-acting to his living situation. All of his friends have mothers." That was another thing he hated—to be nagged.

"But you said Joshua never even knew his mother."

"Mona died when he was two."

He'd never told her about that time in his life, and she was too polite to ask. He wished she had the knowledge without his having to go through the telling.

"Six years ago. So why would he be reacting to her absence all of a sudden?"

They'd been through this before. Joe didn't know why Joshua wasn't happy. God knew he did everything he could think of to reach the boy. But just because none of his ideas worked didn't mean there wasn't one that would. Slapping the Genius Nerd label on him certainly wasn't it. The poor kid already had enough differences to fight on his quest to fit in.

"There's nothing remarkable about my son."

"It's more of a challenge to be bad than to be good." Beth's voice consumed him, so quiet and clear inside a head wrapped with deafening engine noise.

"I think you spend too much time working," Joe said. "You see gifted kids everywhere."

"I've also come across my share of scared parents."

He was not scared. He just didn't want Josh to be labeled, or to have more trouble fitting in with his peers than he already had. He didn't want to subject the little guy to different classes, or maybe even a different school than the rest of the guys in the neighborhood attended. He didn't want there to be yet another reason for the boys that weren't small for their age to make fun of him.

He didn't want to tell his son that his father was dumber than he was.

He was, however, a little concerned about that gas gauge. It had dropped a quarter of a tank in the last fifteen minutes. He was sure it was just the gauge, but…

"Is something wrong?"

Gone was the quiet assured voice of the woman who stood up to him. In its place was the timid tones of the young woman who'd first boarded his plane five years before, clutching her bag as though it would protect her from any evil that might befall her. She'd flown with him for more than a year before she'd started putting the bag down at her feet. Not that he could blame her. A lot of people were afraid to fly.

"Nothing's wrong," he said.

"You're looking at that panel a lot more than you usually do."

"There's some head winds. I'm just making sure we're on course."

And this was why passengers were supposed to sit back in those plush chairs, drink from the bar and watch television.

"You were frowning."

"You know I don't like it when you bug me about Joshua."

"He needs your help, Joe. He needs to be given his chance. Needs to be challenged. Though it's not a stereotypical portrayal, statistics show that prisons are actually filled with geniuses, Joe. Not just for white-

collar crimes like fraud and embezzlement, but rob-
beries, kidnappings and murders. They aren't simply
done out of passion, they all take careful planning by
intelligent people. People who weren't challenged so
they challenged themselves. As I said, in society—or
school—it's more of a challenge to be bad.''

"I know," he nodded, trying to pay enough attention to the conversation to keep her occupied, while
at the same time, watching every single reading on the
panel. If they were losing gas, he was going to have
to land this baby. "It's more of a challenge to be bad
than to be good," he repeated. They'd discussed this
before, too.

"PGK has done studies, followed the lives of genius
children and the statistics are frightening. Suicide rates
for genius teenagers are higher than those for normal
kids. And the numbers that end up in prison are alarm-
ingly high in comparison to control groups.''

Joe heard her. But his mind was on the needle that
continued to drop. "I'd like to see the study," he said,
hoping the response was enough to satisfy her.

When she sat there silently, glancing between him
and the panel, he knew he'd failed to fool her.

"I'm afraid you're going to be late getting into San
Francisco." He told her the worst news first.

"Why?" The question was a thin thread of fear.

"Nothing to be worried about," he said. "Just a
change of course. I'm not getting as clean a reading
as I want and think it would be best to land her and
find out why. If you don't mind, I'd like to go back
to Astoria." Though he'd never had reason to take her

there before, she knew it was his home base. "I've got a second jet that we can take if we need to."

"I don't mind." She sounded like she'd been running. Damn. The last thing he wanted was to scare a passenger, most especially Beth Chenoweth.

So much for making his big move.

With a few short words to air traffic control, he had flight plan number two all set.

Beth hadn't moved a muscle.

"If you'd like, I can call Marta while we're there. If Joshua's home from school she'll bring him down to the strip for you to meet him."

Though Joe's focus was on his plane, the dangerously low gas gauge, the distance he had to travel even more rapidly than normal, he still noticed the turn of her head as she focused on him.

"I'd like that."

He'd been going to tell her she could have her chance to do any testing she wanted to do—to tease her a bit, knowing full well that the kind of testing she spoke of happened in carefully monitored centers, not in the middle of a private, though extremely busy, airport.

But that was when he started losing altitude and his focus turned entirely to getting them on the ground alive.

His passenger's emotional well-being would have to wait.

CHAPTER TWO

BREATHE.

There's no reason to be afraid. You're perfectly safe. Joe is a highly competent pilot and he's not worried. He's just focused, as you'd expect him to be considering the situation. It's simply a faulty gauge. There's no reason to be afraid.

Trust Joe.

You're okay.

Breathe.

The attack had come on so quickly that Beth hadn't had time to reach for the vial of mild sedatives tucked away in the carry-on bag at her feet. Not that she'd ever reached for that bottle in front of another living soul.

It was only in the past six months or so that she'd gotten on Joe's plane without automatically taking a pill. She'd been so proud of herself.

The plane dipped, causing her stomach to flip-flop. Cursing her damn pride, Beth concentrated on blocking the dark shadows from her mind and on thinking only good thoughts. She stared at Joe.

"It's okay," he said, sending her a reassuring smile. "Just an air pocket."

With the intensity he was applying to his craft, an

intensity she'd never seen before, Beth wasn't certain she could believe him. But she wanted and needed to.

And what would it hurt to believe him? If they were going to die, they were going to die. It didn't mean she had to spend the last few minutes of her life panicking. And if they weren't going to die, she'd have wasted minutes of her life in the debilitating swirling vortex of panic she'd been fighting her way out of for as long as she could remember.

Watching him helped. She loved his hands. They were strong, sure, and much larger than hers. And his chin was firm. Masculine. It was freshly shaved, but with enough of a shadow to tell her that his beard was thick. She'd always liked that in a man.

The engine's deafening drone changed and dropped a couple of tones. Did the plane drop, too?

Beth didn't dare look out her window to find out. Light-headed, heart pounding, she didn't dare take her eyes off of Joe, either.

He was wearing blue jeans and a blue-and-white plaid, long-sleeved button-down shirt. But the sleeves were rolled up almost to his elbows. She liked the dark hair sprinkling his forearms. It made them look strong. Capable.

He'd take care of her. Of them. She knew he would.

Another dip. Beth screamed.

"Hang on, we're almost there."

Joe's voice. Beth concentrated on the headset covering her ears because life came from there and from the face of the man next to her.

His gray eyes were alert. Trained. His hair was dark

and clean. It looked thick and silky. She wanted to run her fingers through it.

It was something she'd never admitted before, but at a time like this, if the admission was going to distract her, she was willing to allow it. She wanted to run her fingers through Joe's hair.

The plane was going down. Centrifugal force pushed her body forward against the belt across her chest. She couldn't breathe.

She wanted to run her fingers through Joe's hair.

Her chest allowed an inhalation.

She wanted to do more than just run her fingers through his hair. She wanted to kiss him. To feel those lips against hers. She wanted those capable, strong hands on her skin.

The pressure strangling the air from her lungs let up a little more.

She wanted...

The first bump was so hard it made her bite her tongue, and clamp her eyes tightly shut. She wasn't going to watch her own destruction. The second bump following almost immediately, was softer. The third was barely worth a mention.

Beth slowly peeled her lids open, shocked at the light, the sunshine. They were on a runway, taxiing at an airport, in broad daylight.

She'd been so engrossed in fighting the darkness encompassing her mind that she'd expected it to be night outside.

"Not as fancy as I'd have liked, but safe and sound just like I promised."

"I-Is this Astoria?" Beth asked, survival instincts

coming to the fore. For Beth, survival meant protect-
ing herself from unwanted attention. It meant hiding
the fact that she spent too much of her time fighting
internal demons.

She concentrated as Joe told her a bit about the
historical town, describing the Victorian homes, the
unspoiled beauty. As she used his voice as a distraction, calm settled over her.

She'd made it through an episode, away from home,
with no medication.

AN HOUR LATER, Beth knew she'd let up on her guard
too soon. When Joe had excused himself, leaving her
in the terminal of Astoria Regional Airport, with a
promise to only be a few minutes, she hadn't been the
least bit hesitant about keeping her bag on the plane
as he'd suggested. She hadn't wanted to lug it around,
and had been completely confident, with her newly
won battle, that she wouldn't need it.

She hadn't planned to be trapped in a surprisingly
busy private airport terminal in an unfamiliar town
with strangers for an extended length of time. Joe was
busy getting the plane in order. She knew that so she
bought a book to keep herself occupied.

She read the first page so many times that she lost
count. And she had no idea what it was about.

She went over to a kiosk and bought a snack.

But she had to struggle so much to swallow, and
then struggle again as she convinced her stomach it
wanted the nourishment. She'd missed lunch but she
wasn't hungry.

Toying with a way to get out to the plane to get her

bag, Beth couldn't come up with a scenario that would be easy. She needed a plan that could be implemented without drawing attention to herself, without causing an embarrassing ruckus that she would then be obligated to explain to all of the sets of eyes peering at her.

Most of all, she didn't want to have to explain herself to Joe.

She walked around and looked in the Runway Café—very nice, non-airport-looking—and read the menu. And then walked some more, trying to ignore the pounding of her heart.

And not to think about her breathing. The more she thought about it, the tighter her chest got. There was absolutely nothing physically wrong with her. She knew that.

But she could hyperventilate. And then they'd haul her away.

Looking around, Beth tried to find a place she could hide. A place to wait where she'd be safe from curious eyes. Thoughts of home, Vancouver Island, Victoria, her bungalow, tormented her with their absence. She just needed her own space and she'd be fine. She could go lie down until she calmed down and no one would ever be the wiser. They wouldn't judge her, or put her out to pasture for having personal baggage that she couldn't always control.

They wouldn't haul her away.

Eventually she found a corner seat. With her back to a wall, she only had to guard the area in front of her. The corner was quiet, inconspicuous.

She started to shake anyway. Encompassed by a

sense of doom and unreality, fear took over, stifling her and her thoughts.

With her hands on the arms of the chair, Beth sat perfectly still—trying to look as inconspicuous as possible. She had to tune out all that was going around her, mentally remove herself from the threatening situation, as she had no choice but to bear it. Clutching the arms of the chair to control her shaking, she studied the weave in the carpet. Flecks of color that repeated themselves. And another. And another.

A thread of fear passed through her body, burning her stomach. She couldn't breathe.

She'd have chosen softer pastel shades for those diamonds in the carpet, not the greens she was looking at.

If she had to pass out, she could lean back and close her eyes and everyone would think she was asleep. And then, when she'd calmed down, she'd wake up and no one would know.

Except for her, of course. She couldn't escape the knowing. Which was why she was twenty-eight years old and all alone. In spite of the counseling, the understanding of the reasons for her attacks, she couldn't seem to escape them. They controlled her. Controlled her life, her choices, her environment. It wasn't a life she'd wish on an enemy, let alone someone she loved.

She couldn't go to anyone whole and she wasn't going to saddle anyone with a basket case. She wasn't going to expose herself to the risk of having someone get fed up with her and desert her.

Not ever again.

Her jaw started to chatter. She was so cold. It was

a normal balmy November day outside. The heat was on inside. Pulling the thick chenille of her sweater up against her throat she tried to find comfort in its familiar softness. But she just couldn't get warm.

Oh, God, what was going to happen to her? She'd been there for two hours and she couldn't hide much longer. And in the state she was in, she didn't trust herself to get up from the chair. With her legs as shaky as they were, they'd give out on her. She'd fall down for sure. And they'd come haul her away...

"Beth?"

She recognized the voice, but was beyond figuring out what to do about that.

"I've been looking all over for you. No one has seen you in over an hour and it's no wonder with you tucked away over here...."

It was Joe. Thank God.

No! It couldn't be Joe. He couldn't see her like this. No one other than Lindsay, her childhood guardian—and guardian angel—had ever seen her like this.

"I'm sorry it took so long."

She knew, when he paused, that she had to look up. But how could she? Everything was falling apart and there was nothing she could do to stop it. She had planned so carefully, had kept her world so controlled to prevent just this sort of thing from happening.

But who could plan for a faulty plane?

And why had she ever thought she'd handle it well enough not to need a pill?

"Beth? What's wrong?"

He was sitting beside her, had placed one hand over hers on the seat.

His touch was warm, real. Alive.

Slowly, with so much effort it hurt, she lifted her head and looked at him. She even tried to smile, though she failed miserably. "Nothing's wrong. Are we ready to go?" she asked.

Her voice sounded odd, too high, but he mostly only heard it over headsets and telephones so he might not notice.

What was she going to do when he said, yes, he was ready, and she couldn't yet trust herself to stand?

"No," he said. "Unfortunately it looks like we're going to be stuck in Astoria overnight."

Her heart started to pound harder. Another change in plans.

But stuck with him? Beth was kind of excited about that thought. Life felt good when she was around Joe.

"There was a leak in the gas tank," Joe was saying. "All but one of my planes are already out and the one I knew I had left is on a last-minute pickup this morning. I checked for another charter for you but the soonest anyone can go is tomorrow morning. By that time, I'll be able to take you myself."

She was going to miss the first day of her conference. And she was stuck with Joe.

How was she going to keep Joe from guessing that she was losing it? What was she going to do if she had another attack—in front of him this time?

"Is there a hotel nearby?" she asked, controlling her voice as well as she could. "I need to get a suite."

"I've already called Marta," he said. "We, Joshua and I, were hoping you'd agree to stay with us. We have a separate guest suite at the back of the house. Marta's already planning one more for dinner.''

Marta was his housekeeper. He'd told her that several years before. The woman had a husband, but no children. She was dependable, calm, kept a great house and lived nearby. The only problem was that she just didn't understand Joshua.

Beth looked up at him, intending to insist on going to a hotel. But somehow, when her eyes connected with his, when she saw how much her acceptance meant to him, she couldn't say no.

"Okay, I'd like that," she said. And was shocked to find out how much she really meant those words.

She'd just take a pill. And keep taking them if that was what it took to get her through the evening. It wasn't a way to live life, keeping herself sedated. But it was only for one night.

"Great. I grabbed your bag out of the plane before they took off with it. It's already in my truck, so if you're ready to go..."

Joe stood. Because she had no choice, Beth stood as well, but her knees were too shaky to hold her. She fell against Joe, her hands splayed right in the middle of his chest.

And she wanted to die.

CHAPTER THREE

SHE WOULDN'T talk to him. Wouldn't tell him what was wrong.

Joe hated that. Hated any reminder of the painful part of times past.

"I thought we were friends," he told Beth as he pulled onto his street late that Thursday afternoon. The house he'd bought a couple of years before was at the top of one of the steepest hills in Astoria.

And he felt like the hill he was climbing inside his truck was even higher.

"We are."

"So why won't you tell me what's going on?"

"Nothing's going on."

"You practically passed out back there."

"I missed lunch."

Alarm signals, made more sensitive by his years with Mona, assaulted him.

"Are you diabetic?" he asked, going for a manageable disease. "Or hypoglycemic?"

"No."

"People don't usually pass out from missing a meal."

He should let it go. He knew that. But he'd just feel

a hell of a lot better if she'd tell him what was really
going on.

"I didn't pass out."

He was getting nowhere. But then, there was nothing between them. He could just walk and not take
any of her problems upon himself, and wouldn't have
to worry about history repeating itself. He had a plan.
He wanted there to be more between them and had
been hoping that this trip would be the beginning of
that.

But she didn't know that. And plans could change.

She smiled at him. "I'm fine, really. And I can't
tell you how much I'm looking forward to meeting
Joshua. Thanks for asking me."

Of course, Joe amended the train of thought she'd
interrupted, once you started caring. plans didn't much
matter. Another lesson he'd already learned.

"You might change your mind on the meeting
Joshua part," he told her. "When I called home I was
informed that he'd been sent home early from school
today for setting off a stink bomb in his classroom.
They had to evacuate the room for half an hour."

Rather than seeming put off, Beth sent him a quick
grin. "Like I said, I'm looking forward to meeting
your son."

SHE'D BEEN RIGHT. There was absolutely nothing the
matter with her. He'd been an overreacting fool.

Bemused, Joe sat at the dinner table a couple of
hours later and nursed the bottle of beer he'd helped
himself to for dessert.

Josh and Beth had just finished pieces of the turtle cheesecake Marta had left in the refrigerator.

"So your company must be rich chartering Dad's jet every time you have to travel for work," Josh was saying.

"Oh, they don't pay for it," Beth told the boy. "I do."

Joe froze, the beer bottle halfway to his mouth. She'd always written him a personal check, but he'd just assumed the organization reimbursed her for his fee.

"You sure must be rich then. Are you a millionaire?" Josh asked for the answer his father wanted, but propriety would never have allowed him to ask.

"No," Beth laughed. "You don't have to be a millionaire to do expensive things. It's just a matter of what you choose to spend your money on."

"Most people couldn't afford to charter jets several times a year even if they chose wisely," Joe said, jumping into the conversation for the first time since before dessert.

She glanced over, almost as though she'd forgotten he was there. "I live alone," she said, shrugging. "I don't spend a lot." She paused, staring at him for a second. "And," she added, "I received my adopted father's estate several years ago. He was an artist of some renown, Olson Chenoweth. You ever heard of him?"

"The abstract landscapes with an unusual combination of bold colors mixed with pastel."

She nodded, smiled, but she'd tensed, too. He wondered why.

"I have an invention, you wanna hear about it?"
Josh asked, leaning forward, completely enthralled
with his dinner guest. Joe was entirely taken by the
young man who'd taken possession of his son's body.
This kid was suddenly in possession of all the manners
Joe had tried, most unsuccessfully, to teach his son
over the years.

"Of course," Beth said, giving Josh a smile that
touched Joe in ways a smile meant for a young boy
should never do.

"Well, see, it's a form of thermometer that the police can use on car seats to determine the body temperature of the driver."

Joe grinned. He'd first heard this one about a year
ago. The kid was nuts. Not smart. Joe was kind of
glad Beth was finally getting the chance to see that he
knew what he was talking about where his son was
concerned.

"And why would a policeman want to know the
body temperature of the driver?" Beth asked.

Joe had never seen her look so relaxed, or healthier
and more beautiful.

With her slim body, forest-green eyes and free-
flowing thick curls around her shoulders, she could
have passed for any number of models he'd admired
over the years. He was used to seeing her with a headset on her head. And apprehension in her eyes.

"Well," Josh was saying, hands folded on the table,
gaze glued on the woman sitting directly across from
him, "for instance, in cases of an accident, the police
would be able to tell if a driver was at fault for having

fallen asleep at the wheel. Body temperature changes from sleep to waking.''

Joe frowned. He'd never heard that part. Never realized there was any thought behind Josh's inventive ideas. He'd never asked.

''I had a friend whose grandmother was killed by a trucker who ran her over on the highway,'' Josh continued, his big-eyed expression so serious beneath his short thick dark hair. ''His parents were certain that the trucker had fallen asleep at the wheel, but no one was ever able to prove it.''

''He's talking about one of my pilots.''

Josh and Beth both glanced his way briefly. ''Oh,'' she said, her attention already back on his son.

Marta had long since gone home to her husband and Joe could be occupying himself with clearing the remains of their homemade lasagna dinner off the table, doing the dishes, and cleaning the kitchen.

''I had another invention, too,'' Josh said now, a hint of his usual belligerence in his voice. ''But Dad wouldn't listen to me when I told it to him and now someone else has come up with the very same thing and is making millions off of it.''

The intimate smile Beth sent Joe, as though the two of them shared a secret, took away much of the sting he felt from his son's obvious disdain for him.

''What was the invention?'' she asked Josh.

''A topography computer for cars. You know, the ones that map out where you are. You can type in an address and it'll tell you how to get there. I came up with the idea when I was four. That was four whole years ago. But no one would listen to me and now it's too late."

"I'm afraid it was already too late," Beth said with a soft smile. "Kit the car on that television show *Knight Rider* had one of those."

"Well, still, Dad didn't listen."

"I listened, son." Joe couldn't just sit there and let the truth go unanswered. He was obviously screwing up as a Dad, but it wasn't because he didn't try.

"You laughed," Josh said.

Yeah, he probably had. But not to be mean. It had been kind of funny having a little guy who still sat in a car seat so serious in his belief that he could invent a navigational computer. Spending time with Josh had always been entertaining.

There used to be nothing in the world Joe enjoyed more than spending time with his son.

Giving up, Joe stood and cleared the table, telling Beth not to bother when she offered to help. It was worth doing all the work himself, giving up some time with Beth, to see his son so animated. So happy.

Joe had been right. Josh's problem was not academic. Or chemical. All his son needed was a mother.

JOSH WAS UP an hour past his bedtime. Beth had asked him if he'd ever done logic problems and when he'd said that he hadn't, she'd produced a sample book from her suitcase and shown him how to do them. The boy had been quietly engaged for the rest of the evening, sitting at the table with Beth, occasionally asking questions as he'd frowned over the pencil markings he'd been making.

Joe had vacillated between elation to see his son so tranquilly and pleasantly occupied, and frustration that his time with Beth was slowly slipping away.

And then he suddenly found himself alone with her, in a house that had never seemed so quiet before, and he wasn't sure what to do. Or what to say.

He wanted to ask her to marry him.

She didn't even know he'd be interested in a date.

"You never told me you were adopted." They weren't quite the words he'd meant to say.

Flipping a pencil from end to end on the big antique maple table that filled his dining room, she shrugged. "It never came up."

"You said you were raised by a guardian, Lindsay McNeil. A teacher at the high school in Victoria."

Head bowed slightly, Beth glanced over at him. "I can't believe you remembered that."

He held her gaze, his glance steady. "I remember everything about you."

Beth looked down.

"So what happened to your adopted parents?"

"They died." She pulled a piece of paper over and started doodling.

"At the same time? Were they in an accident of some kind?"

"My mother was. A car accident. I was only three. Olson died several years later."

She spoke without emotion. Joe was suddenly feeling enough of it for both of them.

"He was bad to you?"

"Who?" she asked, glancing up, but only briefly.

The pencil marks on her paper were emerging into an intricately detailed design. "Olson?"

"Yeah."

"No. Olson wasn't mean to anyone."

"So you had a good life with him." Something wasn't right here.

"He was my father."

Which didn't say anything at all. And Joe was right back where he'd been that afternoon after her near collapse at the airport.

It wasn't that he hadn't been up against Beth's walls before; he'd just never before set himself the task of getting by them. He'd never let himself care that much.

"Tell me about your childhood."

"It was good." More lines. And an emerging design that spoke of a talent he'd not known she had.

With one hand on top of hers, Joe stopped her. Without a word, she peered up at him.

"Please talk to me, Beth."

"Why?"

"It matters."

"Why?"

"I don't know," he had to be honest with her. "I'd say because I'm interested in you, but I have a feeling it's more than that."

"You're interested in me?" Her voice was barely a whisper—and an octave higher than normal.

"I didn't meant to blurt it out like that, but, yeah, I guess I am."

"Oh."

"Is that a bad thing?"

With a sideways peek, she studied him, and then the drawing in front of her. "Maybe not."

Joe grinned. And then, catching himself, stopped.

"So," he leaned down until he could catch her gaze. "About that childhood…"

Beth pulled her hand from beneath his and resumed her drawing. "I was born in San Antonio, Texas, but was adopted when I was ten months old. I know nothing about my biological parents, or why they suddenly decided they didn't want to keep me. I just know that I didn't spend time in a foster home. I was adopted by Charlotte and Olson Chenoweth, both natives of Victoria."

Though she didn't look up, Beth's face softened, touching Joe in a way he hadn't expected to ever be touched again. He'd decided long ago never to allow himself to feel so protective of another individual that their well-being meant his own.

"Those first couple of years were bliss," she said.

"You remember them?"

Her eyes focused on him momentarily and then she resumed her doodling. "Not really, but from what I've heard I'm sure they were. And I have vague impressions…"

"And then your mother was killed."

"Yes."

For a long time he thought she wasn't going to say anymore. And he couldn't bring himself to ask again. He sat there watching her draw. Waiting. Wondering. And strangely aching for her.

"She'd been in Seattle, visiting a friend. Olson

spent that whole night down at the pier waiting for her to come home.''

''He didn't know?''

''He knew. He just didn't believe.''

Joe completely understood. ''He must have loved her very much.''

''He did.''

''And you, too.''

''Of course, I was Charlotte's daughter.''

It was an odd thing to say. She was just as much Olson's daughter as she had been Charlotte's. But when Joe asked her a couple more questions about her father, the artist, he slammed into Beth's wall again. He hadn't even seen it coming.

''So have you ever thought about looking up your biological parents?'' he finally asked.

Beth shook her head. ''Charlotte knew the family. She didn't say, but I think my mother died fairly young.''

''What about her husband?''

''Nothing's ever been said about him,'' she said, dropping the pencil as she looked up at him. ''It's more in what's not said. I know for certain that he had no legal rights over me. I have a feeling they were never married. Maybe she didn't even know who the father was.''

Their eyes met and Joe was filled with the urge to pull her into his arms and never let go.

''So how old were you when you went to live with Lindsay?''

''Five.''

''And she was good to you?''

Beth smiled, an expression that lit up her entire face. "The best. She not only loved me as much as a biological mother would have, she encouraged me to always stretch my mind and believe in my dreams. She also spoke of my mother all the time, which was a nice change. Olson would never let anyone mention her name."

As she mentioned her adopted father, some of the joy diminished from Beth's face. Joe wondered if it was grief, if she still missed the man so much, or if there was some other reason the mention of her father made Beth so sad.

He wondered if he'd ever have the right to know the answer to that question.

CHAPTER FOUR

"I DON'T REALLY date much." Beth spoke the previously rehearsed answer into the headset on Sunday afternoon. All weekend long, at the educators convention in San Francisco, she'd prayed that when Joe brought up the subject again—as surely he would—it would be while they were flying.

In a world of their own, maybe, but buffered by engine noise and controls and an entire sky to look at.

"Why not?"

"I don't know," she shrugged, shying away from the major reason she couldn't get involved and thinking of some of the more minor reasons she'd come up with that weekend. "I don't have a lot of time, for one thing. I work ungodly long hours. I don't ever go to bars or places where I might meet someone."

"But when you travel..."

"I meet people who don't live in Victoria," she cut him off, completely prepared. "I can't very well date someone I have to fly to go see."

"Unless he's a pilot with a plane and comes to pick you up."

The roaring in Beth's ears had nothing to do with the plane's engine. "I don't think us dating would be a good idea, Joe."

Most especially considering how badly she wanted
to do just that. All weekend she'd been distracted by
memories of her night with Joshua and Joe. She'd escaped to the guest suite almost immediately after Joe
had questioned her about Olson that night. It frightened her to think of how close he'd been getting.

And yet, at the convention that weekend, every time
she'd thought of him and his son instead of paying
attention to the business she normally found so en-
grossing, she'd felt like smiling. Not crying, or running. This was heady stuff.

She'd spent the three days looking forward to Sunday when he'd be there to get her and take her safely
home.

The landscape below looked the same as it always
did—rugged mountains, plotted plains, tiny lines of
roads.

"You don't think we'd have a good time together?"

His question was so late in coming she'd thought
he'd dropped the subject. Her heart rate sped up and
she didn't think it was from fear. Or dread.

"Of course I do." Beth shivered in spite of the
heavy black turtleneck sweater she was wearing.

"Is Joshua the problem?"

She turned to look at him, appreciating, as always,
the thick dark hair that would not be contained by the
headset, his broad shoulders, and the easy way he sat
in the pilot's seat with his knees open and relaxed.

"Of course Joshua isn't the problem," she said,
horrified that he'd think so. "I told you, it's just the
time and distance...."

How could reasons that had rung with such validity in San Francisco sound so trivial now?

"Because the thing is," he glanced over at her, his brown eyes hidden behind the aviator glasses he wore, "Josh has talked of nothing but you for three days, begging me to make certain that he gets to see you again."

That hurt. A child in need. A gifted child whose father did not recognize his special needs.

"You guys live several hundred miles away."

"An hour's flight." Reaching across the cockpit he grabbed her hand. "What would it hurt to try?"

"I might lose my personal pilot." And that was a major consideration.

"I promise I will still fly you anywhere you want to go even if we decide we hate each other."

"What if you hurt me and I can't bear to get in your plane?" She hadn't meant to say the words loudly enough for him to hear. Hadn't reckoned with the intimacy of the headset which took the words from her mouth straight to his ears.

"It could work the other way, too, you know," he said, his voice soft and husky in her ears.

"Okay."

"Is that a yes?"

Pulling her hand back, Beth slipped it, along with her other one, under thighs clothed in the rough black-and-white tweed that she hated, but wore because it traveled well.

What was she doing? What on earth was she doing? She thought again of the evening she'd spent at

Joe's house. And how that memory had sustained her through a difficult weekend.

She remembered a little five-year-old girl who'd been so lost; life had been one long nightmare from which she couldn't wake. And she remembered Lindsay waking her...

"Yes."

HE'D LEFT HER with a handshake. Somehow that was most reassuring of all to Beth as she walked the few blocks from town to the house she'd inherited from Olson. His studio still stood out back, complete with oils he'd never sold or given away. Someday she'd have to clean it all out.

But not now. Not yet. After all these years she still wasn't ready to face the confusing mass of emotions that awaited her inside those doors. The love she'd craved and might have had. The mother she'd lost.

And the knowledge that ultimately, she was wholly and eternally alone.

Joe had left her with a handshake. Just as he'd done every other time he'd flown her over the past five years. He was a dear friend. One of the few people she felt safe with and trusted. And those were traits she couldn't afford to lose.

Beth soaked up the scent of the flowers all around her as she walked, soaked up the scent of home. There was no place on earth like Victoria, with weather that grew neither too hot nor too cold. Many of the houses had wild flower gardens instead of front lawns during warmer weather.

Turning one street before her own, Beth inhaled the

familiar and amazingly strong scent of the roses trailing along the sidewalk and found herself, suitcase and carry-on in hand, knocking on Lindsay's door.

The woman who'd been a mother to her, a sort of great aunt, a best friend as well as her guardian didn't appear the least bit surprised to find her old ward on her doorstep, luggage in hand.

"You're back!" she greeted, as though she hadn't just seen Beth four days before. "Come on in, tell me all about your night in Astoria."

"You were expecting me," Beth said, wondering why she was surprised.

"Of course." The still slender older woman, wearing navy linen slacks and a white blouse, led her into the living room that looked exactly the same as it had when Beth had grown up there. Chintz sofas, Victorian high back chairs, pastels and flowers. A woman's room. A safe, warm and welcoming room.

Beth, leaving her bags at the front door, followed the retired high school teacher and plopped down on her usual end of the couch, kicking off her serviceable black slip-ons to pull her feet up underneath her.

"He asked me to go out with him."

This was Lindsay; there was no point in prevaricating.

"Did you go?"

"I don't mean on Thursday night, we just went to his house, then. I mean, he wants us to start dating."

Lindsay's brow, more wrinkled now than when she'd come to rescue Beth from the darkness of her own mind all those years ago, was creased, though with concern or curiosity Beth couldn't be sure. As was her way, Lindsay sat silently. Waiting.

She never pressured Beth for answers. Never jumped in with unsolicited advice. From the very beginning, when Beth had been a young child, the compassionate and brilliant woman had simply been the security, and perhaps somewhat the catalyst, that allowed Beth to figure things out for herself.

"I can't have a relationship with him."

Nothing.

"Eventually he'd find out how trapped I am."

Lindsay's eyes clouded, but Beth felt wrapped in the older woman's love. They both knew the demons Beth fought. Knew how handicapped she was by a mind that she couldn't always control.

"You trust him."

"Of course."

"With your life." Lindsay's short dyed-brown hair fell over her forehead as she shot her head forward with emphasis. The older woman had always been one to use her body as much as her words when she had a point to make.

"Yes," Beth said, her mind engaged in the conversation, and also with stepping outside the conversation to figure out, not only the world as she saw it, but also how it differed from her perceived realities.

"So maybe you can learn to trust him with your secrets."

"No." The denial came swiftly. "I will not saddle anyone else with my problems. We've been through this."

"Never to my satisfaction."

Beth frowned. "But..."

"And I don't think to yours, either."

Were anyone else to challenge her like that, Beth's chest would have tightened to the point of making breathing painful. She'd have clammed up and disengaged herself.

Run.

With Lindsay, she was safe. Lindsay knew everything about her and loved her anyway. Together they'd made miracles happen more than once in Beth's life.

"I make life difficult for you sometimes," Beth said.

"Not anymore."

"Only because I'm not living here, because I have my life so organized and controlled that there is generally no opportunity for problems to arise."

Lindsay shook her head, leaning forward in her chair, her elbows on her knees. She scrutinized Beth.

"I don't think so, honey," she said. "You've grown up, taken control even without knowing that you were doing it. Look how well you handled Thursday's mishap."

"I panicked!"

"You kept yourself safe."

"I called you."

"Because you knew what tools you had at your disposal, but still, by yourself, you kept yourself safe. You didn't let yourself down, Beth. You held it together."

"Until Joe finally showed up and I practically passed out on him."

"Again, because you knew he was safe. And look

at how you handled the remainder of the evening. You were a perfectly normal houseguest.''

Beth had called Lindsay again as soon as she'd arrived at her hotel in San Francisco on Friday to let her guardian angel know that she was safe.

''His son's remarkable, Lins,'' Beth blurted. She'd stored up all kinds of things to tell her mentor and friend—things she knew Lindsay would understand. ''He's as smart as you or me, easily. Remember that time when I was about eighteen months old and I wanted chocolate for breakfast and I convinced Mom that since my doll wanted chocolate, too, and we couldn't tell her no because she didn't have any ears, we had to have chocolate for breakfast?''

''Yeah,'' Lindsay grinned. ''Your poor mom! She called me up, crying and laughing at the same time. So proud of you and your amazing reasoning ability. And scared to death at the same time.''

''Because she thought I was smarter than she was?''

''Partially. And partly because you were still a baby and already getting the best of her. How was she ever going to keep up with you, let alone stay one step ahead?''

''Do you think she'd have made the right choices for me when the time came?'' Beth asked something she'd never asked before.

''I'm sure she would have, sweetie. Charlotte was my best friend and I know she wanted only what was best for you.''

Blinking back tears, Beth smiled at the woman who'd been so much more than a friend to her.

''Josh kind of reminds me of that story,'' she said

quietly. "He reasons things out beyond his years. And scares his dad to death."

"It sounds like those two need you, Beth."

"Maybe."

"You can do this."

She wanted to believe that. But knew differently.

"Think back to the times when I lived with you, Lins. How many times did you have to change your plans, not do things you really wanted to do, because I freaked out? How many times were you so embarrassed you wanted to die?"

"A few."

"More than a few."

"They didn't matter."

"Things have a way of settling with age," Beth said. "But I remember times when you looked about ready to give up."

"Never."

"What about the time I wouldn't go with you to Seattle and you missed that weekend with your mother and sister?"

"Beth," Lindsay said, her gaze firm. "Of course there were times I was disappointed. You have those in all relationships. But never once did the problems outweigh the joy you brought to my life. Never."

Hiding behind her hair, Beth peered at her friend. "There weren't times when you regretted taking me in?"

"Not one. Ever."

Beth held Lindsay's gaze for a long time, trying to believe.

And then she looked away. Lindsay was her mother's

best friend. Beth was more her daughter than Charlotte's. Lindsay had responsibilities toward her, obligations. She'd had to put up with Beth's problems. She'd told the courts she would.

But Beth wasn't anything to Joe. He had no reason to put up with the boundaries Lindsay accepted. A good friend she could be. Anything more, any kind of merging of lives, would never work.

CHAPTER FIVE

"IT WAS GREAT of Lindsay to take Josh for us," Joe told Beth the following Friday night as he sat across from her at an intimate table for two at Chandlers—one of Beth's favorite steak-and-seafood restaurants. She was wearing a pair of navy slacks that were tight in all the right places, having already treated him to several enticing looks at the perfect shape of her bottom, and a navy sweater with stripes of white, that formed around her breasts and the indentation of her waist in such a way that made the entire picture a priceless piece of art in Joe's opinion.

They'd had part of the afternoon and all of the evening together.

And it had been everything Joe had figured it would be. Beth had shown him her town—the shops, the history, the homes. They'd toured the incredible Buchart Gardens, window-shopped, walked aimlessly for miles.

He couldn't remember the last time he'd laughed so much.

He'd held her hand. And felt like a school kid when her fingers had wrapped around his.

"I think it was very sweet of Josh to go with Lindsay," Beth was saying, a glass of wine at her lips.

"She uses any excuse she can find to visit the Miniature World. And she might pretend that she's making homemade macaroni and cheese for Josh, but it's really for her. It's her favorite, but she thinks she's too old to make it for herself. And teaching him to play chess? It's only so she'll have someone she can beat."

Beth's lips were spread in a big grin, but it was the smile in her eyes that took Joe's breath away. She was a different person here in Victoria. Still as smart, as composed and assured. But here she was also relaxed. Funny.

The restaurant was on the wharf and, as he looked out the wall of windows behind Beth, he could see lights shining on the water. The entire day was taking on a surreal quality. Like he'd stepped into his own fantasy and found that it was better than he'd imagined.

"Tell me about Josh's mother."

Lulled by the day, by the woman, Joe didn't immediately freeze as he was wont to do whenever Mona was mentioned. "I met her in college," he said, slowly twirling his beer mug. Odd, to be thinking about Mona and not be instantly unhappy. "She was one of those people who was always looking for an adventure and I was captivated from the first moment."

As he glanced up, Joe caught the shadows in Beth's eyes and gave himself a mental kick. It had been a long time since he'd been in a relationship. A long time since he'd tended to a woman's sensitive emotions. He was rusty.

Not for the first time that day, he was too hot in his

dark-green corduroy button-down shirt and tan Dockers.

"What kind of adventures?" she asked softly.

And because she sounded genuinely interested, looked interested, because he wanted to share his life with her, Joe continued.

"Mountain climbing, skiing, hang gliding, parachuting. You name it, she wanted to try it."

There were times he missed her so much he didn't think he could stand to go on. Thankfully, those times were fewer and further between as the years passed.

"Did she have no fear?"

He'd wondered the same thing. "I'm not sure," he said, meeting Beth's gaze across the candlelit table. God, she was beautiful.

And he'd been alone for so long...

"She had such desire to make every minute count, to get the most out of every day. I think that desire was stronger than any fear she might have felt."

"And did you do all those things with her?"

He nodded. Smiled, remembering. They'd had some great times. But that was before Mona became pregnant. After that, everything he'd thought they had, everything he'd thought they were, changed.

He told Beth about some of the more harrowing experiences and it felt good to have someone to share them with. Someone to laugh with.

One particularly loud burst of laughter kicked him right in the gut. He'd been attracted to Beth for years, but never with such a burning need as he'd been feeling that day. Like if he didn't touch her soon he was going to burst.

Because their relationship had changed? Or because he'd finally lifted the rein on emotions that had been stifled for so long?

"I'll bet you guys had an interesting wedding," Beth said, grinning. Like him, her amusement seemed tinged with melancholy, as though she knew exactly how much that time in his life had hurt him. As though she cared.

"Fess up," she teased gently when he didn't reply. "Was it on a mountaintop requiring all the guests to hike in, or jumping from a plane just as you said, 'I do' and landing in the middle of your reception?"

Joe's smile faded. "We were never married."

"But…" And then, as she watched him, "Oh."

He knew there were probably things he should say. He just couldn't come up with them. He looked around for their waiter, figuring it was about time for their steaks to come. They'd finished their salads quite some time ago.

"I just thought, with Joshua…"

If not steaks, he'd sure appreciate some more beer. His mug was almost empty. "We'd been living together for a couple of years when she got pregnant with Josh. I'd asked her to marry me several times, but she'd been afraid to jinx something that was working so well." He finished off the beer in one long swallow, looked at Beth and almost drowned in the compassion he read in her expression.

He'd never have believed he could be so affected by two different women in one lifetime.

"A couple of our friends, couples we'd hung with

in college, had already been married and divorced. She'd said she didn't want that to happen to us."

"I can understand that," Beth said. "I guess. But once Josh came..."

"That's when I started pressuring her to get married. I pressured her right out the door."

"She left you while she was pregnant with your son?"

Turning his attention to the sugar packets in a little glass dish on the table, Joe said, "Only for a week. Until I promised not to mention marriage again."

"Wow."

"Yeah," he shook his head, remembering his confusion—and pain—during those months. He'd thought Mona's aversion to marriage had been because of him, because she hadn't loved him enough.

And he'd about broken his back to try to change that, to make them a happy, normal, American family. When, in reality, it had been out of his control all along.

"When I saw that she was serious, that she was going to have that baby all alone, I agreed not to mention marriage again under the condition that when Josh was born, he at least be given my name. I think I was still holding out hope that at some point she'd change her mind and marry me."

"Who knows? She might have. If she'd been given more time."

Beth had no idea how ironic that statement was. And Joe didn't tell her. Mona's biggest indiscretion, the one that had cut the deepest was still something he couldn't talk about. Not even to Beth—the only other woman he'd ever considered marrying.

"YOU SHOULD HAVE seen it, Beth!" Josh had been chattering nonstop since they'd stopped by to get him from Lindsay's house. "I saw the world's smallest working sawmill. It was awesome...." The boy went on to give her a point by point detailed description of how a tree becomes a table, complete with weights and measures and hours and years.

The three of them were walking from Lindsay's to Beth's house where the Holden men were going to spend the night. Joe was taking Joshua whale watching in the morning and then the three of them were going to take a tour of the Royal London Wax Museum which was just blocks from Beth's house.

"The war scenes were awesome, too, Dad," Josh said, his small-for-his-age body hopping in front of them as he tried to get everything out at once. "There was the Battle of Waterloo, the European Thirty Year War, the US War of Independence, the US Battle of Bull Run, and the War of the Roses. Interesting, don't you think, that Canadians cared so much about American wars?"

"Of course we'd matter to them, son, we're their neighbors...."

"And did you know that the Canadians' National Wonder in the 1880s was the Great Canadian Railway? We walked along it. I never knew about that." The boy, his dark hair bobbing up and down with him, looked at Beth. "It's something isn't it that you guys know about our wars, but we don't learn about your stuff?''

Beth had a sudden and very strong urge to scoop the little guy up and hug him.

She wanted to take him for a month, a year, the next nine years and watch as his mind discovered all the great wonders that were in store for him. Inside his own mind, his own capabilities, but also outside of him, in the world that held such fascination for him. She ached to make certain that he be given the means to make those discoveries.

And she worried about what would happen to him if he wasn't taught to recognize his gift—and also, with the opposition that was in all things—the ways his mind would play with him. He had to be taught how to control his gift so that it didn't drive him insane.

Or lock him inside walls of his own making.

"DO YOU OFTEN work on Saturdays?"

"No!" Beth answered more quickly, and loudly, than she'd have liked. Josh had just gone to bed in one of her two guest rooms. She and Joe were virtually alone in her house and she had idea what was going to happen next.

She didn't even know what she wanted to have happen. Or rather, the warring parts of her had not yet declared a victor on that issue.

She pulled on the bottom of her sweater, then ran her hands along her thighs as she stood uncomfortable in her own living room. Should she sit with him on the couch? Or take a chair?

She never sat in those chairs.

"Then why aren't you coming whale watching with us?"

"I've got things to do here."

He looked around her living room. "This place is spotless. Cleaner than mine and I have a housekeeper."

"I do, too," she admitted. What she didn't tell him was that it was a sort of medicine for her—a pill that she had to choke down—letting someone in her private space, touching all of her things, seeing her dirt. Which is why she did it. She wanted to be normal.

"So come with us. Josh really wants you to."

And so it starts. She had no business allowing anything to happen between her and Joe.

"I have some errands to run," she said, mentally inventing them as she spoke so that the words were not a lie.

Joe grabbed her hand, pulled her down beside him on the couch. "You don't want to come."

She studied his incredibly handsome and very dear face. "You're right. I don't."

With his fingers he lightly traced the top of her hand. She felt him through every vein in her body.

"Because you've seen it too many times?"

That would be an easy answer. It would also be untrue. She shook her head.

"You get seasick?"

She shook her head again.

"You're afraid of whales?"

She wondered what would happen if she told him the truth. That she was just plain afraid.

And then it hit her. Maybe that was the answer. Show him that she wasn't fun and adventurous like Mona was. He wasn't going to enjoy life with her.

He'd go and she'd still be relatively intact. Or at least her secret would be.

"I don't go whale watching because I scare myself out of it every time."

He blinked. She'd surprised him. Beth sat back on the couch, pulling her hand back to her own lap. Not quite how she'd envisioned the evening.

"There's nothing wrong with being afraid." He took her hand again. "Everyone has something or other that scares them."

"Yeah?" she asked, leaning back enough to see his eyes. "What are you afraid of?"

"Many things. Disease, death, things I can't control. But right now, what scares me most is that I'm going to try to kiss you and you're going to pull away." He'd moved closer. The words were little more than breath at her neck.

"Don't be scared." The sensible part of her was angry she'd said the words, but it didn't matter. She'd been fantasizing about his lips, about how they'd feel against hers for more than a year.

And she'd been alone such a very long time.

Beth suffered from desertion phobias. It didn't mean she was sexless.

As Joe's lips came slowly toward hers, she quieted the left side of brain her with a promise that she'd kiss him.

And nothing more.

CHAPTER SIX

THERE WAS NOTHING tentative about that first kiss. As though he'd been waiting as long as she, was as ready as she, Joe kissed her with an intimacy usually reserved for lovers, lips open and possessing hers with more urgency than finesse. It wasn't what she'd been expecting.

The kiss ignited her.

Her lips opened, her tongue exploring as boldly as his. Everything about him was more than she'd been expecting. The taste of him more potent. The touch of his lips, his tongue, telling of a much more primitive joining. The smell of his cologne, the feel of his hands sliding over her shoulders and up her sides was intoxicating her.

She could hardly breathe for wanting him.

He kissed her again and again. Her lips, her cheeks, her eyelids, her neck, they all tingled from his touch. Her entire body was filled with tremors of intense need.

"I've been waiting a long time for this." The husky words came from him, but they could have been hers.

"Me, too."

His lips stilled, though thankfully his hands did not, as he pulled back enough to look at her. "You have?"

She nodded.

"For how long?"

His thumbs grazed the sides of her breasts. "At least a year," she answered, wondering if he could feel how hard her heart was beating.

"Mmm," he kissed her again. "I got you beat."

She meant to ask him how long it had been for him, but those strong, capable hands she'd been watching on the controls of an airplane all those years had just slid on top of her breasts.

"Mmm," was all she managed of the question. She was going to have to stop him. Soon—very soon.

His thumbs found her nipples. They were hard and aching and she almost cried with the ecstasy of that first touch. Self-sufficient and in complete control of her environment she might need to be, but there were just some things she couldn't do for herself.

Still, she had to stop him. Absolutely. Left and right were in complete agreement on that.

The palm of his hand kneaded the tender flesh of her breast as his thumb continued to work magic on its tip.

She'd stop him. But not yet.

Beth groaned, thrust her tongue more fully into his mouth. She couldn't stop him yet.

JOE HAD ONLY meant to kiss her. He'd wanted more. Of course he'd wanted it all, but he knew that with Beth he had to take things slow. She was special in ways he was still only discovering.

And this was something he hoped would last a lifetime.

So how he ended up hauling her off the couch like a barbarian and hurrying down the hall with her to her bedroom, kicking the door shut behind them, he wasn't sure.

There'd never been a conscious decision. Or even a hint of a discussion. One minute she was moaning on the couch, and the next, lying on top of her bed.

From there, pulling off her sweater had been a given. She looked too hot.

"You shop at Victoria's Secret," he whispered unsteadily as he gazed at the sexy wisps of lace that barely covered her nipples. The full mounds of her breasts spilled from those little cups, enticing him to do far more than he should with them.

"Catalog," she choked out.

Joe joined her on the bed, his body stinging with need as he pulled her fully against him, chest to chest, thigh to thigh, heart to heart.

"You are so beautiful," he said, pulling up his shirt so that he could feel the softness of her belly against his hair-roughened skin.

"Joe?"

No. She was going to stop him. She should stop him. And it was going to kill him.

"Yeah?"

"If we make love, it doesn't mean I'm going whale watching."

There was a message in there. An important one. He knew that. But the only words he heard were "if we make love."

It was a possibility.

She wasn't stopping him.

"Okay." His hands were busy, fingers underneath the fabric at her breasts, sliding along the edge. But he still would have stopped.

Beth started to unbutton his shirt. Deliberately. And quite quickly, in spite of shaking fingers.

"It's been a long time for me." The words were torn out of him. Now was not the time to be less than perfect, but he had no idea how long he was going to be able to hold on.

"Me, too."

He rolled onto his back, taking her with him and laid there with his hands on her breasts as she finished unbuttoning his shirt. "How long?"

"A few years."

"Was he here in town?" He didn't know why he'd asked. Especially then. It didn't matter.

He still wanted to know.

She shook her head, her eyes closing languorously as he popped the front catch on her bra.

"He was an educator. I see him several times a year when I travel. He didn't have anyone either and we kind of just fell into helping each other out."

As her breasts came into full view, Joe wasn't even sure what she was talking about. Her nipples were more tan than pink. And large against perfectly shaped milky white breasts.

And then her words sank in. "I'd fly you there, you'd sleep with him, and I'd fly you home."

"Until I started to wish he was you. Then I stopped."

Joe lifted his hips against hers. And when her hips

applied an answering pressure of their own, he lifted
higher.

He was going to make love to her. He had no other
choice.

THE NEXT WEEK Joe had to make a run to L.A. to pick
up a couple and fly them wherever they decided to go.
It was going to be a fun trip. Their destination spur of
the moment, spontaneous. He could be gone for up to
three days and he wanted her to go with him.

Beth escaped that time with the truth. She couldn't
go because she had to work. She missed him so much,
but she'd known from the beginning that a long-term
relationship between them wasn't going to work.

But she'd been in other temporary relationships. For
as long as she could control her environment. Not
many. Not often. But as long as no promises were
made, no one had to get hurt.

And this time, someone could very well be hurt if
she didn't stick around for a little while. Eight-year-
old Joshua who sometimes reminded her so much of
her lost little self when she'd been that age.

A couple of days later Joe called wanting her to go
snowmobiling with him in Jackson Hole, Wyoming.
"It sounds like a lot of fun," Beth said, delaying the
inevitable. "You should take Josh."

"He was sent home from school again yesterday.
He can't afford to miss any more classes. And this is
an adult trip."

"Joe…"

"You're going to say no again, aren't you?"

He'd called her at the office and, sitting at her desk,

she looked out her second-floor window to the wharf down below. She might be trapped on this island, but the wharf that prevented her from driving away, rather than seeming like a cage, always represented freedom to her.

"I can't go."

"Should I quit calling?"

They'd talked on the phone every day since the night he'd spent with her in Victoria. She'd started to live for those phone calls.

"I hope not."

During the long pause that followed, Beth watched the Seattle ferry come in to dock. The day's tourists had arrived. Soon the downtown streets of Victoria would be buzzing.

"Did something happen between the time I kissed you goodbye last Saturday and now?"

"No."

"So why are you brushing me off?"

She turned around and then back, picked up her pen and held it over the report she'd been reading, ready to continue jotting notes in the margins.

"I'm not brushing you off, Joe," she finally said, knowing that she cared for him too much to let him think that. "But I'm not Mona. I don't thrive on adventure. Truth be told, I don't even like to travel much."

Another long pause—more excruciating than the first. She wasn't ready to lose him yet, or to turn her back on every possibility.

And Joshua needed her.

"You're sure that's all it is?" he asked when she'd

begun to think he'd hung up. "You aren't having regrets about our night together?" His voice was soft, seductive, turning her on all over again.

"I'm positive that's all it is." Her regrets weren't an issue.

"Then how about if Josh and I pay you another visit this weekend?"

The weight on her heart lightened far more than was warranted. "I'd like that," she said, smiling. "What time should I expect you?"

"We'll leave right after school on Friday."

Beth's thoughts flew ahead to the dinner they'd have. Activities for Joshua. And for her and Joe, too. She'd wear the red teddy....

"And Beth?"

"Yeah?"

"Don't bother making up the bed in the second spare room."

"I didn't plan on it."

SHE LEFT WORK EARLY on Friday, walked over to the grocery store on her way home and spent a couple of hours making homemade shepherd's pie. And then she worried that Josh wouldn't like it.

Borrowing Lindsay's recipe, she made some macaroni and cheese as well, storing it in the back of the refrigerator in case she needed to pull it out and microwave it in a hurry.

By the time Joe and Josh arrived, Beth had one very firm plan for the weekend. She was going to talk to Joe and make certain that he understood there were no promises between them.

She couldn't continue seeing him otherwise.

The three of them took a walk down to the harbor before dinner. Beth figured Joshua would get a kick out of all the boats. She also planned to take him by her favorite candy store. Even after a lifetime of living in Victoria, she still loved going into the little specialty shops.

"Don't you ever drive anywhere?" Joshua asked, walking on one side of her with his father on the other.

"Nope."

"Never?" He stopped and peered up at her, his short dark hair too thick to lie flat. The boy was wearing jeans and a dark-blue sweater and was so tiny he could have passed for a six-year-old.

"Never." She smiled at him—and then at Joe. The man had been taking her breath away all afternoon.

He was in jeans, too, and an off-white ribbed sweater that accented a body she knew to be next to perfect.

She still had to have that talk with him.

"What do you do with your car, then?" Joshua asked. The questions just kept on coming.

"I don't have a car. I never learned to drive."

"Is something wrong with you?"

"Joshua!" Joe's voice was sharp as he reached behind her and gave his son a tap on the back of the head. "That's enough questions."

"It's all right," Beth said, not just to save the moment, but because it was. "I like his questions." She liked that he was asking them. When she'd been his age, she'd kept all those questions bottled up inside her along with everything else.

"And not having a car is a good idea here. Victoria's relatively congested and there's not a lot of room to drive on many of our streets. Everyone just prefers to walk places."

"You walk to work?" He'd been kicking a rock for the last block and jumped ahead of them to keep up with it.

"Yes."

"And to the grocery?"

"Yes."

"Wow, what's that?"

He'd turned a corner ahead of them.

"The world's tallest self-supporting totem pole," Beth said.

"Cool! Can I go look?"

"Yeah, but don't break anything," Joe said and slowed his step as Josh ran off.

"Sorry he's such a handful."

"He's not," Beth said, peering up at him. She could tell he was really bothered by Josh. Yet it was obvious how much he loved the boy.

His frown clearing from his face, Joe took her hand.

"He just needs to be challenged, Joe."

When he didn't answer right away, Beth held her breath, hoping that she was finally going to get him to listen. And maybe to agree to have Joshua tested.

"Can we just let that go this weekend?" he finally asked.

Disappointed, Beth nodded. She'd let it go for the weekend, but she wasn't sure how much longer after that she was going to be able to keep her mouth shut.

The boy had been in trouble three times that week—

for interrupting class with obnoxious noises, arguing with his teacher about the correctness of a theory she'd spent twenty minutes explaining, and setting off another of the stink bombs he was making somewhere at school.

Her pranks had been different. Not so inventive or bold, but they'd been sending the same message nonetheless.

One that could spell disaster if unanswered.

Knowing what she knew, and caring as much as she already did for both father and son, she wasn't going to be able to stand calmly by much longer and watch the boy constantly wrestling with himself. And losing.

CHAPTER SEVEN

AT DINNER THAT NIGHT Joe and Joshua took turns telling her about a fishing trip they'd gone on the weekend before. Joe had chartered a boat and taught Josh how to fish for salmon. By the sound of things, the salmon were in no danger from the Holden men. Both of them were laughing hard as they told her about the first one that got away—and could hardly get the words out by the time they got to the story of the third. Josh had tried to tell his dad that they were holding their tension too tight, that the fishing hole wasn't exactly as the man who'd rented them the boat had described, adding several other technical things about salmon and salmon fishing that he'd looked up on the internet. Joe got around to listening eventually, and watched as Josh almost immediately hooked a fish. And then got so excited he dropped his pole in the water.

"So somewhere there's a fish swimming around in the Pacific Ocean dragging a two-hundred dollar fishing pole along behind him," Joe said.

"And we had McDonald's for dinner," Joshua added.

Beth was laughing almost as hard as they were. "Because you had no fish?"

"Yep."

For that moment, she had everything she'd always wanted.

HE COULDN'T plunge deeply enough. Lying on top of Beth, skin to skin, her breasts pressed against his chest, Joe continued to thrust and withdraw, to push as hard as he could without hurting her. His body was on fire, seeking and soaring at the same time, filled with a sense of adventure and excitement, risk and promise. Making love had never been so encompassing.

And yet, it wasn't enough.

"Come on," he urged her, though he had no idea what it was he expected from her. She was loving him every bit as fiercely as he was loving her.

And holding back from him at the same time. Giving him everything, including a wall he couldn't seem to penetrate.

"Don't stop," she whimpered when he slowed, her body moving urgently against his, begging him to continue.

The desperate plea sent him over the edge, driving him to satiate both of them in a world of pure sensation. His body shuddered, spilling into her, giving her not only his life force, but his hopes and dreams as well. The light-headed euphoria that consumed him was amazing.

And the comedown was a harder fall than he could ever remember. Probably because he'd never before climbed so high.

Or was it because he was falling farther down? Not

to a security net whose ropes were made strong by the defines of expectations, but to a void that he neither recognized nor understood.

"Mmm…" she snuggled against him, as he rolled onto his back.

He pulled her closer, keeping an arm around her waist. It felt as though she'd been there forever, a part of him. And it occurred to him that perhaps the only thing missing between them was the question he'd been planning to ask for months. The one that would give them a worldly connection to match their spiritual one.

"You tired?" he asked. He wasn't.

"Not exhausted, just drifting."

He thought about letting her drift. About waiting until the morning. But then Joshua would be there and he wouldn't have an unlimited amount of time alone with her. He wouldn't have the time to do this right.

He thought about waiting. He'd been so sure with Mona, only to find out that he'd been the only one on the journey he'd thought they were sharing.

"Are you awake?" Beth's voice didn't sound sleepy at all.

"Yes."

"I need to talk to you about something."

She hadn't pulled out of his arms. She was running her fingers lightly along his upper stomach.

Joe relaxed instantly, thinking she'd felt the emptiness, too, and was ready to fill it.

"Shoot," he said, eager to move ahead.

"I know we haven't said anything about commitment and maybe I'm assuming way too much here…."

She paused and he had to help her out. "You aren't assuming too much."

She sat up. Pulled the covers up around her chest, covering herself. Joe waited.

"I just need to make sure we both understand, before it's too late, that there can't *be* any commitment—or promises—other than what we currently have."

He froze, lying there nude on his back, staring up at her in the shadowy, moonlit darkness of her room. The four-poster bed and matching Victorian bedroom furniture were all silent witnesses to…he had no idea what.

"What is it we currently have?" he asked slowly, promising himself that history was not repeating itself. Beth was not Mona.

"Companionship, friendship…"

He started to relax again.

"No expectations," she finished.

He should sit up, take this on. "I don't know about you, but I have a particularly satisfying lover."

She raised the covers to her chin, her eyes downcast. "That, too."

He didn't know what satisfaction the admission brought, but it mattered somehow.

"So, no expectations," he repeated, as though testing to be sure he'd heard what she'd said.

"Right."

He could just say "okay," pull her down, and have incredible sex with her again.

"Define that," he said, his mind almost numb, slow to come up with any real thoughts.

"No promises," she said, looking up at him. "You

don't expect things from me and I don't expect them from you. When we're together we enjoy every moment that we have, and when we aren't, we don't owe each other anything.''

''Owe each other.'' Still no clear thoughts, but he'd had a surge of bad feelings at that last remark.

''Yeah, you know, like you don't have to think of me, or call me, or tend to my needs....''

''I think of you.''

''I think of you, too.''

''So?''

''But you don't see to my needs.''

''I would if I knew what they were.''

She shook her head. ''You're missing the point.''

''Just what is the point?'' Joe sat up. Somehow he had to engage in this conversation or give up hope of ever knowing how great it would be to have it all.

''That I don't want to hurt you.''

Would it do any good to tell her it was too late?

''So what you're proposing is that we be like that educator you were with. When we happen to be in the same place at the same time we have sex, but there will be no merging or sharing of our lives?''

She frowned. And he was fool enough to find hope in that.

''I'm not going to be like that man, Beth. We've spent five years building something that's real. I care about you, about what's happening in your life. I'd care if you had a problem. And I'd want to help.''

She was watching him, but still didn't say anything.

''What you're telling me is that you don't want to help if I have a problem?''

"Of course I'd help. I've been trying to help you with Joshua for over a year."

Not that he was going to entertain that conversation at the moment, but Joe was glad she'd brought it up. Because she was right. Whether he agreed with her prognosis for his son or not, there was no doubting that she cared.

"Did you care about the educator's kids?"

"He never talked about them."

"Did you tell him about Victoria, or your life here?"

"No."

That had to count for something.

"So what is it that you think I'm going to ask of you that you aren't going to be able to come through on?"

"I can't have a permanent relationship."

"We've been friends for five years, how long does it take before it becomes permanent and our time is up?"

She frowned again. This time Joe waited.

"We've been friends, but not in the same way. You flew me places and that was all. There wasn't any commitment beyond the appointments I made and paid for."

"So you want to pay me for my time?" Okay, so he was being deliberately obtuse, but he didn't understand the problem. She cared. He cared. What else mattered?

"Of course not."

"You're afraid I'm going to drop in on you unannounced?"

"No, I wouldn't mind that."

That was the best thing he'd heard since the conversation had taken such a wrong turn.

"What, then?"

She shrugged, the tips of her breasts peeking up over the edge of the covers. Joe tried not to notice.

"It's like this past week," she said. "I can't have you wanting things from me because I'm just going to disappoint you."

He thought over what he could remember of their telephone conversations that week. "What things?"

He wasn't aware of asking so much of her.

"The trips. You really wanted me to go."

"Yeah, so?"

"I don't do that."

"But you haven't even tried. You might find that you like it."

"I don't travel for pleasure."

Though he found her nonnegotiable tone a bit odd, Joe still didn't understand the problem.

"Okay, you don't travel. This isn't something that's going to hurt me greatly." Joe couldn't just sit there any longer, allowing something so right to slip away from him. He pulled her up against him and knew that he wasn't completely off base when she came willingly. This wasn't just him, here. She wanted him, too.

Sitting with the back of her head resting against his shoulder, snuggling into the arm he'd slipped around her, Beth was quiet for a while.

Joe would have been much more comfortable being privy to her thoughts. He couldn't help her if he didn't know what the problem was.

"Ideally, if you could make things perfect, what is it that you see here?" she finally asked. The question surprised him. "What is it that you want?" she added.

Now was probably not the time to pop the question. "I want this," he said, choosing his words carefully. "I want to have the right to come into your home and be a part of you, or to have you come to me, to know that there is a place for me in your life and to have you accept a place in mine." He paused, staring out over the end of the bed. When she didn't say anything he continued. "I want to know that you care and that you know I care. To know that you'll come to me if I can help you, or even that you'll come to me if all you need is to talk.

"I want to know that you care about Joshua, too, and that you don't resent the time we have to spend with him."

"Of course I don't!" she said, turning to glance up at him. Her eyes were colorless glints in the night and still their touch reached deep inside of him. "I love spending time with Joshua."

Considering the constant challenge Josh presented, he didn't see how. But he was very, very thankful.

"So what is it about what I said that you have a problem with?"

Her answer was slow in coming. "I don't think anything."

He breathed his first easy breath in many minutes, not sure he dared to go back to her earlier statements, but knowing that they were going to haunt him if he didn't.

"So what are these commitments we aren't going to make?"

"Just…"

Joe's fingers slid up her side and back down, and then again.

"What?"

"I don't know," she turned to look up at him again. "I just don't want to hurt you."

He kissed her. A long, soft, slow kiss, taking his time, tasting her. It just seemed like the right thing to do.

"There are no guarantees on that, Beth," he said softly against her lips.

"I know, but…" She kissed him and then turned around, her head on his shoulder again.

She hadn't pulled away from him.

"Why is that you're so sure you're going to hurt me?"

"Because I know what people expect and I know me. A relationship takes compromise and there are just so many places where I can't do that."

If that was all, the problem didn't sound nearly as bad as he'd feared. "What kind of places?"

"Like the traveling, for one."

"Not a big deal," he told her. "Are the others similar to it?"

"I only stay in suites when I do travel."

"Also not a relationship breaker."

Her heart rate had been steadily rising or Joe wouldn't even have known she was getting upset. It reminded him of the first time he'd taken her home after their impromptu landing in Astoria. He'd put his arm around her to walk her into the house, though she'd seemed completely recovered from whatever had beset her at the airport. Her heart had been beating so hard and fast then that he could feel its pulse way down at the bottom of her ribs.

"Tell me this," he said, trying to make things easier for her. "Until we decide otherwise, can you promise to sleep exclusively with me?"

"Of course."

"Will you always be honest with me?"

"Of course."

"And you honestly care about me and my son?"

"I do. Very, very much."

"That's all I need, Beth. Honesty, fidelity and love."

It must have been a Freudian slip, because in no way had Joe intended to say that last word. And he regretted it instantly.

"Okay."

"Okay?"

"Yes."

She didn't sound as sure as he'd have liked. And he hadn't asked her to marry him as he'd intended.

But still, Joe was satisfied.

CHAPTER EIGHT

BETH WAS TAKING her pills more often. Instead of just feeling threatened by the big things, little things were starting to get to her, too. Like walking in crowds of tourists downtown. She'd never liked crowds—at least not since the time she'd been lost in one in downtown Seattle for half a day.

She'd been three at the time and could still vividly remember it.

But she'd always been able to handle them at home.

Until Joe had refused to stay on the outskirts of her life. He called almost every day. She lived for those phone calls.

And she wondered when the time would come that they'd stop, when he'd have had enough of her, of the extra work it required putting up with all of her idiosyncrasies.

She wondered how she'd survive when he did.

Desertion was the one thing she could not handle— the one thing she had to protect against at all costs.

Involving herself in a relationship, allowing herself to have expectations, was not a way to avoid desertion.

After a month of phone calls and weekend visits, Beth was more torn than ever, wanting desperately to find a way to hold on, and looking for reasons she shouldn't. She was allowing herself to be happier than she'd ever dreamed she could be, and guarding against total despair at the same time.

Joe talked her into a visit to Astoria the first weekend in December. Joe and Joshua had come to Victoria to spend their Thanksgiving with her and Lindsay and when Joshua had invited her to his school fair the following Saturday she'd been unable to refuse. He had a project at the fair that he couldn't wait for her to see.

"This isn't fair to Joshua," she blurted out to Joe late Friday night. They were in his bed, having just made love—twice—and she was thinking about the next afternoon when she would be accompanying the boy to his school function.

"I don't think he knows we do this."

She grinned in spite of the heaviness of her thoughts. Joe always had a way of making her feel moments of lightness in spite of herself.

"I mean us in general. Everything."

"You're the best thing that's ever happened to Josh."

Except that she couldn't get Joe to listen to her about his son's needs.

"I'm afraid he's starting to see me as more than I am."

She felt Joe's arm stiffen against her side, but she had to continue.

"You're a part of our lives, that's what he sees."

It was getting harder for her to breathe. "I'm afraid he's going to start seeing me as a replacement for his mother."

"He cares about you. I don't see the danger in that."

Heart pounding, Beth forced herself to focus. "We're raising his expectations. He might start to hope that I'm going to move in here with you some day."

The pause that followed told Beth the worst. Joe had been thinking the same thing, in spite of her attempts to prevent that very thing.

"He's also hoping that he's going to be a linebacker some day," Joe finally said. He didn't sound nearly as upset as she'd expected. "The important thing is that you care about him, Beth. You've made a huge difference in his life. That's reality. And it supercedes nebulous hopes and dreams."

Because she so wanted to be convinced, Beth allowed him to assuage her fears—and to distract her with the kisses that took her outside of herself and all of her problems. It transported her to a world where she never needed pills.

THE NEXT WEEKEND Joe found her pills. They were in the kitchen cupboard, next to the salt he was looking for—he'd emptied the shaker with his attempts at surprising Beth with breakfast in bed.

Hand shaking he stood there staring at the little orange plastic vial and commanded himself to calm down. A vial of pills was no big deal. People took them all the time, for all kinds of nonthreatening reasons.

But he recognized the name of the drug. It was one of the prescriptions Mona had taken.

Joe's stomach filled with dread as so many things fell into place. Beth's rapid heart rate. The near fainting spell at the airport.

Her aversion to commitment.

It was the past repeating itself.

He'd been making breakfast as a way to apologize for the argument they'd had the weekend before after Josh's school science fair. Joe had to admit the boy's project had been spectacular, innovative. But that didn't mean his son couldn't fit in with normal kids. He'd been sharper than he'd intended when he'd asked Beth to mind her own business.

It hadn't been what he'd meant. And he'd thought that was the reason she'd seemed more distant all week.

But maybe that wasn't it at all. Mona had grown more distant, too, when her heart was bothering her.

Was it too spectacular to believe? Two women? One condition?

Except that Mona's way of dealing with her condition had been to do everything she possibly could, to experience life to the fullest even if that meant shortening her life.

Apparently Beth took a more practical approach. She didn't travel, shunned adventure. Was this a way to prolong her life?

With both hands on the counter, head bent, Joe shook his head. He took a couple of deep breaths. And told himself to get a grip.

He was jumping to all kinds of conclusions. Allowing the past to cloud his judgment.

All he had to do was ask Beth about the pills. She'd

tell him what they were for and he wouldn't have to torture himself with this ridiculous notion that she had a terminal illness.

That's all he had to do. Just ask her.

BETH SENSED a difference in Joe the minute he walked in the room.

He wasn't the open, easy man she knew. His posture was too straight and perfect, his expression impersonal. Joe, with his ready friendly smile, wasn't usually even impersonal to strangers. Certainly he'd never looked at her that way. He wasn't so much looking at her as assessing her.

She'd been lying there waiting for him, thinking, upon waking without him, that he'd gone to the bathroom or to check on Joshua. Now she wished she'd gotten up, and put some clothes on. Sitting up, she pulled the covers up to her chin, trying to ignore the pounding in her chest.

"I was looking for the salt."

"Why?" If she could concentrate on something else, she might be able to avoid a full fledged panic attack.

"For eggs. I was making breakfast."

Joe making breakfast sounded good. The dread tightening her lungs loosened.

"I found your pills."

Every muscle inside her stiffened as she stared at him.

"What are they for?"

"They're just a mild sedative for sleeping." Her voice was distant, it sounded foreign to her.

"They aren't—"

"More than fifty percent of the population suffers from occasional insomnia," she interrupted, spouting words almost faster than she could think them. "I'm one of them."

"Your heart rate increases sometimes when there doesn't seem to be any reason for it."

She stared. How could he possibly know that?

"You almost fainted when I found you at the airport in Astoria."

Breathe. Don't sink into the darkness. Don't do that to yourself. With frantic coaching, Beth managed to stay above water—barely.

"Tell me what's wrong."

"Nothing's wrong." The answer was automatic. A survival instinct.

She couldn't bear to watch when he found out what a burden she would be to him if he were to try to "merge his life with hers" as he'd said all those weeks ago.

Or worse, to see his pity as he insisted on standing by her regardless of how much her handicap would stifle his life.

"You don't travel or take risks."

She'd let him get too close. She'd known this was going to happen, dammit. Why in the hell hadn't she listened to herself? She'd *known*.

Self-anger helped tamp down the feeling of ants crawling under her skin. A benefit she hadn't been aware of until then. It was a welcome distraction.

Until Joe came over and took a seat on the edge of

the bed. Then she started to shake inside and knew it wouldn't be long until she was shaking outside, too.

"Please, Beth, tell me what's going on. Let me be a part of your life."

"You are a part of my life."

"Tell me."

Meeting that intoxicating dark gaze, Beth was almost compelled to do just that.

"Nothing's wrong," she bit out, much more strongly than she'd intended. She was in too much danger. She had to get away, to get him away, because he'd come far too close.

"I love you, honey." His soft words were filled with a warmth that left her in no doubt of their truth.

Beth lost the battle then she opened her mouth to confess how very much she loved him, too.

"I want to marry you," he said before she could speak.

No!

Everything inside Beth stopped. Her thoughts. Her breath. And when they started back up again, she was besieged on all sides with more fear than she could cope with. She had a very clear picture of the changes her phobias would make to Joe's life—this man who lived to travel, to see new places. She remembered the ephemeral look on his face when he'd told her how perfect Mona was for him because of her adventurous nature. She saw her and Joe ten years, even one year, down the road, when the newness of loving her had worn off and he started to feel trapped.

"I don't know how you got the idea we're anything more than friends." Her words were strong, sure. The voice was not her own. "I can't marry you, Joe. I don't intend to marry anyone. Ever."

His gaze never flinched as they assessed each other. Nor did hers.

"You sound absolutely certain of that."

"I am."

He sat there another long minute, then nodded. He stood and dressed. All in all, it took him a mere fifteen minutes to raise his son, collect their belongings, and say goodbye. Joshua's eyes were filled with confusion. And fear. He asked if something was wrong. And when both adults gave him a curt "no" he wanted to know when he'd see her again.

Joe had rushed him off before she could answer.

Beth didn't know which hurt more, the way Joe would not look at her—or the way Joshua did.

CHAPTER NINE

"HI, IT'S JOE." He'd debated for a week before he'd made the call.

"Hi!"

"How you doing?"

"I've been better."

God, it was good to hear her voice. Better than good.

"Yeah, I know what you mean."

When Joe realized that the lag in the conversation was his responsibility since he was the one who'd made the call, he started to sweat. What had once seemed like a good idea, didn't seem at all right.

But then, that was the emotional roller coaster he'd been riding for more than a week.

"The thing is, I have a favor to ask."

At least that was the reason he was ready to acknowledge for the phone call.

"What is it?" She sounded so sweet and ready to help. So Beth.

There'd been no spark in life since he'd walked out on her. And no goodness in his son, either.

Surely some time with Beth, in whatever capacity she'd allow, would be better than the nothingness that had consumed their lives the past seven days without her.

"I was wondering if you could point me in the direction of a good testing center for Josh."

Dead silence met his question. Joe wondered if he'd asked it a little too late.

"He's been in trouble nonstop since we left your place. But not the kind of hell I would have raised if I was his age. This is weird stuff. Manipulative."

"It's the challenge he's after." He didn't want to hear any more about the prisons being filled with geniuses.

"A couple of days ago he took apart all of our cable boxes and wouldn't put them back together again unless I promised to call you."

He didn't say anything. He thought he heard her sniffle, but couldn't be sure.

"So do you know of someplace?"

"Of course. There's a place in Seattle. I can probably call and get him in immediately."

That soon. "Okay."

"You're sure?"

"Yes." As sure as he could be while changing his mind every other hour. "I'm sure that he's not being challenged as he needs to be."

"You're making the right decision."

He hoped so. He didn't want Josh ostracized. But he didn't want him in prison, either.

Joe took a deep breath, looked around the darkness of his bedroom. "I'm scared."

He'd never have admitted that in the light of day. Or to anyone but Beth.

"I know," she said. "But it will be so much better when he's in the right classes. For both of you."

"This is more than a job to you, isn't it?" He wasn't ready to hang up, to face another long night lying awake in the dark trying to figure out a way to have some effect on something he had no control over.

"When I was two I made a call from Seattle, where I was visiting a friend with my mother, to my father's workshop. Apparently I just called said, 'hi daddy,' and hung up...."

Her tone was different than he'd heard before. A mixture of vulnerability and resignation. He had a feeling she was telling him something she didn't share with many people.

"My father, who hated to be interrupted when he was in the middle of a project, was really put out and called my mother to find out why she'd called and then just hung up. He was terrified that something had happened to her."

She stopped and Joe waited, afraid to say anything, to interrupt her lest the story stop.

"Of course, she hadn't called. It was me. I must have watched my mother dial him the night before and remembered how. But I was two, and didn't know that, unlike my play phone, I was supposed to have a real conversation."

"At two years old, with seeing it once, you remembered, not only how to dial long distance, but which number to dial?"

"Yes."

"You're just like Josh."

"Yes."

Joe's knee, which had been raised, fell to the bed.

"How old were you when you were tested?"

"Eight."

"So you know how he feels."

"Yeah."

"And you know he'll be happier in special classes, even if the kids he's trying so hard to fit in with make fun of him?"

"Yes."

He should thank her and hang up now. He knew that.

"Mona knew she was dying when she was pregnant with Josh."

"What? How? Did they tell her?"

With thumb and forefinger, Joe rubbed his eyes. This was hard. He didn't really want to do this, did he?

"She was born with a heart defect and always knew that, depending on the choices she made, she could go at any time."

"Yet she did all those dangerous things...." Beth's voice trailed off.

"She'd decided that life wasn't worth living if she had to be a slave to a bad heart. She was going to enjoy it to the fullest while she could and be satisfied with that."

"Wasn't it hard for you, watching her do those things, knowing that they could kill her?"

"I didn't know."

"Maybe not in college, but later, after you were living together..."

"I didn't know. Not then. Not when she was pregnant. It was the reason she wouldn't marry me. She didn't want me that close, didn't want me to have the right to speak to her doctors, or to be involved in her medical decisions. It was also why she agreed so readily to give Josh my last name. She'd planned to all along because she knew she wasn't going to be around to raise him.''

"Having him shortened her life considerably, didn't it?''

"Yes.''

Did she have any idea how much that hurt him? To have contributed to Mona's death with no knowledge of the danger he'd helped create?

"In the end, when she passed out while carrying Josh, I found out what was going on. The very next day, bottles and bottles of pills appeared. She'd been taking them—and hiding them from me—almost the entire time we'd been together.''

He opened his eyes, looked around the room, remembering the bitter, helpless grief of those days. "One of her medications was the same as the one I found in your kitchen.''

"Oh.''

"I'm sorry if I overreacted. I thought you should know why.''

"Thank you for telling me.'' The words were trite, but the warmth in her voice, the slow way she said them, wasn't trite at all.

"The thing is,'' he forced himself to continue because he'd come too far to just hang up, "I know how precious life is, every minute of it, and I think I'd rather see you on your terms, calling it whatever you want, than to be as alone as I've been this past week."

"Can I have a little time to think about that?"

She obviously hadn't missed him as desperately as he'd missed her. "Yeah." What choice did he have? "Okay."

"I'll talk to you soon then."

"Okay...and...Joe?"

"Yeah?"

"I'm not ill. I promise you."

Those words gave him the first good night's sleep he'd had since he left her bed.

BETH COULDN'T SLEEP, she couldn't find any peace. She took pills. She visited Lindsay so much she'd practically moved back home. She worked hard and took long walks. And still the dark threat of panic pervaded every minute of her days. She might not be physically ill, but her heart was dying just the same.

Life without Joe was cloudy, overcast, threatening. Yet, trapped by her own weaknesses, she couldn't find a workable solution for any of them.

The one bright spot in her life was the knowledge that Joshua was going to be getting the help and direction he needed. Her time with Joe had accomplished something priceless.

She tried to think of that often, to remind herself of the good in life when despair threatened to take over. It didn't always work.

After one particularly stressful attempt to see a movie—she got so claustrophobic and light-headed in the theater that she had to leave—Beth walked around her beloved town and wondered if this was all life would ever have to offer her. Would she never find the way to combat the demons in her mind?

One Monday evening while walking up the street toward her front door, she ran through a mental checklist of possibilities for dinner, trying to find something that she actually wanted. She was almost at her pathway when she noticed two people standing on her front step. They were both slim, successful looking.

There was a man, in his sixties she'd guess, and a much younger blond woman. They were staring at the front door as if they'd knocked and were waiting for her to answer. Beth approached slowly, her attention on the couple's clasped hands.

"Can I help you?" she called from the edge of the sidewalk.

The couple turned abruptly, staring at her oddly.

Her neighbors on both sides were home. Both houses were fully lit. If she needed help all she'd need to do was call.

"Are you Beth Chenoweth?" the man asked after an awkward moment of silence. Though he was dressed casually in tan slacks and a brown pullover sweater he carried an imposing air about him. He was tall, with an explicitly straight spine, thick silvering hair cut very short, and striking eyes.

"Yes," she said, facing them with several feet of sidewalk still between them.

Her gaze turned to the woman, who couldn't have been more than five years older than she herself, if that. She was curvy, her hair glowing with golden highlights. She looked vaguely familiar to Beth, though Beth had no idea why. The woman was dressed casually as well in an expensive-looking pair of slacks with matching blouse and sweater tunic, as though she'd just come from modeling for the latest edition of the Neiman Marcus catalog.

"We'd like to speak with you, if you have a minute," the woman said.

Beth took a couple of steps forward, and then stopped. Something wasn't right. These people were looking at her too intently. And then it hit her.

"Something's happened to Joe." She felt the blood drain from her face, as though she were outside herself cataloguing reactions. The air, cool against her skin, was something to concentrate on.

"No," the man assured her, taking a step forward. "Would you mind if we go inside?"

Her couch was in there. Her carpet and wall hangings. Her pillows. All the things she loved. And that gave her comfort.

Glancing suspiciously at both of them as she stepped between them, Beth moved up the walk toward them.

"I'm sorry, I didn't catch your names," she said, unlocking the door and standing between her visitors and the interior of her home.

"I'm Brad Henderson," the man said. "This is Gabriella Petri."

"Are you from around here?"

"No."

"You thinking of moving here?"

"No."

Though she had no idea why her mind was so slow on the uptake, Beth finally started to make sense of things.

"You have a gifted child."

The two shared a long look and then the woman reached out, taking Beth's hand.

"Please, if we could go inside, we'll tell you why we're here."

It was serious enough to need the privacy of indoors. Beth didn't ask any more questions, just silently led the way into her living room, taking the seat she always used on the end of the couch.

"This is lovely," the woman said, openly examining the room. "I love all the flowers." Her words were innocuous enough, but her voice was shaking.

"Thank you."

Brad Henderson took a seat on the other end of the sofa, perching on the edge with his forearms resting on spread knees. Beth might have relaxed if not for the way he was worrying his hands together. He looked up at the woman called Gabriella as if to say "you start."

She took the armchair adjacent to Beth, leaning toward her. Beth was shocked—and frightened all over again—to see tears in Gabriella's eyes.

"I'm sorry," she said, giving her eyes an embarrassed swipe. "It's just so good to see you."

Beth frowned. "We've met before?"

The woman shook her head.

"Have you ever heard of a firm called Finder's Keepers?" Gabriella asked.

"No."

"It's a private investigative firm in Trueblood, Texas, run by a brother and sister team, Lily Bishop and Dylan Garrett. Dylan helped us find you."

She didn't like the sound of that. "Why?"

"What do you know about your birth, your biological parents?"

Probably because she was so confused by the undercurrents, Beth didn't have time to panic. Her attention was riveted on the two people who obviously had something important to tell her.

"I know nothing about my birth," she said. "I was adopted as a baby."

"To good parents?" the man asked, his tone more sharp than casual.

"My mother was the best," Beth said. Not that she remembered many specifics. It was all just feelings. Sometimes they were all that sustained her, even now. "She was killed in a car accident when I was three."

"And your father?" the man prompted, his gaze intense.

He made Beth nervous. And yet, oddly, not afraid.

"Olson was an artist," she said. "He was besotted with my mother. Would do anything for her." Including adopting a child he didn't want just to keep her happy. To give her something to do—someone to love—when he spent long days and weeks in his studio.

"And for you?"

"Sure," Beth said. Though she felt strangely compelled to trust these two strangers, she was not able to bare her soul to them. To anyone.

Gabriella and Brad exchanged another long look.

Frustrated, impatient, and unsure all at the same time, Beth tried to figure out where she'd seen the woman before.

"Have you ever tried to find your birth parents?" she asked.

Beth shook her head. Their rejection of her had been all she'd needed to know. They knew she existed. If they'd wanted her—at any time in her life—they could have found her.

As it was, thoughts of them only fed the desertion complex that haunted her. The people who'd created her hadn't wanted her, so how could she expect anyone else to?

Another long look and Beth stood up.

"What's going on here?" she asked, thinking, for the first time, of the vial in her kitchen cupboard. Or the one in her purse. Either would do.

Brad and Gabriella stood as well, flanking her. Beth had to fight the urge to push them both away.

"I guess there's no easy way to do this," Gabriella said. "Beth, I'm your sister. And this," she turned to the older man, grabbed his hand, tears in her eyes again, "is our father."

Stunned, Beth sat back down. She'd heard about times when people went outside themselves, watched things happening to them from the outside.

She'd never experienced it before. Until now.

"My father," she said, her voice devoid of emotion. Her entire self devoid of feeling.

"Yes," Gabriella's voice answered. Beth stared at the floor, noticing that she needed to wipe the dust off the black low-heeled pumps she'd worn to work. Were she alone, she would have been changed out of the black-and-white pantsuit she was wearing and into a pair of jeans and a sweatshirt.

She had people in her house. People claiming to be the family she'd never had. Her father...

MAJOR BRAD HENDERSON struggled to keep himself in his seat. Emotions that had been under wraps—dead and gone he'd thought—for twenty-eight long years were clamoring inside him.

He'd gone from no hope, from cynicism and heart-lessness to an overabundance of faith in the possibility of real happiness. All in the space of a very few days. It was as though his precious Lorraine, and the promise of eternal love she'd made him, were back with him.

In a sense she was, in the eyes and hearts of the daughters she'd borne.

Or at least in one of them. Gabriella had been as delighted to find him as he had her. That first meeting with her had played itself out far differently than this second one.

Of course, she'd come looking for him—the meeting on his terms, through proper legal counsel.

Beth, his youngest, hadn't even known of him.

That hurt a great deal.

"I've been in prison, Beth," he said now, his mat-ter-of-fact and to-the-point military training coming to the fore. It had seen him through twenty-eight years of hell, surely it would get him through this, too.

Because get through it he would. And, eventually, one way or another, he was going to bring this beautiful and tentative woman around. His heart couldn't accept any less.

"You might have seen the story in the papers," Gabriella interjected, her eyes shadowed as they passed between her father and newfound sister.

Brad almost smiled at the natural protectiveness his eldest daughter had already begun to implement where he was concerned.

After so many years completely alone, it was odd to have such a champion. Odd, but very, very nice.

"The major who'd been erroneously accused of selling plans for a top secret fighter jet to the Soviet Union." Beth sounded as though she were reading the article aloud to a group of strangers. Her beautiful eyes were turned on him, but there was no life in them.

If not for the vacant expression, she, too, like her eldest sister, could have been a younger version of his sweet wife. Her blond hair was longer than Ella's, but had the same flowing curls.

"He'd been accused of betraying several US agents as well," she continued. "They finally found proof, a name, of the man who was really guilty and Major Henderson was released from prison on Thanksgiving Day."

Brad's heart lurched as his youngest daughter continued to speak of him in the third person. She had walls built higher than his own.

And he wanted to know why. Had to know why. Had to know what he could do to help her.

The anger was suddenly riding him, the need to hurt whoever had done this to her. Anger didn't help, so he clamped it down.

He had learned to do that long ago.

Since being reunited with Ella, with the life he'd lost, he was into believing and having faith. And using the strength he'd gained over the past twenty-eight years to live as much as he could of the life that had been stolen from him and from his precious daughters.

"YOUR MOTHER IS DEAD." Beth looked down. Her mother? She glanced back up at the man and couldn't look away.

"She was pregnant when I went to trial. The stress was too much for her and she gave birth prematurely. To you." And died in the process.

"Oh, my God."

"I only saw you once, briefly, at your mother's funeral. They wouldn't let me hold you."

Tears filled his eyes, dripped slowly, silently down his face. "Every day for twenty-eight years I've wondered how you were growing up—and prayed that God would always keep you safe."

Beth couldn't believe what they were telling her. She couldn't make sense of anything. It was all too much to take in at once.

Except that her house was overflowing with an emotion she'd always been denied. She stood. She stared.

Gabriella looked familiar. She stood more calmly than Beth would have done under Beth's scrutiny. Beth met her gaze unflinching, though her lips trembled with an emotion Beth was only beginning to understand.

Gabriella looked like the face she'd been staring at in the mirror for twenty-eight years.

Her sister. Her flesh and blood.

She almost broke then, almost gave in. But she couldn't let herself believe.

Slowly her head turned back toward the man. His tears had stopped. His eyes were filled with compassion and understanding. And a determination that was stronger than her own.

Compelled by something beyond her, outside her and inside as well, Beth stumbled forward, wrapped her arms around the tall man's rock-hard middle section and held on tight.

She felt his arms wrap around her as though in slow motion, aware of every nuance, of every part of her he touched. And when he had her firmly in the safety of his embrace, she started to cry. Deep racking sobs that didn't stop for a long, long time.

CHAPTER TEN

TWO DAYS LATER, after paying an exorbitant fee for a limo drive from Seattle to Oregon Beth stood in front of Joe's house in Astoria and willed herself to move forward. She could do this. She had to do this, for herself and Joe and Joshua. But for her father and Ella, too. Her happiness, as well as that of her sisters, was all her father cared about. Only by being happy could she bring peace.

He'd traveled across the country—but more, across a lifetime—for her. She could do this for him.

There were lights on in the house. It was close to dinnertime, but Beth figured they hadn't eaten yet. Marta had just left.

Standing outside, shivering in her jeans and off-white wool sweater, Beth had waited to see her go.

Be honest. Ella's words came back to her, giving her strength. Beth had spent many hours over the past two days confiding in this sister of her heart, telling Ella everything. About her childhood. Her weaknesses.

And found nothing but love and acceptance in return.

She'd decided having a big sister was far more than the miracle she'd always dreamed it would be.

Their father's appearance gave both of them a very

certain conviction not to waste a minute of their lives. And while Ella had had nothing to say about Beth's situation that Beth didn't already know, just having a sister to talk to showed Beth how very precious every moment was, every relationship. And that she had to do whatever she could to not lose those who meant the most to her.

That meant Joe.

"Beth?"

He'd come outside and she hadn't even realized it. He found her standing there like an idiot on the sidewalk outside his home.

Ella had said that she had to be honest with Joe, to let him decide what he could and couldn't deal with.

Standing there so close to him, feeling him, needing him, she sure hoped Ella was right.

"Can we talk?"

"Of course." His arm slid around her quite naturally, leading her up the walk. "Josh is over at a friend's house for dinner. We'll have the house to ourselves."

"At a friend's?" she looked up at him.

Joe nodded, tried to act calm and unaffected, but she saw the relief in his eyes. "He has a new friend. Someone he met at the testing center in Seattle. He lives right here in Astoria."

Beth had tried to tell him that if he got Joshua help, his son wouldn't feel so alone. But she understood how some people just had to figure some things out for themselves, in whatever time it took.

JOE DIDN'T WANT to let her go. He wanted to keep walking with her around the block, around the world, if only he could continue holding her. He'd learned how important every day was during those last couple of years with Mona. It was an awareness he'd never forgotten.

The lost days with Beth had been eating away at him, taunting him with his inability to fix whatever had gone wrong between them.

Stepping away from him, she went into the house ahead of him and headed straight to the living room to sit on one end of the leather sofa. He'd never seen her quite so purposeful.

And he warned himself not to let hope spring eternal.

"I have a story to tell you," she said, meeting his eyes, and then not.

He didn't want to, but Joe sat on the other end of the couch. Away from her. "Okay," he said, "I'm listening."

"My father—adopted father," she corrected, "never wanted a child. He'd never needed anything but my mother and his art."

Joe's chest filled with anger, probably beyond what was warranted. He had a sudden premonition that this story was not going to be an easy one, for either of them.

He had no idea where this conversation was going to lead, or why they were having it. He knew only that he was with her, ready to take on whatever she had to give him.

"Why did he adopt you then?"

"Because he adored my mother, and understood

how badly she wanted a child. He just never had much to do with me himself.''

''He wasn't mean to you, then.''

''No. Not in the traditional sense, anyway. He was content to let my mother take care of her 'toy,' her 'hobby.''

His chest tightened a little more, almost imperceptibly, with every word. ''That must have hurt her, to not have him share in any of the responsibility of raising their child.''

''From what I've been told, she loved and understood him, and was perfectly happy to care for me by herself. I guess he worked long hours—sometimes weeks at a time and I filled up the gaps in her life.''

Her eyes dropped as she fell silent. Joe ached to pull her into his arms.

''When my mother was killed, Olson was so bereft, he spent that first night down at the pier, waiting for the ferry that he was sure was going to bring her home. He was convinced that the report of her death had to be a mistake.''

While a distant part of him could relate to the other man's grief, could feel a deep sympathy with the pain of losing a young wife, Joe heard something else in Beth's story. In what she hadn't said. What about the child whose father didn't come home?

''Who took care of you?''

''No one.''

''What do you mean no one?''

''Olson left me alone at the house after the call came.''

''You were three years old!''

"I know."

"You stayed home alone all night."

"It's my first concrete memory," Beth said. "Being all alone in the house for a long time, hungry, sure as I watched it get dark that my mother would be home soon. And then it just stayed dark forever..."

He swallowed. And threw caution and reason to the wind. In one movement he had her against him, cradling her against his chest. There was more to come, he knew that now.

"The second time he forgot me was in an art supply store in Seattle. I was four. I don't know why he took me with him, but it was the first time I'd ridden the ferry since my mother died. He bought me a hamburger for lunch. And then later, he was so busy choosing the perfect tools, oils, watercolors, he didn't notice that we got separated. He paid for his supplies and left."

With a jaw clenched with rage, Joe remained silent. There was nothing he could say that would do her any good.

"When I couldn't find him in the store, I was sure he'd be right outside and I ran out looking for him. By the time I realized he was really gone, I'd made several turns and had no idea where I was."

"What happened?"

She shrugged her shoulders. "I don't remember it all, but some woman figured out I was lost and took me to the nearest police station. I was able to tell them where I lived and somehow ended up back at home with Olson."

"They gave you back to him?"

As she nodded, Beth's head rubbed against his chest. The movement steadied him some, though it couldn't dispel the fury her words were igniting.

That Beth, his precious, beautiful, generous Beth had been treated so harmfully...

Olson Chenoweth didn't deserve the air he breathed.

"He was properly contrite, and told a good enough story, apparently saying he'd been frantically searching since I ran off...."

"He blamed you."

"Yeah."

"Why, if he never wanted you, did he want you back?"

"Because he coveted everything that had belonged to my mother."

"Was he at least better about keeping track of you after that?"

She shook her head.

Why wasn't he surprised?

"He left me at day care. And at church. And when I was five, he left me in a hotel room all by myself for almost twenty-four hours. I kept calling the front desk, wondering if he'd called and left a message. But it wasn't until I ordered room service the next day, and it was delivered to this little kid, that the hotel staff took action. They called the number on the registration—our home number—and Olson was there. They were going to remove me from Victoria, but that was when Lindsay stepped in. She got full custody of me and life was better after that."

Joe heard what she wasn't saying. The years of desertion. Of loneliness. Belonging nowhere and having no control.

Though he didn't, as of yet, know how he figured into any of this. Or even if he did.

"You don't go through something like that, especially when you're old enough to know the fear, but not old enough to help yourself, and escape without scars," he said.

"You're right." Beth sat up, scooted over closer to him, and faced him. "I have scars, Joe. Big ones. Day to day I'm fine, above average in every way," she tried to grin with that, but failed. "But anytime I leave the island, am in an unfamiliar place with people around, I have panic attacks. My heart pounds. I can't breathe. I get light-headed and nauseous. I've even passed out a time or two."

Joe's heart ached for her, wished there was something he could do, some way he could give her enough of his strength to ensure that she never had to suffer like that again.

"That's what the pills are for. They're a sedative to calm me down when I feel an attack coming on."

"You've had help then."

"Oh, yeah," she said, her gaze steady on his, as though, now that she'd made up her mind to come clean, she was hiding nothing. "We figured out why I have the problem, years of abandonment do tend to take their toll. Many adopted children suffer irrational feelings of abandonment just for having been born to biological parents who didn't keep them. It's also quite common for children who lose a parent to death at a young age to suffer those same feelings. To follow all of that up with two years of Olson's constant and frightening abandonment, the cause is textbook. We were just never able to cure me of the attacks, only to try to prevent them with medication.''

Something struck Joe. ''This isn't why you refused to make promises, is it? This isn't what's keeping us apart?''

And yet it made sense. Nothing else did.

''Yes,'' she answered, and then frowned. ''I love you, but love isn't strong enough to control the attacks. Don't you see, Joe? Something like this will stifle you to the point of claustrophobia. Sooner or later, you're going to need to escape.''

''You think I'll abandon you, too.''

''I did.'' She stopped, her gaze filled with an odd light as she looked up at him. ''Now, I just don't know.'' She ran a hand along his chin. ''It wasn't just that, though. I can't bear to subject you to a life that holds less than you desire.''

He had some things to say about all of that, but first, ''You said you *did* think that. What changed?''

''I found out I wasn't abandoned by my birth parents. It doesn't take away the sting of Olson's neglect, but at least the chain of abandonment was broken enough for me to see that there might be other choices. I've missed you so much. You and Joshua. I keep thinking of our times together. They were the happiest moments I've ever known on my island. I had to take a chance.''

His heart started to pound. ''Is that what you're doing here? Taking a chance?''

"Yes." The word was soft, half whisper, half squeak.

"Enough of a chance to marry me?"

The look in her eyes gave him enough hope to sit still. "It's not fair to you, Joe, or to Josh, to be saddled with someone who might rain on every parade you ever try to attend."

"Or maybe what's not fair is to deny us both the love of our lives."

When she didn't immediately come back with another negative, when it looked as though she were actually ready to consider giving them a chance, Joe jumped in hard.

"We'll get through this together, Beth. If it takes the rest of our lives, we can work on things and maybe someday they'll get better. Maybe they won't. But we'll always be trying. And most importantly, we'll be trying together."

She shook her head, and Joe's spirits plummeted. There was that damned wall of negativity he slammed into every time he ventured into her private territory.

"I've already tried everything there is to try."

"But you've tried alone, honey. I have a feeling that not being alone is going to go a long way toward your chances of beating this thing. We can travel in my plane, get you more and more used to being in new places, and for as long as you need me, I'll be glued to your side when we're not at home."

"I don't know...." There was real hope in her eyes. He saw it and wanted to do a double loop in the sky.

"We can make love in every single place, keep a tally...."

"What about Josh?"

"He'll be busy in the hotel room next door, watching his baby brothers and sisters."

She grinned, and slumped back against him. "That many, huh?"

"Only if you marry me first."

"About that…"

A thread of darkness shot through him. "What?"

"I was wondering…would you mind terribly if we have a double wedding?"

He frowned. "What?"

"My big sister is getting married in New York later this month and last night, very late, after I told her about you and she promised me that everything would work out, we made up this fantastic fairy tale where our father gave us both away.…"

Joe grabbed her, turned her around so she was cradled on his lap where he could see her face. He'd been so caught up in their chance, that he'd forgotten the comment she'd made about finding out that her birth parents hadn't abandoned her.

"Your birth family came and found you?" It made sense. Wonderful, bizarre, glorious sense. There was opposition in all things. Horrendous things happened. And so did miracles.

Joe thought about the circles that always come around if only there is enough faith and hope to sustain them, as he held the woman he loved and listened to her tale of her newfound family. Beth was still obviously dazed, exhausted and a little dreamy as she told him about every minute of the past two days.

She and Ella had talked until their throats hurt,

catching each other up on the basic details of their lives with promises of years worth of catching up to come.

Lindsay had taken to her new family immediately, welcoming them into her home, cushioning Beth's identity change as she tried to fit herself into the unfolding events. Joe had a feeling, from a couple of things Beth said, that Beth's guardian and her father might just find more in common than the daughter they shared.

The family wasn't done searching yet. There was one more sister to find. The middle one.

But they'd find her. Beth was sure of that. And so was Joe because they had faith, hope and love.

The circle would definitely come around.

Dear Reader,

Another holiday season has arrived, and once again I have the pleasure of giving you a Christmas story for your Christmas stocking. It always seems so odd to write these stories at different times of the year, sometimes in the heat of summer or while the daffodils are poking their heads out in spring. But when the holidays roll around, it's fun to reread them. Christmas is a time for glad tidings and great joy, but most of all it's a time for love—and sometimes even a little romance.

For Georgiana's story, I went back a year, to the novel I did for the TRUEBLOOD, TEXAS series. I had a chance to return to a character that readers loved—Dylan Garrett—and to a story that brought together three sisters who'd been lost to each other many years before.

I hope that you enjoy my contribution to *Trueblood Christmas* and that it brings just a bit more love to your holiday season. And to keep up with my other releases, please visit my Web site at www.katehoffmann.com.

Warmest wishes!

Kate Hoffmann

GEORGIANA

Kate Hoffmann

CHAPTER ONE

"SURPRISE!"

Georgiana Hewitt cried out in alarm as lights blinded her eyes and dark figures jumped from behind hay bales. When her vision finally cleared, she saw her four older brothers standing in front of the crowd, clapping and howling at her stunned expression.

As the party guests broke into a raucous rendition of "Happy Birthday," Georgie felt the color rise in her cheeks. Her sun-streaked hair was tangled by the wind and she knew her face was smudged with grease from the windmill she'd just finished fixing. If they had given her the least bit of warning, she might have managed to walk into her thirtieth birthday party without looking like some deranged rodeo clown.

"Are you surprised, George?"

Georgie forced a smile, then nodded to her oldest brother, Ben. "Very. Did you and the boys cook this up?"

"It was Jace's idea," Ben said. "He thought a barn dance might be fun. Ma helped with the food and Seth hired the band. What do you think?"

"I think it's great," she lied. She pushed up on her toes and gave him a kiss on the cheek. Her three other brothers collected their thank-you kisses before other guests rushed up to offer their own birthday greetings. Georgie pasted a smile on her face and acted as if a surprise party were the very thing she wanted for her birthday.

As the last guests offered their best wishes, Georgie could think of only one thing—how to make her escape. On any other birthday, she might have enjoyed a celebration, but this was number thirty and for someone not usually introspective, she'd spent the entire day riding the perimeter of the Crazy H Ranch and evaluating her life so far.

She'd always felt she had a handle on her goals and priorities. She loved working the ranch, spending her days under the blue Colorado sky. And she looked forward to the day when her father might consider her alongside her four brothers as the next person to run the Crazy H. Professionally, she was doing fine. But when she moved on to an evaluation of her personal life, she came up short, realizing that she didn't have a life outside the boundaries of the Crazy H.

Georgie wandered over to the gift table and pretended to study the brightly wrapped packages. Everyone had come to the party, relatives, friends of the family, people she hadn't seen in years. But though they'd all come to celebrate her big day, not one of the party guests really knew who she was—not deep down, beneath the confident and competent facade she let the world see. To them she was good old Georgie Hewitt, smart, sassy, the kind of gal who could outride and outrope any man in the county.

A lump of emotion tightened her throat and she scolded herself inwardly for giving in to her feelings.

But the realization was almost too much to bear. Not one person at the party knew her, that was true. But what was even more true was that she didn't really know herself. She was thirty years old and she was still living the same life she'd lived at twenty.

Georgie sighed softly. Exhausted and saddle sore, all she really needed was a long, hot bath and a soft bed. Just the thing to drive away the last traces of birthday self-pity. She listened to the band for a short time, then strolled over to the huge buffet set up along one wall of the barn. Her mother and two aunts stood behind the table, helping to dish up barbecue from huge aluminum pans and potato salad from brimming bowls.

"Happy birthday!" they all shouted in unison when they saw her.

Delores Hewitt leaned over the table and gave her daughter a kiss on the cheek. "You may want to run a comb through your hair, Georgiana. And maybe put on a clean pair of jeans." She licked her thumb, then wiped a smudge off Georgie's cheek, the same way she'd done since Georgie was a little girl. "You look like you just got off your horse."

"I did, Mom. I've been working all day." She forced a smile. "The food looks great."

Though she knew mothers and daughters were supposed to share an unusual bond, she'd never really been able to figure out what her mother wanted from her. Throughout her childhood, Georgie had been allowed to run wild, dressing in her brothers' hand-me-downs, taking any dare or bet they offered, riding with fearless abandon.

She'd always thought her mother accepted her choices, until she was old enough to notice the strained smiles and the thinly veiled disapproval. For some reason, when she'd turned thirteen, she'd been expected to stop doing all the things she found fun—riding, roping, wrestling with her brothers—and become a young lady. But the whole "lady" thing had never taken with her.

As she worked her way around the barn, she greeted more guests, refused invitations to dance, and grabbed a bottle of beer. When she reached the barn door, she slipped through the narrow opening, making an escape into the crisp December night. She found her father nearby, sitting on a hay bale, smoking a cigarette. She handed him the beer.

"Mom would have your head if she saw you with that," Georgie warned.

"I'm down to three a day," Ed Hewitt replied. "Next month I cut down to two a day. Let me enjoy my vices while I can."

Georgie plopped down next to him. "I rode the north fence line today all the way to the river. It's in good shape. I can't figure out where those strays from Marshall's herd got through. I also repaired the windmill on the corner section."

Her father chuckled. "It's your birthday, little girl. Can you stop talking about ranching for just a few hours and enjoy yourself?"

Georgie sighed. "I'm not so little anymore, Dad. I'm thirty years old. Not exactly a birthday I planned to celebrate."

"Thirty years old?" Her father frowned.

"You were there," Georgie said. "Don't you remember?"

Her father nodded. "Right. I was." He stood up and snuffed out his cigarette, then pulled her to her feet. "We'd better get back inside. I'm sure there are all sorts of folks who want to dance with my girl."

"But you get the first dance," she said, hugging his arm.

As Georgie took a whirl on the dance floor, she scanned the crowd. The guests had thrown themselves full tilt into the festivities, the barn warming to the point where most of them had thrown off jackets and sweaters. There weren't many chances to socialize in ranch country, so a barn dance, even in December, was a rare treat.

When the song ended, she started off the dance floor with her father, but a stranger stopped her and asked her for the next dance. "My name is Jim Lang," he said, tipping his cowboy hat. "I'm a friend of your brother, Ben. He thought you might like to dance."

Reluctantly, Georgie agreed to one more dance and he swept her into a country waltz. "So, Jim, what do you do?"

"I own the feed store over in Lamar," he said. He looked down at her. "I make a good living. I've got my own house. Three bedrooms, two baths."

"That's nice," Georgie said, puzzled by the direction of his conversation.

"You'd like Lamar. It's a nice little town. Did anyone ever tell you that you're real cute?"

Georgie continued to dance, trying hard to seem interested in the price of feed and the real estate market in Lamar. She was almost relieved when she and Jim started off the dance floor. Until another man came up to her and invited her to join him.

This time, the guy was a friend of Jace's named Roy Benedict, who worked as a salesman for an implement manufacturer. During their dance, he talked about his hunting cabin west of Pueblo and his last vacation to San Diego. He also complimented her on her appearance, telling her that she had the bluest eyes he'd ever seen.

Georgie wasn't sure whether the compliments were sincere or whether she looked so horrible they felt compelled to make her feel better. Loy Maxwell, the guy who made Will's saddle, told her she had great legs and Kevin Deinow, an old college buddy of Seth's who practiced law in Rocky Ford, mentioned that he'd always been partial to blondes.

By the time she'd worked through a two-step, a line dance and another waltz, she was ready to call it a night. She slipped outside and started toward the house, until she noticed her brothers gathered in a group, engaged in a heated debate. As she approached, she assumed that they were discussing the trouble they were having with Wade Marshall and the water rights that they'd been promised by his grandfather before he died. Marshall had been the only topic of conversation to cause such anger. But that's not what they were talking about.

"She's gotta like Loy," Will said. "He's really into horses and he makes a good living with his saddle shop. He's exactly George's type. Kind of shy and quiet."

"Hell, he's a wimp. George eats guys like that for breakfast," Ben said. "Jim Lang is the kind of guy who can talk a little sense into her. He'd be a steadying hand."

Jace shook his head. "Roy Benedict could get her off this ranch. He's got the kind of job where he travels a lot. He could show George the world."

"You're all wrong," Seth said. "Kevin is a professional. He's got the best future and he does a lot of water rights work. He could help us with our lawsuit against Wade Marshall."

Georgie gasped. Her temper flared and she strode up to the group, her hands hitched on her waist. "I can't believe this! This isn't a birthday party at all. It's a chance for you four idiots to parade me in front of the county's eligible stallions like some prize filly. Do you think I'm so pathetic that I need your help to find a man?" Tears pushed at the corners of her eyes and when one dribbled onto her cheek, Georgie brushed it away angrily. She'd never let her brothers see her cry and she wasn't going to start now.

"Hey, come on, George, it's not like that," Ben said. "We only wanted to make the party fun for you."

"By humiliating me? Did you tell them to shower me with compliments, too?"

"No one humiliated you," Seth said. "And no one at the party knows anything about our plan."

"Those four men do," she said. "And you do. And now, so do I." Georgie turned on her heel and started toward the stable. She'd fought so hard to gain her brothers' respect, trying to prove that she was as capable of running the Crazy H as they were. But this only proved to her that she would never be one of the boys. All they wanted was for her to get married and get out of their hair.

"Hey, Georgie, come on. Come back to the party. We promise we won't do any more matchmaking."

"You can all go to hell!" she shouted.

When she got to the stable, she quickly saddled Jess, tossed her bedroll over his back, then hopped on. Her backside still ached from a day in the saddle, but she didn't care. She wanted to get as far away from the barn and her brothers and their damn bachelors as she could.

A FULL MOON SHONE overhead as Wade Marshall rode through the night. His warm breath clouded in the crisp night air. Though he could have kicked his horse into a slow gallop, he wasn't in any hurry to get back to the ranch house. He'd been riding fence line all day, trying to find the break that had allowed a dozen of his cattle to wander onto Hewitt land.

He wouldn't have been so anxious to find the problem if it had been any other rancher in the county. A few stray cattle and a broken fence line were common occurrences. But considering his rather antagonistic relationship with the Hewitts, he didn't want to give them any excuse to complain.

The fight began the day he'd moved in, nearly three years ago. He'd inherited Lone Rock Ranch from his grandfather. He'd also inherited a dispute over water rights. According to the Hewitts, Jeb Marshall had promised them access to the water in Kettle Creek, which wound along the south edge of Marshall properties. The rights were held by Lone Rock, but with an agreement between the two ranches, the Hewitts could divert a share of the water for their cattle in that section.

But in his last days, Jeb Marshall had never mentioned a word about the Hewitts or water rights, nor had he put anything down on paper, something that Wade found troubling for a man who kept meticulous journals on every facet of life at Lone Rock. Jeb had been fighting with the Hewitts for as long as Wade had been coming to the ranch, nearly twenty-five years. Why would he suddenly change his mind?

Even if they had made a gentleman's agreement, Wade knew it probably wouldn't stand up in court. The last few years of Jeb's life had been peppered with crazy opinions, forgotten responsibilities and unexplained decisions. Wade had suspected the early signs of Alzheimer's and when Jeb had succumbed to a heart attack, he'd almost been relieved that his vibrant and sharp-witted grandfather wouldn't have to suffer.

It probably wouldn't kill him to come to some type of accommodation with the Hewitts. But he knew the financial value of the rights he held and the Hewitts insisted that the water rights be granted for free, as promised. Why should he give away for free what he'd be better off leasing? So he'd ignored calls from the Hewitts' lawyers and stalled them until he could figure out what he really wanted to do.

Wade drew his horse to a stop and stared out into the darkness. He loved Lone Rock. He'd spent every summer on the ranch when he was a kid, learning everything his grandfather was willing to teach him. Though his parents had preferred city life in Denver, Wade had always yearned for the endless vistas and wide open sky of east central Colorado.

His parents had forced him to go to college and had been proud when he'd started work as a stockbroker in New York. But he had put in eighteen-hour days for ten years, socking away a small fortune, for one reason only—so he could one day turn Lone Rock into the most successful cattle ranch in Lincoln county.

For Wade, this was the perfect life—the only true freedom a man could have on earth. He stared up at the sky, awash with stars and alive with moonlight, then turned Charlie toward the Rock River. He'd follow the river until he got to the south fence line, then follow that back to the ranch house. But as he looked across the river, he noticed a small campfire burning on the opposite side, just beneath a cottonwood grove.

He sat in the dark and wondered if he ought to go check it out. Though it wasn't unheard of to camp out on the range, December nights could get downright frigid. He gave Charlie a gentle kick and guided him across the shallows of the river. When he got within twenty yards, he shouted. "Hey! Are you all right?" The figure sitting next to the fire didn't move, so Wade slid off his horse, grabbed the reins and slowly approached. When he reached the fire, he squatted down and only then, realized that the person was a woman. "Are you all right?"

She jumped as if startled by his voice, then scrambled back from the fire, knocking her cowboy hat off in the process. A wild mane of hair tumbled from beneath, falling around a startlingly delicate face. At first, Wade wondered if this was all a mirage, some strange vision caused by the wind and the cold. But she was real and she was quite possibly the most beautiful woman he'd ever seen.

"It's all right," he said. He held out his hand to calm her, like he would a skittish colt. "I just saw your fire and I wanted to check it out. What are you doing out here on a night like this?"

"I'm trying to be alone," she muttered, brushing her hair out of her eyes. "I was doing pretty well until you showed up. What do you want?"

"My name is Wade Marshall," he said.

She stared at him, then retrieved her hat and pulled the brim down over her eyes. "I know who you are."

"But I don't know who you are," Wade said.

"Georgiana Hewitt," she said. "Ed Hewitt's daughter."

Wade sucked in a sharp breath. So this was Georgie Hewitt. He'd heard that the Hewitt boys had a sister, but he'd just assumed that she lived somewhere other than the ranch. He'd also assumed she was some burly, broad-shouldered woman who closely resembled her brothers. "Can I share your fire for a few minutes?" he asked.

He took her shrug as invitation rather than indifference. Wade sat down beside her, upwind from the smoke, then held his hands out to the warmth. "It's a cold night to be camping out."

Georgie turned to him and upon closer view, Wade could see her tear-streaked face and red-rimmed eyes. "You can share my fire if you can manage to keep

your mouth shut.'' She drew her knees up to her chin
and wrapped her arms around her legs.

''No problem.''

A long silence grew between them, broken only
when a ragged sob slipped from her throat. A few
seconds later, her saw her shoulders shake, and then
she dissolved into tears, pressing her face into her
knees.

''Hey, hey,'' Wade murmured, moving closer.
''What's wrong?''

''Nothing,'' she said. ''I—I'm not crying.''

''You are crying.'' Hell, Wade had never been good
with overly emotional women. And once they started
weeping there was usually no stopping them. He
reached out and gently patted her shoulder. ''It's all
right. You'll be all right.''

''No, I won't,'' she said in a ragged voice. ''I—I'm
thirty.''

Wade chuckled softly. ''That's what you're crying
about? Because you're thirty? Well, I'm thirty-four.
You don't see me blubbering about that, do you?''

''I'm not blubbering,'' she snapped, her tears instantly forgotten, replaced by indignation. ''You're a
man. It's not the same for you. Everyone thinks because I'm thirty and I'm not married that there's something wrong with me. Hell, I think there's something
wrong with me.''

Wade reached over and took off her hat, then placed
it on her lap. ''Let me look at you.''

Georgiana sniffled, then brushed her hair back with
her gloved hand. ''I look like hell,'' she murmured.

Wade reached out and tipped her chin until her features were fully illuminated by the fire, allowing his fingertips to linger for a long moment on her face. He'd been right the first time. Even through the grime and the tears, he found a face of absolute perfection, each feature in perfect balance with the others. "Wow," he murmured.

"That bad?"

"No," Wade said. "There's definitely nothing wrong with you. You're pretty. Beautiful. Hasn't anyone ever told you that?"

She bit her lower lip to keep it from trembling, then she smiled hesitantly. "Just about everyone I've met tonight. But you're the first person I believe." She frowned. "At least I know my brothers didn't send you out here."

"Do you want to tell me what sent *you* out here on a night like this? It can't be simply because you're thirty."

"It's my birthday. Today. Or maybe it's yesterday now. My brothers threw me a huge birthday party and they invited all these single men so that I could find myself a husband. I guess they don't want to be saddled with a spinster." She cursed softly. "I don't know why I have to get married. None of my brothers are married and no one is pushing them toward the altar."

"You don't want to get married?" Wade asked. He reached into his pocket and pulled out a folded bandanna, then held it out to her.

"No!" She paused and blew her nose. "Well, maybe. But that's not the point."

"What is the point?"

"I have goals in life. Someday, I want to run the Crazy H. But my father is never going to turn the business over to me. He and my mother don't think of me as an equal to my brothers. And my brothers, well, they just think I'm good old George." She drew a ragged breath and straightened her spine. "I know everything about the ranch. I can rope cattle and fix a windmill and break a horse as good as any man."

"I don't think that's really your problem," Wade said.

"What do you know about my problems?"

"If you really wanted your own spread, you could make it happen. So what's really bothering you?"

She sighed, then cursed beneath her breath. "I don't know. I feel like I'm paddling against the current. My—my life is flying by and I'm not even living it. I—I'm stuck in a rut and I'm getting older by the minute and I'm afraid I'm going to be in the same place when I turn forty." She sent him a sideways glance, as if embarrassed by her revelation. "I shouldn't even be talking to you. On the Crazy H, we consider you the enemy."

"Do you think I'm the enemy?" he murmured, staring into her eyes.

She met his gaze for a long moment. "I think you're probably being nice to me for your own reasons. Your grandfather did promise us water rights. We had a gentleman's agreement with him."

"Well, maybe I'm not a gentleman."

She refolded his bandanna and handed it back to him. "Oh, I don't know about that."

Wade glanced around her campsite. "Did you bring any food out here, Miss Hewitt?"

"Georgie," she said. "And no, I didn't. I left as fast as I could."

"I've got some stuff in my pack. You hungry?"

"I'm starved. Do you have coffee?"

"No, but I have some whiskey." He reached inside his jacket and handed her a small flask. "That should warm you up."

Georgie unscrewed the top, then took a long swig, wincing as she swallowed. "Good."

"It'll put hair on your chest," Wade teased.

She laughed softly. "That will probably seal my fate as a spinster then. But it might make me one of the boys."

Wade smiled. Who was this woman sitting next to the campfire, dressed in her rugged clothes and cowboy hat, her face grimy and her hair tangled and her beauty so disarming it took his breath away? He'd met the Hewitt brothers, a sour-tempered group if he'd ever known one. But Georgie wasn't anything like those four.

She was wild and untamed, and completely real. This wasn't a woman who frantically searched for her lipstick the moment a man walked in the room. Her clothes were worn, her hair unkempt, her face dirty, but she didn't care about appearances. Hell, she'd just opened her heart to a complete stranger without hesitation. That kind of honesty was something rare.

He returned to the fire with his pack. Inside, he found a can of beef stew, a can of SpaghettiOs and his thermos, half-filled with chili left over from his lunch. "What'll it be?"

Georgie pointed to the beef stew. Wade took out his Swiss army knife and opened the can, then set it at the edge of the fire. When he sat down again beside Georgie, he stretched his legs out and sighed softly. She handed him the flask and he took a swallow, then gave it back to her. "Are you planning to spend the whole night out here?"

"I could. I've done it before." She sighed and shook her head. "I'll head back after I'm positive the party is over."

"Isn't your family going to wonder where you are?"

"I come out here a lot. I like being alone. And they know I can take care of myself."

"I believe you can," Wade said.

Georgie pulled her tattered wool blanket up around her shoulders. "I *know* I can."

They both stared at the fire, watching the flames dance in the darkness. The flask of whiskey went fast, the liquor warming his blood and making Georgie sleepy. As they talked about inconsequential things, she leaned closer and rested her head on his shoulder. "I'm glad you're here," she said. "You're not such a bad guy."

Pleased by her compliment, Wade slipped his arm around her shoulders. "No, Georgie Hewitt, I'm not."

She stared up at him, her gaze drowsy, her lips parted. He wasn't sure what possessed him, but whatever it was, the temptation was far too great to deny. He bent nearer and touched his lips to hers, allowing his tongue to gently probe, surprised when she opened beneath the tender assault.

He deepened the kiss, craving the taste of her, so sweet and exotic. Her hands slipped beneath his jacket and her fingers splayed across his chest. He'd lived a pretty solitary life for the past three years. He'd been working so hard, he hadn't had time to think about the lack of female companionship. But the moment she put her hands on him, a flood of desire raced through his body.

He finally forced himself to draw away, knowing that he'd soon reach a point where a full-scale seduction was the only option. Georgie sighed, a tiny smile curling the corners of her mouth. "What was that?" she asked.

"A birthday kiss?"

Her grin grew wider as she wrapped her arms around his neck. She reached up and brushed his hat from his head, then pulled him closer. "They say good things come in small packages. But I don't believe that applies to birthday kisses."

This time, Wade didn't think about the consequences of kissing Georgie Hewitt. She certainly wasn't thinking of the consequences. Like her, he simply allowed himself to enjoy the soft warmth of their lips meeting, the sweet taste of whiskey they shared, and the heat of two bodies in the December night.

He'd kissed a lot of women in his life, but he'd never remembered it feeling quite so good. Maybe it was the cold air that sharpened his senses, or the darkness just beyond the light from the fire that made it seem as if they were the only two in the world.

She kissed him passionately, lacking in all inhibition, the way he imagined she lived. Wade slowly pushed her back onto her bedroll, covering her body with his. Though they both wore so many layers of clothes, it didn't matter. Wade knew there was a beautiful body beneath the canvas jacket and the thick wool sweater and the faded jeans. A feminine form, strong yet wonderfully soft.

He felt like a teenager getting his first real taste of a woman. He was almost afraid to touch her, afraid to hope that she might offer him more. For now, kissing her was enough. And he did that until she fell asleep, wrapped in his arms and her old wool blanket.

As they lay under the night sky, curled together to keep warm, Wade stared up at the stars, wondering what twist of fate had brought them both to the same spot on such a cold night. Whatever it was, he wasn't going to fight it. He enjoyed the feel of a woman in his arms, even if her family considered him the enemy.

CHAPTER TWO

"SO WHAT DO YOU have planned for today, George?" Seth asked.

Georgie looked up from her lunch of ham and scalloped potatoes. She shrugged, trying to appear completely indifferent. "I've got to grease the windmill in section twelve. I'm going to ride out there and see to it."

"I'll come with you and give you a hand," Will offered.

Since the debacle at her birthday party, her brothers had been trying hard to mend fences. "No!" Georgie glanced back and forth between her brothers. "No, I'd rather do it on my own."

Jace groaned. "Aw, come on, George. You can't still be mad at us because of that birthday party. That was almost a week ago. And we've been apologizing until the cows come home."

"I'll forgive you when I'm ready to forgive you," she said.

"Well, at least let us take you out tonight. We're going to the Happy Boot after dinner. Maybe shoot a little pool with the guys, have a few drinks. Come with us."

Georgie paused. They rarely asked her to join them.

And when they did, it was always to get ice cream or go shopping, never to visit the local watering hole. "All right." She tossed her napkin beside her plate, then stood up. "I'll be back before sunset."

She grabbed her jacket and her hat and headed out of the house. Her horse waited near the stable, already saddled from the morning's work. Georgie jumped on and turned Jess to the north, toward the river…toward Lone Rock Ranch…toward Wade Marshall.

With a sharp kick, she set Jess off at a gallop, the cold wind stinging her face and making it hard to catch her breath. That morning after her birthday party, she'd woken up beside the river alone. At first, Georgie had wondered whether she'd dreamed the whole thing. But then she noticed the fire, stacked with fresh wood and the two extra blankets carefully tucked in around her.

They'd met every day since that night. At first, they'd pretended that the meetings were sheer coincidence. But then they began to make plans, setting a time and place. Sometimes, they'd sit down and talk. Sometimes all they did was kiss. And other times, they'd simply ride. But from the moment they parted until they met the next day, Georgie could think of nothing but Wade Marshall.

She suspected that all the sneaking around added to the excitement. But she wasn't about to tell her family about her little trysts. The brothers thought they knew what was good for her, but they were wrong. Even if they paraded every bachelor in Colorado in front of her, she wouldn't find a single man as fascinating as Wade Marshall.

There hadn't been many men in Georgie's life. In high school, she'd dated a friend of Seth's. During college, she'd made up for her lack of social life with a long string of young men. But once she'd returned to the ranch, the dating pool had pretty much dried up. She had a brief affair with a rodeo rider she'd met on a trip to Colorado Springs and another failed relationship with a ranch hand who had worked on the ranch the previous summer. But overall, she'd been caught in a very long drought.

As she rode over the rolling plains, Georgie couldn't help but wonder where this whole thing was going. They'd become more and more intimate with each other, yet neither one of them had asked that question, nor offered an answer. But it didn't matter. Right now, all she cared about was the present, the excitement of meeting him every day, of falling into his arms and kissing him, of giving way to overwhelming desire. She felt as if she were finally living her life and she wasn't going to question her good fortune.

She spurred Jess on, over a small rise. When she got to the top, she saw him riding toward her, his horse at a full gallop. Georgie slipped off her horse and stood beside Jess, the reins clutched in her fist. He dragged Charlie to a stop just a few feet away from her, then jumped down.

A moment later, she was in his arms, kissing him as if they'd been apart for twenty-four days rather than twenty-four hours. Wade pushed her hat off her head, then threw his gloves on the ground. His fingers furrowed through her hair as he molded her mouth to his. "Mmm, you taste good," he murmured, his lips hot on hers, his tongue delving deep. "I've been thinking about you all morning."

She shoved his jacket aside until her fingers reached the warmth beneath. Then she worked at the buttons of his canvas shirt, pressing a kiss into the spot below his collarbone. "You know, sooner or later, it's going to be too cold to meet out here. We've had a warm December, but January is coming. There'll be snow and—"

"We need to come up with another plan," Wade murmured, tipping his head back. "Maybe I should just show up at your door tonight and take you out."

"No, don't do that. We'll think of something else. There's a little camp shack about a mile from here. We could always meet there."

He drew back and looked down into her eyes. "We could meet in town."

Georgie shook her head. "My brothers would find out. They know everyone in Reynolds and everyone in Reynolds knows about your feud." She sighed. "They're taking me out to the Happy Boot tonight. I think they're trying to make up for that mess at my birthday party."

Wade wrapped his arms around her and pressed his lips to her temple. "I don't like the idea of you going out alone."

"I'll be with four men." She stepped back, then laughed. "Are you jealous?"

"No," he said. "Well, maybe. I just don't like to think that there will be fifty guys out there who are going to spend a whole evening with you in a warm bar, while I get a few hours in a freezing field."

"I kind of like the field," Georgie teased. "It's much more exciting. A little dangerous."

"And damn cold," Wade said. "So why don't we go out, Georgie? I'll call you up and ask you on a date and pick you up at the door. What could they say? You're an adult. You can make your own choices."

Georgie pulled out of his embrace and walked back to Jess. "I suppose they make my life completely miserable," she said as she fiddled with a strap on her saddle. "They could call me irresponsible. And they could refuse to give me a shot at running the Crazy H. And that's all I've ever really wanted."

Wade came up behind her and slipped his arms around her waist, pulling her body against his. "You wanted a life, remember? You can't say this hasn't been exciting."

Georgie stiffened at the words he seemed to throw back at her. What was she doing here? This was a dangerous game she was playing, risking her future—and her heart. True, Wade Marshall had brought excitement back into her mundane existence, but at what price?

"I should go," she murmured. She bent down and grabbed her hat, then pulled it on "I have to get back."

"But you just got here," Wade said.

"I just need some time alone—to think." She hooked her foot in the stirrup and pulled herself up on Jess's back. Then she looked down at Wade. "I'll see you."

"When?" Wade asked.

Georgie shrugged. "I don't know." She kicked

Jess's flanks and the horse took off, flying across the
rolling landscape. When she reached the top of the
rise, she drew Jess to a stop, then turned around. But
Wade was no longer standing below. He'd ridden off
in the opposite direction, just disappearing over another rise.

She pressed her palm to her heart, hoping to subdue
the ache that grew there. This whole thing with Wade
had been a mistake from the start. She'd been hurt and
angry and he'd offered her comfort. But now he'd
made his demands clear—he wanted more. And allowing herself to fall in love with him would be a huge
mistake. It was better to walk away now, before she
got hurt, than to continue in a hopelessly futile
relationship.

"That's it. I'm done with men. From now on,
you're the only man I wrap my legs around, Jess."

WADE OPENED THE DOOR of the Dinner Bell Café, the
only restaurant in the tiny town of Reynolds, population six hundred. The town served the surrounding
ranches in Lincoln County by providing a grocery
store, post office, gas station, restaurant and three taverns. It had once been on the railroad line, but now
the tracks were rusted and paved over and the town
worn away by time.

Though Wade usually ate supper with his ranch
hands, every now and then he craved variety. What he
really craved was Thai food or Szechwan or Indian,
the kind of food he used to eat in New York, instead
of the meat and potatoes usually served at Lone Rock.

The Dinner Bell offered variety—and a passable Cajun-fried catfish.

Tonight, the café was quiet, with only a few diners lingering in the booths along the wall. He sat down at the end of the counter and studied a menu. But the sound of soft laughter drew his attention to a booth on the far end of the restaurant—a laugh he'd know in a crowd of thousands.

"Georgie," he murmured.

It had been nearly a week since they'd seen each other. Every day, he'd ridden the fence line that adjoined Hewitt property, hoping to run into her, but every day he'd gone back to the ranch house disappointed. He'd considered calling her. Hell, he'd even considered driving over to the Crazy H and knocking on the door. But she'd made her feelings pretty clear. Their little affair, however passionate, was now over.

Wade had always known women to be a fickle sex, but he'd never imagined Georgie Hewitt would display such a tendency. Still, he couldn't ignore the fact that she was dining with a date. He picked up his menu and moved down the counter until he was only a few feet away from her. Her back was to the door, so she couldn't see him, but Wade had a perfect view of the man she was with.

Wade knew almost everyone in Reynolds and this guy didn't register. He looked like city folk, dressed in a tidy sport jacket and khaki pants. Of course, Georgie hadn't bothered to put on airs. She wore faded jeans, a heavy wool sweater and scuffed cowboy boots.

He was close enough to eavesdrop, so Wade pretended to study the menu as he listened to the conversation. Georgie's date was trying hard to impress her with his knowledge of horseflesh and his sense of humor, but he could hear the boredom in her responses. Her laughter was forced and her contributions to the conversation less than enthusiastic.

Wade was just about to go over to the booth and say hello when she excused herself to go to the ladies' room. Never one to pass up an opportunity, he waited a few seconds, then wandered to the rear of the café. He stood outside the bathroom in a small hallway, well out of sight of the rest of the restaurant patrons. When the door opened, Wade caught Georgie around the waist and kissed her.

She cried out in surprise, but then, when she saw who he was, she smiled and kissed him back. "What are you doing here?"

"I'm here to save you from that bozo you're dining with," he said.

She wriggled out of his arms. "Andrew is my date. I met him at the Happy Boot last week."

"You got back on that horse pretty darn quick," Wade teased. "Have you forgotten me already?"

She gave him a sideways glance. "You're hard to forget. I just thought it might be good to date someone a little more…"

"Short? Bald? Paunchy?"

"Appropriate. Andrew is very nice. He's a veterinarian in Pueblo and he loves horses. And he isn't feuding with my family."

"He should love horses. He's resembles the back

end of one. All he does is talk about himself and stare at your chest.''

"How do you know that?''

"I've been watching him, and listening to him, for the past ten minutes.''

Georgie sighed, then glanced down at her breasts. "He does seem to have a particular fascination with my bosom.''

"I can sympathize,'' Wade muttered. "It's a very nice bosom.''

She shook her head. "And he can't stop talking about himself. Honestly, if I could figure out a way to get him to take me home early, I would. I'm getting a headache listening to him.''

Wade grabbed her by the shoulders and turned her around, pushing her back toward the dining area. "Go back to your table and wait for me.''

"You can't—''

"Don't worry, I won't embarrass you.''

Wade waited until she'd found her place, then slipped out the back door of the restaurant. A minute later, he walked through the front door and strode directly to her table.

"Miss Georgie?''

She looked up at him, her eyes wide, her expression uneasy. "Yes?''

"Sorry to interrupt your date, but your daddy sent me. He said I'm supposed to bring you back to the ranch. Your favorite mare is about to foal. He said you'd want to be there.''

Wade reached out and grabbed her hand, pulling her out of the booth and to her feet. He quickly helped her into her jacket, allowing his fingers to linger on her shoulders for a long moment. "Sorry about this, buddy, but it's her favorite mare." Georgie turned and made a quick excuse to Andrew, then hurried out of the restaurant with Wade.

When they reached the sidewalk, Wade pulled her out of view of the front windows and pressed her back against the brick wall of the building. He braced his hands on either side of her head and kissed her long and hard, tasting her as if she were food to a starving man. Then he pressed his forehead against hers. "That was pretty easy," he said.

"I can't believe we did that! What if he drives out to the ranch to help out. He *is* a vet."

"Come on," Wade said, grabbing her hand again. "My truck is parked down the street. We've got the rest of the night, we can at least have some fun. I hear there's a band over at the Spur and Saddle. Why don't we go get a few drinks and kick up our heels."

They headed toward the pickup. Wade pulled open her door and helped her inside, then ran around the front and got in. Their breath clouded in the cold night air as they stared at each other for a long moment. Wade tossed his hat into the back seat, then Georgie threw herself into his arms and kissed him.

He groaned and pushed her back until they both lay across the front seat of his truck. Stretched out beside her, he slowly began to tug at layers of clothes until he found a spot of bare skin below her collarbone. He pressed his lips to the spot. "I've missed you," he murmured.

Georgie smiled. "I've missed you too."

"I've missed this." He slipped his hand beneath her sweater and then her T-shirt, finding the soft swell of her breast. "Being close to you, touching you, listening to your voice."

She arched against him, sighing softly as he began to tease her nipple with his thumb. "I rode out yesterday afternoon to find you, but you weren't in our regular spot."

"I've been watching for you, too." He pushed her sweater up and nuzzled her belly. "This is crazy."

"Mmm. But it's a lot warmer in your truck than it was out on the range."

Wade drew back. "That's not what I meant."

Her fingers furrowed through his hair and she pulled him close until she could kiss him again. "I know what you mean. But we have a whole night together. Let's just have some fun and forget about everything else."

Wade nodded. She was right. They had precious little time to spend together as it was. Why spoil it with long-winded discussions about the future of their relationship? Hell, he should just accept things the way they were and be happy with that.

He sat up and started the truck. Georgie sat beside him, running her hands through her mussed hair and trying to restore order to her clothes. Maybe he was trying to make things more complicated than they really were. Hell, he'd spent most of his adult life trying to avoid love and commitment. Why go looking for it now?

He steered the car toward the north end of town. Reynolds had three taverns, or more appropriately, roadhouses. The Happy Boot was a favorite among the ranch hands who played pool. For music and dancing, the Spur and Saddle was the first choice. And the Lucky Ace was the place that cowboys went to lose their paychecks in a game of poker or bar dice, or to pick a fistfight. Not the kind of spot to take a beautiful woman.

As he pulled the truck into the lot of the Spur and Saddle, he heard Georgie draw in a sharp breath. ''What is it?''

''We can't go in,'' she said.

''Why not?''

''That truck. That belongs to my brother Seth. He's probably inside with the rest of the boys.''

Wade's jaw twitched and he tried like hell to hold his temper. He was damn sick and tired of sneaking around like some schoolboy. He was thirty-four years old! This kind of behavior was for kids. ''So what?''

''I—I just can't. Not now.'' She opened the door and hopped out of the truck. ''I'll get a ride home with my brothers.''

''Dammit, Georgie, get back in here.'' Wade slid across the seat and jumped out after her, slamming the door behind him. He caught up to her halfway to the entrance, then grabbed her waist and picked her up off her feet. ''We are going to talk about this. I'm not going to let you walk away again.''

''Put me down!''

''Not until you tell me that we can fix this,'' Wade insisted. He carried her back to the truck and set her down, then trapped her against the passenger door with his arms.

"You want to know how to fix this?" she asked. Her eyes were ablaze with anger and she brushed her hair back with a soft curse. "This is very easy to fix. You want me, then you can give my daddy the water rights your grandfather promised him. Once you do that, you're going to be the finest neighbor in all of Lincoln County. My parents and my brothers won't be able to find enough nice things to say about you. And when you come calling, they'll just open up that front door and show you in." She drew a ragged breath. "That's what's standing between us, Wade."

He stepped back. Suddenly, everything became crystal clear. "That's what this has been about? The water rights? Who put you up to this? Was it your brothers or your father?"

"You think I—" Georgie balled her fingers into a fist, then punched him squarely in the stomach. "You can just go to hell, Wade Marshall. If that's what you really think I'm capable of, then you don't know me at all."

This time, Wade let her go. She ran across the parking lot and disappeared inside the Spur and Saddle as the effect of her punch wore off. He rubbed his belly, his anger dissolving. She'd answered that accusation with brutal honesty. "That girl has a mean right jab," he muttered as he circled the pickup. "You gotta love a woman like that."

He chuckled softly, and climbed back inside the truck. Though a betting man might think things were over between him and Georgie Hewitt, Wade knew that they'd just begun. A woman didn't get that angry over a man she didn't have feelings for. "I think she might just love me,'' he murmured as he turned the key.

And for the first time in his life, he didn't wince at the possibility.

"So, SWEETHEART, how was your date last night?''

Georgie looked up from setting the table. Her mother held a bowl of mashed potatoes in her hands, smiling hopefully. Though Delores Hewitt had given up her dreams of having a daughter she could dress in crinolines and lace, she hadn't given up her desire for grandchildren—the more the better. "It was fine. We had a nice time."

"Yeah, right,'' Ben said. "Then why did you show up at the Spur and Saddle an hour after your date started?''

She turned and gave her brother a withering glare. "Like I said, we had a nice time. He's very interesting.''

Jace shook his head. "You're thirty years old, Georgie. It's time you settled down and had a family.''

"And what about you guys? Ben, you're thirty-seven. Where's your wife and children? None of you are any closer to tying the knot than I am, and I'm the youngest in the family. Don't talk to me about settling down.''

"Men can wait longer than women,'' Ben said. "We don't have one of them—what do ya call it—biological clocks.''

Georgie slammed the rest of the silverware on the table, then returned to the cupboard for napkins. "Well, maybe I don't want to settle down. Maybe I have higher aspirations than looking after some man and a bunch of screaming kids." She drew a shaky breath, ready to admit what she'd kept a secret for so long. "Maybe I want to run the ranch after Dad retires."

Ben and Jace stared at her for a long time, as if she'd just told them she wanted to become an astronaut and go to Mars. Jace was the first one to laugh. "You want to run the ranch? Georgie, you're a girl."

"I'm a woman. I'm thirty years old and I have just as much right to run the ranch as you do. Besides, I know this ranch inside and out *and* I've been doing the books for Mom for the last four years. So don't you dare tell me I'm not qualified."

"What about Andrew?" Will asked. "Now that you're dating him, what if you decide to get married? He lives over an hour away. How are you going to run the ranch from—"

"What do you care about Andrew?"

Will shrugged. "Don't be so quick to toss him aside. He mentioned he was looking for a permanent relationship, marriage and a family and he'd make a fine hus—"

Georgie gasped, unable to believe what she was hearing. A permanent relationship? Marriage and a family? "You did it again, didn't you? You took me to the Happy Boot that night to meet another one of your friends. You just sat there while I introduced him as if you didn't even know him." She tossed the pile of paper napkins at his face, then headed for the door.

"Where are you going?" her mother asked.

"For a ride," she said as she yanked on her jacket and grabbed her hat.

"It's freezing out, Georgiana. And it's going to snow. You are not taking Jess out at this time of night."

Frustrated, Georgie grabbed the keys to her father's pickup. "Don't wait up for me."

The weather had turned since she'd come in from feeding the horses. Snowflakes swirled in the frigid wind and settled in soft mounds on the porch railings. Georgie ran out of the house and jumped into the truck, then sped out the long gravel drive. At first, she wasn't sure where she was going. She considered heading all the way to Colorado Springs to see a movie. Or maybe she'd just head into Reynolds for a beer at the Happy Boot. Or maybe...

Georgie knew the turnoff for the Marshall ranch, but she missed it the first time in the dark. When she realized she'd gone too far, she turned around and slowly retraced her tracks. She found the dirt road marked by a weather-beaten sign. The house was about a quarter mile off the main road, the lights blazing in the snowy night.

She shut off the truck, but stayed inside, her fingers gripped around the steering wheel. The ranch house was a rough affair, the wide porch sheltering a low building. A yard light illuminated the approach, casting the house and outbuildings into stark relief.

She slowly stepped out of the truck and walked toward the house. "What am I doing here?" Georgie climbed the steps, then stopped. For the first time since she'd driven off, she wondered if this was really where she wanted to be. Her feelings for Wade were becoming more and more complicated. She felt as if he were pulling her in, so strongly that she'd never be able to escape.

The porch light flashed on and Georgie's breath caught. She spun on her heel and ran for her truck, slipping and sliding in the snow. But the front door opened before she even got halfway there. "Georgie?"

She stopped short, then cursed softly. "Yeah?" Turning around, she pasted a smile on her face.

Wade stood in the doorway, dressed only in jeans, his chest and feet bare. He crossed his arms over his chest to ward off the cold. "What are you doing out here?"

"Nothing. I shouldn't have come. Go back inside."

"No," he said. "Come on in. It's cold."

Georgie reluctantly accepted his invitation and stepped inside his house, her fears replaced by curiosity. To her surprise, the interior of the house was a startling contrast to the outside. A huge stone fireplace dominated one end of the living room, the chimney rising up through the hewn-timber construction. The furniture was heavy and expensive and very masculine, with lots of dark colors and leather. Everything was perfectly accessorized. "Very nice."

"I had the help of a decorator who did my co-op in New York. I just moved everything here after I inherited the ranch. It fit pretty well." He grabbed her hand and pulled her toward a blazing fire. "Do you want a drink?"

Georgie nodded and watched him move to a pretty

wood cabinet filled with bottles and glasses. He sloshed some whiskey into two tumblers, then carried them over and handed her one. ''Drink,'' he said. ''You look like you're freezing.''

''I am a little cold.''

''So, tell me what brings you over here. Running away from home?''

Georgie gulped down the whiskey, grateful for the warmth that spread through her body and the nice little buzz it gave her. ''I hate my brothers,'' she muttered.

''And why is that?''

''Remember that man I was with at the Dinner Bell? Andrew? He was another one of their setups. Here, I thought I was actually meeting a man all on my own, only to find out they'd arranged it all. Like I'm some pathetic spinster who can't find a man without a road map.''

''You found me,'' Wade said.

''Actually, you found me,'' she corrected.

''Yeah, but you could have sent me away from your campfire. Instead, you invited me over, and the rest is history.''

Georgie gave him a reluctant smile. ''That's not the way I remember it, but it sounds better than the way it really was.'' She drew a deep breath. ''You know, I should just run off with one of those men they found for me and get married. Just to show them what their meddling can do.'' She grabbed his tumbler from his fingers and downed his share of whiskey, then coughed softly. ''More?''

''Don't you think you might be overreacting?'' Wade asked as he retrieved the bottle.

"No! It would serve them right."

She dumped a good measure of whiskey into her glass and took a big gulp, her nerves starting to numb and her anger abating with every swallow. The fire danced in front of her and she stared at it, wondering at the flush of heat that warmed her cheeks. Was it the whiskey or the fire? Or was it the fact that Wade had pulled her against his body and now twisted his fingers through her hair?

"If I really wanted to make them pay, I could marry you," she muttered. "We could drive over to the Judge Warren's place in Reynolds and get married right now."

"Well, we probably could," Wade said with a chuckle.

She looked up at him with wide eyes. "Then let's do it. Right now. You and me." She scrambled to her feet, knocking her glass over, dumping the rest of it on the oriental carpet.

Wade slowly rose. "Georgie, I think maybe you've had a little too much to drink."

"I'm not drunk. I'm angry. And I'm sick and tired of them trying to run my life. What's wrong? Don't you want to marry me?"

"We've only known each other for a few weeks."

"Haven't you ever heard of love at first sight?" she asked. "Or maybe you don't love me at all. Maybe my brothers were right. I'm just going to end up an old spinster sister, living on the ranch for the rest of my life until I die all alone, never knowing the love of a good man." Tears sprang to the corners of her eyes and dribbled down her cheeks. "I am a spinster.

I'm thirty years old and I'll never get married. I won't have a man, I won't have the ranch, I'll just have my horse and a clock that's all wound down.''

''A clock?''

''Yeah, my biological clock.''

He chuckled, then wiped a tear from her cheek. ''All right, I'll marry you. Just stop crying.''

''You will? You'll marry me?'' Georgie threw her arms around his neck and gave him a fierce hug. ''Let's do it then. Let's go get married right now.''

CHAPTER THREE

HE'D BEEN AWAKE since sunrise, but Wade didn't have any intention of crawling out of bed for chores. He turned his face into Georgie's tousled hair and drew a deep breath, letting the scent of her shampoo fill his head. How many nights had he lain in this exact spot, staring at the ceiling and wondering what it would feel like to have Georgie lying next to him, curled up against his body?

Last night had been the strangest night of his life. From the moment she showed up at his door until her impulsive marriage proposal, he felt as if he'd stepped onto some crazy carnival ride. Wade had never been a very spontaneous person, but with Georgie, he'd learned to enjoy the unexpected. She seemed to live life at full tilt, wearing her every emotion on the outside and letting her heart rather than her head make her decisions.

Wade pressed a kiss to her temple and sighed. Mr. and Mrs. Wade Marshall. It had taken him almost an hour to talk her out of her crazy idea. But that didn't mean he wasn't intrigued by the possibility. Hell, if they had gone to the judge to marry them last night, they certainly wouldn't have spent the night together in bed, fully clothed.

Of all the women he'd dated, he'd never met one who he'd consider marrying. Forever was a long time and he couldn't imagine a woman who could keep him interested that long—except maybe Georgie. She had qualities that he found undeniably attractive. She was honest and enthusiastic, sexy and spontaneous. She was stubborn, yet tender, tough but vulnerable. And to his eyes, she was the most beautiful woman he'd ever met.

But he wasn't ready for marriage any more than she was. They'd only known each other a few weeks. That didn't mean they couldn't embark on a passionate affair, though. Women were in short supply in Colorado cattle country and it would be nice not to have to drive a hundred miles for good sex. Hell, great sex. With Georgie it would have to be great.

Wade touched his lips to hers and she stirred slightly, then opened her eyes. For a moment, she looked at him as if she didn't know him. Then her gaze became more lucid and she slowly drew back. "Morning."

"Good morning."

"Am—am I in your bed?" she asked, a frown furrowing her brow.

Wade nodded.

She released a tightly held breath. "My head feels like it's going to explode."

"Too much whiskey."

Georgie slowly sat up, then brushed her hair out of her eyes. "I'm still wearing my clothes, so we must not have—"

"Nope. Not much of a wedding night."

She groaned softly, then buried her face in her hands. "Oh, God. I was hoping I'd dreamed that. I asked you to marry me, didn't I."

"You did."

"I'm sorry. I really didn't mean to. You have to understand it was the liquor talking. We barely know each other. Not that you wouldn't make a great husband. Just not a great husband for me." She rolled her eyes. "No one would make a great husband for me. I'd make a horrible wife. I can't do anything that wives are supposed to do."

Wade shrugged. "Even if we would have found someone to marry us last night, it never would have been legal. No marriage license."

"Right." She rubbed her forehead. "So, we can just forget I ever said it?"

"It's forgotten," Wade said. "At least, the marriage proposal is. Not everything else that happened before that."

"There was something else?"

"You did spend the night here. And we have been meeting secretly for a while now. And you have to admit, as hard as we've both tried, we can't seem to keep our hands off each other."

She glanced over at him and graced him with a tiny smile. "All right. Maybe we should tell my family. It might be nice to go out on a real date."

Wade grinned and drew Georgie into his embrace. "And I guess I could think about talking to your daddy's lawyer about those water rights. We've got to be able to come to some compromise."

Georgie rolled over on top of him and kissed him,

taking time to linger over his mouth, drawing her tongue along his bottom lip. But Wade wasn't satisfied to leave it at that. He wove his fingers through her hair and returned her kiss, a warm flood of desire pulsing through his body.

"This is something new," he murmured. "I'm not freezing my butt off on frozen ground or twisting myself up into knots in the front seat of my pickup truck."

"It is nice to be warm."

"Maybe we should forget about your parents," Wade murmured, kissing the curve of her neck. "We could spend the whole day in my bed getting warmer."

Georgie braced her hands on either side of his head. "That sounds like fun," she said.

But even though Wade was tempted to slowly undress Georgie and make love to her, he wanted to clear things up with her family first—before she changed her mind again. She'd opened a door for him and he wasn't going to waste any time stepping through it. After that, they'd have days, weeks, maybe even months to enjoy each other.

GEORGIE STEERED the truck onto the long gravel road that led up to the ranch house. Her stomach lurched with each bump, the effects of her hangover mixing with a bad case of nerves. Maybe she should have stayed in bed with Wade. She could have eased into the day with a bland breakfast and a short nap, followed by some serious kissing.

But she was as anxious as Wade was to set things

straight with her family. Now that Wade had decided
to go through with the deal on their water rights, how
could they possibly object to their friendship? She
could imagine it now, her father shaking Wade's hand,
her brothers clapping him on the back. And her
mother, happy at last that Georgie had a man in her
life.

As she pulled the truck to a stop, she glanced in the
rearview mirror to find Wade following close behind
in his own pickup. A strange car was parked in front
of the house. This was not news she wanted to give
in front of guests. She fought the urge to go back to
Wade's house and come back another time.

"Stay calm," she said to herself. "Everything will
turn out just fine. All will be forgiven and Wade will
be welcomed into the family." Georgie crawled out
of the truck and joined Wade at the bottom of the
kitchen steps. She sent him a wavering smile, then
nodded. "Ready?"

"Are you?"

She nodded, then reached out and opened the
kitchen door, dragging Wade in behind her. But the
scene in front of her caused her to stop short. Her
mother sat at the table, her eyes moist with tears. Her
father sat beside her with his arm around her shoulders, softly consoling her. And her brothers gathered
in a small huddle near the kitchen sink, their expres-
sions grim. The only person she didn't recognize was
the handsome man sitting opposite her parents. He
wore jeans and a denim jacket and looked like every
other rancher in Lincoln County—except maybe a bit
more attractive than most.

Georgie ground her teeth. Her brothers just wouldn't give up! "Good morning, everyone." She turned to the stranger and held out her hand. "I'm Georgiana Hewitt. And you must be the bachelor of the day." She glanced at her brothers. "You're starting a little early, don't you think?"

They all stared at her, speechless, then turned their attention to Wade. She'd spent nights away from home before, but now it was quite obvious where she had slept. She slipped her arm around Wade's, steeling her resolve. "I suppose you want an explanation why I didn't come home last night." She laughed, but the sound was forced. "Wade and I have been seeing each other for some time now. And I really don't care what you have to say, but I'm going to see him again. Whenever I want." She looked at the stranger. "I guess that means you can leave now."

Ben stepped forward. "What the hell are you talking about, Georgie?"

She blinked. "Wade and I. We're…an item."

"Oh, my God." Georgie's mother covered her mouth with her hand and sobbed.

"You and Wade Marshall?" Jace asked, his words dripping with disdain.

"Hey, I'm an adult. And I can choose the men in my life, without your help." She sent the stranger a pointed glare. "And if I want to see Wade Marshall I don't need to ask your permission." She drew a deep breath, ready to play her ace. "Besides, there won't be a feud now that—"

"Georgie, stop," Ben said. "This is really not a

good time. Maybe you'd better ask Wade to leave while we talk as a family.''

"No," she said, gripping his arm more tightly. "I want him to stay."

"Dammit, Georgie, this is a family matter," her father shouted.

She jumped, unused to hearing her father raise his voice. Suddenly, she regretted her heedless rush to introduce Wade to her family. She'd expected a negative reaction, but not this kind of hostility.

Wade turned to her. "I'll wait outside." As if to prove his place in her life, he tipped her chin up and kissed her, a sweet lingering kiss that set her pulse to racing and caused her brothers to take a threatening step forward. Wade looked at each of them in turn, then walked out.

After he'd closed the door behind him, Georgie moved over to the table and pulled out a chair. "I know this is a big shock, but once you hear what I have to—"

"Georgie, this is Dylan Garrett," her father began. "He's come here to see you."

She frowned. "I thought I made my feelings clear about this matchmaking. I don't need—"

Her father reached out and grabbed her hand, squeezing it so hard that her fingers ached. "Mr. Garrett is a private investigator from San Antonio, Texas. He owns a company called Finders Keepers. And— and he's been looking for you." Her father swallowed hard and she saw tears moisten his eyes. "I—I'm not sure how to tell you this, Georgie. I guess your mother and I always thought we'd find the right time. But the right time never came."

A sick feeling grew in the pit of her stomach. "Are you all right?" She looked over at her brothers, but they avoided her gaze. "Are you sick? Did someone die? What's wrong?"

"I can't," her mother said, fresh tears spilling from her eyes. She shoved her chair back and ran from the room.

Ed Hewitt cleared his throat, then continued, though Georgie could see that the effort was costing him dearly. "After Will was born, the doctors told your mother she couldn't have any more children. Your mother wanted a girl so badly that we decided to look into adopting. We found a beautiful little girl. She was two years old when we adopted her."

Georgie's heart froze and for a long time, she forgot to breathe. Her first impulse was to ask what had happened to the little girl, but she already knew. "No," she said.

Ben stepped up to the table and placed his hand on her shoulder. "It was so long ago, George. We all just forgot how you came to live with us."

"No. I don't believe you," she said, her words desperate with denial. "This is all some cruel joke to pay me back for bringing Wade here. Well, it's a nasty joke. It's not funny!"

"It isn't a joke, Miss Hewitt," Dylan said. "Your biological father and your two sisters have been looking for you."

Georgie shook her head. "No. You must be looking for someone else. There must be a mistake. I mean,

I…'' Her voice faded as she glanced between her father and her brothers. She'd noticed the differences before. Everyone in the family had dark hair and brown eyes, yet she'd been fair-haired and blue-eyed. Her mother had always claimed she looked like her grandmother, a woman Georgie had never met. But now…

Dylan Garrett stood and she saw sympathy in his eyes. "I know what an intrusion this must be, Miss Hewitt, but bringing this type of news is never easy. If you'd like time to consider all of this, we'd be happy to come back another time."

"We?" Georgie asked.

Ben grabbed her hand and wouldn't let go. "Georgie, your father is here. Your biological father. He's waiting in the dining room with your sisters. They came here to see you."

"No," she said, yanking her arm away. "I don't want to see them. They're not my family. I don't want to see them."

"You have to," Ben said. "They came a long way." He took her hands and gently drew her toward the dining room door. "Come on."

"Please don't make me do this," she said, her eyes filling with tears. "This isn't true."

But the moment she stepped into the dining room, all of Georgie's doubts dissolved. The two women, who slowly stood as she entered, looked startlingly familiar. Their eyes, their mouths, every feature reminded her of the woman she saw in the mirror every morning. The older man looked uneasy, as if he weren't ready to deal with the raw emotion that seemed to permeate the room.

Dylan Garrett stepped between them. "Georgiana Hewitt, this is Brad Henderson and his daughters, Gabriella and Beth."

Henderson nodded and gave her a weak smile. "I'm sorry if we've upset you. And I know this news is very difficult to take. But in time, I hope you can accept—"

"Why?" Georgie murmured.

Henderson blinked. "Why?"

"Why did you give me up? That's all I need to know. Just tell me that and then you can leave."

His expression softened. "That's a very long story and probably best left for another time. It's enough to say that I never meant for you or your sisters to be separated. I didn't give you up. You were taken from me."

Georgie looked at the two young women who watched her expectantly. "I remember, once, I was supposed to bring a photo of myself to school, a photo from when I was a baby. And Mom couldn't give me one. She said the camera had broken right before I was born and they didn't have money to get a new one." Georgie pressed her palm to her forehead. "But there were pictures of all my brothers during that time. I don't know why I never made the connection."

Gabriella stepped forward. She reached into her purse and withdrew a photo of three little girls, pale-haired and pretty. "This is you," she said, pointing to the middle child, a girl of about two years old. "I'm the oldest. And Beth was just a baby when this was

taken.'' She pressed the photo into Georgie's hand.
''You can keep it. We didn't mean to barge into your
life, but we've been desperate to find you. We've had
Mr. Garrett looking for you and when he finally located you, we just had to come.''

''I know it's a lot to take in,'' Beth added. ''Both
of us have been through it. But we both knew we were
adopted, so the news wasn't quite so devastating.''

Georgie shook her head. ''Am—am I supposed to
just smile and accept this? Where's your proof?''

Brad Henderson cleared his throat. ''You have a
little strawberry birthmark just above your right elbow,
don't you?''

Her breath caught in her throat and her mind spun
wildly. For a moment, Georgie was sure she was going
to be sick.

''We had to come, to make sure it was really you.''
Gabriella handed Georgie a business card. ''That's my
number in San Antonio. When you're ready, you can
call. I've also written our father's number down and
Beth's. Or you can call Mr. Garrett at Finders Keepers
and he'll answer any of your questions...when you're
ready.''

She gave Georgie's hand a squeeze, before the three
of them said a hasty goodbye. As they headed toward
the front door, Georgie watched them numbly. She
knew she ought to stop them from leaving, but she
couldn't seem to speak. Why was this happening to
her—today of all days? For God's sake, she thought
she'd been stepping into disaster when she brought
Wade home. She was so determined to start living her

own life. And now that life had been turned upside down in a matter of minutes.

She spun and hurried back into the kitchen, where her father and brothers waited expectantly. "I have to go. I have to get out of here."

Ben grabbed her hand. "Georgie, you need to stay and talk to Mom. She's very upset."

"No! Don't you tell me what to do. Don't any of you tell me what to do ever again." She looked around the room at each one of her brothers. No, not her brothers. Her—an idea suddenly occurred to her, one so startling it caused her heart to ache and her stomach to twist. "That's why," she said softly. "That's why you refused to consider my interest in running the ranch. It's a family ranch and I'm not really family, am I."

Emotion overwhelmed her, but she wouldn't allow herself to cry in front of them. She grabbed the door and yanked it open, then ran outside. She headed for the truck, but changed her mind and turned toward the horse barn.

"Georgie!" Wade's voice echoed in the crisp morning air.

"Leave me alone," she shouted. "Just go home."

When she reached Jess's stall, she didn't bother with a saddle. She pulled the bridle over his ears and settled the bit in his mouth, then slowly backed him out of the stall. She led him over to a bale of hay, then stepped up on it and threw her leg over his back. The moment she got to the yard, she kicked his flanks and he bolted, taking off over the frozen ground.

Shouts from Wade and her brothers were drowned

out by the sound of Jess's hooves. Georgie's temples throbbed from the clamor in her head and the wind whistling past her ears was the only thing that could silence it. She'd ride until she could make sense of it all—even if she had to ride all the way to the Pacific and back.

"WHAT THE HELL did you say to her?" Wade shouted.

Georgie's brothers all stood on the back porch, watching her ride off to the north. None of them made a move to follow her. "None of your damn business," Ben said.

"What the hell are you still doing here?" Jace asked.

"I was waiting for Georgie. Tell me what you said to her. So help me, if you said anything to hurt her, I'll tie up those water rights so tight you'll never get a drop from me."

"This is family business," Ben said. "So it's none of your business." He turned and walked back into the house. Jace followed him along with Seth.

But Will stayed on the porch, still staring at Georgie as she rode toward the rise. "Is it true you and Georgie have been seeing each other?"

Wade shrugged. "Yeah."

"Do you love her?"

Wade didn't even have to think about an answer. It came automatically. "Yeah." He paused, then reconsidered. "I don't know. Maybe. I care about her and I don't like to see her hurt."

"Does she love you?"

"She asked me to marry her last night."

Will's eyebrows shot up in surprise. "Then you'd better go after her. She's not going to listen to any of us right now. And she needs someone she trusts."

Will held out his hand and Wade took it, shaking it firmly. "Thanks." His thoughts immediately turned to Georgie. He knew where she'd gone, or at least he suspected. But the only way to get there was on horseback.

He made it back to his house in just minutes, roaring down the road toward the ranch house and skidding to a stop in front of the horse barn. A few minutes later, he had Charlie saddled with two wool bedrolls strapped to the back.

A wicked wind roared out of the north, stinging Wade's face as he rode. He steered Charlie toward the river, praying he'd find Georgie in the same spot where they'd met. He saw her horse before he saw her. Jess stood near the river, nuzzling the snowy ground. Georgie sat huddled beneath an old cotton-wood, the branches clattering in the winter wind. Wade slipped off Charlie, grabbed a bedroll, and slowly walked toward her. "Georgie?"

"Go away."

Wade could see she was cold. The wind whipped at her hair and her whole body trembled along with her voice. He slipped his arm around her shoulders and pulled her against him. Gently, he rubbed her back. "We have to go back in. You're going to freeze out here."

"I—I don't care."

"Well, I do. I guess you're my girlfriend now and

I don't want to have to take care of you when you get sick.''

Georgie looked up at him, her eyes rimmed in red. A tiny smile touched the corners of her mouth. "I'm freezing."

He untied the bedroll and wrapped a blanket around Georgie, pulling it tight around her ears. "Why don't we go back to my place? You can have a nice hot bath and a cup of tea and you can tell me all your troubles—or our troubles."

"Th-That sounds pretty good," she murmured, a fresh round of tears coursing down her cheeks.

Wade grabbed a rope from his saddle and tied one end to Jess's bridle and the other to his saddle horn. Then he helped Georgie up onto Charlie's back and settled in behind her, her body pressed against his. He urged his horse into a slow walk and they started back to the ranch house.

She sobbed softly the entire way back to the house. Pulling her more tightly against him, he whispered soothing words in her ear. The protective instinct he felt surprised him and he contemplated all the things he could say or do to make her forget her hurt feelings. When Georgie hurt, he felt it just as acutely. Wasn't that all a part of loving someone?

When they got inside, he helped her out of her jacket, then drew her along with him to the bathroom. She followed him numbly, as if her emotions had completely exhausted her. As he filled the whirlpool tub, Georgie sat on the edge staring into the water. Wade looked around for something to add to the bath, but bubbles or bath salts weren't part of his beauty regimen. Instead, he grabbed a bottle of liquid soap from the sink and squirted a fair amount into the swirling water.

"Why don't you get undressed? I'll go get you some tea." He smoothed his hand over her cheek, then tipped her gaze up to meet his. "Go ahead. You'll feel a lot better."

THE WHIRLPOOL TUB was too tempting to resist. In truth, Georgie could have moved into Wade's bathroom and lived the rest of her life there. Compared to the rough surroundings of the ranch, the bathroom was like an oasis, the kind of thing she'd only seen in magazines, and the perfect place to forget who and what she was.

She quickly shrugged out of her jacket, then stripped off her clothes. Hesitantly, she stepped into the hot water, then sighed softly as she sank beneath the bubbles. A push of a button activated the jets and they hissed softly. Tipping her head back against the edge of the tub, Georgie closed her eyes. For the first time since she'd walked out of the Hewitt house, she was able to calm her mind and overcome the chaos of her thoughts.

Her world had changed forever, and no matter how much she wanted to go back in time, to forget everything she'd learned, it wasn't possible. She wasn't really Georgiana Hewitt but someone entirely different. If she wasn't having an identity crisis before this, she certainly was on the road to a major crisis now. The only comfort she could take was that she felt safe here, at Lone Rock. She knew who she was—she was the woman Wade Marshall loved to kiss and touch, the woman who could make him laugh and drive him to distraction. For now, that's all she really needed to be.

When he returned from the kitchen, Georgie was so relaxed she didn't want to move. He set the mug of tea on the edge of the tub and she smiled, but didn't open her eyes. "Thanks."

"Are you warmer now?"

She looked up at him, only to watch as his gaze drifted down her body, from her shoulders to the soft swell just above her breasts. A tiny shiver of desire raced through her as Georgie realized that the tub was made for two. An image of them together, two naked bodies amidst the bubbles, flashed in her mind. "This is heaven," she said.

"So I take it your family reacted badly to our news?"

She glanced away, focusing on her fingertips as she swirled the bubbles. "Not at all. They had big news of their own to share." She reached up and traced an imaginary headline in the air. "Georgiana Hewitt Is Not A Hewitt At All."

He blinked in surprise. "What?"

"I'm adopted," she murmured. "I'm not really a Hewitt but a—a Henderson."

"You told them you and I spent the night together and they came back with 'you're adopted'? Jeez, Georgie, how cruel is that?"

"That's not the way it was. My birth father and two sisters showed up at the ranch shortly before we got there. They were waiting in the dining room. They wanted to meet me."

Wade squatted down beside the tub and placed his hands on the edge. "I'm so sorry."

She shrugged, trying to appear nonchalant. "Don't be. It explains a lot. It's just so strange. This morning I thought I knew who I was. Or at least, I was making an effort at finding out. And then everything changed. I was two years old when my—when the Hewitts adopted me. I've been racking my brain trying to remember the time before that, but I can't. The very first thing I can remember is a red cowboy hat I got for my fourth birthday. Why can't I remember my real family?"

"What are you going to do?" Wade asked.

"I'm not going home, that's for sure. I just can't face them right now. My mother can't look at me without crying, my father doesn't know what to say to me and my brothers keep trying to make excuses." She turned to him. "Can I stay with you tonight?"

Wade reached out and smoothed his hand over her damp cheek. "Sure."

Grateful, she leaned over the edge of the tub and brushed her mouth against his. But Wade wasn't satisfied with just a brief kiss. Before she could draw away again, he wove his fingers through the damp hair at her nape and pulled her closer.

She lost herself in the taste and warmth of his kiss. Every worry slipped from her head and she focused on the wild sensations that raced through her body. Need pulsed through her veins, and rather than pull Wade into the tub with her, she slowly rose, drawing him up with her.

She stepped out of the tub and stood before him,

naked, aching for the touch of his hands on her body. He stared at her for a long moment, then began a gentle exploration—first her shoulders, then her arms, then her waist and hips. She deepened their kiss, an unspoken invitation for him to take more.

Georgie had never thought much about her body, especially in a sexual sense. If all her limbs were in working order and her jeans fit without binding, she was happy. But now, she wondered whether her hips were too narrow or her breasts too small. Would a figure that she considered unremarkable be attractive to Wade?

He slipped his arm around her waist, then slowly moved up to cup her breast in his palm. When he drew his thumb across her nipple, she shuddered as a wave of sensation washed over her.

"You're beautiful," he murmured, his mouth hot on her neck.

"My brothers tell me I'm too skinny. They used to say I looked like a boy."

"You definitely don't look like a boy," Wade said with a soft chuckle. "You look like a woman. A sexy, desirable woman."

Georgie felt a blush warm her cheeks. She met his gaze and gathered her resolve. She knew what she wanted and it would be silly to pretend that she didn't. "Make me feel like a woman," she murmured.

"I like that," Wade said. "No coy games." He reached down and grabbed her waist then gently lifted her up, settling her legs around his waist. Then he slowly walked into his bedroom.

Georgie's heart slammed in her chest as he lowered

her onto his bed. It had been so long since she'd been with a man and then, it had been just a fling. She wanted to believe that what was happening between her and Wade was more. But if it wasn't, she was determined to enjoy every moment regardless.

She watched as he quickly shrugged out of his shirt, then kicked off his boots and socks. Her breath caught when he unzipped his jeans and slid them down over his hips and legs. But when he stripped off his boxers and kicked them aside, she stopped breathing altogether.

His body reflected the work he did, wide shoulders and a muscular chest, arms sculpted by hard labor, long legs toned by hours in the saddle. His body also betrayed his desire, his shaft hard and ready. Wade stepped to the bed, then slowly stretched his body out alongside hers. Skin met skin and a shiver raced through Georgie's body.

Though she'd been with men before, she felt nervous and unschooled, almost frightened by the undeniable need coursing through her. But the moment she ran her hands over his chest, she realized the power of her touch. Wade groaned softly, closing his eyes and drawing her nearer. Emboldened, Georgie let her hand drift further, to his belly and then to his smooth shaft.

The instant she touched him, he sucked in a sharp breath. But she wasn't about to stop. She rolled on top of him and straddled his hips, then bent down to kiss him. Her wet hair created a curtain around them as she slowly teased at his lips with her tongue. When she drew away, he arched against her, his erection pressing into the moist spot between her legs.

With a low growl, Wade grabbed her waist and flipped her beneath him. Then he reached over to the bedside table and grabbed a condom from the drawer. He held it out to her. "Take care of this, would you?"

Georgie hadn't wanted to think about protection; her mind was occupied with more sensual matters. But she was glad that Wade was still thinking clearly. With trembling hands, she tore the package open and slowly sheathed him.

As he slipped inside her, Georgie let out a tightly held breath, allowing the sensation of their meeting to sweep the troubles from her mind. Nothing existed beyond the two of them, beyond the whirl of sensation that rocked her body as he moved inside her. She'd never wanted a man the way she wanted Wade Marshall—and now she had him.

For now, that was enough.

CHAPTER FOUR

THEY SPENT the rest of the morning and the early afternoon in bed, making love, dozing, talking quietly as they lay next to each other. Wade had never been one to linger after lovemaking, but he couldn't seem to get enough of Georgie. Just touching her, running his hands over her silken skin, and listening to her voice seemed to provide endless fascination.

He'd initially thought of her as uncomplicated and honest, but the more he got to know her, the more he realized there were many facets of Georgie Hewitt's personality that he hadn't even discovered. The one thing he had learned was that beneath that tough and competent exterior, Georgie was vulnerable and uncertain. Her family's revelation had shaken her world and she wasn't sure how to deal with it.

"We should get up," Georgie murmured.

Wade chuckled softly. "I suppose we have to eat sometime."

"I have to go."

"Now?" He groaned and drew her closer. "Why don't you wait until tomorrow morning? Spend the night with me and you can deal with your family tomorrow."

She met his gaze, her expression serious. "Not

home. I have to go to San Antonio. I have to find out why this happened. The man—my father, my *real* father—said that I'd been taken from him. I need to get all the facts straight before I talk to my parents—my *adopted* parents.''

Wade frowned. "Why San Antonio?"

She crawled out of bed and padded to the bathroom. He watched her, admiring the slender beauty of her body, the perfect breasts, the narrow waist, the long legs. A few moments later, she returned, clutching a slender billfold and a business card in her hand. He held up the bedcovers and she snuggled back into her spot against his body.

"My sister gave me this. Dylan Garrett owns Finders Keepers. It's a detective agency in San Antonio. He's the one who found me. He knows everything about the case.''

"How are you going to get there?"

She pulled a credit card out of the billfold. "I have this, although I've never used it. And I have money in the bank. Since I turned eighteen, I got a split of the profits of the ranch every year, and I've put it all in my checking account. I have almost fifty thousand dollars saved for a rainy day. I guess this would qualify. I don't even have to think about it. I just have to figure out how to get a plane ticket and go.''

Wade cursed inwardly. He wasn't about to let her walk out of his life. Not before he knew how he really felt about her—and how she felt about him. "Don't worry about that," he interrupted. "I can call and make a plane reservation for us and we'll need a hotel.''

She shook her head. "Not we. Me. I have to do this on my own."

Wade reached out and idly smoothed his hand over her shoulder. His mind wandered back a few hours, to the sweet feel of her body beneath his, to the wonderful sensation of moving inside her. As he'd made love to her, he'd imagined that they might have found something together. But now, he had to wonder at how easily she could put it behind her.

In just moments, a distance had seemed to open up between them, a gap that felt as if it were growing with each word they spoke. Georgie had a new and different life waiting for her. Was she about to walk out of his and never return? Every instinct warned him to harden himself against such a possibility. If he didn't allow himself to feel anything for her, then he wouldn't miss her when she was gone.

He'd always been so indifferent when it came to relationships with women. They'd had their place in his life, but never a permanent one. But from the instant he'd met Georgie, he thought she might be something special. He could ask her to stay, but what was he ready to offer her? Promises of happily-ever-after had never been part of his game plan.

"Even if you want to do this alone, we're friends, and friends help each other out."

She glanced up from the business card. "Are we friends?"

He bent closer and kissed her gently. "Of course we are." But friendship wasn't what Wade really wanted. Hell, he could make friends anytime. Friends were a dime a dozen. He wanted more. But just how much, he wasn't sure.

Georgie smiled tentatively, apprehension filling her expression. "I need to know who I am and where I belong. I feel like I've been living someone else's life. I'm not Georgie Hewitt. I'm Georgiana Henderson."

"The name may have changed, but you're the same person you were this morning when we woke up in each other's arms."

She sat up and pulled the sheets up around her naked body. "I don't feel like the same person. I never used to be afraid of anything, but now everything scares me. I feel...lost. I can't go back to the Hewitts' and yet I don't have anywhere else to go." She gave him an odd look. "Maybe we met that night out near the river for a reason. Did you ever think that it might have been fate?"

"I'm sure it was," Wade replied. "Two weeks ago, we didn't even know each other. And now we're..."

"Friends," Georgie said. A faint blush colored her cheeks. "Actually, I did know you. When I was about thirteen years old, I was out riding along that north fence line and I saw you. You must have been about seventeen and I thought you were the most handsome boy I'd ever seen. I had such a crush."

"Really?" Wade said.

"I even wrote your name all over my geography notebook. I was sure that I was going to marry you. And when I heard you were coming back here to take over your grandfather's ranch, I had this strange fantasy that maybe I'd see you again and we'd fall in love. But then you stirred up all that trouble with my family." She drew a shaky breath. "So much for fantasies."

Wade reached out and took her face between his hands, then kissed her gently. He tried to memorize the way she tasted, knowing he'd crave her kisses once he was without her. The thought of letting her go caused an ache in his heart. But he knew that he could never force her to stay. Georgie Hewitt was like the wind, blowing in and out of his life at will. And no matter how hard he tried to hold on to her, she'd always slip through his fingers.

"Maybe I should see about that plane ticket," he said. "You might be able to get a flight out tonight. And I can drive you to the airport."

Her expression brightened. "I can call Dylan Garrett when I get there. Maybe he'd be able to see me tomorrow."

Wade nodded. He said a silent prayer that there would be a plane—any plane—headed from Colorado Springs to San Antonio. And that there would be a seat available for Georgie. If she spent another night in his bed, he wasn't sure he'd ever be able to let her go. "Why don't you get dressed and I'll make a few phone calls?"

But as he crawled out of bed, Georgie jumped up beside him and threw herself into his arms, hugging him fiercely. Wade held her tight, their naked bodies pressed together, his face buried in the curve of her neck.

"I don't know what I'd do without you." She drew away and looked up into his eyes. "I love you."

Wade felt his breath catch in his throat. The words

were so simple and honest, said out of impulse rather than carefully considered emotion. He wasn't even sure if she realized what she'd just said, or if she did, whether she was aware of the impact of her words. Unable to bury the instinct to reply, he answered her. "I love you, too, Georgie."

THE RESTAURANT overlooking San Antonio's River Walk was bustling with business during the lunch hour. Christmas decorations glittered from above the windows and a huge artificial Christmas tree stood in the entryway, draped with lights and ribbons. A soft Christmas tune from the restaurant's stereo system drifted through the hum of conversation. In all the chaos of the last few days, Georgie had almost forgotten the holiday.

If she was back on the Crazy H, the boys would be heading out to find a Christmas tree right about now. Her mother would start baking cookies soon and every night, when she returned for dinner, the entire house would smell of Christmas treats. And she'd be frantically flipping through mail order catalogs for last-minute gifts.

Christmas just wouldn't be the same this year. How could they possibly gather around the tree on Christmas Eve and act as though nothing had happened? She wasn't even sure where she'd be on Christmas Eve— at Wade's place, at the Crazy H, or maybe even in San Antonio with her new family?

She could always stay at Lone Rock. Wade had made that clear last night when they'd spoken on the phone. As for her parents, she hadn't bothered to call them yet. They probably suspected she was staying at Lone Rock. If they called there, Wade would explain where she'd gone. Besides, she was thirty years old. They didn't have to know her every move.

Georgie ignored the line at the hostess stand and went right to the front. She shrugged out of her new coat, then smoothed her hands over the skirt of her new dress.

After arriving without any luggage, Georgie had spent her first full day in San Antonio shopping for basic necessities. She couldn't meet with Dylan Garrett or see her sisters and father again wearing faded jeans and cowboy boots. After that, she'd placed a call to Finders Keepers, making an appointment with Dylan for the next day.

"Do you have a reservation?" the hostess asked.

"I—I'm meeting someone here. Actually, I'm a bit late. His name is Dylan Garrett. Has he—"

"Right this way," the hostess said.

She hurried after the hostess, weaving through tables and dodging waiters bearing trays of tempting food. Georgie had never spent much time in a city, with the exception of her college years in Fort Collins, but she found it almost comforting to lose herself in the crowds of people. No one knew her here and it was easy to pretend she was someone else. Someone with a life less confusing.

The hostess led Georgie to a table in a quiet corner of the restaurant. A man sat at the table, a cowboy hat resting on the table beside him. His attention was focused on the contents of a file folder he had spread out in front of him.

She hadn't taken much notice of Garrett that day at the ranch house, but now that she had a chance, she realized he was about as far from her image of private investigator as anyone could be. Where was his trench coat and the fedora pulled low over the eyes, the care-worn face and the cigarette dangling from his lips? Instead, she found an incredibly attractive man not much older than she was, with a rugged build and sun-streaked hair. "Mr. Garrett?"

He looked up, then quickly stood and held out his hand. "Miss Hewitt. It's good to see you again." He gazed at her for a long moment with arresting blue eyes and Georgie shifted uneasily. "You look like your sisters," he finally said. "The resemblance is quite amazing."

Georgie quickly shook his hand, then slipped into the chair he pulled out for her. The moment she sat down, she felt the need to make conversation. "I've never been to San Antonio before. It's a lovely city. The River Walk is wonderful." She reached out to grab her napkin and nearly knocked her water over, catching it just in time. A warm blush crept up her cheeks. "I'm sorry. I'm really nervous."

"I'm glad you decided to come," Dylan said.

"I didn't have much choice. I'm not quite sure where I belong right now. This was as good a place as any." She took a sip of water, then cleared her throat and spread her napkin on her lap. "You told me you could fill me in on everything that happened to me when I was a baby. I thought it would be easier to hear it all from you."

Dylan nodded. "I understand. But before we start,

I want you to know that I've handled a lot of these cases and if I can give you any advice, it would be to take things slowly. It's a lot to absorb all at once.''

"I'm ready to hear it all. I need to know everything.''

"All right,'' he said, fixing his gaze on her. "You were born to Air Force Major Brad Henderson and his wife, Lorraine Fletcher, thirty years ago in Silver Spring, Maryland. He was working at the Pentagon. Your mother was a housewife.''

Just that fact alone caused Georgie to blink in surprise. Maryland? She'd always thought of herself as a native of Colorado. In truth, she'd been born on the East Coast. What did that mean?

He pulled out a wedding photo of a handsome couple and placed it in front of her. "These are your parents.'' He laid another picture down, this of a smiling family, a husband and wife, a flaxen-haired toddler and an infant wrapped in a pretty baby blanket. "Your sister Gabriella was born two years before you and your mother was pregnant with your younger sister Beth when your father was convicted of espionage. The government had an open-and-shut case. He was sent to Leavenworth.''

Georgie gasped. "My father was in prison?''

"He worked for the Pentagon and had access to highly classified material, plans for a new fighter jet that they believed he had passed on to the Russians. He was falsely accused. He spent twenty-eight years in prison for a crime he didn't commit. The government recently learned that a man named Ronald Muir was responsible.''

"Is that why we were taken away from our mother?"

"You were with your mother until she died from complications after the birth of your sister Beth. Since your father was in prison at the time, he turned over guardianship to your mother's sister, Heather Cooper, who lived on Long Island in New York. We're still piecing together exactly what happened, but it appears that a Fletcher family trust fund that was intended for your care was diverted into Heather Cooper's bank account after she offered you all up for adoption."

"How did I get to Colorado?"

"Heather Cooper worked with a rather unscrupulous lawyer to break the trust. He was the one who arranged for your adoption and he took you all the way out to Colorado to cover his tracks. He died a few years ago, but his unsuspecting law partner let us access his records. The lawyer collected part of your trust for arranging the adoption with a nice fee from your adoptive parents."

"And my sisters?"

"Your sister Beth ended up in Victoria. Gabriella was placed with a woman Heather Cooper knew on Long Island in New York."

The waitress appeared at the table to take Georgie's drink order. She considered a double whiskey, straight-up to settle her nerves. "I'll have a club soda," she said. The waitress turned to Dylan and he ordered the same. "You said my father went to prison. When did he get out?"

"He was cleared of the charges and released on Thanksgiving Day."

Georgie closed her eyes and rubbed her temple with her fingertips. If she thought her own life was in crisis, she couldn't imagine what Brad Henderson had gone through for the past twenty-eight years, stuck in prison for a crime he didn't commit. ''I have so many questions. I don't know what to ask next. Didn't my father suspect we were missing?''

''He couldn't do anything from prison to find you. Then, right after Thanksgiving, your sister, Gabriella, came to me with a photo and a suspicion that Brad Henderson might be her real father. She'd seen him on the news after he'd been exonerated and recognized him. I contacted Major Henderson and Gabriella was indeed his daughter.''

''How can you be sure I'm the right person? I mean, my parents admit I was adopted, but how do you know my father was Brad Henderson and not some other man?''

''We're certain,'' Dylan said. ''Your father and sisters wouldn't have gone to Colorado if they weren't. I think seeing you reassured them. You have to admit, you look an awful lot like your sisters. And there is the birthmark. But a DNA test would be proof positive. I can help you arrange for that, if you'd like.''

The waitress returned with Georgie's drink and asked if they were ready to order, but Georgie shook her head. Her stomach was tied so tightly into knots she wasn't sure she'd be able to keep anything down. She sipped at the club soda and tried to focus.

Dylan pushed the file folder across the table. ''Everything is in there. My report, some more family photos from your childhood. And a couple of letters from your sisters. They suspected you might come to see me, so they faxed me a couple of messages. Your sister, Gabriella, lives here in San Antonio and I believe Beth is staying with her this week. Your father has been in and out of town on a pretty regular basis, so you might be able to see him as well."

"And what about this Heather Cooper? Has she been punished for what she's done?"

"It's been twenty-eight years and I'm not sure you'd find a court willing to prosecute her. From what I've been able to discover, life has not been kind to Heather Cooper. She squandered all the money she embezzled from your trust fund in pretty quick order. She had a drinking problem and she gambled away a lot of the money on a series of get-rich-quick schemes. She's living in a run-down apartment in the Bronx. Maybe that will have to be justice enough."

Georgie paused for a long moment, her gaze fixed on the file folder. Though she wanted to exact some revenge for what this woman had done to her all those years ago, she knew she couldn't focus on the past any longer. That was over and there was nothing she could do about it.

"You're right. This is a lot to take in all at once." She glanced around. Suddenly, the restaurant seemed to close in around her, the sound of chattering patrons hurting her ears and smell of food nauseating. "I need to go." She picked up the file folder and tucked it under her arm. "Thank you for everything you've done, Mr. Garrett."

He stood and shook her hand. "Good luck, Miss Hewitt."

''Henderson,'' Georgie said. ''My name is Georgiana Henderson.''

She turned and hurried out of the restaurant, her heart pounding, the sense of claustrophobia nearly choking her. When she got outside, she drew in a deep breath, the smell of the river thick in the air. She started off toward her hotel, then decided that she couldn't wait. She found the nearest park bench and sat down, opening the folder on her lap.

As she slowly read through Dylan Garrett's report and flipped through the copies of old photographs, Georgie couldn't help but feel a strange detachment. Though these people were her family, she couldn't seem to make a connection. They were strangers to her.

But then, she pushed aside a copy of a newspaper report on her father's trial to find a photograph of a beautiful young woman. Her breath caught in her throat as she stared at a face that looked hauntingly familiar. In the deep recesses of her mind, she recognized the face, and though Georgie knew the memory was probably false, she let it wash over her anyway.

This was her mother, the woman who had given birth to her, the woman who had nurtured her for the first two years of her life. Georgie traced a finger over the features of her mother's face, stunned at how many of those features resembled her own.

Tears swam in her eyes, tears brought on not by sorrow but by frustration. She'd never know this woman, never hear her voice or smell her perfume. They'd never be able to sit on a porch swing and share a glass of lemonade or bake cookies together in a cozy kitchen. She'd never be able to tell Georgie about life and love.

Georgie drew a ragged breath, an image of Delores Hewitt drifting through her mind. She shared all that with her adopted mother, and though she knew she ought to be grateful for those times, she still couldn't ignore the deep sense of betrayal she felt toward the Hewitts. Why hadn't they told her? Why had they continued to pretend all these years?

Closing the file folder, Georgie fixed her gaze on one of the pretty bridges that spanned the river. She'd have to come to terms with that betrayal sooner or later. The Hewitts had raised her and made her into the woman she was today. She owed them at least some gratitude for that. And she couldn't expect to live the rest of her life without seeing them again. Sooner or later, she'd have to face them with her questions.

They'd raised her to be a strong, independent woman. Her brothers had challenged her to be just as tough and stubborn as they were. But they'd also sheltered her from many of life's more difficult moments. She'd been living in a fairy-tale world on the ranch, where she never had to face anything more upsetting than an argument about her dirty jeans or her tangled hair.

But now that she'd stepped out of that world, Georgie knew that she really hadn't been living her life atall—at least not until the night of her birthday party. Her mind flashed an image of Wade Marshall and she closed her eyes and let the image focus.

She fought the urge to call him. It was so easy to

need him, so easy to…love him. The words she'd said
to him that morning in bed had been so carelessly
given and returned. But how did she really feel? Had
she mixed up love with need? He'd given her shelter
from the storm raging in her life and for that, she was
grateful. But once the storm subsided, would he still
be there? And would she still need him? Or would
they drift apart? Georgie reached up and touched her
lips with her fingertips, imagining the feel of his
mouth on hers, remembering the desire they'd shared.
Though it had only been days, it seemed like years
and years ago and a million miles away.

GEORGIE PULLED her feet up on the bed and reached
for the phone. She punched in Wade's number, then
leaned back into the pillow. He answered after three
rings and the sound of his voice instantly soothed her.

They talked of inconsequential things at first, the
weather, his ranch, what she'd had for dinner. "I met
with Dylan Garrett today," Georgie finally said. "It
wasn't too bad. I learned a lot about my adoption."
She paused. "But I still need to see my sisters. And
maybe my father. I'm not sure when I'm going to do
that. Or what I'm going to say."

"You could always come home for a while," Wade
suggested. "Your brother, Will, called today. I gave
him the number for your hotel. Your parents want to
talk to you."

"I can't talk to them yet. Not until I know what
happened. And I can't come home."

"I could come there," Wade suggested.

"No," Georgie replied. "I have to do this myself.

This is my life, not yours." She twisted her fingers through the phone cord, aching to tell him how much she loved him, how much she needed him. But in the end, she just sighed. "I'll call you again soon."

They said their goodbyes and Georgie gently replaced the phone in the cradle. It would be so easy to go home, to pretend nothing had happened. That's what her parents would no doubt want, for their lives to go back to the way they were. But there were too many questions that still needed to be answered.

She picked up the phone, determined to call Gabriella. She'd spent most of the afternoon figuring out what she wanted to say, writing everything out on hotel stationery. She'd grown up with four brothers, emulating them at every turn. What could she possibly have in common with sisters?

She imagined Gabriella as smart and sophisticated and confident. That was the first impression she'd created at the ranch house. She'd been dressed so perfectly and her hair and makeup looked as if she'd taken great care with it. Beth was just as pretty and probably good at whatever it was she did.

Georgie grabbed the file folder. "Gifted children," she reminded herself. Beth ran a nonprofit organization and Gabriella managed a hotel. "And what do you do, Georgiana? You herd cattle and grease windmills and muck out the stables. How glamorous."

She'd always been satisfied with the life she led, but in comparison to the important jobs that her sisters did, working a ranch was nothing. She'd devoted her life to putting a decent steak on someone's dinner table. Georgie set the phone aside, crawled off the bed and walked over to the mirror above the dresser. She stared at herself critically, trying to discern what kind of first impression she'd created. Her hair always seemed to be in a tangle and her face was tanned from all the time she'd spent outdoors. Spanning her waist with her hands, she slowly turned around. Her body wasn't too bad, though it was hard to see beneath the bulky sweater and the faded jeans she usually wore.

A knock sounded on the door and Georgie frowned. Peering through the peephole, she gasped softly. Gabriella stood on the other side. Cursing, Georgie ran over to the mirror and quickly ran a brush through her hair. Then she smoothed her hands over her sweater. For an instant, she considered not opening the door. Was she really ready to face her sister? But when Gabriella knocked again, Georgie had no choice.

Her sister greeted her with a warm smile. "Hello, Georgiana."

"Hi," Georgie replied. She stepped aside. "Please come in."

"I hope you don't mind me coming. But I spoke with Dylan Garrett this afternoon and he mentioned you were in town. I called every hotel until I found you."

"I—I was planning to call you," Georgie said, frantically trying to restore order to the room. She pointed to the bed. "Sit down."

Gabriella looked around the room. "This is nice."

"It is. It has a nice view of the river. Would you like to—" Georgie swallowed. Her sister wasn't interested in looking at her view.

"If you're planning to stay longer, I'd love it if

you'd stay at the Sedgwick. I can comp you a room since you're family. We have very nice amenities and our rooms are a bit bigger than these.''

"I—I'm not sure how much longer I'll be staying.''

Gabriella straightened. "I know how hard this has been for you, Georgiana.''

"Georgie," she said. "Everyone calls me Georgie.''

"And everyone calls me Ella," her sister replied. "As I was saying, it was difficult for me to take all this in and I was aware that I was adopted. And I had memories of my childhood.''

"You did?''

"Actually, I had memories of you. We used to play in this little swimming pool together. And I remember being very protective of you.''

Georgie moved closer, then sat down on the edge of the bed next to Ella. "We did?''

She nodded. "Our father tells me that you and I were absolutely fearless. We made quite a pair, climbing and jumping all over things. We had our share of scrapes and bruises. Two little tomboys.''

For the first time since she'd learned about her real family, Georgie felt a sense of belonging. "I was a tomboy?'' She smiled. "I *was* a tomboy. I still am. I've never been interested in girly things. There's not much room for that living on a ranch.''

Ella nodded. "My adoptive mother used get so frustrated with me. Skinned knees and grass stains and tangled hair.''

"Me, too.''

"See, we do have something in common.'' Ella

stood up. "I'm getting hungry. Why don't we pack up your things and we'll go over to the Sedgwick? Our father will be staying there for the next few days. He'd really like to see you when you're ready to see him. I'll get you a nice room and call Beth and we'll get room service and spend the rest of the night getting to know each other."

Georgie couldn't help but smile. Though she was certain she'd feel intimidated by her older sister, that wasn't so at all. Ella was kind and warmhearted and so easy to talk to. And in truth, she looked forward to knowing her better. "I'd like that."

"So would I," Ella said, grabbing her and giving her a quick hug. "So would I."

CHAPTER FIVE

WADE BALANCED on the tailgate of the pickup as he heaved the bales of straw off the truck into a pile in front of the barn door. The weather had turned bitter cold and the gray sky signaled a coming snow, but Wade had worked himself so hard that he was sweating beneath his flannel shirt and insulated vest.

He looked up as a truck rumbled up the drive. The truck was from the Crazy H, the same truck that Georgie had driven that night she'd come to visit him. Wade pulled off his hat and raked his hand through his hair. It had been three days since she'd last called and nearly a week since he'd put her on the plane to San Antonio.

He'd thought about calling her, but each time he got the urge, he'd convince himself that she should be the one to contact him. Then he convinced himself that she was too busy to call. By the end of the week, he was certain that Georgie hadn't ever really cared, that her profession of love had simply been empty words.

"But she's here now," he murmured as he hopped down off the truck, his heart pounding a little faster in anticipation. "That's a start."

The excitement lasted only a few seconds, until the moment when Delores Hewitt stepped out of the pickup—alone. She approached him slowly, shading her eyes against the low winter sun. When she got within ten feet of him, she stopped as if she were afraid to come any closer. "Mr. Marshall."

Wade nodded. "Mrs. Hewitt."

She reached into her jacket pocket and withdrew an envelope. "I know we haven't been the most cordial of neighbors and I have no right to ask you for a favor, but I'm hoping that you might be able to help me. My husband and sons don't know I've come. I'm not sure they'd approve but I have nowhere else to turn."

"What can I do for you, Mrs. Hewitt?"

She held out the envelope. "I wrote Georgie a letter. I was hoping you could give it to her. It explains everything. How we came to adopt her. Why we didn't tell her. I know she probably doesn't want to talk to me, so maybe a letter is a good thing."

"Mrs. Hewitt, Georgie isn't here. She hasn't come back from San Antonio yet."

A tiny gasp slipped from her throat. "Wh-what do you mean? She's been gone for almost a week." Mrs. Hewitt slowly drew the letter back, clutching it to her chest. "Do you know when she's coming home?" She paused. "*Is* she coming home?"

"I'm not sure," Wade said. "But I've been thinking that I might take a little trip down there, just to check up on her. Make certain everything's going all right. Maybe convince her to come back."

Her expression brightened and she took another step closer, gazing at him with hopeful eyes. "You care about my daughter, don't you."

In truth, Wade really didn't know how he felt. A

week ago, he would have said yes. Hell, he'd even admitted he loved her, said the words right out loud. But now, he could only wonder if what he felt back then was true emotion or unvarnished lust. "I suppose I do. I'm just not sure how she feels about me. She's got a lot going on in her life right now."

Delores Hewitt crossed the distance between them and pressed the letter into his hands. "You're a good man, Mr. Marshall, even though my husband would like to lasso you and drag you across Lincoln County by your feet. Give that letter to Georgie when you see her. And tell her we love her. Her home is at the Crazy H. And Christmas wouldn't be the same without her."

"But I'm not sure if—"

"Even if you don't go to San Antonio, she'll probably come back here first. That last week, before Mr. Henderson and his daughters showed up at the ranch, I've never seen her look so happy. Whatever was going on between you two, it must have been something special."

"I guess it was…for a little while, at least."

"Good. Then I know she'll be coming home soon."

Wade watched as Delores Hewitt got back into the pickup and drove off. He glanced down at the envelope in his hand. Maybe it was time he stopped waiting. What was wrong with making the first move? He'd at least know where he stood. He couldn't bear living in limbo like this, every day spent wondering whether this was the day Georgie would walk back into his life.

Wade strode to the house and grabbed the cordless phone, then sat down on the sofa in front of the fireplace. The number for Georgie's hotel was scribbled on a pad on the coffee table. He punched it in, but when he asked for her room, he was told that she had checked out.

"Try Georgiana Henderson," he said. "She might be registered under that name."

"I'm sorry, sir," the operator replied. "We have no Henderson or Hewitt staying with us. It looks like Miss Hewitt checked out three days ago."

"Can you tell me where she went?" Wade asked.

"I don't have that information. She didn't leave a forwarding address."

Wade hung up the phone, then flopped back on the sofa, tipping his head back and closing his eyes. Three days ago? Maybe she was on her way home. Or maybe she'd decided never to come back to Colorado. "Aw, hell," he muttered. Why was he so worried? She obviously didn't care enough about him to call.

Pushing himself up from the sofa, Wade angrily threw the phone across the room. He should have married her when he had the chance. At least then there would be something holding them together, something he could call on to make her recognize what they shared. But neither one of them had made any promises. No, he'd been much too prudent for that.

He cursed softly. Why make a fool of himself? They'd shared a brief but passionate affair and now it was over. It was time to put her in the past and get on with his life. There had been other women before her and there would be plenty more after her.

With renewed determination, Wade strode to the door, prepared to finish his chores. But he stopped when he saw the phone, still intact, lying on the plank floor. He squatted down and picked it up.

As if his fingers had a mind of their own, he punched in the number for San Antonio information, then scrambled to remember the name on the business card she'd had.

"Finders Keepers," he said to the operator. "I'd like the number for Finders Keepers Private Investigations in San Antonio."

GEORGIE ORDERED A DRINK from the bartender, then plucked a few cashews from the small bowl that he'd slid in front of her. Soft music drifted through the bar off the lobby at the Sedgwick.

She'd spent the day with her sisters, beginning with a morning of beauty at a local salon. Ella and Beth had talked her into a new haircut and once they got her in the chair, they'd convinced her to add hair color to the equation. Before the morning was out, she'd had a facial, a brow wax, a manicure and a pedicure. After a sumptuous lunch of lobster salad and mimosas, they took off for an afternoon of shopping. They'd all indulged in a cosmetic counter makeover, then spent the next three hours buying pretty dresses and matching shoes.

Georgie had always thought of these things as "girly" activities, meant for women who had nothing better to do with their time. But she'd had fun with her sisters and she felt great about herself. Her new hairdo, cropped to shoulder length and colored with warm blond highlights, made her look more sophisticated than she'd ever thought possible. And the dress she'd chosen to wear to dinner that night showed off her figure to its full advantage.

She couldn't help but wonder what Wade would say if he saw her. He'd been the first man in a long time to notice that there was a woman beneath the dusty jeans and the baggy flannel shirts. But now that his woman actually looked like a woman—the kind of woman he probably was used to dating—he might be surprised.

She stared at her reflection in the mirror behind the bar, tucking her hair behind her ear. His woman. A tiny ache settled around her heart. She missed him more and more with each day that passed. So much had happened in the past few days, so much that she wanted to tell him. But she'd stopped herself from calling, determined to set one part of her life right before she moved on to the next, knowing he'd ask about her return and aware that she still wouldn't have an answer.

Life at the ranch seemed like a distant memory, a dream that belonged to another person. Georgie felt as if she'd stepped into a new world the moment she'd arrived in San Antonio. And now she looked different and she felt different, she even spoke differently. And though she hadn't decided where she belonged, she wasn't ready to return to Colorado—not yet.

She wanted to believe her reasons had to do with her new family, but in a secret corner of her mind, Georgie knew it was more. Gabriella and Beth both had fiancés and plans for their futures. They talked of their double wedding at Christmas and their honeymoons and the children they wanted to have. It was as if they'd been waiting for this moment since they were girls.

Georgie had never even thought about marriage. She'd grown up wanting to be a rancher. And because of her singlemindedness, there had been little room in her life for romance—until Wade had come along. But how was she supposed to know if he was the one? Though they'd shared an incredible passion for each other, what guarantee did she have that their passion would last?

She took a sip of her champagne cocktail and closed her eyes, conjuring up a picture of Wade in her head. Her mind wandered back to their last hours together, hours they'd spent wrapped in each other's arms. He'd made her feel safe, provided a haven when she needed it. But now it was time to stand on her own two feet.

"Georgiana?"

Georgie turned as her father slid onto the bar stool beside her, startled to see him. He'd planned to join her and her sisters at dinner. He looked much more relaxed than when she'd seen him at the ranch—and more rested. "Hello," she murmured, uncertain of what to say. They'd been introduced once, but she felt as if she were staring into the face of a stranger.

"What are you drinking?"

She smiled. "A champagne cocktail. Ella and Beth introduced me to these," Georgie explained. "I don't think I'll ever drink whiskey again." He ordered a Scotch. A long silence grew between them as she searched for an appropriate topic of conversation. "I want to apologize for my behavior at the ranch that day."

He held up his hand. "No need. We surprised you. I guess I'm doing the same tonight. Ella and Beth told me you were here and I asked your sisters if I might have some time with you alone, before we all met for dinner. I thought we might get to know each other a little better. I sort of feel as if you've been avoiding me."

Georgie shook her head and forced a smile. "It's not that."

"What is it then?"

She paused for a moment, grasping for the words that might make him understand. But she didn't know Brad Henderson, so she didn't know how he might react. Perhaps total honestly was the best course. "It's easy for me to accept the fact that I have two sisters. But when I think of my father, I can't help but think of Ed Hewitt."

He nodded. "I understand, Georgiana. Ed and Delores Hewitt raised you and I'm grateful for that. I can't take their place and I don't want to. But I would like to get the chance to know you. And maybe someday I could be a part of your life."

"Well, that's pretty straightforward," Georgie said. "I guess I got that trait from you."

"Your parents aren't straight talkers?" he asked.

"They kept a pretty big secret for nearly thirty years."

Henderson took a long sip of his scotch. "I wouldn't blame them for that, Georgiana. They had no idea I'd be barging back into your life. For all they knew, you were an orphan in need of a loving home. They chose you to be a part of their family and never wanted you to think any less of yourself. I understand completely, and I'm glad they spared you all the questions and doubts.''

"But I had a right to know."

"You also had a right to a carefree childhood without any concerns about who you were or where you belonged. And I understand you've grown into a determined and confident woman. You're the kind of daughter any man would be proud to claim as his own. I think Ed and Delores Hewitt made the right choice.''

Georgie turned her champagne flute around and around, watching the bubbles rise to the surface. "Then they could have told me when I got older. I'm just so angry with them. I want to blame someone and they seem to be the best choice.''

"I spent a lot of years in prison assigning blame and venting my anger. But that's no way to live, Georgiana. What happened, happened. We can't change it. We can only live with the life we've been given. You need to come to terms with this, then move on. And part of that is going to mean going home and talking to your parents.''

"I guess it's not too late for you to give me a little advice," she said.

"I sure hope not," he replied. "Because right now, I'm afraid that's all I could possibly offer you. You're past the stage where a new doll or a pretty dress might buy me some points.''

"I wouldn't be so certain about pretty dresses. I'm beginning to like them as much as champagne cocktails.''

"But I get the feeling you prefer dusty jeans and a good whiskey a lot more, don't you?"

Georgie forced a smile. "That's the old Georgie."

"Oh, I think there's a lot of the old Georgie that's worth keeping, don't you?"

For a man who barely knew her, he'd managed to cut right to the heart of her dilemma. Sooner or later the new Georgie would have to go back to the old Georgie's life and make things right again. And the sooner she faced that fact, the better.

THE LOBBY OF THE Sedgwick Hotel was elegantly serene, filled with green plants and floral arrangements and finely upholstered furniture. A huge Christmas tree stood in the middle of the lobby, soaring up through the expansive atrium. Footsteps echoed on the marble floors and somewhere a pianist played a jazzy holiday tune.

Wade had done a bit of detective work of his own to find her, but it had been pretty easy once Dylan Garrett had told him to contact Georgie's sister at the Sedgwick. He'd hopped the next flight to San Antonio and arrived just before the dinner hour.

When Georgie hadn't answered her room phone, Wade had checked in. He'd grown impatient ringing her room every half hour between bouts of pacing, so he'd decided to wait for her in the lobby. He watched the guests as they moved in and out of the lobby doors. Even though the clientele at the Sedgwick was upscale, Wade didn't feel out of place in his denim shirt and scuffed boots.

San Antonio was a cowboy town. And it felt good

to be back in the city, to have everything there in front of him—good books, decent coffee, Chinese food, and pretty, sweet-smelling women. He'd seen more attractive women in three hours than he'd seen in the last three years spent at Lone Rock.

Yet, even though he'd tried to convince himself that any of those women was just as attractive as Georgie, the notion was a hard sell. Georgie was unique, a woman who didn't look like every other woman on the planet. She had a pure and natural beauty, an inner light that shifted and spun like sunshine on prairie grass. To his eyes, she was perfection.

Wade reached down and picked up a newspaper from the table in front of him, determined to focus on something other than Georgie Hewitt's attributes. But as he opened to the second page, the sight of a woman entering the hotel caught his eye. He stared at her for a long moment, until he was sure it wasn't Georgie. But he had to look again as she walked down the steps into the lobby. There was something about her, something in the way she moved that seemed so familiar, so... Wade slowly rose. It *was* Georgie...only it wasn't.

He stared at a woman he'd known intimately, whose body he'd explored with his lips and his hands, whose face he'd memorized. But the woman he saw before him now could have been a complete stranger. She'd cut her hair, the sun-streaked waves now brushing her shoulders. Beneath her open coat, she wore a figure-skimming dress that clung to her body like a second skin. Hell, she'd even put on makeup!

Wade watched as a man came up behind her, tall,

dark-haired, dressed in an expensive suit. He tapped her on the shoulder and she turned around, then grabbed his hands and kissed his cheek. A surge of jealousy shot through Wade and he took a step forward, his jaw tight.

Suddenly he regretted whatever stupid impulse had put him on the plane to San Antonio. He knew how fickle women were, yet he'd managed to convince himself that Georgie was different. But in the course of a week, she'd come to San Antonio and met someone else, leaving her life in Colorado for some joker in Hugo Boss.

Wade buried his anger, knowing that he had a task to complete before he walked out of her life for good. He slowly approached, drawing her mother's letter from his pocket. Two more women walked into the lobby and joined her, then they all started toward the front desk. But when Georgie saw him, she stopped short.

"Wade?"

He didn't say a word. Nothing that he'd prepared to say made any sense now.

She hurried over to him. "What are you doing here?"

"This is for you," he said, handing her the envelope. "It's from your mother. She asked me to deliver it."

Georgie frowned, then took it from him. "You saw my mother?"

"She's worried. You might want to call her just to let her know you're still alive. After all, she gave you thirty years of her life. The least you could give her in return is a few minutes on the phone.'' He rubbed his palms together, then forced a smile. ''Well, I'd better get going. I'm sure you want to get back to your new friends.''

He started toward the elevators, happy to escape with his pride intact. But Georgie reached out and grabbed him by the arm. ''Wait,'' she said. ''You're just going to walk away?''

''I got what I came for,'' he said. ''And what I deserved.''

Georgie stared at him for a long moment, confused by his behavior. ''At least let me introduce you to my sisters.'' She quickly motioned the two women over and Wade ground his teeth as the man Georgie had hugged followed them. ''Wade Marshall, this is my older sister, Gabriella and my younger sister, Beth.''

Wade shook both their hands and mumbled an appropriate greeting.

''And this is Ella's fiancé, Josh Hunter. He and Ella both live here in San Antonio. Josh owns a very successful packaging material company. And this is Ella's hotel.''

Gabriella laughed, slipping her around her fiancé's waist. ''Not my hotel,'' she said. ''I'm the assistant general manager.''

''Close enough,'' Georgie teased.

Wade glanced back and forth between the three women and the man who stood among them. Righteous anger and uncontrolled jealousy gave way to a feeling of utter stupidity. Her sister's fiancé. Hell, a week apart from Georgie had made him crazy enough to get jealous of an innocent man. The first thing he planned to do when he got back to Colorado was to get his head examined.

He reached out and shook Josh's hand. "It's a pleasure to meet you all. I really have to get going. I've got to catch a flight back to Colorado in a few hours."

As he walked through the busy lobby, he heard Georgie make her excuses to her sisters. Then she ran after him, catching up just as he reached the elevators. When the doors opened, she walked in right behind him, then stood against the back wall. "Seems kind of weird that you'd rent a room here if you weren't planning to stay overnight."

"Well, I'm a strange guy," he said, his voice edged with sarcasm. He gave her a sideways glance, then turned his gaze back to the numbers over the door.

Georgie sighed. "Are you angry at me?"

He shook his head. "Why would I be angry?"

"I meant to call, but so much was happening."

"Fine," Wade said. "No problem."

"It seems like a problem for you." She sighed softly. "That's not true. To be honest, I didn't want to call. I was afraid if I talked to you, I'd find any excuse to come running back to Colorado, where everything was easy and safe. Being with you is the easiest thing I've ever done in my life. And this is the hardest. I'm trying to figure out where I belong, so I had to stay."

"It's pretty obvious where you belong, Georgie. Just look at yourself." The doors to the elevator opened and he stepped out, striding toward his room.

Georgie followed, nearly running to keep up with him. "What's that supposed to mean?"

"That hairdo won't last long squished up under a cowboy hat," he said, his voice dripping with sarcasm. "And that dress would be rags after a day mending fences." He stopped and grabbed her hand, laughing derisively at her painted fingernails. "I won't even comment on these."

He strode to his room door and unlocked it, then stepped inside. For a moment, she didn't follow him. But just as the door was closing, she barged in. "I like the way I look. Ella says I'm pretty and Beth told me I have a body that most women spend hours in the gym to get. And when I walk down the street, men notice me. And if that makes you angry, then tough."

Wade stopped and drew a deep breath. Then, without warning, he grabbed Georgie around the waist and yanked her against him. His mouth came down on hers in a deep kiss and he continued until she went soft in his arms. A tiny moan slipped from her lips. When he was certain he'd proved his point, he let her go. Her eyes fluttered open and she stared up at him, her lips still damp, her breath coming in quick gasps.

Wade laughed softly and shook his head. "Well, I guess that answers one of my questions. How about another one? Are you planning on coming back to Colorado? Because if you aren't, it might be good to let me know. Then I won't waste any more time thinking about you."

"Do you want me to come back?" she asked.

"We're not going to play this game, Georgie. Both of us waiting to see how the other person feels before we make a move." He raked his hands through his hair. "Hell, I don't expect you to come back. Look at yourself. You're not the same Georgie that I knew."

"I put on a dress and some makeup and suddenly I'm not the same person?" she asked.

"Haven't you changed? Tell me the truth."

"I spent twenty-eight years on that ranch, certain that I knew who I was. And then, everything changed. Maybe I'm *not* the same person. Maybe I'm the person I was always supposed to be."

Wade cursed softly, then stepped away from her. As he walked to the bed, he grabbed his duffel and began to stuff clothes back into it. "You're hiding here, Georgie, the same way you hid at the Crazy H. You may be having the time of your life, but you have people back home who care about you. You're going to have to face them sooner or later."

"You can't tell me what to do," she said. "Or how to feel. This is my life and I have to live it."

"Here? With the traffic and the noise, the crowds of people all pushing to get somewhere they really don't have to be? If that's what you want, then you stay here. But I outgrew that world a long time ago, Georgie. I chose a different world, one where the sky is big and the air is clean." He shoved the last of his things into the duffel then zipped it up. "And I'm going back there on the first plane out of here."

He walked out of the room, leaving her standing inside with her pretty dress and her red lips and the perfume that seemed to fill his head with images of naked bodies and tangled sheets. The elevator doors opened up a few seconds after he pushed the button.

Wade hesitated, wondering if she intended to follow him. But the hall remained empty and silent.

He slowly stepped inside, knowing that if he left now, it would be over between them. An ache settled in around his heart, an ache that could only be dispelled by hard work and sheer determination to put her out of his mind. He'd go back to Lone Rock, to the place where he belonged, and start his life over again, as if they had never met that night on the river. And maybe, over time, he'd be able to get through an entire day and then a week and then a month without wondering what might have been.

"HE CAME ALL THE WAY to San Antonio to see you," Ella said. "That must mean something."

Georgie took another bite of her hot fudge sundae and sighed. Her sisters had gathered in her room after they had bid their father, Josh, and Beth's fiancé, Joe Holden, goodbye in the lobby. Earlier, they'd dined at one of San Antonio's best restaurants and shared a perfect family meal, relaxed and easy. But it had been followed by a blistering argument with Wade.

He'd been so angry with her, hurling accusations at her. His feelings must run very deep to cause such a reaction. She should have gone after him, but she was so stunned by his behavior she'd reacted with indignation rather than understanding.

"I'm not sure," Georgie murmured. "Maybe he just came to deliver this letter from my mother."

"Sure," Ella said. "A postage stamp is much more expensive than the round-trip ticket to San Antonio."

Georgie flopped back on the bed and reread the last

paragraph of the letter, her mother's words causing a surge of guilt to wash over her. "I've got to go back," she said.

"What did the letter say?" Ella asked.

"My mother tried to explain how she felt the day I came to live with them. How much she wanted me and how it was so easy to believe I was really her daughter. She talked about how she tried to turn me into the perfect little girl and how she realized that I was going to be the person I was meant to be, without her help. And she told me that if she could do it all over again, she wouldn't have done anything differently." Georgie sighed softly. "When I was talking to our father earlier this evening, he said the same thing. We have to live the life we were given." She drew a ragged breath. "Heather Cooper took away our life together. And maybe it wasn't fair. But Ed and Delores Hewitt raised me. And loved me. And no matter how angry I am at what happened, it's not their fault. Heather Cooper is to blame. And Ronald Muir. And a justice system that took twenty-eight years to learn the truth."

Ella nodded. "It's time for you to go home. To talk to your parents and Wade."

"And Wade," Georgie said. "But what about the three of us? We're just getting to know each other. I feel as if there's so much more that we have to talk about. I always wanted a sister and now I have two. I don't want to let you go."

"You're going to see us at the wedding. You did promise to be our maid of honor, didn't you?" Beth slipped her arm around Georgie's shoulders. "And we're always going to be here for you, even when we're not together. We can talk on the phone and visit. Joe has his charter business. He can fly you guys to visit me at the drop of a hat if we want.''

"We just have to make plans to spend time together," Ella said.

Georgie sighed. "Do you ever wonder how different things might have been if we grew up together? Would we be living next door to each other? Would our children play on the same Little League team?"

"We'll never know," Ella said. "All we can do is start from now. We're together now and that's all that matters."

"And we'll be together in New York next week. Joe has arranged a plane for you and your family.''

"My family?"

Beth nodded. "Our father wants them to be there," Ella said. "He called the Hewitts yesterday and they said they'd be happy to attend—if you wanted them to. So go home and fix things with your family. Beth and I want a perfect wedding. And it won't be perfect unless you *and* your family are there to celebrate with us. I'll have the bridal shop here in San Antonio send the dress and shoes we ordered for you directly to my parents' house in New York.''

"And I'll have Joe call you and find out where and when he should send the plane," Beth added.

Ella jumped up from the bed and set her dessert plate on the dresser. "And you should ask Wade to come, too."

"I don't know about that," Georgie said. "We have our problems to work out as well." She crawled off the bed. "I guess I'd better call the airline and get a flight back."

"No, you'll fly with me," Beth said. "Joe is flying me to Vancouver tomorrow morning so I can take care of some business there before we go to New York for the wedding. We can easily drop you off in Colorado. It's right on the way."

"All right," Georgie said. "I'd like that."

Ella picked up the phone and punched in a number. She ordered three more sinful desserts from room service, then crawled back onto Georgie's bed. "We've got until tomorrow morning before we have to say goodbye. Let's settle in here, pig out on sweets and have ourselves a slumber party."

"And our first topic of conversation has to be Wade Marshall." Beth rolled over on her stomach and gave Georgie an inquisitive look. "Tell us everything and spare no details."

CHAPTER SIX

GEORGIE STOOD on the back porch of the ranch house, her hand on the door. The driver that Ella had arranged for had picked her up at the airport in Colorado Springs and driven her all the way to the Crazy H. But she'd been hesitant to pull up to the house in a limo, so she'd made him drop her off halfway down the drive.

She set her new suitcase down next to her, wondering how she'd managed so many purchases in such a short time. Her life had certainly changed since she'd left the Crazy H a little more than a week ago. She'd gained two sisters and a father, she'd stayed in a fancy hotel and eaten gourmet food at famous restaurants. She'd drunk wine that cost more than she could ever imagine, she'd flown in a private jet and ridden in a limousine.

But all that seemed so unreal now, like a dream. What was real was right in front of her. The house that she'd grown up in, the blue sky that went on for miles and miles, and the crisp, clean air that smelled of snow. Wade had been right. She belonged here. The Hewitts were her family and like it or not, this ranch was in her blood. She knew every inch of land, every rise and hollow, every fence post and every windmill. But even more, she knew that her family loved her.

Georgie shivered, then drew her jacket more tightly around her. She'd come back to the ranch in the same clothes she'd left in, her fancy city things packed away in her luggage. She slowly opened the door, grabbed her suitcase, and stepped inside. The scent of fresh-baked cookies filled the kitchen.

Her mother bent over the open oven door, her back to Georgie. "Wipe your feet," she called. "I just washed the floor."

She set her bag near the table. "Hi, Mom," Georgie said, her throat tightening with emotion.

Delores Hewitt slowly straightened and turn to face her. For a long moment, she didn't speak. Tears filled her eyes and a tremulous smile touched her lips. Then she slowly crossed the kitchen and drew Georgie into her embrace. "You're home," she said.

"I'm home," Georgie replied, tears tumbling from her eyes.

Her mother stepped back and took Georgie's face between her palms, then kissed both of her cheeks. "You look so pretty. What did you do to your hair? Do you have mascara on?"

Georgie laughed through her tears. "I knew that would make you happy. I even bought a few dresses." She held up her fingers. "And I got a manicure. But I'm still the same old Georgie, Mom." She gave her mother another hug. "I'm so sorry. I shouldn't have run out like I did. But I was scared and confused and I—"

"You don't have to explain, sweetie. I understand.

I'm just glad you're home. Come and sit down. Your father and the boys should be back in a few hours. They're moving the herd from the southwest pasture. I've just baked some cookies and I'll put on a fresh pot of coffee and we'll—'' Her mother stopped, then smiled apologetically. "You don't need cookies, do you. I'd suspect you need to go see that man of yours, if you haven't stopped there already."

"Wade?"

"What other man? You didn't fall in love with someone new in San Antonio, did you?"

"Mom, I don't love Wade Marshall. And I'm not sure he's going to want to see me. We had a fight when he came to San Antonio to deliver your letter."

"Of course you love him," Delores said. "You just haven't admitted it to yourself yet. And a little fight is nothing to worry about." She turned Georgie around and pushed her toward the door, grabbing her cowboy hat from the hat rack as she passed and plopping it on her daughter's head. "We'll talk later. And take the truck. It's too cold to ride all the way over there on Jess."

Georgie turned around before she stepped out of the door. "I have so much to tell you," she said.

"It will wait. We have plenty of time."

"I love you, Mom. And Daddy, too. And the boys, even though they drive me crazy.'

"And we love you, sweetie. Now get going. I want you back here by dinnertime."

Georgie walked outside and adjusted the brim of her hat against the sun's glare. It felt good to be back. But instead of jumping into the pickup truck, she headed to the horse barn.

Jess was waiting in his stall and she murmured soft words to him as she saddled him up. He almost seemed happy to have her on his back again, and when they got out of the barn, he strained against the bit, anxious to run. Georgie pointed him in the direction of the north rise and gave him a gentle kick.

She wasn't sure what she'd find there, only that she had to go back to the place where it began. As she came over the last rise, the wind stinging at her cheeks, her breath coming in gasps, she saw him. He sat on his horse on the other side of the river. She paused, uncertain whether he saw her. But when she urged Jess forward, Wade did the same with Charlie.

They approached each other slowly, warily, as if neither one of them was sure of what they'd say. When they were close enough to speak, Georgie slid out of her saddle and stood silently beside Jess. A moment later, Wade did the same. They watched each other for a long time.

Georgie's heart hammered in her chest and she tried to speak. But words wouldn't come. In the end, she raced across the short distance between them and threw herself into his arms.

Wade picked her up off her feet and spun her around as he kissed her. And when he drew away to catch a breath, Georgie laughed, nuzzling her face in the curve of his neck. "I'm back," she said.

"I'm glad."

She gazed up into his eyes, certain that everything was going to be all right. Home wasn't just a house.

Home was in Wade's arms and in his kiss and in the sound of his voice. "And I'm sorry about what happened in San Antonio. I was so surprised to see you and when—"

He kissed her again. "Never mind. You're home now. You are home, aren't you?"

"I am. At least for a little while. My sisters are getting married in New York over Christmas. I'm going to be maid of honor for the wedding. My whole family is invited, and so are you."

Wade took her face between his hands and kissed her over and over again. "I'm so glad to see you. And I'm sorry about San Antonio. I said a lot of stupid things. I liked your red fingernails and your new hairdo. And you can wear that dress any time you want."

Georgie laughed and hugged him hard. "How did you know I'd come out here?"

"I called the hotel this morning and they said you'd checked out. I took a chance you were on your way home. I'm glad you finally turned up because I was getting damn cold. Have you seen your parents yet?"

"I talked to my mom. My father and brothers are out working. I'll see them in a few hours at dinner."

Wade smoothed her windblown hair out of her eyes. "They'll be glad to have you back."

"So, is everything all right between us? Are we still friends?"

Wade's eyebrow quirked up. "Is that what you want? Because friends don't meet at the river and kiss. And friends don't spend long afternoons in bed. And friends don't accompany friends to New York to their sisters' wedding. Are you really sure you want to be friends?''

''If we're not friends, then what are we?''

''Maybe we should just start here,'' Wade suggested, ''and see where it leads us.''

Georgie nodded and looked around, happiness filling her heart. How could she ever have doubted her feelings for Wade? ''I like this spot. In fact, I was thinking about asking my father for a little bit of land. I thought I'd build a cabin right here on the river. A place of my own. Then, when we meet, we wouldn't have to stand out in the cold. It wouldn't be anything big. Just something warm and cozy with a big soft bed. What do you think?''

''I think that anything that keeps you in Colorado is fine with me.''

''Good,'' Georgie said. She gave him a quick kiss. ''Now that we have all that settled, maybe we should find someplace warm where we can talk. I've got a few hours before I have to head back to the house for dinner.''

''Why don't you ride back to Lone Rock with me and then I'll drive you back to your parents for dinner. And maybe, if I'm lucky, they'll invite me in.''

''That sounds like a good plan,'' she said. ''I'll race you.''

He walked Georgie over to Jess, then helped her into the saddle. ''It's good to have you home.''

She turned her horse around and looked over her shoulder at him. ''It's good to be home.'' With a loud whoop, she kicked Jess in the flanks and the horse took off toward Lone Rock. As she rode over the gently rolling land, she wondered how she'd ever doubted her place in the world. This land was in her blood, maybe not by birth, but by the sheer power of her life here.

She was home and she was with a family who loved her and a handsome, sexy man who might just love her if she let him. Life couldn't get much better.

"ARE THEY ALL HERE?"

Will Hewitt nodded. "They are, though I can't tell you how long Ben will stay once he sees the reason I asked them to meet me. I think they all assume I asked them here to discuss Georgie."

"Well, we are discussing her, aren't we?" Wade asked.

"Actually, we've been working out a way that Georgie can run the ranch," Will replied. "It's what she's always wanted, and to tell the truth, none of us are much good at the book work. She'd probably make a bigger success of it than we could. So we've decided to go to my Dad and see if he'll agree to put it all down on paper."

"Do you think he'll do it?"

Will shrugged. "Maybe. It's the only way to make sure Georgie stays on the ranch. If she leaves, I'm not sure my parents will be able to handle it."

Wade nodded. "It's a good plan. But I might have a better one." He motioned toward the feed shed where Ben, Jace and Seth waited. "Why don't we see what they think."

Georgie had been back for three days and was due to leave again in two. They'd spent nearly every minute together, mending fences during the day and making love by night. But before they left for New York, he wanted to clear up a few important points in their relationship.

Will opened the door to the shed and stepped inside, Wade following. The three older brothers were waiting, sitting on sacks of horse feed. The moment they saw Wade, they all stood up, creating a menacing wall of muscle and bone. Wade instantly regretted his choice to meet them here. He should have found some neutral turf.

"What are you doing here?" Jace demanded.

Wade took off his hat. "I came to talk to you. All four of you."

"We don't have anything to say to you," Ben mumbled, clenching and unclenching his fists. "You may have snowed our parents, but we know what kind of man you really are, Marshall."

Will stepped in. "I think we should listen to him, guys."

Wade reached in his pocket and withdrew a packet of papers, then handed them to Will. "I was going through my grandfather's journal a few days ago and I found an entry for attorney's fees. I called the attorney and found out that my grandfather had talked to him about a water rights agreement. So, knowing that, I had my lawyer draw this up. I think you'll find it in keeping with my grandfather's promise to you. For as long as a Hewitt lives on the Crazy H, that contract is in force."

Jace eyed him suspiciously, then snatched the papers from Will's hand. He slowly unfolded them, his eyebrows rising as he read through the first page. Then he looked up. "Is this real?"

Wade chuckled. "It better be. I don't pay my lawyer a hundred dollars an hour to draw up fake contracts."

"All right then." Ben nodded before reluctantly offering his hand to Wade. "It's a deal."

"Good," Wade said, shaking each of their hands in turn. "And now that we have business out of the way, I wanted to talk to you about something personal."

Jace's eyebrow quirked up and Ben frowned. "Personal?" Seth asked.

"It's about Georgie."

"I told him about our plan to give her the ranch to run," Will said. "He says he's got a better one."

Wade sat down on one of the feed sacks and the brothers followed suit. "I'm just as interested in having Georgie stay in Colorado as you are," he explained. "But I have my own plans. And I'm going to need your help."

Jace slapped the packet of papers on his hand. "So this water rights thing has a price attached to it?"

"Not a price. More like a simple favor." Wade drew a deep breath. He wasn't sure how his request would go over. Either he'd find himself a human punching bag in the next minute or he'd have the support of four very important allies. "I'm going to ask Georgie to marry me. And I figured it might be best if I got your approval first."

Ben laughed. "You want to marry Georgie?"

"Good luck," Jace said. "She's not exactly the marrying type. We tried to find someone for her, but she wouldn't have it. And these were decent guys. A few of them had money. What makes you think she'd want you?''

"And she doesn't cook or do housework," Ben added. "And if you think you'll wear the pants in the family, you've got another guess coming."

"I won't know unless I ask her," Wade said.

"But you gotta ask her the right way," Will countered. "She won't go for any big romantic gestures. And she won't like a flashy ring."

Wade groaned, then reached in his pocket as he fingered the small velvet box. Though the ring wasn't exactly flashy, it was big. Wade had bought it thinking she'd enjoy showing it off to her sisters when she went back to New York. Maybe he'd made a mistake.

"We know Georgie. If you want her to say yes, you're going to have to listen to our advice."

The door to the feed shed opened, sunlight streaming in. They all turned to look at the slender figure that stepped inside. Georgie glanced back and forth between the five men sitting in a circle on feed sacks. "What's going on in here? Wade, what are you doing here?"

Ben cleared his throat and Jace shifted uneasily. "We're just talking, Georgie."

"Will made us come," Seth added.

She strolled up to Wade. "And who made you come?"

Wade grinned. This was the Georgie he loved, with her fiery temper and her stubborn streak. "I came on my own. I had a deal I needed to talk to your brothers about."

"Yeah," Seth said. "A deal. And he's got an offer for you, too."

Jace cursed. "Geez, Seth, will ya shut up?"

"It wasn't our idea," Ben said, stepping forward. "We didn't have anything to do with it. He came to us. But that doesn't mean we don't think it's a great idea. We do think it's a great idea, don't we boys?"

They all nodded. Wade forced a smile. This was not exactly the way he pictured his proposal going, but maybe this wouldn't work out too badly. "Georgie, I came here to ask you something."

"Go ahead," Ben said. "Ask her."

Wade looked over his shoulder and sent Ben a quieting glare. "I will, if you let me get to it." He slowly lowered himself to one knee and reached in his pocket for the ring. "Georgie, I love you. I know you asked me to marry you a while back and now I'm asking you. Will you marry me?" He flipped open the box and held it out to her.

In the history of marriage proposals, it wasn't the smoothest or the most romantic, but he'd said what he'd come to say and knowing Georgie, she'd have to appreciate the simplicity of the whole thing.

She stared at the ring, dumbfounded. She opened her mouth once, as if to speak, then snapped it shut again. Her gaze darted between her four brothers and she narrowed her eyes. "I thought you'd learned your lesson," she murmured. "This is exactly what you did that night of my party."

"I wasn't at your party," Wade said.

"I'm not talking to you," Georgie snapped. "I'm talking to them. What did you offer him? How did you manage to convince him to come over here and propose? Because I don't think for one minute that pitiful proposal was his idea."

Wade slowly stood. "Pitiful?"

She wagged her finger at her brothers. "This is the final straw. Either you four stay out of my life or—or I'm going to run off and marry the next man that sets foot on this ranch."

Georgie turned on her heel and stalked out of the feed shed. "Wait a second," Wade called. He turned to her brothers. "What was that all about?"

"She thinks we set this up," Ben said. "Maybe you ought to go tell her that this was your idea. She's not in any mood to listen to us."

Wade rolled his eyes and cursed softly. Then he hurried out of the feed shed and followed a smaller set of footprints to the Hewitt's horse barn. He found Georgie inside, furiously grooming Jess. She wielded a curry comb with short, efficient strokes, as if all her anger were contained in that simple movement.

"Georgie, I—"

"Go away," she muttered.

"Hell, no. I proposed to you and I think I deserve an answer. I'm not going anywhere until I get one."

"What did they give you so you'd marry me? I can't imagine how my brothers could convince you to do anything. But once they've set their minds to something they're like a pack of wolves at a dinner table. Get out of the way or they'll eat you alive."

Wade walked into the stall and grabbed her curry comb from her hand, then tossed it into the straw at Jess's feet. "Come with me," he said, taking her hand

and pulling her along behind him. He pushed her down onto a bale of hay, then sat down beside her. "Your brothers didn't convince me to make my marriage proposal. In fact, I had to convince them to support me on this. Hell, I gave them the contract for the water rights just to make sure we had their blessing."

"Then this is real?"

Wade nodded. "And I know it wasn't very good. But if you give me another shot at it, I think I can make it better." He got down on one knee and retrieved the ring from his pocket. "Georgie, we belong together, for now and forever. And if you agree, then I'm going to put this ring on your finger and we're going to get married. Say yes and I'll be the happiest man in the world."

She stared at the ring, her eyes wide.

Wade cursed. "That wasn't very good either." He pulled the ring away. "Just give me a few minutes here and I'll come up with something really good."

"No!" Georgie said.

"No?"

She reached for the ring and snatched it out of his hand. Then she slipped it on her finger. "Yes."

"Yes?"

"Yes, Wade Marshall. I'll marry you."

He grinned. "Then I don't have to think up another way to propose?"

"No," she said, wrapping her arms around his neck. "That won't be necessary."

"Good. Because I'm fresh out of material. I'll say this, Georgie. I promise to do everything in my power to make you happy. I love you and that's something you can depend on.''

She ran her fingers through his hair. ''And I love you, Wade. Now kiss me and let's make it official.''

Wade stood and grabbed her up in his arms, and did precisely as ordered. And when he was finished, he set her back on her feet. ''So, I guess we're getting married. Husband and wife.''

''Wife and husband,'' Georgie corrected. ''And speaking of wives, you should probably know that I'm not much of a cook. And the last time I did laundry, everything came out pink. And forget about cleaning the bathroom. But I can help you run a ranch.''

Wade gaze down into her eyes, knowing that whatever Georgie brought to the marriage would be more that he could have ever imagined. ''We're going to be great together,'' he murmured.

''Yes, we are,'' she said in a quiet voice.

BRAD HENDERSON STOOD in front of a mirror in the hotel hallway, just outside the reception room, staring intently at his reflection. Behind him, a huge Christmas tree glittered with tiny white lights and shiny ornaments. His thoughts wandered back years, to the last Christmas he'd spent with his wife and family.

He didn't remember growing old, but there it was—the telltale gray at the temples, the deep wrinkles at the corners of his eyes, the wide shoulders that were now slightly stooped. Where had all the time gone? So much of his life spent sitting in a cell, waiting for the day when someone would discover that he was there for all the wrong reasons.

He'd made a vow to himself that if he ever got out of Leavenworth he'd never look back. But now that he'd been freed, he couldn't seem to put all the regrets behind him. He'd found his daughters and this morning had walked Gabriella and Beth down the aisle to their waiting grooms. Georgiana was engaged and would be married in the spring. They'd grown up without him and now they'd begin lives of their own, families of their own. But he still mourned for every moment of their lives that he missed.

He smiled ruefully. "Lorraine, I wish you could be here to see this day. Your daughters are so beautiful. I'm sure you would have cried because you always had a soft heart. They're fine women and each of them carries a bit of you inside their hearts."

"Dad?"

Brad turned to find Georgiana coming toward him, her deep-green dress rustling around her feet. He had wondered if she'd ever be able to call him father, but they'd spent a few days together before the wedding, getting to know each other even better, and gradually she'd dropped her defenses. Though she hadn't stopped calling Ed Hewitt "Dad," Brad was happy to share the title.

He reached up and straightened the bow tie he wore with his formal shirt and tuxedo. Georgie joined him at the mirror and smiled. "What are you doing out here?"

"Nothing," he said. "Just gathering my thoughts."

"Everyone is waiting inside. You're supposed to make a toast." She turned to him. "Are you all right?"

Brad nodded. "I am."

"Ella told me you got word this morning that the authorities caught Ronald Muir in Argentina. That must make you feel good."

He shook his head. "It doesn't change the past."

"No, I suppose it doesn't," she said. "But there's no use moping over the past. You convinced me of that. We have the future. Lots of years left, full of love and family and maybe a few grandchildren."

Brad smiled. He could always count on Georgiana and her direct nature to put things in perspective. "You're right. Today is a new beginning. A fresh start. I have my girls all together and everyone is happy. I'm happy, too." He paused. "You know the Air Force has offered me a new job. I think they're trying to make up for the mess they made of my case. They're hoping I don't write a book."

"What kind of job?"

"They want me to teach at the Air Force Academy."

"In Colorado Springs?"

Brad nodded. "Just a few classes a week to start. First-year military history. But I think I might accept. I'm going to need something to do with my time. I'm not ready to retire."

Georgie slipped her arm through his and gave it a squeeze. "That would be wonderful. You could come out to the ranch whenever you want. Wade and I have plenty of room at Lone Rock. You could spend weekends with us."

"You know, I don't care for you two living together before you get married."

"The world had changed a little in the last thirty years. Lots of couples live together. Besides, it's too crowded at the Crazy H. I get my own bathroom at Wade's house. And it's about time I started living my own life, don't you think?"

"I still don't care for it and I might just have to have a talk with that fiancé of yours."

Georgie hitched her hands on her waist. "Well, then maybe we'll just have to get married before you visit. I'd imagined a June wedding beside the river, under the cottonwoods. There's a beautiful spot right at the bend. But if we have to stand out there in the freezing cold with the snow blowing just to make you happy, I suppose we could."

Brad chuckled. "When did I turn into such an old fuddy-duddy?"

"All fathers are fuddy-duddies." She gave his arm a tug. "Come on, it's time to go back inside. Do you know what you're going to say?"

"I'm sure I'll think of something once I get in front of everyone."

They walked together back into the small reception hall. Relatives and friends sat at round tables set with crystal and silver and lit with tapered candles. Brad and Georgiana walked to the head table where the two grooms, the two brides, and the rest of the wedding party sat. Brad stood between Ella and Beth, picked up a champagne flute, then cleared his throat.

The guests quickly quieted and turned to him, listening intently. He took a moment to look at each of his daughters, first Gabriella, then Georgiana, then Beth. Then he faced the guests and smiled. "I never thought this day would come. I used to dream about it, but in my dreams, my girls were still children, the same age they were when I last saw them. Now I look at them and see the fine women they've become.''

He stared down at his glass for a long moment, swirling the champagne distractedly as he tried to fight back a wave of emotion. "First, I'd like to toast my late wife, Lorraine.'' His voice cracked, but Brad drew on his resolve and carried on. ''She gave birth to these three wonderful girls and if she were here today, she'd be very proud. Secondly, I'd like to toast some special folks—the people who raised our girls. Frank and Mary Petri, Charlotte and Olson Chenoweth, Lindsay McNeil, and Ed and Delores Hewitt. I owe these people a debt of gratitude that I can never repay.''

A round of applause broke out and Brad nodded. ''And finally I'd like to toast my three girls and the men in their lives. May you all find the love and happiness you deserve. And may you give me plenty of grandchildren. Soon.''

The guests broke out in laughter, then applauded the couples when they stood and kissed. As Brad made his way back to his table, Georgie grabbed his hand and gave it a squeeze. ''That was very eloquent.''

He pressed her hand between his. ''I had a lot of time to think about what I'd say to you three when I finally found you. But I've never been very good with words.''

''You don't have to tell us, Dad. We already know.''

Brad nodded, fighting back the tears that had threatened all day long. He'd spent a lot of Christmases sitting in his cell and wondering what his daughters were doing for the holidays. He'd eaten too many tasteless Christmas dinners on plastic plates with dull cutlery. And he'd made so many futile Christmas wishes, knowing full well that they might never come true.

But from now on, whenever he thought of Christmas, he'd have this memory to savor. For faith and hope had given him the best Christmas gift of all— the love of his three daughters and a future full of many more happy holidays.

Two women in jeopardy...
Two shattering secrets...
Two dramatic stories...

VEILS OF DECEIT

USA TODAY bestselling author

JASMINE CRESSWELL

B.J. DANIELS

A riveting volume of scandalous secrets, political intrigue and
unforgettable passion that you will not want to miss!

*Look for VEILS OF DECEIT in April 2003
at your favorite retail outlet.*

HARLEQUIN®

Makes any time special ®

Visit us at www.eHarlequin.com

A visit to Cooper's Corner offers the chance for a new beginning...

COOPER'S CORNER

Coming in December 2002
DANCING IN THE DARK
by Sandra Marton

Check-in: When Wendy Monroe left Cooper's Corner, she was an Olympic hopeful in skiing...and madly in love with Seth Castleman. But an accident on the slopes shattered her dreams, and rather than tell Seth the painful secret behind her injuries, Wendy leaves him.

Checkout: A renowned surgeon staying at Twin Oaks can mend Wendy's leg. But only facing Seth again—and the truth—can mend her broken heart.

HARLEQUIN®
Makes any time special®